THE NIMBUS

THE NIMBUS

A Novel

ROBERT P. BAIRD

Henry Holt and Company

New York

Henry Holt and Company
Publishers since 1866
120 Broadway
New York, New York 10271
www.henryholt.com

Henry Holt® and ⒽⒽ® are registered trademarks of Macmillan Publishing Group, LLC.

Excerpts reprinted with permission: Peter O'Leary, "Ebulliences," *Luminous Epinoia* (Cultural Society, 2010); *The Epic of Gilgamesh*, translated by Andrew George (Penguin Press, 1999); Juvenal, *The Satires*, translated by A. S. Kline (Poetry in Translation, 2001).

Library of Congress Cataloging-in-Publication Data

Names: Baird, Robert P., author.
Title: The nimbus : a novel / Robert P. Baird.
Description: First edition. | New York : Henry Holt and
    Company, 2025.
Identifiers: LCCN 2024048440 | ISBN 9781250392657 (hardcover) |
    ISBN 9781250392640 (ebook)
Subjects: LCGFT: Humorous fiction. | Novels.
Classification: LCC PS3602.A5745 N56 2025 | DDC 813/.6—dc23/
    eng/20241015
LC record available at https://lccn.loc.gov/2024048440

Our books may be purchased in bulk for promotional, educational, or business use. Please contact your local bookseller or the Macmillan Corporate and Premium Sales Department at (800) 221–7945, extension 5442, or by e-mail at MacmillanSpecialMarkets@macmillan.com.

First Edition 2025

Designed by Gabriel Guma

Printed in the United States of America

1   3   5   7   9   10   8   6   4   2

This is a work of fiction. All of the characters, organizations, and events portrayed in this novel either are products of the author's imagination or are used fictitiously.

Noi siam venuti al loco ov' i' t'ho detto
che tu vedrai le genti dolorose
c'hanno perduto il ben de l'intelletto.

—Dante, *Inferno*

It cannot be denied that the university is a place of refuge, and it cannot be accepted that the university is a place of enlightenment. In the face of these conditions one can only sneak into the university and steal what one can.

—Fred Moten and Stefano Harney,
"The University and the Undercommons: Seven Theses"

The light lies
Deep within your vision of it and
Can't satisfy your demands.

—Peter O'Leary, "Ebulliences"

THE NIMBUS

TO THE READER

When I was in college, a long time ago, I enrolled in a survey course on the history of religion. My professor was an austere and grumpy ex-Lutheran, a historian of Christianity who held his subject in roughly the same regard that an oncologist looks upon cancer. He was a Nietzschean, this professor, which meant that he was—in his own mind, anyway—a realist of the most uncompromising variety. Like his intellectual hero, he was the sort of person who took both pride and pleasure in shredding what he saw as the comforting illusions that kept his fellow human beings from seeing the world as it truly exists.

The professor began our class, as he began all his classes, by announcing that every story starts with a lie: the lie that it's possible to start somewhere. To admit the appearance of something new under our very old sun, he declared, suggested not merely a lack of intellectual rigor but also a cast of character that he despised above all others: sentimentality. He believed—no, he insisted—that a clear view of religion required a clear view of history. And anyone who wanted to understand history had to dispense with any hope of finding meaning therein.

Not providence, not destiny, not the slowly-but-surely, bending-but-not-breaking arc of justice that Martin Luther King Jr. promised, not even (much as he hated to contradict his beloved Marx) the legible workings of the dialectic were to be found in the annals. Instead there was only the bottomless human appetite for power, coupled with the onrushing stampede of entropy: two thrashing, witless forces that were locked in an unremitting death match, the comprehensive depravity of which most people could not bear to contemplate even for an afternoon.

Contingency, blind and bloody contingency, was the only iron law of history, he argued. Thus it followed logically that true beginnings—meaningful beginnings, of the sort religions liked to claim for themselves—were impossible. They were, in short, a category error, a deception of the most fundamental kind. Even Tolstoy, a Christian, knew this to be true. "There is and can be no *beginning* to any event," the great Russian wrote in *War and Peace*, "for one event flows without any break in continuity from another."

Every story starts with a lie: if I can't help but recall my professor's mantra, please do not imagine that I thereby endorse his bleak philosophy of history. But since you'll have every reason to distrust what follows—I still hardly believe half of it myself—let me confess, here at the outset, that I have taken certain liberties with the truth. Though I have tried to accurately record the most unbelievable of the events that I witnessed, I have changed some names and scrambled some personal characteristics in recounting their context: to protect the innocent, yes, but also to protect myself, who am far from innocent.

RPB

FALL QUARTER

ONE

He was on fire. Adrian's son was on fire.

That, at any rate, was what it looked like the first time Paul Harkin saw . . . well, the first time he saw whatever it was. Luca Bennett, a burly, bubbly two-year-old with gray eyes that drooped a little in the corners and a rumpled haystack of yellow hair atop his oversized head, was sleeping soundlessly in a jogger's stroller in the corner of his father's office, and he looked like he was on fire.

It was not a big fire, to be sure. Not a bright fire. Certainly not a blaze or conflagration. More like the flame you see on the underside of a broiler, something low and close. At once lucent and translucent, it traced Luca's baby-fat contours in three dimensions and extended a half inch or so into space, dissolving into wispy filaments that rustled according to a rhythm that appeared impervious to the motion of the air around them.

To Paul, that first time, the light appeared deep yellow. Later, others would say that they saw it as blue or pink or even clear, like the fumes from an open gas tank. One woman compared it to the radiant fuzz that clings to the outer edge of a lit neon tube. A college sophomore said it reminded him of a dense and luminous fog, of the sort that settles onto a city after a rain in the lamplit dead of night. A little girl said the glow looked like the stuff that seeped out when you popped a firefly open between the nails of your thumb and forefinger, while her mother said she was put in mind of the blue blur of atmosphere you see in photos of Earth taken from space. A man who'd lost his eyesight thirty years earlier in a boiler explosion swore up and down that he could see Luca in a sort of reverse silhouette as he moved. The boy's entire tiny being, the man said, appeared to pulse, flare, and churn in tempestuous whorls like the movies he remembered watching that showed the roiling surface of the sun.

Around the Divinity School—where Luca's father, Adrian Bennett, was an associate professor, and Paul was that lowliest of human entities, a graduate student—there was much debate about what to call it. This was hardly surprising. The faculty included experts on all five of the world's major faith traditions, as well as scholars fluent in another dozen or so minor religions besides. There were more than a handful of professors and doctoral students at the Div School, in fact, who could speak eloquently, extemporaneously, and at considerable length on the visible charismata of the Gnostic pneumatics; the dazzling, variegated splendors of the Buddhist saints; Apollo's glistering halo at Hadrumetum; the glamours of the Sumerian *melam*; the Uncreated Light of the Neoplatonic hierarchies; the swirling aureolae of the Tibetan *thangkas*; the mysteries of the divine *kavod*; and the gold-leaf almonds and fish bladders that enveloped the holy fools in medieval Christian manuscripts. They knew their archons from their arhats, their saints from their tzaddiks, their wali from their kami. Being scholars of religion, they also, of course, knew their share of charlatans, cons, and infamous frauds: the golden plates buried on a hill in upstate New York; the mass hallucinations in Medjugorje; and the collective pareidolia that saw Hanuman in a mahogany tree in Singapore.

For a time, Adrian tried to get everyone to call his son's glow a *khva-renah*. As a professor of religious studies and a specialist in comparative mythology, he knew, as most people did not, that the word was Avestan, that Avestan was the sacred language of Zoroastrianism, and that Zoroastrianism was the world's oldest extant monotheism. He knew, too, that according to Zoroastrian scripture and tradition, *khvarenah* described a divine radiance bestowed upon the righteous and the holy—and most of all upon the ancient Persian kings.

Of course Adrian also knew that his two-year-old son was not a Persian king—any more than he was, by any definition, ancient. Nor did Adrian count himself among the 150,000 or so remaining devotees of Ahura Mazda, the benevolent and wise creator of the world, whose gift the *khvarenah* was traditionally understood to be. He was, rather, by his own account, the product of a secular upbringing in Southern California, the only child of an overworked aerospace engineer and a high school librarian who'd flatly and finally rejected her parents' Presbyterianism at the age of sixteen. The nearest Adrian had ever come to any formal religious affiliation was nine months on the trail of the Grateful Dead in 1992, and behind that, in high school, a brief flirtation with a nondenominational youth group that had put him off institutional religion, and especially Christianity, for good.

And yet for all that Adrian couldn't bear the banalities of American religious life at the turn of the second millennium, he felt an almost equal abhorrence for his parents' desert-dry rationalism. He liked to say that he believed in belief—the odder and more esoteric, the better. The only point of studying religion, he told his students, was to examine it in all its bizarre profusion. Forget what you know or think you know. No one cares if you grew up Catholic or Jewish or Southern Baptist. No one needs to read the six hundred thousandth dissertation on Augustine or Spinoza or John Calvin. Why not make yourself a world expert on the Etruscan religion, or the Nahuatl pantheon? Or if you must study Christianity, why not address yourself to the majestic Valentinian cosmology, which posited a vast pleroma full of aeons and syzygies, along

with a Christ so inhumanly perfect that his holy rectum was never convulsed by the flutterings of even a single urgent bowel movement?

Paul had heard this little speech enough times that he initially wondered if Adrian's insistence on the *khvarenah*'s Zoroastrian provenance
was a private joke. Later he would learn better. At some deep level,
Adrian had always been a serious person, though it was not always
obvious to those who knew him casually. He was friendly and direct,
but also often aloof in a way that suggested a certain fundamental laxity
of character. Handsome, in a San Diego sort of way, he gave the impression of a person who didn't watch himself too closely, largely because
he'd never had to.

In recent years, however, the people closest to Adrian had noted a
change of timbre, a tightening of his attitudinal tone. He was not immune
to humor or lightheartedness, and he did not lose his talents for banter
and light teasing that composed an essential part of his inoffensive charm.
But as he approached fifty he'd become increasingly suspicious of anything that smacked of whimsy or uncomplicated glee. More and more
he seemed like the kind of serious person who speaks seriously about the
importance of being serious.

Yet despite his best efforts, no one took Adrian up on *khvarenah*. The
word was too hard to pronounce, the notion too bizarre to comprehend.
This was frustrating, he admitted, but it was not entirely unforeseeable.
He'd been around academia long enough—he'd been around life long
enough—to recognize how warily most people, especially the sort drawn
to the life professorial, reacted to any sort of anomaly. They liked what
they knew and rarely took the trouble to get to know anything they
weren't going to like. As Frege once said, an academic confronted with
novelty is like an ox confronted with an unfamiliar gate: it will gape, it
will bellow, it will try to squeeze through sideways—anything to avoid
going through.

Adrian was therefore disappointed, but in the end not all that surprised that it wasn't *khvarenah* that people used to describe whatever was
happening to Luca. Instead it was another word—one that, thanks to

Harry Potter, even Max, Adrian's other son, had heard before. Instead they called it the nimbus.

The day Paul first saw the nimbus, which was the first time anyone saw it, was an ordinary Thursday in mid-October. It was a few weeks before his twenty-eighth birthday, a little less than a month after the start of a new academic term. By some measures it was not all that long ago, but it was far enough back that Paul and his friends still had every reason to believe that George W. Bush would be the worst president they'd see in their lifetimes.

That fall, Paul was arcing high in the weightless apogee of life. He was in his sixth year as a graduate student at the Divinity School of a well-respected but not particularly well-known university on Chicago's South Side. Six years—call it five, even, if you only wanted to credit time served—was longer than anything else he'd done in his life: longer than high school, longer than college, far longer than all of his postcollegiate jobs put together. Five years was serious business, the length of world wars and Soviet economic plans. Five years is what it took Justinian to build the Hagia Sophia, or Flaubert to write *Madame Bovary*.

Paul had done nothing nearly so impressive with his time at the University. Nevertheless, he wore all the marks of an able young man at the peak of life: dense black hair that crowded close to his dense black eyebrows, sturdy shoulders and calves traversed by visible, vigorous blood vessels, joints that never ached for no reason, and a bladder that let him sleep unmolested for ten long hours at a stretch. He had dark eyes that still glistened under thick lashes, a bright face that neither sagged nor sank. His skin, a firm Sicilian fawn in the coldest months, was burnished to a fine copper hue after a long summer of early-morning runs and late-afternoon beers. Not once, not even for a second, had he forgotten the name of his best friend, or for that matter what to call the kitchen utensil he was just then holding in his hand.

Paul had been in graduate school long enough to know that the first

rule of being a graduate student, at least a graduate student in the humanities and soft social sciences, was that one must always insist on the hor-
rors of quaternary education. *It must be nice*, people liked to say, when they
heard how Paul spent his days, as though getting a PhD were like taking
an extended beach vacation in Bali. And who could blame them? Any time
grad students featured in a book or a TV show, their occupation tended to
serve as a placeholder, an excuse to let a character wander around the city
all day thinking deep thoughts or doing expensive drugs or having complicated polyamorous affairs, without the narrative drag of a job or other
ordinary adult responsibilities.

No, no, it's not like that, Paul was supposed to say. *Grad school's not like
that at all.* He knew the whole spiel, could rattle it off without thinking:
the work was limitless, the hours were awful, the pay was atrocious, the
stress was enormous, the whole system ran on bureaucratic caprice and
professorial whim—and now there were no jobs on the other side of the
gauntlet to redeem all that torment. Possibly you could justify grad school
in the name of pluperfect desire, which was to say that for some people it
was, like chemotherapy or learning German, something worth wanting
to have done. But no one in their right mind looked forward to actually
doing it.

To complete a PhD in the humanities, after all, was to forfeit the best
decade of your life to a state of quasi-monastic abstention, to spend years
writing a thesis that ten people in the world would understand and four
people in the world would ever read, to take on a small nation's worth
of student debt, and to come out of it at the end—if you were lucky!—
with a degree of such mind-boggling inutility that it would make you less
employable than you were when you started.

And yet.

And yet for all his very real gripes, for all that he spent most of his time
feeling unripe and overspent—somehow simultaneously both wet behind
the ears and past his prime—Paul also often felt like the luckiest person on
Earth. The secret was that he loved being a graduate student, loved it so
much that he sometimes wondered if being a graduate student was, in fact,
his true calling in life.

This was absurd, of course. He understood that. The point of graduate school was that you weren't supposed to stay forever. The idea was to take your courses, do your exams, write your dissertation, and then, five or ten or a hundred years later, to get on with your life. But Paul didn't want to get on with his life. He didn't want to leave.

Of the many books Paul had read during his five years of graduate school, one of his favorites was a nearly forgotten rhetorical manual for students that was produced during the High Middle Ages. The manual consisted, for the most part, of sample letters meant to be used as models by young men at the universities of Paris or Oxford or Bologna. They included missives aimed at fathers, mothers, uncles, brothers, sisters, priests, archdeacons, feudal lords, and bishops—any potential benefactor who might be susceptible to a lucrative guilt trip. "I am studying at Oxford with the greatest diligence, but the matter of money stands greatly in the way of my promotion," said one letter, speaking essentially for all of them. "The city is expensive and makes many demands." Or, as another letter put it—this one written as a model response from a father to his pleading son—"a student's first song is a demand for money, and there will never be a letter which does not ask for cash."

Thanks to the letter manual, Paul could appreciate his membership in a hallowed lineage of impoverishment. For he, too, was broke—and not in the way that Carrie, his sorta-kinda girlfriend, liked to say she was broke when the monthly transfer from her trust fund arrived in her high-interest savings account a few days later than she'd expected, or even in the way of his less ostentatiously appointed colleagues and peers, the ones who poor-mouthed endlessly yet always seemed to find the means to fly off to Park City for a ski vacation, or down to St. John to attend a friend's wedding. Paul was broke in what the right-wing professors at the University's law school liked to call the original public meaning of the term: when he said he was broke, he meant that his money was gone.

Unlike his ancient predecessors, however, Paul had no father he could beg for money. He had no father at all, in fact, none he'd ever known, and a mother only in blessed memory. He did have an uncle back in Northern California, his mother's younger brother, Steve. But Uncle Steve was a sixth-generation farmer—almonds and walnuts, some rice, and, for a narrow, humiliating stretch, a little weed—who'd been working the orchards since he was eleven years old. In Steve's view, which he never hesitated to offer, his late sister had been the perfect example of someone who relied too much on her head. She had always been the smarter of the two of them, he conceded without hesitation, but all you had to do was look at her life to see where all that thinking had gotten her. At twenty she'd dropped out of college, sold off her share of the family business, and nearly got herself killed hanging around Communists in Bolivia. A few years later, finding herself broke, unemployed, and unmarried with a newborn—she was enough of a Catholic to make abortion unthinkable—she'd had no choice but to move home and mooch off her hardworking kid brother.

To Steve's mind, Paul's decision to go to graduate school was proof that he had learned all the wrong lessons from his mother. If Paul really wanted to learn something about religion, Steve insisted, he could do what a billion Catholics the world over did every Sunday: he could haul himself off to church.

Paul was a heavy agnostic who could pass for an atheist six days out of seven. He had not attended Mass since his mother's funeral, and he was about as likely to go to church on a random Sunday as Uncle Steve was to write his wayward nephew a check. But he was not entirely at a loss. The reason Paul saw the nimbus—which is to say, the reason he was anywhere near Adrian's son in the first place—was that Adrian had offered him a job. *It'll be easy money,* Adrian promised, and though Paul couldn't guess how that was going to translate into numerical terms, he had little choice but to find out. The city is expensive and makes many demands, and the last time he could bear to look, his checking account was down to sixty-four dollars.

Like many of humanity's highest achievements, the University where Paul was getting his PhD had been conceived under the spell of a powerful self-loathing. Bought and paid for by Chicago's leading industrialists to crown what was then one of America's leading industrial cities, it was constructed to evoke everything opposed to the grubby churn of industry: age, authority, wisdom, calm, quiet, and tradition. Even the buff-colored facades of the campus's original neo-Gothic buildings—including Harrison Hall, the home of the Divinity School—spoke of a past so unfathomably antique as to be roughly equivalent to eternity. Built of Salem limestone, the pride of Indiana stonemasonry, Harrison's portals, spires, and window traceries were a literal graveyard for trillions upon trillions of tiny oysters, snails, and clams who died in the vast inland sea that gave Illinois oceanfront views in the years when sharks were still a new sight on the Earth.

The University was now nearly a hundred years old, but it had been designed from the start to look like it was a thousand. Rumor had it that the architects had so painstakingly copied the medieval European originals that they'd drawn the imperfections of age right into their plans. The copper roofs were installed with preexisting chemical patinas. The limestone was stained and scuffed to disguise its fresh-from-the-quarry shine. Even the slate stairs in the main buildings were sanded down along the nosing to suggest centuries of ponderous treading. By American standards, the University was now legitimately old, and despite the corporatizing pressures of the contemporary academy, it was still holding fast to its reputation as the guarantor of what one chancellor had unironically called "traditional traditions." The truth, though, was that the University was and always had been, like fundamentalist Christianity or *haredi* Judaism, that purest and most perverse of modern institutions: the sort that cannot bear the thought of its own modernity.

Paul pulled open the heavy front doors of Harrison Hall and climbed four flights of old-but-not-as-old-as-they-looked slate steps to the top floor. He walked down the long tiled hallway to the end, where, as one of the newer and younger faculty members, Adrian had been assigned a small office under the building's sharply slanting eaves.

At the sound of Paul's knock, a gentle rap of two knuckles against the glazed oak, Adrian opened the door almost instantly. His eyes were wide in silent alarm. He put a hand out, miming Hold On, and disappeared. A minute later he was out in the hallway, easing the door closed behind him with a nearly inaudible click. Paul noticed that while Adrian was otherwise dressed in standard professorial attire—a crisp white shirt with the sleeves rolled to the elbows, dark cotton pants with a brown leather belt—he wasn't wearing any shoes.

Sorry about that, he said. *Luca was up all night and I just got him to sleep in his stroller.*

Paul didn't know what to say to that, so he lifted his eyebrows and twisted his mouth into an awkward smile. Young children were a mystery to him—not a deep and intriguing mystery but a boring, mundane one. It wasn't that he liked kids or disliked them. He simply didn't know anything about them. Life as he'd been living it had given him no reason to think about children since he'd been a child himself, and so he hadn't.

Adrian looked over his shoulder, back at his door. *Hang out here for a few minutes, will you? Once I'm sure he's out, I can show you what I'd like you to take care of.*

Paul had met Adrian nearly a decade earlier, after signing up for Adrian's Introduction to Religion class during the fall quarter of his sophomore year. He'd taken the class, frankly, because he thought it would be easy—as easy as beginning French for the child of a native Parisian. Probably the "religion" of the course's title would cast a wider net than his mother's idiosyncratic American Catholicism—surely you couldn't spend a whole quarter on acoustic-guitar hymns, antinuclear activism, liberation theology, and unprintable imprecations against the Vatican. But sixteen years of being dragged to Sunday-afternoon Masses at St. Zwingli had to count for something. How much more, really, could there be?

Adrian was, at the time, an adjunct professor. He was not in those years the lecturer that he would be half a decade later, when Paul first started at the Div School. Yet even back then, during his first postgraduate teaching gig, it was obvious that Adrian had an unusual gift.

His Intro to Religion class had started on a late-September day that was already starting to feel like fall. The maple and elm trees on campus had begun their autumnal transfiguration, as had many of the girls, who'd traded their shorts and sundresses for jeans and sweatpants. Paul remembered parking his mountain bike outside the Humanities Building, finding a seat high in the terraced auditorium, and waiting, with fifty or so others, as the three o'clock start time came and went.

As the rustle of half-whispered conversations in the lecture hall grew into a proper din, Paul considered bailing on the class. But just as he made up his mind to leave, he saw a young-looking man in a brown corduroy suit stride aggressively down the central aisle. Back then, Paul hated wearing the glasses he needed to decipher a face more than ten feet away—it was one of his few concessions to vanity—and so he couldn't make out much about the man's expression. Still, it was obvious even at a distance that the man was desperately, and not very successfully, trying to catch his breath.

Once he was able to regain some portion of his lost composure, Adrian began his lecture with a nervous joke about his tardiness. He was new to campus, he explained, and had gotten so lost that he'd very nearly ended up delivering a lecture to an empty gymnasium in the fitness center. After that halting start, which diminished but did not extinguish the ambient chatter, Adrian grasped the rails of the wooden lectern and closed his eyes. In a deep, clear voice that bore no obvious relation to the shaky tenor the students had heard a minute earlier, he recited strange verses in a strange language. The language, as it turned out, was ancient Akkadian, and the verses were part of the lament that Gilgamesh poured out to Utnapishtim in the tenth tablet of the epic that bore his name. When he finished his recitation in Akkadian, Adrian opened his eyes to an auditorium whose attention he now possessed completely. He recited the verses again, again from memory, but this time in English:

My friend Enkidu, a wild ass on the run,
donkey of the uplands, panther of the wild,
my friend Enkidu, whom I love so dear,
who with me went through every danger:

the doom of mortals overtook him.
Six days I wept for him and seven nights.
I did not surrender his body for burial,
until a maggot dropped from his nostril.
Then I was afraid that I too would die,
I grew fearful of death, and so wander the wild.
What became of my friend was too much to bear,
so on a far road I wander the wild.
How can I keep silent? How can I stay quiet?
My friend, whom I love, has turned to clay,
my friend Enkidu, whom I love, has turned to clay.
Shall I not be like him, and also lay down,
never to rise again, through all eternity?

From there, and for the next forty-five minutes, Adrian was off and running. Without pausing for breath, he spun out a lecture that connected the existential agony of Gilgamesh to the Iraq War, forty-two centuries later. His theme was "the doom of mortals"—death, he explained to the undergraduates in the auditorium, lest there be any confusion—and the efforts, which appeared in *The Epic of Gilgamesh* as they would in every age and society—to evade, overcome, or accommodate that fate.

In the years before he arrived at the Divinity School, Paul often referred to Adrian as the best teacher he'd ever had. As proof, he offered his own vocation: Adrian's Intro to Religion course had persuaded Paul not just that religion was more than his mother's Catholicism but that the academic study of religion could be something other than a dilettant-ish and somewhat disreputable antiquarian pursuit. In Adrian's hands, religious studies was every bit as urgent and impressive as the world's great religions were for their original practitioners. That one class had changed the course of Paul's college curriculum, redirecting him from the major in English Literature, Communications, and Media that he had been contemplating to a degree in the college's catch-all World Stud-ies Department, with a specialization in Religion. It was Adrian himself who had first talked to Paul about the possibility of graduate school, and who had later written him the recommendation letter that, in the words of the Dean, had been so impressive as to almost single-handedly win Paul admission to the master's program at the Div School.

After a few minutes, Adrian reappeared in the doorway of his office. *We're good*, he said. *You can come on in.*

Paul picked up his bag. *Are you sure?*

Once he's down, he's down. As long as we whisper, we should be fine.

Adrian's office was anchored, at its center point, by a broad wooden desk with a black walnut chair on rollers parked behind it. Each flank of the desk hosted a minor mess of books, papers, and colored folders, and in the center was a clearing where an open laptop supervised an undisturbed calm. The six rows of simple bookshelves that ringed the walls were about three-quarters full. In one back corner of the office was a double file cabinet, in front of which were two columns of cardboard bankers boxes. In the other back corner was a three-wheeled jogging stroller. Besides the books, the only personal touches in the office were a framed photograph of Adrian's wife and children, and a framed PhD diploma, both of which hung in the slender space of wall that divided two slim latticed windows.

It didn't take long for Adrian to show Paul what he wanted done. His books needed sorting—*Nothing intricate*, he insisted, *just group them by author and alphabetize by the first letter of the last name*—and the files in his bankers boxes needed to be scanned into PDFs and unpacked into his filing cabinets. Adrian took a key from his pocket and handed it to Paul. *Thursdays I work from home, and Fridays I'm usually gone by three, so you should feel free to work either of those days without checking ahead of time. Mondays, Tuesdays, and Wednesdays are my class days, so you should probably avoid those.*

What about the weekends?

All yours if you want them, but don't feel obliged. Adrian turned and looked at the bankers boxes. *I'll see if the Div School has a scanner we can borrow.*

I can take them to the library, Paul said.

You sure? I can pay you time and a half, but I don't know if I can afford a worker's comp claim.

Paul smiled. *I'll be fine.*

Adrian walked over to the desk and ran his finger over the laptop's trackpad to wake it up. *Let me see if there's anything I'm forgetting.*

Paul turned to the bookshelves and pretended to care intensely about the first book his eyes settled on, the twelfth volume of the *Encyclopedia Iranica*. He turned back around when he heard Adrian typing.

Hey, listen, Paul. I know this wasn't in the job description, but I just got a note from the Dean. Do you think you could stay in here with Luca while I go talk to him for a minute?

Paul felt his brow furrow.

You won't have to do anything. You can just sit here and read or whatever. He's so tired it wouldn't surprise me if he slept through to tomorrow morning.

Sure, Paul said. *Sure, no problem.*

Adrian tapped his trackpad a few times and his laptop screen went black. *Thanks. It shouldn't be more than a few minutes. If he happens to wake up, just rock the stroller back and forth a couple of times, he'll probably go right back down. If that doesn't work you can shoot me a text.* He slipped on his shoes, offered Paul a half-ironic salute, and rushed out.

It was about six minutes before Paul saw the nimbus. He could say this with some precision because the first thing he'd done when Adrian left his office was to pull out his phone. What he'd intended to be a quick glance at his email became, as it always did, a total immersion in the ethereal underworld of Online. Within the space of a few short minutes, Paul had gotten himself emotionally entangled in a days-long fight between two packs of roving social-media mobs. He knew none of the people involved, cared nothing about the ostensible subject of their dispute, but still that didn't stop him from getting wrapped up in the tortuous intricacies of their feud. He first caught sight of the nimbus only because one participant in the fight had said something of such egregious stupidity that Paul had to look away from his phone to give himself a moment to ponder how humanity would ever survive when it was filled with so many obvious idiots.

Luca's glow snapped him out of it. Paul's despair at the state of the Internet, so easily confused for the state of the world, turned to a more acute form of desperation when he saw the boy's two-year-old body enveloped in a strange soft light. Luca was still breathing, still sleeping; except for the nimbus, in fact—in fact, even with it—he looked perfectly content. Paul, meanwhile, was on the verge of panic. He sent Adrian a text—something's happening with Luca, can you come up?—and when that didn't bring a response in thirty seconds, he took what was for him the radical step of calling Adrian directly.

Paul, we're almost done here. What's wrong?

I think you need to come up here. There's something you need to see.

TWO

As she kick-turned into another lap in the pool in the basement of the University's Undergraduate Athletic Center, Renata Bennett decided that Plato was right: the poets are full of shit. This was a lesson long in coming, a lesson she'd spent most of her life resisting. Now, though, on this Thursday morning in the thirty-eighth fall of her one wild and precious life, the wisdom of Plato's complaint struck Renata with the force of what one of those poets, being full of shit, might call an epiphany, or possibly a revelation.

Coming off the wall, Renata let herself feel the force of her momentum before she began her breaststroke in earnest. In her husband's estimation she had a bad habit of humility: Adrian was always pushing her to claim more credit for her accomplishments. When it came to the full-of-shitness of poets, however, Renata needed no prompting. She knew she knew whereof she spoke.

She was, after all, that rare thing, and maybe that unique thing: a serious reader of contemporary poetry who was not herself a writer, a publisher, or a teacher of contemporary poetry. She read poems the way her husband read blogs, the way the women in her moms group read Facebook and watched TV, the way her mother's latest boyfriend still read the print editions of the *Wall Street Journal*, the *FT*, and the *New York Times*. She read poems the way she used to read novels, back before she had children, which is to say that she read poems like reading them was the most ordinary thing in the world.

Renata's expertise did not stop there. For when she looked back at her pre-Adrian dating life, among the wry ectomorphs and the hyperverbal mama's boys, the would-be secretaries of state and the overearnest blerds, it was not difficult to pick out a red thread of real and aspiring poets running through her romantic history.

In high school the trend had started with the black-eyed scion of a Greek shipping dynasty who had plied her with ridiculous verses that were at once mawkish and curiously effective at encouraging her body to try things it had never attempted before. During her freshman year at Harvard, she'd had a brief fling with one of the mama's boys, a curly-haired experimental poet who had already started cataloging his correspondence for the benefit of future scholars and was certain that his furious, unparseable compositions were going to hasten the end of war, capitalism, and every other form of human misery. That arrangement, a not-quite-relationship that transpired entirely in the sleep-drunk and drunk-drunk hours after midnight, had ended abruptly after what she'd thought was a one-off hookup with a thirtysomething bartender from Somerville. (Only later would Renata learn that the bartender, who worshipped at the doorframe of Adrienne Rich and ran a small feminist press out of the basement of her apartment building, had a well-earned reputation for attempting to rescue guileless coeds from the grubby clutches of heterosexuality.)

Still later, after she moved out West, for a master's degree at Stanford, there came a one-night farce with a wrinkled Argentine émigré whose overtures she'd indulged on the chance (100:1, according to Ladbrokes) that he would win the Nobel Prize in Literature before his death. That affair, the most ridiculous of her life, was followed within days by the beginning of the most intense: a torrential entanglement with the only person who'd ever persuaded Renata that the idea of tortured genius was something more than a marketing ploy—the extravagantly brilliant, extravagantly depressive daughter of Palestinian exiles who lived alone in a lichen-covered cabin in Portola Valley.

It was because Renata was that rare thing, and maybe that unique thing—because she knew poets so well, both biblically and otherwise—that she felt competent to say that they were full of shit. With this new truth in hand it was possible to conjure any number of justifications to defend it, but what had caused Plato's wisdom to strike her afresh was her recognition that not once, in all the years that she'd been reading poetry, had she ever read a poem that sang the praise of the sort of day like the day she'd been having.

The poets had written reams about beauty and death, about nature and war. They had composed odes to drinking, drugs, dreams, derangement, seduction, sex, silence, and subways. They had exalted poverty and idleness, pain and regret, old stoves and menstruation. They had written about love—god, had they written about love, so many lies about love.

But what bard had described the satisfaction afforded a woman—and not just a woman but a wife, a mother of two young boys, and the sole proprietor of a profitable nonprofit consultancy—who was able to catch up to her manifold responsibilities for once, or even outpace them a little? Where were the sestinas in praise of competence and hard-earned confidence? Who had turned a neat sonnet or a witty villanelle that captured the exultant feeling of making things happen, of getting stuff done?

Key to the day's triumph—the capstone, the flourish—was convincing Adrian to watch Luca for a few hours. Like much good art, Renata's blazing pièce de résistance was born of necessity: her babysitter Mariela had texted early to say that she was feeling congested and feverish. Renata insisted that she stay home, even though she understood, as she was tapping the words into her phone, that she was courting disaster. Thursday mornings were Adrian's scheduled writing time, and by long-standing agreement they were, or were supposed to be, inviolable.

If it were any other Thursday, Renata might have managed the disruption entirely herself. Adrian could take Max to school on the way to his office, while Renata ditched every last one of her previously scheduled plans to take care of Luca until Max got home, at which point she would watch both boys for hours upon endless hours until they went down to sleep. This morning, however, she had an unmissable call with one of her most lucrative clients planned for eight o'clock, which meant that the day's success would depend entirely on Adrian's willingness to give up his Thursday writing time to take care of his younger son. This was not impossible, but it was also far from a sure thing.

Renata had fallen in love with Adrian over email, during the course of a long-distance correspondence that started after they'd spent an evening together, and then spent the night together, at a wedding of mutual friends. She'd been flattered by his easy charm, impressed by the obscurity of his interests, and drawn to the warm fluency of his conversations. He was likable but not cloying, funny but not obnoxious, at once sincere and ironic in an echt Gen X sort of way. A decade older than she was, he knew a lot about a lot, and obviously loved learning, but he wasn't a prick about it. He wasn't uptight. Not much seemed to get under his skin.

Renata liked his looks, too, which answered a primordial fantasy involving beaches and lifeguards that she'd carried around since she was a girl. She also liked it when he had sworn, early on, unprompted and with evident honesty, that she was the most beautiful woman he'd ever dated.

But what had really taken her—intimidated her, really, albeit in an intensely attractive way—was the depth of feeling and intensity of resolve she found waiting under his veneer of SoCal disaffection. Though she felt very old at the time, Renata was not yet thirty when she and Adrian started trading long emails after their wedding rendezvous. He was nearing forty and working as an adjunct in Ohio, with no visible prospect for improvement. No one wanted to hire him. No one wanted to publish him.

Even his first lucky break—which would come when a senior scholar at Indiana University happened upon his dissertation and invited him to apply for a tenure-track job—was still hiding up ahead in the unseeable future.

Yet none of these setbacks had defeated Adrian's ironclad self-assurance. At Harvard Renata had known plenty of would-be future presidents, corporate titans, and Pulitzer Prize winners, all of them as exasperating as they were confident they were headed for world-historical renown. Adrian shared their sense of a grand personal destiny, but in him it was both complicated and intensified by the belief that he'd nearly missed his chance. He was certain that he'd wasted a precious bolus of time in his twenties—certain, too, that the soulless debasements of late-imperial America had conspired to keep him from discovering his vocation in religious studies until it was almost too late. In his own half-ironic telling, by the time he started his PhD, at the ripe old age of twenty-nine, he was as desperate for redemption as any sinner in the hands of an angry god.

Feeling herself substantially adrift in the doldrums of postcollegiate life, Renata had felt an immediate attraction to Adrian's purpose and drive. She admired the way he never let his feelings of belatedness get him down—the way he used them, in fact, as a spur to his ambitions. Most of all she was impressed (impressed and not a little envious) that he seemed to know exactly what he wanted to achieve, and exactly what he needed to do to achieve it.

A decade later, Renata could identify more than a few things she'd gotten wrong about her future husband. She could only laugh at herself for ever believing him free of neuroses, for example, and especially for imagining that his fondness for hippie rock was a prophylactic against, rather than an expression of, an abiding psychological unease. It was also true that what she'd once taken for his impossibly comprehensive erudition had far more gaps, holes, and blind spots than she'd ever suspected. In several

areas, in fact—including modern history, twentieth-century art and literature, and music by any composer or band you couldn't see at a summer festival drowning in tie-dye—she had known far more at twenty-five
than he did even now.

It was also the case that the rigors of parenting Max and Luca had
taken Adrian, as they had taken Renata, completely by surprise. They
talked about this a lot, so much that it sometimes seemed it was their only
real subject of conversation anymore: how nothing in their lives—not
their families, not their friends, not their acquaintances, not the culture at
large—certainly not the poets—had prepared them for the unrelenting
effort required to raise small children. Renata had of course appreciated
that motherhood in general would be difficult. (She was not the sort of
woman who needed *The Atlantic* to tell her that having it all, whatever
that was supposed to mean, was a ludicrous fantasy.) She felt she'd been
adequately informed about the ways infancy would be a strange and tax-
ing time for her mind, body, and sanity. But she was staggered utterly, as
Adrian was, to discover how hard parenthood got after that, once both
her boys were no longer babies.

Why had no one told them it was going to be like this? Why had no
one warned them that they would be giving up not only the ability to go to
a movie on a rainy weeknight or to fool around on a lazy Sunday morning
but whole swathes of what they'd taken to be ordinary existence? They'd
been interesting people once, they reminded each other. Interesting people
with interesting friends, and fascinations, and hobbies. They'd listened to
new music and read old books. They'd thrown parties. They'd gone dancing. They'd enjoyed the fizzy delights of spontaneous conversation and
the deep pleasures of solitary thought. They'd believed, and had reason
to believe, that it was possible not to be tired. And now they had nothing.
Nothing but their boys.

Why had nobody warned them? Renata had a theory: to raise a young
child was a little like drowning. Not drowning as it appears in movies,
with loud thrashing and desperate cries for help. Renata meant actual
drowning, the kind she'd learned to watch for during the two summers

in high school when she'd worked as a lifeguard on Martha's Vineyard. At the Vineyard Haven Y, she'd seen kids slip silently to the bottom of the pool not five feet from their unwitting guardians. She'd seen others with their mouths bobbing at the waterline, their hands working frantically underwater and their mouths too busy sucking air to scream for assistance.

The tribulations of parenthood had only exacerbated Adrian's feeling that he was falling hopelessly behind. It was his bad luck (and therefore, of course, also Renata's) that the peak of his sons' physical dependency coincided with—competed with, really—the demands of the most consequential stretch of his academic career. Max was born while Adrian was applying for the job that brought him from Indiana back to the University's Div School, where he'd done his PhD, and Luca arrived one nail-biting year before his father went up for tenure. It was a lot to take on all at once, and Renata recognized that. She recognized that, even though motherhood had thrown its own hurdles up—and not a few of them—in front of her attempts to get a freelance consultancy off the ground after she finally escaped McKinsey. Because she loved her husband, because she believed in him, she had never grumbled too much that theirs was not a perfect division of household labor, or really anything close to one.

On any other day of the week, Renata would have had no trepidation about asking Adrian to fill in for Mariela so that she could handle her call. He was regularly exhausted, often irritable, and sometimes ornery. But he was not unreasonable. In theory, if not always in practice, he wanted to carry his share of the parental burden, and any day that wasn't a Thursday he was generally willing to try.

But Thursdays were special. Sacrosanct, even. For all that Renata had gotten wrong about Adrian when she first met him, she had not been mistaken about his sense of purpose. Of his potential for greatness he was still certain, and at forty-eight, with teaching requirements, academic-service responsibilities, and two young children under wing, the one crucial question that remained to be answered about his life, as he had once put it to Renata, was whether he would be able to find enough minutes in each hour, enough hours in each day, and enough days in each year to produce the work that would allow that potential to be actualized. One morning a week was not enough—neither of them pretended otherwise—but it was something he could count on, something that was very definitely better than nothing.

Mariela's text had arrived that morning a little after six, a solid hour before Adrian had slumped down to join Renata and the boys for breakfast. Still groggy from too little sleep—on top of everything else, he was a hopeless insomniac—he had kissed her on the top of the head, and then had gone out to the living room to kiss the boys, and then had returned, shuffling, to the espresso machine, which he probably would have kissed as well, if its chrome surface weren't already too hot for human contact.

Renata made small talk while he made their cappuccinos, steeling herself mentally for a potential blowup. When he handed over the completed coffee, she took a sip and thanked him with an exaggerated murmur of satisfaction. She placed the coffee on the Caesarstone countertop, leaned back beside it, and steadied herself with a foot against the kickboard of the kitchen island. Though Adrian was known to acquaintances and colleagues as a portrait of calm, Renata was familiar enough with his private intensities that some part of her thought it wise to be ready for the worst.

I got a text from Mariela, she said.

Adrian looked up. *Already? That can't be good.*

An hour ago. She's sick.

Adrian appeared to consider this, and then he took a long drink of his cappuccino.

Renata wanted him to answer, but when he didn't say anything she couldn't stop herself from going on. *It sounded bad enough that I told her she should stay home. For her sake, obviously, but also for ours. The boys just got over that other bug. I don't think either of us is ready to do it again.* She added that last part for Adrian's benefit, even though it wasn't strictly true. He liked Mariela—liked her very much, he regularly insisted—but he'd made it clear that he thought Renata was too generous in portioning out sick days and personal time.

It's up to you, he said finally. *It's Thursday.*

Renata pushed her foot harder into the base of the island. *I know it is,* she said. *I know it is, and I know I promised . . .*

Adrian watched her while she tried and failed to find the words she needed. *But . . . ?* he offered.

Renata let out a loud sigh. *But . . . I was wondering, I was hoping . . . I can clear stuff later on, but I've got a call at eight . . . It's pretty important . . .*

Adrian took another long drink from his coffee and again appeared to consider something. For a moment, she was certain her fears were about to come to fruition. She watched Adrian set his coffee down, felt her body tense as he approached, and dipped her head when he stood over her. She couldn't bear to look at his face.

It's no problem, he said. *I can take Luca to the office. We'll drop Max at school on the way.*

You can? You will? Now Renata looked up. Her husband, already smiling, wrapped her in a big hug.

Yeah, of course, he said. *I've got a light day. It's no problem at all. I'll bring him back at lunch.*

The surprise of Adrian's acquiescence set the tenor for the morning, or at least for its first half. With the boys taken care of, the other demands on Renata's day fell swiftly into place. The call with her client, a grant application she'd needed to review, and a passel of emails she'd left unanswered all gave way without friction or complaint, as though touched by the lightning-strike application of genius. She had time, too, to turn over the laundry and start another load, to text her cousin's wife about her cousin's son's upcoming birthday, to order online the Star Wars Lego set and military-grade squirt gun that occasion would require, to speak to a repairman about their ceaselessly rattling refrigerator, to confirm Max's playdate with the mother of his new kindergarten friend, and to call three separate programs that offered piano lessons for kids in the neighborhood.

By ten thirty, Renata was so far ahead of where she'd expected to be a few hours earlier—she'd been able, even, to check in with her mother for ten minutes on the phone, and to read, while she drank down a vegetable smoothie, a solid third of an article a friend had sent her about a TV show written by a guy they'd both known in college—that in the absence of a poem to consecrate her good fortune, an hour in the pool seemed the next best reward.

Renata slid down the lane for her final half lap, feeling the warm buoyancy of the water as a confirmation of her accomplishment. She touched the wall, lifted her goggles to her forehead, and worked out her pace with the help of her trusty Timex, a near replica of a waterproof model her father had given her before sending her off to camp the summer after third grade. She climbed out of the pool and padded quickly across the slightly tacky floor to the locker room, where the air was several degrees warmer and somehow smelled more intensely of chlorine than it did in the main hall. After a brief shower, she found her locker and twisted the blue dial on the combination lock, another Proustian artifact from her distant past. She pulled on her clothes and dug into her bag for a hair clip. It was only then, when she saw her phone's screen light up to announce her eighteenth missed call from Adrian, that she saw how much her triumph had cost her.

According to the Timex, it took Renata nearly ten minutes of running flat out to get from the Undergraduate Athletic Center to the emergency entrance of the University-affiliated children's hospital. The receptionist in the lobby called an orderly over to her desk and directed him to take Renata down to the Radiation Oncology Department. Renata knew what that meant, or thought she did—this was not the first time she'd been sent to Rad Onc, not even the first time for Luca—and as she followed the orderly into the gurney-sized elevator and down a wide hallway, she felt numbed by the terrible certainty of what she was about to discover about her son.

The orderly brought her to a door labeled "STAFF ONLY" and asked her to wait outside. He was gone before she could object, and back before she made up her mind to disregard his instructions. When he returned, he handed her a plastic face shield and a heavy blue apron.

What are these for?

The orderly shook his head. *Hospital protocol.*

Renata donned the gear and followed the orderly to another door. This one said "THERAPY ROOM" alongside several "HIGH RADIA-TION" warnings. The orderly held the door open for her and let it close behind her.

Inside was a dim room with an elevated table in the center and a huge machine of some sort at one end. Luca was sitting on the table, smiling broadly at a group of twenty or so people gathered around him. All of them were wearing lead aprons and transparent face shields, but he was not. Renata pushed her way through the loose crowd until she was stand-ing nearly face-to-face with her son. He appeared to be okay: his olive skin was neither flushed nor pale, his gray eyes were lively and bright. Besides the hospital bracelet on his wrist and the Mickey Mouse gown on his body, Renata saw no other evidence of medical intervention.

Luca clapped his hands excitedly when he recognized his mother. He'd been playing some sort of game on the table with his red toy race car, a recent favorite that he'd found in one of Max's old toy bins. Now he ran his left hand over his head as though pulling a strand of hair behind his ear. It was his sign for Renata, a mimicry of a gesture she'd barely known she made, which had become, in his hands, a visual metonym.

Adrian stood up from a stool near the machine end of the metal table. With a hangdog half smile visible through his shield, he gave his wife a one-armed hug. *Yeah, buddy, Mama's here. I told you she was coming.*

Renata pulled Luca into a full-body embrace. She held him hard against the vinyl-coated apron until he squirmed free. She bent down to look at him square in the face—no, to study him: she wanted to be sure that nothing was amiss, nothing awry. Luca thought it was funny, this sudden intensity, and lifted his car to drive it across her face shield. She let him, but she didn't stop looking, not until she could be certain that every last freckle was in its proper place.

She was crying before she knew it, and then she was sobbing. Fat runnels spilled off her cheeks as she stroked Luca's thin blond hair. Through the fog on her face shield she saw Adrian gazing at her expectantly. Everyone else in the room was, too: they were not just looking at her, they were watching her, like they were waiting for something.

What? she said, finally. *What are you all looking at? What's wrong with him?*

Adrian turned to examine the other faces in the room. Renata, a notch or two calmer now, had the presence of mind to note that there were five or six doctors wearing white coats beneath their aprons. All but one of them looked younger than she was. There were as well at least as many nurses in pastel scrubs and Crocs. *You tell me,* Adrian finally said.

Adrian, she demanded. *Tell me what's wrong.*

You can't see? Adrian asked.

The question pushed her fear over into an anger that was checked only by Luca's blithe obliviousness. *What are you all staring at? What the hell is going on?*

After clearing the room of most of the medical staff, Adrian endeavored to explain to his wife why he'd rushed Luca to the hospital. It was not cancer, he assured her quickly; one of the doctors had suggested the radiotherapy room merely as a precaution.

A precaution against what? Renata said. *What's happening to Luca?*

Adrian appeared to be at a loss. His face was pale and his blue eyes betrayed a deep exhaustion, as though he were the one who'd run a mile after swimming two. He looked sheepish, almost embarrassed. Until he started speaking, Renata was sure he was responsible for whatever was going on.

Finally Adrian told her what he'd seen—what he could still see, he said, though it was much fainter than it had been ninety minutes earlier. He used his hands to show her, holding them about an inch from Luca's skin.

It might be easier if you move your head a little, Adrian said. *When I first saw it, it looked like a sort of viscous light. It was brighter near his body, and faded into these little trembling wisps. Now the color is gone but I can still make out the wisps.*

Renata looked down and assured herself three times over that she had no idea what Adrian was talking about. Luca's forehead was warm to the touch, but if anything he looked even healthier than he had when Renata left the house this morning.

When Renata turned back to Adrian, she saw that the look she had taken for embarrassment was something closer to fear.

Adrian, are you all right?

Almost as soon as she asked the question, Renata felt a presence behind her. Without letting go of Luca, she turned to see the attending physician, a dark-haired woman with chestnut skin. Through their face shields, Renata could see that the doctor had a small, circumspect mouth, a sharp, aquiline nose, and eyebrows so neatly threaded that they looked as though they'd been painted on with a calligrapher's brush.

I'll be honest with you, Mrs. . . .

Renata, call me Renata, please.

The doctor smiled sympathetically. Her voice was high and clear, and she spoke with the casual assurance of someone who knew that she was very good at her job. *Anita. Anita Krishnamurthi. I'll be honest with you, Renata, when your husband brought Luca in, we had the same question. When Sam, Dr. Partridge—he's my resident—presented the case to me, he wanted to send your husband up to the Neuro wing. Or maybe Ophthalmology. We get that occasionally: a parent who doesn't understand that his child is not the one who needs a doctor.*

Renata's eyes narrowed. Her head felt light, almost dizzy. *But?*

Dr. Krishnamurthi thought for a moment before looking past her, to

Adrian. Renata tried to read her gaze—what it offered, what it sought—but the effort came up blank. After a few seconds, Dr. Krishnamurthi spoke again. *But then I came in and saw it for myself.*

You can see it, too?

Dr. Krishnamurthi put a hand to her mouth and nodded almost imperceptibly.

What do you see?

Like your husband said, it's faded since Luca got here. It looked at first like a faint glow. White-yellow, with little tendrils. They wave a bit, like they're suspended in some sort of fluid. It's pretty much gone now, though. She turned to Adrian. *You can still see it?*

It's almost like I can see where it was, he said. *The air is clearer there than it is everywhere else in the room.*

Dr. Krishnamurthi pulled her phone from her lab coat and made a note before continuing her explanation. *It's a very strange case. At first, I thought it might be some form of electricity. Static, plasma, maybe something like St. Elmo's fire. Then we wondered if it might be some kind of radiation, which is why we ended up in here, with these loathsome aprons on. But we've tried every instrument the hospital owns—EEGs, skin impedance, several different varieties of Geiger counter. Nothing registers.* She let out a quiet sigh. *Nothing registers at all, really. His temperature is just under a hundred degrees, but that's hardly unusual. The glow itself isn't warm. You can't feel it if you put your hand in it. The good news is that whatever it is doesn't seem to be bothering Luca one bit. Right, Luca?*

At the sound of his name Luca looked up and smiled. He held out his toy race car and hooted in her direction.

Dr. Krishnamurthi didn't need to be told that he was looking for her admiration and approval. *Yes, it's a very nice car,* she said in an ingratiating singsong. *Does it go very fast?* For the first time, Renata caught a hint of an accent in Dr. Krishnamurthi's voice: a hollowness in the word "go" that testified unmistakably to formative years spent in Wisconsin.

Luca, who hadn't started talking yet despite his age, hooted vigorously to answer the question in the affirmative.

Can he see it? Renata asked Adrian. *The, the—glow, or whatever it is. Can Luca see it?*

I think so, her husband said. *I mean, yes, I know he can. He was very interested in it at first, but not so much anymore.*

So I'm the only one who can't see it?

No, Dr. Krishnamurthi said quickly. *Dr. Partridge couldn't see it, either. And not just him. As you saw when you got here, your son's case attracted some—well, some attention. And not all of them—*

That doesn't strike me as a good sign. A hospital isn't a place you want to get famous.

Dr. Krishnamurthi's small mouth crumpled into a frown. *No, it isn't usually, you're right. But in your son's case—*

Could you not use that word, "case"? Renata regretted the remark as soon as she said it. *I'm sorry, I just, I'm just trying to figure out what's wrong with my son, and no one seems to be able to tell me.* Renata felt her tears coming again and reached up to wipe them away. As she did, she saw Adrian and Dr. Krishnamurthi trade a silent, significant look.

We don't know, Adrian said finally. *Nobody knows. All we know is that right now Luca seems to be fine.*

Though everyone who'd seen it agreed that the glow had disappeared within four hours of its first appearance, Dr. Krishnamurthi asked to keep Luca at the hospital overnight for observation. She was confident that whatever was happening to Luca was not radioactive, and saw no reason he couldn't be moved to a private room on the pediatric floor. Renata was reluctant at first: still stunned by the day's events, she wanted nothing more than to be home with her boys away from all this madness. She did assent, however, as Adrian did, to just about every sort of test that Dr. Krishnamurthi and her colleagues could think to suggest.

The early results came in over the course of the afternoon and showed nothing—or nothing concerning, anyway, beyond a slightly depressed platelet count. Tests that were supposed to come back positive came back positive. Tests that were supposed to be negative were negative. And test results that were supposed to land, à la Goldilocks, within some blessed intermediate interval all did exactly that. Along with the test results arrived a parade of specialist doctors and nurses—half of whom, Renata came to suspect, were essentially rubbernecking—who generated hypotheses that were dashed nearly as soon as they were formulated. Finally, around five, Dr. Krishnamurthi confessed to Adrian and Renata that only one unsatisfying possibility remained: Luca was a perfectly healthy two-year-old who had somehow lit up like a glow stick for a few hours one Thursday morning.

But of course that's not the only possibility, right? Renata said, after the doctor handed Adrian a thick folder full of printed lab results.

Dr. Krishnamurthi pursed her lips and lifted an eyebrow.

It's like you said this morning, Renata continued. *Maybe it's not Luca who's having . . . you know, some kind of issue. Maybe it's the rest of you.*

Adrian looked up from the folder. His face under the fluorescent lights appeared gray and bloodless. The bags under his eyes were as big as quarters. *Oh, hon, come on. You saw it yourself—*

I didn't see anything. That's the point. I didn't see anything, and I wasn't the only one.

You saw how many people saw it, though. Saw something. You think we were all making it up?

I didn't say that. But how do you know . . . Renata caught herself before she went too far.

How do I know what?

Renata looked hard at her husband, trying to signal with her intensity that this wasn't the time.

Ignoring the tacit message, Adrian looked over at Dr. Krishnamurthi, but the physician, no rookie, refused to acknowledge his glance. Adrian turned back to Renata with widened eyes and raised his hands in a gesture of exaggerated befuddlement. *What is it?* he insisted. *Whatever it is, you can say it. Anita needs to know anything we know. Right?* Once again Adrian looked over at the doctor, who once again refused to offer him even a hint of silent support.

Renata folded her hands and took a deep breath. *I just wondered if, you know, it was some kind of flashback. You told me you used to get them after you did drugs sometimes in college.*

Adrian was watching her carefully. *And . . . ?*

And, well, what about the river trip? You guys did mushrooms a couple of times, right? A few months earlier, as a much-delayed reward to himself for getting tenure, Adrian had left Renata and the boys to spend a week rafting down the Colorado with a college friend.

He barked a loud disbelieving laugh. *That's what you think this was? You think I'm having a psilocybin flashback? What about everybody else? You think Anita was tripping, too?*

Adrian's last question landed with the force of an accusation. It succeeded in making Renata feel more shame than she deserved. She was therefore grateful when the doctor contradicted her husband in a calm and authoritative voice:

No, Adrian. Your wife is right to wonder. We always tell our medical students that when you hear hoofbeats, you should think horses, not zebras. By the same logic, even a zebra is more likely than a unicorn. At the same time—here Dr. Krishnamurthi turned to Renata—*there were a lot of witnesses, and they all saw the same thing. I can appreciate that that's not dispositive. Maybe you're right that it was some sort of mass hallucination, however unlikely that might seem. Maybe it was something else. But precisely for that reason, precisely because we don't know what's happening, I'd like to keep an eye on Luca for at least a little longer.*

Okay, Renata said at last. *Okay. I can live with that.*

Renata wanted nothing more than to stay with Luca for every minute that he had to remain in the hospital, but Adrian argued that Max, who'd spent the afternoon and early evening at his hastily extended playdate, would demand her presence far more than Luca would. This was not quite the clinching argument he wanted it to be: what finally convinced Renata to let her husband stay behind was her continuing suspicion that he, and not their son, was ill.

Still, she knew Adrian was not wrong about Max. Luca was a cheery people pleaser who toddled through the world with the rollicking ease of the second-born. His brother was his opposite, a classic oldest child. He was careful and conscientious to a fault, outwardly quiet while inwardly wracked by a conflict between a bone-deep anxiety and an equally unshakable sense of self-possession. (Before she'd had kids, Renata had treated birth-order theories as so much maternal mumbo jumbo, but her two sons had made her a true believer.)

That night, at home, Renata let Max sleep on Adrian's half of their king bed. Max treated this as the rare privilege it was, performing the whole run of his evening ritual—pajamas, teeth, pee—with an exaggerated display of good behavior. Renata read him a chapter from *Superfudge*, and then sang him a truncated version of "Southern Cross," which she'd introduced to the bedtime rotation when he was two, not realizing that she'd be stuck with it forever after.

Mama, Max said, calling Renata back after she'd tucked him in and shut off the light. *Is Luca going to die?*

Without much thinking about it, Renata rushed over to the side of the bed and squatted to eye level. The faces of her boys looked enough alike that she felt a sense of déjà vu as she examined Max for any sign of psychic injury. *No, sweetie, of course not. Why do you say that?*

Never?

Renata took a deep breath. *Well, someday, buddy. Someday we all have to die. But not now. Not for a very long time.*

Max was quiet again, and then he curled his body to fit his head on Renata's lap. *So why is Luca at the hospital?*

Suddenly, it clicked: both of Adrian's parents had passed away recently, one after the other, and Max had said goodbye to each of them in the hospital. Renata explained to him that while older people sometimes did die in the hospital, usually it was a place where people went to get better. He accepted the explanation without further questions, but she could see that he was not finished chewing it over.

Renata pulled herself up onto the bed next to her son. She had not intended to put herself to bed at nine o'clock that night—she had a vague idea that she wanted to get on the Internet to see if she could find anything that would help explain what was happening to Luca—but the stress of the day was too much to resist. Still in her clothes, with her face unwashed and her teeth and her hair equally unbrushed, she fell into a deep and dreamless sleep.

The next morning, Renata did everything she could to reinforce Max's continuing belief that he, and not his younger brother, was the one getting special treatment. She made him pancakes with blueberries and whipped cream, let him watch ten minutes of his favorite TV show before school, and promised him pizza for dinner.

After dropping him at the door of his kindergarten, Renata went straight back to the hospital. Adrian looked like he hadn't slept so much as an hour, but Luca was full of energy. He climbed into her arms and kissed her repeatedly, like a woodpecker, and then he pointed at the rolling stool on the far side of the bed.

He's spun himself dizzy on that thing a dozen times already this morning, Adrian said. *I think he thinks it's his own private merry-go-round.*

Luca started squirming, but Renata refused to let him down. In that moment she wasn't sure she'd ever let go of him. *Anything new?* she asked her husband, as she had over the phone a half an hour earlier, before she'd left the house with Max, and an hour before that, when she decided she couldn't wait any longer to call Adrian at the hospital.

Adrian rubbed his eyes. *Still nothing,* he said. *Except they want to keep him here. At the hospital.*

Renata felt her stomach drop. *What? For how long?*

I don't know.

Instinctively she put a hand to the back of Luca's head. *Oh, Adrian . . . Really?*

They said it would be the safest course of action, just in case . . .

In case what? Who's "they"?

I guess in case it happens again. Dr. Krishnamurthi suggested it, and then she brought another doctor in this morning, an expert of some sort, and he said the same thing.

An expert in glowing children?

Adrian allowed himself a tired smile. *He's a pediatrician who deals with rare diseases.*

So now they think it's a rare disease?

I don't know, he said. *I guess they're considering it.*

They have no idea, do they? Luca twisted violently away from Renata. With no minor reluctance, she set him down on the bed. When she looked up, she saw Dr. Krishnamurthi waiting in the doorway.

You're right, Renata, the doctor said, after seeing that she'd been noticed. Her face wore an expression of unsentimental sincerity, a thin smile that said she was not going to insult the Bennetts with sugarcoated nonsense. Renata wanted to believe it, and nearly did. *Trust me, I wish I could tell you I've figured it all out. I was up all night looking for any hint that might help us understand. But, frankly, we still don't know—Oh!* Her voice jumped an octave when she saw Luca clapping for her attention. *Well, hello, sir.*

Luca had been playing with the chunky remote that controlled the movements of his bed, and now he held it up for the doctor's approval.

Dr. Krishnamurthi walked over to the bed and put her hands on her slender thighs. *Yes, isn't that interesting? Watch this!* She took the remote from Luca and held a button until his bed was taller than she was. Luca laughed and clapped as he rose, and when she brought him back down he put his hands together in his signal for "more." Dr. Krishnamurthi didn't need a translator. *Let me talk to your parents first,* she said, *and then we'll do it again.*

None of us know what this is, Adrian said to the doctor. *Nobody knows what caused it. We don't know what made it stop, or what might make it start again. It's like you said yesterday, maybe there's a chance Renata was right, and it's not even really happening to Luca at all. If we keep him here until the next time, it could be days, or weeks, or months—*

We wouldn't keep him for months, Dr. Krishnamurthi said quickly, a comment that was less reassuring than she seemed to think.

But even a few weeks, Adrian said. *I mean, Renata and I both want what's best for him, obviously, but we can't just, I mean, we both have jobs—*

We have another son, Renata interjected.

Anyway our house is barely a mile from here. If it returns, if something happens, we could always bring him back.

You could, Dr. Krishnamurthi said. *And, look, I'm not going to pretend to know more than I do. But I would remind you that we are a state-of-the-art pediatric facility. We can keep a close eye on Luca here. As you saw last night, we have staff who work around the clock. If the phenomenon returns, we'll be here to monitor it. If any other symptoms develop, we'll be able to immediately manage those. Really, it's better in just about every way.*

Better? Renata heard the sharpness in her voice but did nothing to soften it. *Better than having him home, where he's comfortable? Where he's familiar? Better than letting him sleep in his own bed? Better than having his family around, when we can't even be sure—*

I'm not suggesting it would be easy, Dr. Krishnamurthi said. *But I've spoken to a number of colleagues, and we do think it's what's best for Luca.*

And what if we don't agree? Renata was pleased to hear her husband emphasize the plural pronoun.

Perhaps seeing her visions of a write-up in the *New England Journal* turn to smoke, Dr. Krishnamurthi put her hand up in a conciliatory gesture. *It's up to you*, she said finally. *We can make recommendations, but ultimately it's up to you.*

Later that night, once they'd gotten Luca home and both boys in bed, Renata and Adrian had sex for the first time in a month. It was her idea, not his, and the urge surprised her nearly as much as it surprised him. The previous thirty-six hours of excitement had been wholly exhausting, and though she'd slept straight through the night, as Adrian had not, she felt the undertow of a deep weariness that she recognized as aftereffects of too much cortisol and adrenaline.

Probably because she was so tired, Renata felt none of the throbs or tingles that were her body's usual way of telling her she needed to get laid. But even though she was still terrified about what had happened to Luca, or maybe because she was still terrified, she felt a deep desire—a compulsion, really—to be physically close to her husband. She walked up behind him while he was wrapping the last of the pizza in tinfoil and pressed herself up against his back. Eschewing even a minimum of subtlety, she reached her arms around his torso and began to stroke the flat planes of his chest and lower abdomen.

Adrian shut off the water and turned around. He looked down at Renata with a skeptical smile. *Tonight of all nights, huh?*

Renata stood on her toes and kissed him lightly. *Not in the mood?*

Adrian scoffed. *I didn't say that.* He put both hands on Renata's butt and pulled her toward him, and the throbs and the tingles kicked in.

Oh, she said, her voice a little hoarse. *Thank god.*

Now now. Let's not be too hasty. God might be the one who got us into this whole mess.

Very funny, Professor.

I'm just saying.

Well, I'm just saying thank you.

For what?

For agreeing with me. About bringing Luca home. I don't know what those doctors had in mind, but I don't think I could have handled watching them do the whole E.T. routine on him.

Adrian leaned down and kissed her. *I don't think we had to worry about that,* he said. *I was pretty impressed with the way they treated us, actually. Anita was very good with Luca. But I agree there wasn't any point in us staying.*

Upstairs, in the bedroom, Renata stripped herself naked and climbed on top of Adrian as soon as he took off his jeans. Still desperate to close the gap between them, she rode him hard and came quickly, much faster than he did. As she repositioned herself so that he could get behind her, a consolation for her haste, she nearly broke out laughing at the memory of something Max had said earlier in the week, back when their lives were still normal. Max had finished his breakfast cereal a few minutes before his brother, and he rattled his spoon to get Renata's attention. *It's not a race, Mama*, he exulted. *But I won.*

After kissing each other good night, Adrian and Renata both fell fast asleep. Renata woke what felt like minutes later to the sound of her bedroom door opening. Max shuffled in with his Star Wars fleece blanket in hand.

Hey, buddy, she said drowsily. *Everything okay?*

Yeah, but Luca won't turn out his light.

You can sleep on the mattress if you want, Renata told him. She reached under her bed and pulled out one of the toddler-sized mattresses they kept to accommodate the kids' midnight visits. After Max pulled back the top sheet, she covered him with his blanket and kissed his head. *Good night, buddy*, she said softly.

Renata was nearly asleep again when a stray thought jolted her awake. She got out of bed and ran quietly down the hallway. The boys' room was dim but for the plastic clock they used as a night-light. As usual, Luca had wandered far from where she'd left him earlier in the evening, and was now curled up, like a puppy, at the foot of his bed. He was breathing normally, his pink cheeks inflating like little puffer fish with each exhalation. Renata saw nothing out of the ordinary.

Back in her bedroom, she kneeled next to Max and put her hand on the side of his head. *Max? Hey, buddy. Max, wake up.*

Max didn't move.

Renata stroked the side of her son's face more intensely. *Sweetie, I need you to wake up. I need you to tell me something. What did you mean about Luca's light?*

Max yawned like a tiger cub, without opening his eyes. *He was making a light on his face, and he wouldn't turn it off, even though I asked him.*

What do you mean, "He was making a light"?

A light. Like, I could see him in the night.

Are you sure, Max?

Yeah, Mama. That's why I came in.

Renata felt her heart race. *What kind of light was it, Max? Did he have a toy? A flashlight?*

I don't know, Mama. Can I go back to sleep now?

Yeah, sweetie, of course. Sleep tight.

Renata stood and crossed over to Adrian's side of the bed. Her heart was beating hard now, like it was trying to escape the confinement of her ribs. She shook her husband roughly on the shoulder.

What? he said finally. *I'm just, I'm just so tired.*

I know, I'm sorry. But I need you. It's Luca. Max says he saw it.

Adrian opened his eyes. *Saw what?* he said. A few seconds later, he understood. *Oh. Oh, okay.*

Renata followed Adrian to the boys' room. She knew in an instant that what she most feared had come true. While Adrian ran his hand out over Luca's sleeping body, as though checking for heat, Renata strained and squinted, hoping to see whatever her husband appeared to be seeing.

Finally she couldn't take it anymore. *What is it? Is it there? Did it come back?*

Adrian was still for a moment. Then his face broke into a wide and terrifying smile.

THREE

Warren Kaylia was well into his second meal of the morning—a slab of stale cream cheese on a disk of canned brown bread, an unsliced apple, a glass of cold buttermilk—when he noticed, across the street from his apartment, a car that looked like his car but couldn't be. For most of his post-breakfast snack, or pre-lunch appetizer, Warren had been sitting at the small table beside the small window in the corner of his small apartment, reading a not-so-small refutation (769 pages of text, plus endnotes, appendices, and a vicious, score-settling index) of John McTaggart's argument for the unreality of time. It was only by chance that he'd looked up, and looked down, at the street below.

What he saw outside resembled his sedan in several respects. The cars were the same make and the same model. They shared an identical and ruthlessly sexless design. Both wore a hue of accidental tan that was the result, at least in Warren's car's case, of too many sunny Midwestern summers and too many salty Midwestern winters. Just like Warren's car, the car on the street had a rainbow's worth of University-issued parking passes affixed to its rear window, as well as a bruise of glittery blue paint on its front right door, in exactly the place where a teenaged yahoo in a pickup truck had sideswiped Warren when he was driving home one night on Lake Shore Drive. Most eerie of all, this new car was sitting in exactly the same spot where he had parked his own three days before.

Yet there were also differences. For one thing, the car down below was dented tip to tail, with more and more various indentations than a golf ball. For another thing, in all the places that Warren's car had windows, this car had dense spiderwebs of shattered safety glass. The wing mirrors on this other car were busted, as were the brake lights, and the rear bumper, and the muffler, which had somehow dislodged from its moorings and was now resting on the asphalt a solid six feet away. Then there were the wheels, which is to say, there weren't: though this car, like Warren's car, was propped up on a toy-scale spare tire, that was the only thing keeping its undercarriage off the street. The other three wheels, as best Warren could tell, were missing entirely, leaving the vehicle clumsily atilt and making it, officially, a unicycle.

Sensing, perhaps, that to resolve his confusion would cost him the tranquility of his morning off—he didn't need to be at work till noon—Warren decided there was no need to rush down to the street. After reopening the heavy hardback volume to the page he'd marked with a grocery mailer, he ate the rest of the brown bread and cream cheese. He finished his glass of buttermilk. He chewed the apple down to the core and wiped its juice from his chin with a paper towel. He remembered the thought he was about to have when the car on the street had stolen his attention: a conviction, really, that for all its barely concealed vituperation, the book he was reading had not laid so much as a pinky on McTaggart's logical demonstration of the incoherence of past, present, and future. Warren could say this even though he despised McTaggart's argument and would like nothing more than to see it reduced to ashes.

He closed the book and stood up from the small table. He brushed the crumbs from his chest and his lap. He deposited his dishes in the sink and returned the would-be refutation to the top of a precariously balanced tower of books in the far corner of his living room. He found his pants folded over the back of his easy chair, where he'd left them the night before, and recovered a clean but slightly damp pair of socks from a towel bar in the bathroom. He collected his black leather loafers from the front hall. He put them all on. He took his keys from the hook next to his heavy metal front door and was about to leave when he realized he'd forgotten a sweater. Once he got his sweater he realized he'd forgotten to pee. Once he peed he realized he'd forgotten his phone. (He had a hard time remembering things when he was tired, and he'd stayed up too late the night before playing The Mace of Wintermere, a medieval-themed online computer game that had lately become all-consuming.) He took the stone stairs down to the first floor, glanced at the sagging folds of his face as he passed the mirror that hung in the cracked-tile foyer, and left his building.

Warren, amigo. Cómo estás?

Warren looked up at the sound of his name. Still out of sorts, he needed a moment to recognize his neighbor Gabriel coming up the sidewalk. The old Mexican, a bricklayer in a previous life, lived down the hall from Warren and was now the pastor of a storefront Pentecostal church nearby. He had a wide face with deep lines running from his nose to the corners of his mouth. He was dressed in a gray suit and a dark felt fedora, and on his back he wore, somewhat incongruously, a bright orange backpack.

He grasped Warren's hand and shook it slowly while he gave Warren a once-over. He did not appear to like what he saw. *Todo bien, amigo? Enfermo? Sick? No te ves bien.*

Warren grunted. *I didn't sleep well*, he said. *Lunga noche. Demasiado lunga.*

Aha, the pastor said. *Larga noche. Comprendo. No dormiste bien.* He tapped his chest. *Me, too. Es difícil para mí también. Es difícil ser viejo, no?* He laughed and patted Warren on the shoulder.

Warren dipped his head, as much to signal his goodbye as to acknowledge their shared infirmity. Before he could step away, Gabriel put a hand up to stop him.

Viste a tu amigo? Te encontró anoche?

I'm sorry, what? Cómo? Between Warren's high school Spanish and Gabriel's construction-trade English, the two men usually found it easy enough to exchange pleasantries and minor building gossip, but their rapport was not built for serious conversation.

Your friend, he find you?

My friend?

Gabriel lifted a hand about a foot over his head. *Tipo alto. Gringo delgado. He says he is your friend.*

Un gringo? Warren felt a pressure in his chest.

The pastor nodded. *He comes last night. Asks me if you live here.*

He did? What did you tell him? Qué dices?

Gabriel looked stricken for a second, but then his face relaxed into a smile. He put his large hand on Warren's shoulder. *Don't worry so much, amigo. I know he is not your friend. I no tell him nothing.*

When he reached the car, across the street, Warren found a message waiting for him. Two messages, really, one inside the other. The inner message took the form of a scrawled slip of paper that had been insinuated somehow (the options were many, given the perforated state of the car's windows) and then dropped onto the stained fabric of the driver's seat. Warren could not decipher the note through the tempered-glass crazings, but he was certain that it was important he see what it said. He unlocked the door and recovered the paper slip from the front seat.

The inner message, which was scrawled on the paper, addressed the outer message, which was the car. The author of this impromptu explication de texte had neither the grace of a Cambridge practical critic nor the subtlety of a deconstructionist at the Sorbonne. But he was clearly a person (he was also clearly a he) who understood that any sign—even a dramatic sign, such as a half-demolished car in the middle of a city street—depended on its context for meaning:

Warren—I told you when we met that I liked you. You remind me of your mother. (RIP.) Much better than your dead old man. So consider this a gesture of friendship. You know it could have been worse. You know it still might be. Get me what's mine so that doesn't have to happen. —W8

With the note in hand, with the double message unequivocal—*a gesture of friendship!*—the belated recognition of Warren's original misinterpretation fell heavy upon him. It was not a cold day, not by Chicago standards, but he was cold nevertheless. His muscles felt weak, and his chest once again felt tight. He heard himself breathing hard, almost panting. Not wanting to faint, which suddenly seemed a real possibility, Warren leaned heavily on the roof of what he now knew, indubitably, was his car.

The Weight, or W8, as he liked to style himself, was a loan shark who hailed from one of the quasi-Canadian counties of northern Minnesota. He was a tall man, with long, ungainly limbs, a thatched tuffet of thin blond hair, and a face dominated by the shaft of his sharp, arrow-shaped nose. Seeing him walking down the street, pale and skinny as a cocaine rail, you might think, as many people mistakenly did, that he'd earned his *nom de crime* back in the days when he used to speed bricks of coke and bales of Chicago Green across Lake Superior in the hulls of deep-V pleasure craft. Or maybe, you might imagine, it was the result of the outlaw's customary affection for nominal perversity—one more thuggish paradox to set beside all the idiot Brains and ponderous Slims and neckless Giraffes.

In fact, however, Warren had it on good authority that The Weight had literally made a name for himself thanks to a particular talent he was said to possess. Blindfold his eyes, hand him a stack of paper currency from any country, and to a startling degree of accuracy he could, or so the story went, tell you exactly how many dollars, drams, or dinars he was holding. Even more impressive, it was said, when it came to American and Canadian currency, The Weight was somehow able to discern by feel the minute differences between counterfeit and legitimate bills. These days this talent was little more than a party trick, like working out the payout on a four-race parlay without a calculator or a computer. But back before portable bill counters were common, The Weight's skill at assessing the integrity of a cash handoff during a moonless midnight exchange off the coast of Thunder Bay had conferred a significant professional advantage.

Prior to his entanglement with The Weight, Warren's awareness of the greater Great Lakes crime world had been next to nonexistent. As a young kid, he'd grown up in frank terror at the thought of doing anything to encourage his father's anger and disappointment, a fear that the teachers at his mostly white public elementary school had misinterpreted as a natural complaisance. He had worked hard to maintain his reputation as "one of the good ones" long after the perniciousness of the tag became unignorable, and this self-image, or self-delusion, had followed him into adulthood. More than a few times, Warren had decided that he was too risk-averse for his own good—too cautious, too meek, too ready to defer to anyone in a position of authority—and so it seemed a vicious irony that he had ended up in hock to The Weight.

Of course this was not his fault, not exactly. If it hadn't been for his mother's late-in-life discovery of Texas Hold 'Em (she had learned to play the game, but not well enough, watching ESPN) and his father's unwillingness to pay the many debts she incurred after he stopped funding her "hobby," Warren would have had no reason to make The Weight's unfortunate acquaintance. Much less would he have reason to learn anything about the breadth, depth, and depravity of the multiethnic free-for-all that had sprung up, like a toxic fungus, to feed on the rotting corpse of the Chicago Outfit.

Warren ran his fingers over the dimpled body panels of his wrecked car. With the scuffed toe of his loafers he shifted the shattered glass that littered the pavement. In his left hand he cradled the driver's-side mirror, which dangled, like an incompletely severed head, from a single electrical cable. He told himself, not for the first time, not for the five thousandth time, that he needed to think. He needed to concentrate. John McTaggart was not going to help him now.

What was going to help him? Money was the easy answer. Money was always the easy answer: that's what makes it money. But if money was the easy answer, it was also insufficient.

The amount that Warren's mother—and then Warren's father, and now Warren—owed The Weight was not abstract. It had a quantity, albeit one that, thanks to the magic of compounding usury, jumped alarmingly every week. As of now, that number was a little more than sixty thousand dollars, which worked out to three kilograms of fresh twenties, twelve hundred grams of fresh fifties, or six hundred grams of hundred-dollar bills, roughly twice the mass of a human heart.

But who was it who said that quantity made its own kind of quality? Surely that person would have understood Warren's predicament. For it was no longer possible for Warren to think of his obligation as merely financial. The debt had become existential, maybe metaphysical: it was fundament and firmament, alpha and omega, alkahest and void, hyle and Pradhana, *tohu wa-bohu*, holy the firm.

The weather outside, it finally occurred to Warren to notice, was much better than it had any right to be. It was an almost springlike fall day, with a gentle white sunlight mingling unobtrusively with the last low layer of the morning chill. Warren's street and the lots that lined it were not dense with trees or other tall vegetation; what plant life they had tended toward the low and weedy. In this respect, as in so many others, the area was nothing like Fell Gardens, just a few blocks to the north. Even so, the trees that had survived the decades of institutional neglect looked vibrant today, almost giddy, as if the leaves had roused themselves for one last display of boisterous defiance against their imminent demise. The birds on the telephone lines were hyperactive as well, chirping a tune with multiple harmonies that sounded to Warren's ears mysteriously close to what a chorus of castrati might sound like if they were forced to sing "Ode to Joy" backward in triple time. It was a weekday, so all the bigger kids in the neighborhood were at school, or at least pretending to be, but on the brick stoops and in the chain-link yards up and down his street, Warren saw children nonetheless: babies and toddlers, mostly, who were lit by the white light of the great hydrogen bomb in the sky and were being watched over by their mothers, grandmothers, aunties, sisters, and stepsisters.

It was typical, Warren told himself, that the world would spite him like this. Typical that it was not content to make him the unfair victim of somebody else's bad debts. It was entirely typical that the world had to rub it in, to show him exactly how little it or anyone cared. By rights, Warren deserved the indulgence of the sympathetic fallacy, an external *Sturm* to echo and amplify his internal *Drang*. At the very least he should get a foul fog to match his melancholy mood. But Warren had seen enough of life—he had seen enough of *his* life—to know it was not to be. The way his life worked was that bad things happened, and then more bad things happened, and then maybe for a brief time slightly fewer bad things happened before even worse things started happening, and the cycle rolled over again. All the while the world went on its way, sometimes merrily, sometimes not, but always without even the slightest care for his state of mind.

Though the sun wasn't that hot, and though Warren had felt chilled just a few minutes earlier, he realized he was sweating under his sweater. His eyes were bleary, and his sinuses were clogged, making it impossible to breathe through either nostril. All this anguish was making Warren woozy. But more than anything, it was making him hungry.

After deciding that he needed a proper lunch before it was time to report to the library for work, Warren walked north. When he reached the grassy median of the Midway, the broad four-lane boulevard that divided his neighborhood from Fell Gardens, Warren was still pondering the ontology of his debt to The Weight, still plotting what to do with the tortured remnants of his car. (If it wasn't dealt with by nightfall, the scavengers in his neighborhood would surely strip it to the frame.) He stepped into the road and looked up just in time to see a city bus bearing down upon him. He jumped back fast enough to miss the bus, but before he could congratulate himself for this spurt of unaccustomed agility he saw a woman on a bike headed straight for him. He heard the woman yelp, and then he felt a tremendous pressure, followed by an even more tremendous pain, on the right side of his body.

When he opened his eyes, Warren couldn't breathe. He couldn't see anything, either—the room he was in was darker than a pocket—and what little he could hear was at best a faint burble. He was no longer in pain. That much he could tell. In fact, he felt no sort of physical sensation whatso- ever. His mind, as though soothed by a cool light mist, was quiet for once. For once it was not skittering this way and that, readying itself anxiously in preparation for the next onslaught or insult. But his mind noticed the breathing—i.e., the lack thereof. It told Warren he needed oxygen. It told him he needed to expel the carbon dioxide that was already strangling his blood and poisoning his flesh. In this strange state, Warren's mind still felt as though it were a distant appendage, reporting in from the outer extremities of his body. It said that something must be done, that Warren should give anything—anything, really, it insisted; this was not hyperbole—for a single deep breath. One hard pump of the bellows. One firm stroke of the oars. Warren did not disagree. He was fond of breath- ing. He liked it in theory and liked it even better in practice. More than anything right now (again, this was not hyperbole), he wanted to feel his lungs expand, wanted to see his chest heave. But it was no use. Though he could sense the existence of his body now, he still could not feel it, not in any ordinary way. It was impotent, incapable, immobilized.

The mist began to dissipate. The room (but was it a room?) began ever so barely to brighten. As the darkness resolved into dim shapes, matte black against dark gray, Warren thought he understood what was happening. He thought he could see: he was trapped, pinned beneath the undercarriage of a passenger sedan. Above him now he could see the serpentine twists of the exhaust piping, the heavy dimple of the fuel tank. To each side stretched the shadowy arms of the rear axle. They were stripped down, wheelless, to the naked lugs. The car, Warren understood, was balanced on a single point, and that point was his chest. His breath didn't stand a chance. The darkness yielded another few degrees. Of course: it must be dawn. Earliest dawn, before the birds and the colors come out. The faint commotion he'd heard before began to untangle itself into a murmur of recognizably human voices. Off to his right Warren was able to make out a small crowd, gawking at something he couldn't quite see. They appeared not to notice him. No one seemed to care that he was trapped and well on his way to dying. Warren tried to speak, but his lips were as useless as his lungs. Anyway, if he couldn't breathe then how could he be expected to talk?

Warren felt himself blink. He closed his eyes and opened them again. After a few more experiments in this vein he looked to his right and saw that the crowd was gone. In its place were two figures, two women, whose dim monochromatic features were only barely visible in the twilight. They were talking face-to-face. One of them was moving her hands energetically as she spoke.

You haven't seen him yet? Oh, he's adorable. A total sweetheart, the hand-waving woman said. *You should go see him, he's down in 115.* The clarity of her voice surprised Warren, given how far away she appeared, as did her accent. She sounded like she was from Boston. Was Warren in Boston?

He's back? I thought they sent him home? The other woman's accent was Midwestern, which was reassuring but did little to ease Warren's growing confusion.

They did, but then it happened again. And then it kept happening.

His poor parents.

I was on the floor when they brought him in last time.

Wait, you saw it? What's it like?

What do you mean, what's it like? The first woman's voice sounded coy, almost teasing.

Come on, you know. The second woman held up her silhouetted hands in a gesture of exasperation

I already told you. I don't know how to say it otherwise.

But you saw it? You're sure? I heard a bunch of people tried. Lizzy, Ryan, Tracey, Lucas, Sarah. It didn't work, not for any of them.

Forget them. Just go and see for yourself.

I'm still not sure I want to.

Why not? the Boston woman said. *It's nothing to be scared of.*

How do you know? It could be contagious. How do you know you didn't catch whatever the kid's got?

Look at me. Does it look like I've got it?

I don't know. Maybe you do. Maybe I just can't see it.

As the women spoke, the sky, strangely, seemed to darken again. The women and their accents seemed to recede. Warren could tell he didn't have much longer. *It's not a disease*, he heard the Boston woman say, just before she and her friend disappeared. *It's just a sweet kid. That's all . . .*

The bad news *is that it's going to feel worse before it feels better.* Warren peered up into the lean, angular face of the man who was talking to him. The man looked young, with a smooth, unlined complexion and a full head of jet-black hair, but the deep tenor of his voice belied his appearance. He was wearing a white lab coat, with "Dr. Ryan Campos" stitched in scarlet over the hospital logo. Warren remembered him now. This was the attending physician who had seen him when the paramedics brought him into the ED—what? An hour ago? A day? A week? Warren glanced around the curtained emergency bay without moving his head. He saw cabinets, computer stations, instrument carts, IV stands, all of them on wheels. Overhead were several blank black monitors, as well as a large white contraption, a light of some kind, that resembled a satellite dish. But there were no windows, no clocks. It was like a casino: nothing to indicate the time. Warren could appreciate this. Time was real; that much McTaggart had gotten wrong. But time was also the enemy. A good idea to keep it in its place.

Just now, however, he needed to know if he was late for work. He reached for the pocket where he usually kept his phone. A dull throb of heavy pain stopped him from moving his arm.

How long have I been here? he said finally. *What time is it?*

The doctor gave a dry laugh. He looked at his watch, an ancient digital model with a tiny calculator keyboard built into the face. *It's a few minutes after one. You dozed off after we gave you the Percocet.*

So what's the good news?

I'm sorry?

You said that was the bad news. What's the good news?

Dr. Campos looked down at Warren's arm. Warren noticed for the first time that his forearm was immobilized in a Velcro splint. *Oh, well. Your arm's definitely fractured. Looks like you hit the ulna pretty hard. You've also got a collapsed lung and a couple of bruised ribs. I guess the good news is that it could have been worse. Much worse. You were pretty lucky.*

Warren grunted. *Easy for you to say.*

You want to hang around here for a few hours and see what comes through our doors, you might change your mind.

The thought of staying longer than necessary made Warren queasy. As a rule he didn't hate hospitals. He wasn't scared of them the way some people were. Until he was in his twenties he'd planned to be a doctor, and a few of his best memories from early boyhood had been the Saturday afternoons his father let him hang out in his office while he did his weekend rounds. Still, even though Warren had medical insurance through his job, he had every faith that this little detour was going to cost him something, and something was nothing he could afford. *When can I leave?*

We want to make sure you're secure on your feet with the Percocet, but I don't see any reason to keep you. Your head scans looked clean, your vitals are normal. We got your forehead stitched up. You should see an orthopedist in a few days for your arm, once the swelling goes down. They'll probably want to put that in a real cast. For now you just need to take it easy. It's going to hurt when the Percocet wears off.

Dr. Campos typed some notes on the rolling computer workstation and said goodbye. He turned back just before disappearing through the patterned curtain that made the wall of Warren's bay.

Mr. Kayita, one more thing. Do you mind if I ask you a personal question?

Warren felt himself tense. *Go ahead.*

You wouldn't happen to be related to Dr. Kayita, would you? Used to work up at Mercy North?

That was my father.

The doctor's expression brightened. *I thought that might be the case. I can see the resemblance. I was a resident there, back in the day. Heard him do grand rounds once. He was very smart, your dad. How's he doing? Enjoying retirement, I hope? Or is he still working?*

Neither, I'm afraid. He passed away last year.

A shadow fell over the doctor's face. *Oh, I'm sorry to hear that*, he mumbled. He looked down and then eased himself backward toward the curtain. *Really sorry to hear that.*

An hour later, after a nurse in foam clogs and purple scrubs said he was clear to leave, Warren dropped his feet off the side of the hospital bed. He collected his sweater and his shoes and glanced over the sheaf of paperwork the nurse had left behind. Among the disclosures and insurance forms and instructions for wound care was a printout of a prescription for three days' worth of Percocet. Warren wondered if he should ask for more. Between the car, The Weight, his arms, and his ribs, he figured he was a good candidate for permanent pain relief.

When he stepped out of the curtained bay, Warren thought again about what Dr. Campos had said about his resemblance to his father. Certainly in physical terms Warren could concede the point. His mother's genes had given him skin light enough that he was often assumed to possess some sort of Caribbean or Hispanic ancestry, or occasionally even South Asian. In other respects, however, he had inherited most of his father's distinguishing anatomy. They were both on the short side of five foot eight, both mesomorphs with broad chests and round bellies, both the victims of early balding and intense myopia. Both men had large heads with wide noses and narrow, almond-shaped eyes. They were each left-handed, they shared the same low blood pressure that encouraged them to keep their feet up, and when they walked side by side, it was impossible not to notice almost identical pigeon-toed gaits.

In every other way, however, Warren was, or felt himself to be, the opposite of his father. If he needed to be reminded of that fact, today was good proof. Though his dealings with The Weight had to count as another of his unfortunate inheritances from his father, it was entirely typical that it was Warren, and not his dad, who had ended up with the busted car. Warren was certain that his father never would have let such a thing happen to him, not least because he never had let such a thing happen to him. Warren's father had a craftiness about him, a wariness and a wiliness, that he often described as his instinct for trouble. In saying this he meant the opposite of the usual American idiom: if the instinct helped him find trouble, it was only so that he might better avoid it.

The instinct for trouble had taught Warren's father how to reassure the colonial educators that he was the exception to the rule that medicine was no business for a black African; it had allowed him to survive as an ambitious Muganda during the Mengo Crisis and the first Obote regime; it showed him the path out of his native Uganda before it was taken over by the shark-suited madman who filled lakes and clogged dams with the bloated corpses of his rivals; and it had helped him make a home, and a career, and a family in a country that was indifferent at best to his arrival. For his father it was a given that you had to be smart and work hard to succeed in life. But he also insisted that these were not enough. A crystalline intelligence coupled with a bullheaded diligence might suffice for someone who was rich or lucky, but for everyone else—for Warren, it did not go without saying—an instinct for trouble was imperative.

Warren found himself now in the middle of a broad beige hallway. On the wall to his right was a decorative tribute, in dark wood and brushed nickel, to the millionaires and billionaires who had contributed to the hospital's most recent capital campaign. On the wall to his left was a row of framed photographs of pseudo-abstract landscapes. In front of him was a set of heavy swinging doors. He realized he had no idea where he was. He'd been trying to leave the hospital but something (the Percocet? the meditation on his filial failures?) had led him astray. He turned back, made a right turn where he thought he'd made a left before, and then another right, and then a left, and discovered that he'd managed to make himself even more lost.

While Warren was looking around for some indication that would help him leave the hospital, his eyes fell upon a small panel next to one of the patient rooms. The sign said 115, and for a moment the number gave Warren pause. Then he remembered: 115 was the Dewey number for Metaphysics—Time. He must have recalled it from the spine of the anti-McTaggart volume, which he'd picked up for three bucks at a local library sale.

Warren was a few steps past the room when he heard the door open behind him. He looked back and saw a man put his head out suspiciously, as though casing the hallway. It took Warren a couple of long seconds to recognize him. It was Adrian Bennett, a Div School alumnus who'd been hired back as a professor a few years earlier.

In the space of an instant, Warren saw a flash of surprise cross Adrian's face, then disappointment, then a weak, second-thought smile. Adrian stepped out of the room and approached Warren, a little awkwardly. He stopped short when he saw the blue sling that was holding Warren's splint-stabilized arm.

Adrian and Warren had known each other in graduate school—they'd overlapped at the Div School in the nineties—but they'd never known each other well. Adrian was already a doctoral student when Warren started his master's degree, and because of this Warren had always thought of Adrian as several years older than he was. Looking at him now, though, Warren wondered if he himself wasn't the elder between them. Adrian had the features of a lean man in middle age—the sharp facial structure, the hollowing cheeks, the eyes that were just starting to recede—but he was tan and fit in a way that suggested a lively extracurricular life. It seemed impossible he was a day over fifty.

Hey man, Adrian said. *I know we know each other, but I can't remember how. Forgive me. I'm a little distracted today. I'm Adrian Bennett.*

I know, Warren said hoarsely. *We were at the Div School together. A long time ago. Warren Kayita.*

Warren! Right, of course. Warren, sure. I thought it might be you, but then I thought, no, that can't be, there's no way. Adrian nodded at Warren's sling. *You all right there?*

I've been better, Warren said. *Also worse. But definitely better.*

You get jumped or something? I keep hearing about these teenagers in the neighborhood playing knockout.

No, no, it was nothing like that. Girl on a bike ran into me. White girl, he couldn't stop himself from adding.

Adrian missed the message. *Oh, that's unfortunate, man. I'm sorry. Sounds like an unlucky day.*

Warren shook his head. *Believe it or not, this is what luck looks like. I was almost hit by a bus.*

Oh, Jesus, man. Hooray for the bike, then, huh? He laughed a nervous laugh.

Warren tried to chuckle along with him, but the pain in his ribs stopped him. *What about you? Everything okay, I hope?*

Adrian made an exaggerated shrugging motion. *Yeah, all good, man. Everything's fine. Just a routine visit. You know how it goes.*

Warren saw something moving behind Adrian. He bent his head to get a better view. It was a boy, a little boy, maybe two or three years old. He was toddling fast toward Adrian with his hands outstretched. He looked happy, and relieved, to have found his father. But there was something strange about him, too: he was glowing. Not brightly, not from within. The light seemed instead to envelop him. But the boy definitely looked like he was glowing.

Adrian saw Warren squint at the strange intrusion. He spun on his heels and scooped up the boy, blocking Warren's view. *Luca, buddy!* Adrian was nearly back in the room before Warren could quite appreciate what was happening. *Good seeing you, Warren!* Adrian shouted with a little too much eagerness as he rushed away. *Hope that arm gets better soon!*

That night in bed, before he fell asleep at the end of a very long and very awful day, Warren assured himself that he'd made some sort of mistake about the boy. Probably it was the Percocet messing with his mind, or maybe some delayed neurological consequence of his collision with the bike. One or the other would make sense. One or the other would explain the inexplicable.

There was a time in Warren's life when he would not have doubted himself so severely. Twenty years earlier, he would have thrilled at the possibility of witnessing something genuinely weird. That time, it was not too much of an exaggeration to say, had ruined Warren's life. Just look at where it had left him. At twenty-three, everything his father had wanted for him had been laid out in front of him. He had a biology degree from Stanford, a good postgraduation job, and a clear path to medical school. Ahead of him lay a successful—or at least normal—American life: all of it was his for the taking. But he'd thrown it all away. He'd left it all behind. His father had warned him. *I regret this already but I will not be alone,* his father had said, his baritone thundering. *Mark my words. You will rue the day you made this decision, just as I rue the day I let you anywhere near that high school.* The worst part was, his father was right. Just look at Warren now: deep into middle age, he was wasted and worn out, a broke and broken man. He was ridiculous. It was ridiculous. Ridiculous to think he could have possibly seen whatever it was he thought he saw.

FOUR

Paul told no one about Luca. Not at first. In part this was because he wanted to do right by Adrian, who had called a day after the incident and asked him to keep it a secret. *It's just, you know*, he'd said to Paul. And Paul did: he knew. Though he still sometimes felt terribly naive about the world, he did not need to be told what would happen—to Luca, to Adrian, to their family—if word got out about what he'd seen.

Anyway, what would he say? What could he say that wouldn't make it sound like he was the one suffering some sort of strange ailment? For reasons he couldn't entirely explain, his memory of the incident was soaked through with a peculiar kind of embarrassment, as though he'd been caught spying on something he was not supposed to witness. In his mind Paul had replayed the scene dozens if not hundreds of times. On each playback some part of him hoped that a new detail or aspect would make itself known, something that would let him write the whole thing off as misunderstanding, or maybe a weird trick of the midmorning light.

Of course Paul knew that it was too late for that. Adrian had seen the glow, too, after all, and he'd told Paul over the phone that another twenty or so people at the hospital had seen it as well. That was one reason for his call: Adrian didn't want Paul to worry about his sanity or his neurological well-being. The glow, he said, had come back several times since its first appearance, and each time it had lasted for several hours before fading. Not everyone could see it—Adrian's wife, Renata, for instance, could not—but a series of informal experiments had established that the people who saw it generally agreed when it was there and when it was not.

Adrian told Paul that the doctors' increasingly desperate attempts to determine what was happening had turned the Bennetts' lives upside down. He and Renata were essentially living at the hospital while the doctors continued to test and monitor Luca. Unfortunately, he said, what they'd learned about the glow so far was mostly negative knowledge. The doctors couldn't explain why it was visible to some people and not to others. They couldn't understand why cameras couldn't record it, or why other instruments failed to register its presence. They couldn't guess what was causing it, and nothing they'd tried had succeeded in making it go away.

At the same time, Adrian said, there was a bit of reassuring news that he wanted to pass on to Paul. So far there seemed to be no reason to think that the glow was in any way harmful. It was not radioactive. It was not electrical or magnetic or infrared or ultraviolet. It did not cause Luca any pain, and in fact did not seem to cause any physical feeling at all. It had no detectable effect on his biochemistry or his mental status. Best of all, there were no signs of contagion or spread: though many people had by now spent a lot of time in near proximity to Luca when he was glowing, Adrian first among them, it remained a unique phenomenon.

Paul was more relieved than he expected to be by this news. He wasn't a hypochondriac, and he was still young enough to assume as a matter of course that his health was a permanently renewable resource. Still, every morning since the incident, he'd examined himself naked in the mirror, checking among his freckles and scars for any sign that something odd had developed overnight. Every evening, once the sun went down, he closed himself in his room with the blinds pulled and the lights off to see if he could discern any hint of a burgeoning luminescence.

Yet there were other effects. Without really meaning to, Paul found himself avoiding campus, blowing off Billy, his best friend, and inventing excuses not to see Carrie. For a while he could tell himself that there were good reasons for this, not least since the production deadline for a new issue of the *Graduate Review* was rapidly approaching. But after Carrie called him on it—after she told him she was taking him out for a fancy dinner to celebrate his birthday, and wouldn't take no for an answer— Paul realized that Adrian's secret was wearing on him. It was too heavy a burden to carry alone.

Paul made up his mind to tell Carrie about Luca at his birthday dinner. He couldn't guess how she would take it, and he knew there was a decent chance she'd think he was losing his mind. But he also knew that this would not be a black mark in her book. Quite the opposite. Carrie often teased Paul for being the sanest person she'd ever slept with more than twice, and it seemed possible that she might see in his story the proof of the hidden freak she was always half hoping to find.

Like Paul, Carrie was a graduate student at the University. She was a doctoral student in the Committee for Social Research, an idiosyncratic academic entity known internationally for the preponderance of Nobel Prize winners it counted among its faculty and known locally for its astounding success in rendering its graduates unfit for the academic job market. This latter fact was not a problem for Carrie, for she was the semi-estranged daughter of an executive at a Canadian mining concern, which was to say, she was rich in a way that Paul couldn't really comprehend.

It was one of Carrie's charms that she took a special pleasure in the wanton redistribution of her father's ill-gotten gains. (She liked to joke, not really joking, that it was proof of her commitment to socialism.) For Paul's birthday, she booked a table for two at the James Steakhouse, a flamboyantly unhip throwback to the days when streetcars clanged under the Chicago River and millions of hogs, horses, sheep, and cattle passed through the Union Stock Yards on their way to the agricultural afterlife. Designed to satisfy the psychic and gastronomic needs of the peak-lapel-and-pinstripes set, the restaurant was the spiritual opposite of the ultramodern molecular-gastronomy outfits that had lately swarmed Chicago with edible menus, spherified cocktails, and gilded scallops.

It was a place that offered aldermen, defense attorneys, union bosses, and the third-rate sons of second-rate business owners the chance, after their fifth vodka martini, to imagine themselves into the blurry black-and-white photos of Paul Ricca and Frank Sinatra that hung on the walls. There they'd be, sitting at the far end of a long table, busting a raucous gut at every one of the boss's bad jokes. They stayed for the plate-sized toma-hawk steaks, the bloated massifs of mashed potatoes, and the dessert cart larded with enough sweetened milk fat to clog the carotid of a Clydesdale.

Paul and Carrie did it, too, the whole mid-century haut-gangster shebang: they ate steamed clams and fried calamari, they drowned huge calving quadrants of iceberg lettuce in opaque seas of blue cheese, they choked down tennis-ball hunks of filet mignon. They drank two marti-nis each, and followed those with two bottles of hundred-dollar Barolo, and followed that with a dessert of cheesecake and limoncello.

All through the evening, Paul kept meaning to tell Carrie about Luca. But the evening had a velocity and a vector that he found impossible to steer. By the time they got back to Carrie's apartment he'd lost his chance. Both of them were drunk, happy, and horny—and too much of the former to do much about the latter. His last conscious flash of the evening, after they'd shared a joint and brushed their teeth and dutifully gulped down three Advil each, was being startled when a half-naked Carrie leapt off him mid-hookup and sprinted for the bathroom in the hallway.

Paul woke up the next morning to the double agony of a headache and a hard-on. It was early, he could tell, early even for the early riser he tended to be. The big picture window in Carrie's bedroom was streaked from an overnight rain. The sky was yellow gray. Through the glass he could hear the hiss of air brakes from the delivery trucks out on Ashland, as well as a high-pitched commotion from the birds in the magnolia tree next door. With his phone nowhere in sight, he guessed it couldn't be much later than seven o'clock.

Carrie lay next to him, her body curled against the mid-November chill. Her torso rose and fell in long, languorous heaves. Envious, Paul buried his head in his pillow, hoping against hope that he might join her again in the bliss of oblivion. It was no use. His stomach was in open rebellion against the beef he was still digesting, his dick was throbbing with the previous night's unfinished business, and his head felt as though a spike had entered his skull just below his right temple.

Uncomfortable in about six different dimensions, Paul rolled across the bed and pressed himself against Carrie's body. It was cruel, he knew, but he couldn't help himself. He reached down and stroked the bare skin of her thigh until Carrie took his hand and pulled it around her T-shirted belly. She mumbled something that Paul couldn't make out.

He leaned in close. *What was that?*

I said I should fucking murder you right now. What time is it?

I don't know.

Carrie reached across her bed to her nightstand and peeked at her phone. *Jesus Christ, it's not even seven thirty. Why are we awake?*

I don't know, Paul said again. *But since we are . . .*

Carrie's scoff was palpable, a whole-body rebuff. *If you think you're getting laid after waking me up at seven thirty in the morning, I have some bad news for you. Anyway, if I have sex right now I'm going to throw up all over again.*

You puked?

A couple of times. I tried to get you to get me some water, but you were passed out.

Paul chuckled. *I barely remember getting home.* He got out of bed, found his phone, and collected his boxer shorts from the floor.

Where are you going?

I've got to pee.

Carrie nodded at his erection and smiled. *Careful of the ceiling. I just had it painted.*

Paul carried his phone into the bathroom. Standing splayed, with one hand holding his phone, he managed to flip through a few dozen

tweets on Twitter without making a mess of Carrie's bathroom. When
he returned to the bedroom, he pulled on his pants and his undershirt.

Carrie rolled over. Her face was pale, and the whites of her eyes were
shot through with tiny pink threads. Her hair was tangled in strange,
weblike constructions. *Now where are you going?*

Paul was confused. *I thought we were done here.*

Carrie shook her head. *I said I wasn't going to have sex with you.
I didn't say you couldn't make me breakfast. Come on, stay. It's been too
long.*

*I've got to get back. I'm meeting Adrian in a few hours. I need to look over
some stuff beforehand.*

What's this for, the dissertation?

Paul examined Carrie's face for any sign that she suspected otherwise.
Unfortunately.

How's my buddy Fra?

Not good, Paul said. *Not good at all.* "Fra" was Fra Dolcino, the medieval heretic who was supposed to be the subject of Paul's research.

I don't believe it. You're just dooming again.

*I'm not, actually. It's kind of a disaster. You want to know how many other
dissertations I've found in the last month that did exactly what I want to do?*

I'm guessing this is going to be a number larger than zero.

*Three. Six months ago when I looked there was nothing. And now all of
a sudden there are three. I'm fucked.*

What does Adrian think?

I don't know. That's why we're meeting.

You said he loved the idea, though, right? That's all that matters.

He loved the idea when no one else had written about it.

I'm sure it will be fine.

Paul collected his sport coat and put on his socks and shoes. He kissed
Carrie on the forehead and said thanks for the dinner and was halfway
out the door when she called after him.

In the taxi, last night, you kept saying you had something you wanted to tell me, but you said you didn't want to do it drunk.

I did? Paul dropped his hand from the doorknob.

You said it was really important, something you'd been waiting a long time to say. You said I deserved to hear it sober.

Paul walked back to the bed and sat down on the edge of the mattress. He made a decision that he regretted immediately. *Do you want me to tell you now?*

Carrie reached for Paul's hand. *I think there's something I should tell you first. It's one of the reasons I wanted to talk.*

Paul was puzzled, and he didn't make much effort to hide it.

I, um . . . I've been hanging out with somebody recently.

Hanging out or, like, hanging out?

Carrie bit her bottom lip. *I don't know. Hanging out, I guess.*

I see, Paul said. *So who is he? What's his deal?*

Her deal.

Oh.

Yeah. She's a she. She's also a law student, if you can believe it. I met her in my Dostoyevsky class.

Paul thought for a long moment. *Good for you*, he said finally. *That's great.* The words came out sounding less sincere than he intended. He and Carrie had been sleeping together quasi-casually for years, a habit that had persisted comfortably alongside the rest of their respective dating lives. *Maybe I can meet her someday. Maybe sometime, you know, we can all hang out together.*

Paul tried to soften the skeeze of his insinuation with a smile, but Carrie seemed not to notice. She looked off in the direction of her picture window and then turned back to Paul. *I wanted to tell you because things have started to get kind of serious between us. I like her a lot. And she likes me. I don't think she'd like me so much if she knew . . .* Carrie squeezed Paul's hand, letting the gesture finish her sentence.

So don't tell her, Paul said. *I certainly won't.*

I know, but . . .

When has that ever been a problem before?

This one feels different, Paul. The other day I mentioned that I was going to take you out for your birthday. Without missing a beat she started grilling me about you. She's an excellent interrogator. She's going to be a terrifying lawyer someday. It wasn't long before she asked me if we'd ever hooked up. I told her we had, in the past, but not since she and I got together. And that was pretty much true, you know. Maybe not to the day, but pretty close. It's been a while.

Paul pulled his hand back out of Carrie's grasp. *I'm sorry*, he said. *Like I said, I've been super busy.*

No, I know. It's fine. It's fine. Whatever. But we were seeing so little of each other, I just assumed you were off doing your own thing, too. Which of course is your right. You don't have to tell me.

Paul felt hot in the face. *But I wasn't. I'm serious. I wasn't trying to avoid you. I mean, you could have just asked.*

I tried! I wanted to hang out. I mean, not like that. I wanted to actually hang out. You were MIA. Anyway, I asked her if it was a problem if we went to dinner, and she thought about it for a minute. And then she said, "No. You should go. I trust you not to hurt me."

Paul lifted his eyebrows. *Whoops.*

I know. But I didn't want to hurt her. That's the thing. I don't want to.

A little late for that, don't you think?

I appreciate that it doesn't make a lot of sense.

You are correct about that.

I really did want to see you. I really did want to celebrate your birthday. And I really didn't want to hurt her. The rest, I guess, was red wine and old habits. I don't know. Carrie sat up against the headboard of her bed. She pulled her naked knees up to her chest. *Honestly, until last night it didn't even occur to me that you might feel differently.*

Would it matter if I did?

No, I mean, that's why I wanted to tell you before . . .

Before what?

Carrie turned to him with a look of pure pity on her face. *You know I like you, Paul. I do. And of course I love you in a way. But not like that.*

It's never been like that for me. Carrie reached for him again. She took his hand. *I'm sorry. I'm really sorry.*

Paul had many questions for Carrie. He understood that most of them would have to remain unanswered, at least for the time being. But he couldn't let himself leave without asking her one.

Out of curiosity, he said, *what did you think I wanted to tell you this morning?*

Carrie looked at Paul like she'd been wounded. *Please, Paul. I didn't want you to have to say it. There's no reason to do it now.*

Really, I'd like to know.

You were going to tell me you're in love with me, right?

Paul declined Carrie's offer—a guilty one, clearly, and of uncertain earnesty—of a ride back to Fell Gardens. He took the Blue Line to the Loop, changed to the Red Line, and rode the bus in from the Garfield station. When he reached McGinley House, whose second floor hosted the headquarters of the *Graduate Review*—which was also now Paul's hemisemidemipermanent place of residence—he worked the key in the tricky front-door lock.

Stepping through the foyer to the black-painted stairs, he glanced quickly at the former dining room of the fin de siècle mansion. There was broken wood and glass everywhere, toppled bookcases, maimed tables, desks, and chairs. The carpet—a seventies-vintage sea green—was stained with dark spots that strongly suggested a second gig as state's evidence. A chandelier that still hung, or dangled, from the cream-colored ceiling was bereft of most of its arms, not to mention all of its bulbs and fake candles. Even the wainscoting had been stripped inelegantly from the walls: the dark wooden slatting, splintered and cracked at rough angles, was deposited suspiciously in the charred fireplace.

When Paul first joined the *Review* staff, four years earlier, the editor of the journal, a PhD student in the Committee for Social Research named Ross Dering, had told him that the scene on the first floor was not in fact the aftermath of a violent melee. The *Review*, he explained, was old enough that it had escaped the purview of bureaucratic authority. It belonged to no department or school. It subsisted, to the extent it did, on a minor annual stipend supplied by a long-forgotten endowment, as well as on a few work-study positions that an executive assistant in the Humanities Division always approved without question. Ross liked to say that his most important task as editor was to preserve this policy of benign neglect, and so he maintained the apparent rapine of the first floor as a useful prophylactic against any sort of administrative curiosity.

To Paul, now, the mess looked like home. He had moved into McGinley the previous summer, in the midst of a particularly dire cash crunch that had left him officially homeless. The possibility of living in his office at the *Review* had struck him with the force of a life-altering inspiration, and the reality of it was, he still felt, an ingenious arrangement. He got a couch for a bed, a pair of locking file cabinets for dressers, and a pink-tiled bathroom with a working sink and only moderately off-putting shower. For food preparation he could rely on the *Review*'s microwave, water cooler, and dorm-sized refrigerator, as well as on the electric hot plate and rice cooker he'd inherited from his friend Billy.

With his head in pain and the rest of his body still numb from whatever had just happened with Carrie, Paul climbed the stairs, unlocked his office, and collapsed on his couch-bed. He tried to remember what he wanted to tell Adrian about Fra Dolcino.

WITHIN THE UNIVERSITY, the Div School was often seen by other disciplines, including in the humanities, as obsolete. You could study dinosaurs in the English Department, or reality television in Comp Lit, and no one would bat an eye. You could even study religion, so long as you understood it as epiphenomenal, something that needed the fundamental theories of psychoanalysis, or Marxism, or economics, or anthropology, to be comprehensible to the modern mind. But religion as at least half the Div School's faculty and students tended to approach it, religion as a constructive enterprise and a going concern, was something else entirely.

Over the years Paul had assembled a clever-sounding rationale to deflect the barbs and befuddlement that came his way. To his mind, there was no great mystery why religion persisted in a modern world that professed to have no need for the supernatural. Forget what the rigorists would tell you: that the most important question for any religion was who was in and who was out, what it took to be counted good or bad, which beliefs or practices or prayers would make you a saint or a heretic. Forget, too, any thought that the universe stood ready to reveal its deepest mysteries, if only we could ask our questions in just the right way. Paul felt strongly that people would always want a mental box to hold their hopes and fears and desires about the muddle of existence. They would always seek out some way to address questions to their confusion that they could formulate in no other manner. You could call that ultimate concern, if you wanted, or the feeling of absolute dependence, or you could just call it religion.

Of course it was true that the answers people found in religion were often terrible, chief among them the answer that said that the demands of heaven overruled any ordinary claims of human solidarity. That was how you got Isaac on the rock, that was how you got the Crusades, that was how you got burning witches and kamikaze monks and pedophile-protecting churches. Yet the bad answers were also, in their way, beside the point. As long as there was longing there would be disappointment. As long as there was love there would be heartbreak. As long as there was life there would be death. And as long as there were any of those things, Paul believed, religious feeling would always be able to find itself a foothold.

For these reasons, Paul let himself say in his more pretentious moments, religion was the specter that haunted modernity, the wraith in the rafters that was as embarrassing as it was unevictable. You could try to leave it behind, you could try to use science or philosophy or *Ideologiekritik* to make a clean break on unhallowed ground, but you couldn't escape it. Maybe Nietzsche was right. Maybe God is dead. But this was not tantamount to saying that God was gone. He was, truly, the holy ghost.

That was Paul's pitch, anyway. That was the little speech he kept in his back pocket for whenever he was annoyed or drunk enough to snap back at the condescension that came with the academic study of religion.

In the dissertation he'd been planning to write on Fra Dolcino he had
seen a chance to expand the notion more seriously. He would write about
Dolcino's life, sure, and there would be plenty of fun in that. Dolcino
was a proto-anarcho-communist who opposed feudalism and the Church
hierarchy, as well as being an apocalyptic visionary who led his followers
on guerrilla raids from his mountaintop redoubt.

More important, though, Paul could write about Dolcino's long afterlife. The heretic had been mentioned by name in Dante's *Inferno*, he had
a cameo in John Stuart Mill's *On Liberty*, and he was claimed as a fore-
runner of modern socialism by Karl Kautsky. He also had an important
role in Umberto Eco's *Name of the Rose*, which is where Paul first came
across him. Paul figured he could turn this to his advantage. He could
show how the ideas of a man who believed that he was the Angel of Thy-
atira, the sixth of the seven churches of Asia mentioned in the Book of
Revelation, had been taken up by people who wanted nothing to do with
religion of any kind.

Adrian loved the idea when Paul first suggested it. He said it hit all
the right notes. Communism was always in academic fashion, the hint of
prophetic madness lent the subject a thrilling shudder of anti-rationalism,
and of course everyone lately was eager for work that flattered their apocalyptic moods. The next step was to put together a dissertation proposal.
The document was not supposed to be a major obstacle, just something
that would give Adrian and the other two professors on Paul's committee a
sense of where the project was heading. (One of those professors was Marcus Doran, a cruel and arrogant scholar in the History Department who
was the world's expert on the cruel and arrogant reign of Pope Urban VI.
The other was Thomas Hart, a genial ex-priest who was a sort of mascot
around the Div School.) They needed to see that Paul had surveyed the
existing scholarship, and to be reassured that there was enough space for
him to stake out a plat of provably new research.

Despite the distraction caused by Luca's glow, Paul had made decent
progress on the proposal throughout the fall quarter. Or at least he had
until he discovered the three recent dissertations he'd mentioned to

Carrie. Not wanting to bother Adrian, Paul had tried to deal with the problem himself, seeking out a research path that would give the other dissertations a wide berth. Finally, though, he decided he couldn't get any further on his own. A few days before his birthday, he'd written Adrian a long email laying out what he'd found and why he was worried.

Don't freak, Adrian wrote back. We'll figure it out. Why don't you come by my house on Saturday morning. We'll talk it over. I bet there's something you can still do.

Adrian lived in a graystone town house on a quiet street a few blocks east of the University. Paul had only been there once before, and then only briefly, but he found it without trouble. He climbed the steps of the front porch and heard a child shriek inside the house when he pressed the doorbell.

There was another shriek, and then a woman's voice shouting *Max, chill, please!* and then the sound of approaching footsteps. The front door opened to the taut extent of its security chain. A woman—Renata, he assumed—appeared in the open gap.

Can I help you? she said.

Hey. I'm one of Adrian's students. I'm here to see him? The woman looked at Paul as though the information he'd provided did nothing to answer her question. *He asked me to come by.*

Are you sure? the woman said.

Paul nodded. *I guess I'm a few minutes early.*

Can you hold on for a second?

Of course.

Another shriek from inside escaped through the gap just as the woman closed the door. Paul heard Renata yell *Max, leave your brother alone!* and then he heard her talking sharply to someone else. The door made it impossible to hear the whole conversation, but Paul picked up snatches that conveyed the general tenor: . . . *he says he's supposed to meet you here . . . I thought we agreed . . . wait, it's him? . . . still, I wish you'd told me . . . what should I tell him . . . how long? . . . you're sure about that? . . . I'm not really in the mood to play hostess . . . yeah, Max is being a pill . . . no, it's fine, it's fine, just come straight home please . . .*

Paul heard the chain scratch the lock, and then the door swung open again.

The woman was smiling now, though not comfortably. She was pretty, with blue-gray eyes and thin, brown hair and smooth, clear skin. But she also looked tired, deeply tired, in a way that suggested a culprit other than a lack of sleep. She put out her hand. *You're Paul. You should have said so. I'm Renata. I've heard a lot about you.*

Same, Paul said, shaking her hand, even though it wasn't really true. Adrian was garrulous on a wide range of arcane subjects, but except for the odd anecdote or sarcastic aside, he almost never talked about his family life. Paul knew almost nothing about Renata besides her name.

Please, come in. Adrian had to run out for something, but he's on his way back now.

Paul stayed where he was standing. *I can wait out here till he gets back. Honestly, I don't mind.*

No, come on. He said he wouldn't be more than five minutes.

Paul still didn't move. He was not eager for even five minutes of awkward small talk with his adviser's wife, but Renata, on seeing his hesitation, misinterpreted his reluctance. *It's okay,* she said. *Luca's not . . . it's not happening right now. At least I don't think so. Hold on.* She looked over her shoulder. *Max, is your brother shining? Max, stop touching him, please. Please leave him alone, Max. I asked you a question. Is Luca shining?*

From inside, Paul heard a boy's high voice. *Nuh-uh, Mama. He's not shining now. He's annoying now.*

See? she said with another weak smile. *Nothing to worry about.*

At Renata's request, Paul took off his shoes in the foyer. He followed her into the Bennetts' living room. Inside he saw Luca and another boy— Max, presumably—standing together. Unlike his older brother, who was dressed in a brown T-shirt and jeans, Luca was wearing only a diaper. The skin on his naked belly was so white that it seemed to redouble the ambient light, but there was no sign of any unusual incandescence.

Can you say hi, boys? This is Paul. Though it seemed pretty clear that Luca had no idea who he was, the boy started hooting energetically at his mother's prompting. Max bent his face into a scowl at his brother's enthusiasm.

Max, what do we say when we have guests?

The boy was silent, as though he were considering the question, and then he howled and ran into a hallway toward the back of the house. Luca, sensing a game afoot, clapped excitedly and chased after him.

Luca and I go way back, Paul said. *I don't know if Adrian told you, but I was there, the first time . . .*

Oh, I know. He told me everything.

Adrian said it's still happening?

A couple of times a week. Or so I'm told.

Is it true you can't see it?

Paul hadn't meant to pry, but it was immediately clear to him that he'd crossed a line. Instead of answering, Renata said she'd better check on the boys. She offered him drinks—water, lemonade, beer if he wanted it—and after he turned these down she told him to make himself comfortable. With a prim smile she said, *Adrian should be back any minute.*

ADRIAN'S HOUSE WAS A NICE HOUSE, which was to say: it was an expensive house. That was obvious as soon as Renata stepped away. What Paul knew about architecture and interior decoration could fit on a scrap of confetti, but he knew very well what money looked like. He was particularly good at knowing what money looked like when it was trying to look like something other than money: when it wanted to dress itself up as taste, or style, or art, or a scholarly passion for comparative mythology.

In the Bennetts' house, money's efforts to camouflage itself were helped by a layer of kid mess that covered everything. The floors, the tables, the countertops: all of them were buried under the half-deconstructed ruins of plastic marble runs and wooden train tracks, the panchromatic splays of markers, paints, and crayons, and the ubiquitous tyranny of spilt Lego. Still, he could tell. The wallpaper was the tip-off. Paul's residential résumé was a long list of illegal squats and off-lease sublets, where the best you could hope for from a wall was a splash of eggshell white and sufficient density to keep the sound and the smell of your roommates' flatulence to a tolerable minimum. The Bennetts' wallpaper, with its intricate blue-and-white pattern, was as foreign to him in its splendor as the Hall of Mirrors at Versailles.

The Bennetts had interesting furniture, too—a winningly eclectic assortment of velvet sofas and leather reading chairs and reclaimed-wood tables—and framed art that looked like real art. The star of the room, however, at least as far as Paul was concerned, was a run of built-in bookshelves that stretched twenty feet or more along the longest wall. If the wallpaper signaled terrestrial luxury, the bookcases offered up a vision of supernal magnificence that even Aquinas might have appreciated. (*Summa Theologica*, II.IIae.134.3: "It belongs to magnificence to intend doing some great work. Now for the doing of a great work, proportionate expenditure is necessary, for great works cannot be produced without great expenditure.") Paul's life as a grad student sometimes felt to him like an extended survival test, in which the central challenge was not to get brained, or buried alive, by this or that stack of teetering library books that he'd had to pile up beside his bed. This was just how it went, Paul had assumed without thinking, a vocational hazard of the life of the mind. Now he saw that it was possible to live another way.

Paul walked over to a shelf in the middlemost case, where he saw several copies of Adrian's two books. Next to them was a run of anthologies and assorted scholarly journals—likely, Paul guessed, the remainder of Adrian's academic output. At the end of the shelf was a much smaller collection of literary magazines, including a single copy of the *Graduate*

Review. After glancing down the hall, he took the latter off the shelf. It was an issue from the early 2000s whose cover Paul recognized but whose innards he had never examined. He scanned the table of contents three times before discovering the name he hadn't known he was looking for, and then he flipped forward to the page number indicated. At the top, in the same self-serious sans serif the magazine had used since its founding, he read: "Six Stories / By Renata Parker."

Paul was only four sentences into the first of the stories when he heard Renata advancing down the hall. *I'm so sorry, Paul. I texted Adrian again. I don't know where he is. He should have been back by now.*

Paul looked up. *Is this you? Renata Parker?*

Renata looked nonplussed for a moment, took a long breath, and composed herself. With a thin, wordless smile she took the issue out of Paul's hands.

I'm sorry, Paul said, *I should have asked. I don't know if Adrian told you, but I work there. At the* Review.

The Graduate Review? *What do you do?*

A little of everything. Sometimes a lot of everything, depending on the day. Editing, production, mailing. It's a pretty small operation. Officially I'm the managing editor. I didn't know you were a writer.

Renata gave him a look that suggested he was again straying into unwelcome territory. *I'm not.* She stepped forward and put the issue back on the shelf. When its spine was once again flush with the others, she turned to Paul. In a quiet voice, she said, *I didn't answer your question earlier. I wasn't trying to avoid it, or at least I don't think I was. But the answer is no, I can't see Luca's . . . Luca's thing. The boys can. Adrian can. Luca's doctor can. Sometimes it seems like everyone can except for me.*

I'm sorry, Paul said. He was apologizing for bringing up a sore subject, but Renata misinterpreted him for a second time.

I'm not, she said immediately, with a tone that sounded like a long-pondered defiance. *Part of me still thinks you've all gone sick in the head. But even if that's not true, I can't say I'm sorry to be missing out. I like Luca just the way he's always been.*

A loud wail, uttered as though in objection to that last sentence, went up from the back of the house. Renata exhaled heavily. *I'm sorry. I've got to go deal with them. I don't know what to tell you about Adrian, but you're welcome to stay if you want to, on one condition.*

What's that?

Renata nodded at the bookshelf. *No more snooping.*

Adrian arrived a few minutes later, breathing hard and steaming visibly. His face was pale and splotchy. His hair looked wet and deranged. Without taking off his coat or his shoes, without even setting down the fabric grocery bags he was carrying in the crook of each elbow, he stepped quickly into the living room. *Paul, god, I'm so sorry.*

It's okay, Paul said. *It hasn't been long.* He let his gaze loop around the living room. *It's a nice place you've got.*

Adrian looked confused. *What do you mean? You've been here before. Haven't you?*

Just once to drop something off. I hadn't been inside.

Now Adrian looked incredulous. *Seriously? You'd met Renata, though, right?*

Paul shook his head.

Aw, man, now I'm really feeling like a terrible adviser. I'm sorry, I'm still not really used to having graduate students. When this all settles down, you'll have to come over for a proper dinner, okay? I want you to hold me to that.

Begging thirty more seconds—*and then I'm all yours, I swear*—Adrian put his bags in the kitchen and disappeared into the back hall to say hello to Renata and the kids. When he returned, he led Paul upstairs, to a home office that doubled as a guest room. He offered Paul the room's single available chair, an ergonomic rolling model tucked under a cluttered wooden desk, and took the couch for himself. He slipped off his shoes, straightened his back, and crossed his legs, as though he were getting ready for a yoga session. *So. Renata said you saw Luca again. It's the first time, right? Since . . . since . . .*

Yeah, Paul said.

And?

Paul frowned. He didn't know how to answer Adrian's expectant tone.

What did you think? How'd he seem?

Oh! Fine, I guess. He was only there a couple of minutes. But he looked okay to me.

Adrian nodded. *Good, good. I'll be honest, that's part of why I wanted you to come over here. I confess to an ulterior motive.*

Paul was still confused. *You wanted me to see him? Renata said it . . . the thing . . . the glow . . . is still happening, but I didn't see it.*

Yeah, no. No. It is happening still, in general, but I just went back there. It's definitely not happening now. That was kind of my point, though. I wanted you to see Luca without it. You know, just in case.

In case what?

I know you said you weren't worried about it, but I thought, you know, just in case you were worried about it being harmful somehow. The glow, I mean. Honestly the truth is, even though Renata has a hard time accepting it, Luca's completely fine. Except for the glow, his doctors say he's as healthy as he's ever been.

Paul couldn't hold back a little smile.

Adrian spotted it, and smiled himself. *Okay, fair. Right. I get it. "Other than that, how was the show, Mrs. Lincoln?" Right?* He laughed. *It's not like that, though, really. They kept him at the hospital for almost a week straight. They ran all kinds of tests. They used all these instruments. They tested me, too, and Renata and Max.*

That sounds expensive, Paul said.

Adrian smiled again. *It's funny you should say that. That's why we finally decided to bring him home. Luca's doctors were thrilled to have him, but the hospital started wondering out loud who was going to pay for us to keep coming back in. It turned out our health insurance doesn't cover glowing children.*

Wait, seriously? Paul couldn't tell if Adrian was kidding.

Totally serious. We could have fought it, but it just would have made the whole thing a bigger deal. As you know, we've been trying very hard to keep this thing under wraps, and the last thing we wanted was a paper trail that pointed to something definite. It's not easy, though, even with the privacy laws. Rumors were definitely getting around the hospital, and we decided we were not comfortable with how many people knew something already. So now we just call the doctor whenever it starts happening, and every second or third time we bring him in for a checkup. The doctor figured out a way to get us in through one of the loading docks. We try to make it fun for Luca. We call it the Sneaking Game.

Anyone have any idea what's causing it?

Adrian smirked and shook his head. *I mean, sure. Everybody has ideas. You can imagine. I'm sure you have some guesses.*

Given the ostensible reason for their meeting, Paul wasn't eager to let Adrian know how much time he'd spent chasing references to auras, ethers, and other forms of occult luminescence on the Internet and in the library. *Only crank stuff,* he said. *Well, crank stuff and religious stuff. But that may be the same thing.*

Adrian laughed. *Gimme your best shot. I want to make sure there's nothing I missed.*

You found Walter Kilner, I assume?

He of The Human Atmosphere? *Oh yes.*

And Charles Leadbeater?

Come on, that's too easy. It's like straight from Wikipedia.

Okay, how about the Tabor Light?

Adrian cocked his head. *I'm listening.*

It's from Eastern Christianity. It's what they call the divine radiance.

Oh, like the khvarenah.

I'm sorry, the what?

Never mind. Go on.

The Tabor Light is supposedly what lit up Jesus during the Transfiguration, and the burning bush that Moses saw. Also it's the fire that makes hell so unbearable.

Adrian smiled. *Fuck, man. That's good. Even Renata might like that one. I keep trying to tell her that everything's okay, and she doesn't want to hear it. But if I tell her that Luca's glow is actually the fire of hell, she just might believe me.*

Adrian adjusted himself against the back of the couch. *Okay, look, much as I'd like to just sit here and chat, unfortunately I've got more errands to run soon. So I'm just going to cut to the chase. I looked at those dissertations you sent me, and the bottom line is, I unfortunately have to agree that the space for what you want to do has narrowed pretty considerably.*

Paul felt something snap in his innards, and then a visceral plunge, and then a rough commotion as his stomach crashed painfully into his bowels. What Adrian said was not a surprise, but that was just it: only in that moment did Paul understand that he'd come here hoping to hear he'd been wrong to worry.

Paul looked up and caught Adrian watching him. For the briefest of instants he could have sworn he saw in his professor's face a flash of exhausted disappointment, but the expression was quickly replaced with a consolatory grin. *I'm not saying it's impossible. If you really want to do something on Dolcino, I'm sure we can find a way. But there's another thing I should say, and . . .* Adrian stopped himself here to consider something. *I want you to promise not to panic about it. I probably should have looked into this sooner, to be honest. But if you do do something on Dolcino, I think the Div School is going to insist that a medievalist—Doran, probably—should be your main adviser.*

There was another snap of another something and Paul's stomach was once again in free fall. Confirmation of the bad news he'd been anticipating was bad enough, but this was many times worse.

From his position on the couch, Adrian was still watching Paul. He tilted his head and squinted, and when he spoke again he sounded like he was offering an invitation to a conspiracy. *You get what I'm saying?*

Paul made no effort to hide his irritation. He let fly a bitter little laugh. *It sounds like you're breaking up with me.*

Adrian threw his hands in the air. His fingers made dueling pistols that he touched to his temples. *No. No. That's not it at all. I'm saying maybe we should forget Dolcino. Forget anything Doran can claim as his own.*

Okay, Paul said, hesitantly. *What am I going to write about then?*

I don't know. I wish I had something I could hand you. But with all this stuff with Luca, I've been more than a little distracted. I'll keep thinking, I promise. But I want you to promise me something in return: don't despair. Okay?

Paul looked up. *Sure, yeah. Sure. Okay. I promise.*

Back at McGinley again, Paul climbed the stairs slowly. His head felt no better than it had when he left. Possibly it was worse. He dropped his backpack inside his office-bedroom and walked back down the hall to a small room lined with steel bookcases that served as the *Review*'s archive. Tracking the spines with a finger, he quickly found the issue with Renata's stories. He pulled it from the shelf and went back to his room. He lay down on his couch and started reading. They weren't bad. Everything else in his life right now was terrible, but the stories—the stories weren't bad.

FIVE

Max, moving briskly, scaled a geodesic play structure on all fours. At the top, he dangled his feet through one of the steel triangles before dropping himself onto the crushed bark below. He brushed the crumbling mulch from the knees of his fleece-lined jeans and looked up eagerly at Renata, who was standing about twenty yards away.

Did you see that, Mama? Did you see me jump?

Renata flashed him a vigorous thumbs-up. *That was great, sweetie. Was it scary?*

No, Mama, it was so easy. Watch. I'll do it again. Take a video.

We don't need a video, buddy. I want to see it with my own eyes.

It was around ten o'clock on a chilly Saturday in November. Gray clouds made an undulating roof of the upper troposphere. The sun, barely visible, was smudged and astringent. In the avenues and alleyways of Fell Gardens, a damp wind swirled leaves and paper litter into miniature tornadoes. Renata and her family were at the playground a block from their house, in the corner of a wide, empty ball field that was still muddy from the previous day's rain.

Across the playground, in the corner nearest the sidewalk, Adrian was pushing Luca on what Max insisted on calling the baby swing. With a technique honed over thousands of hours on this very piece of equipment, Adrian was reading something on his phone while keeping the swing moving with a clocklike consistency. Luca, slumped in the bucket seat and wholly oblivious to his father's distraction, wore a look of narcotic satisfaction.

Satisfaction was not the word for what Renata was feeling at the moment, but seeing both her boys happy allowed her at least a momentary equilibrium, which was something. After the frenzied first weeks with what they were not yet calling the nimbus, Renata had made the important discovery that it only felt like Luca's condition was overwhelming everything. Though it appeared from a middle distance that everything in their lives had been submerged or set adrift by the glow—they had given Mariela an unexplained and indefinite vacation, and Renata had suspended her consulting business in what was beginning to look like a permanent hiatus—she discovered that there were still islands of ordinary existence to be found: feeding the boys; keeping them entertained, or at least occupied; trying not to rely too much on the TV to take the place of their absent sitter. Even Renata's attempts to get through the seemingly endless back catalog of bills and insurance paperwork that she'd ignored when Luca first started glowing offered a reminder of what normal life had been like. These islands became her fallback position, her last-ditch line of retreat, and Renata took it as her central task to protect them as best she could.

In some ways it was easier than she might have expected. Max could keep going to kindergarten, Dr. Krishnamurthi had assured them, and there was no reason—no medical reason—that Adrian couldn't keep teaching at the University. As for Luca himself, Dr. Krishnamurthi had endorsed Renata's general inclination to keep him close to home, but she also said that there was no reason to believe the nimbus posed a danger to other people. Walks were fine, she said, and so was the playground, even with other kids around. *He's a little boy, with a growing brain*, she said. *He needs to see more than the inside of your house.*

There were no other kids around now. Just Max and Luca, who snapped to attention when Max called him and gestured at Adrian to be let down from the swing. Renata was pleased to see that Max was in an expansive big-brother mood this morning; he seemed glad to have Luca for a sidekick. She watched the boys cycle through one invented storyline after another, in playacted spurts that lasted no more than four or five minutes each. Sticks became swords, light sabers, machine guns. Stones became missiles, meteors, hand grenades. The tree's trunk, as ever, was the long-suffering enemy. When they tired of their undiminished military dominance, they played two-man tag, drafted Adrian for a game of monkey in the middle, and then started digging in the soggy bark of the playground. Max said they couldn't stop till they made it to China, and Luca, his mouth already caked somehow with dark wood pulp, hooted his enthusiastic concurrence.

Adrian drifted over to Renata and put his hand in the small of her back. Misinterpreting the gesture, she pulled the hand farther around her waist and leaned into him, tipping her head onto his bony shoulder. Through his jacket she felt him stiffen against her.

I think I'm going to head home, he said. *Try to catch up on some stuff while they're playing.*

Renata felt her own body go tense. She said nothing, but Adrian read her expression immediately.

What? They're fine. They're having a good time together. Look. They don't need two of us here.

No, but they need one.

Adrian pursed his lips and exhaled a long visible breath through his nose. *I'm sorry, hon. I'm just so behind. I'm already a week late grading my midterms.*

Renata pulled away, putting an air gap between them. *A week? You realize I haven't spoken to any of my clients for more than a month, right?* She tried not to sound upset, and did not succeed.

Adrian shook his head and closed his eyes. *Please don't do this,* he said quietly. *Not now. We've been having such a nice morning.*

Renata crossed her arms.

What? Adrian said again. His voice was strained now. *You want me to stay? Okay, I'll stay.*

I didn't say that.

You know I didn't ask you to stop working. That was your decision.

My decision was to take care of Luca. To take care of the boys. Which is what I'm doing now. I'm sorry if you think that means I'm not taking my work as seriously as you take yours. Renata kept her eyes on the boys as she said the last part. It was a callback to a fight they'd had many months earlier, when Adrian had said something casually belittling about her consulting work.

Renata.

What?

You know that's not fair. You know I apologized, and anyway you know that's not what I meant.

Maybe, Renata allowed, turning now to face him. *But we both know it's what you said.*

Adrian looked at her with a plaintive expression. *So what do you want me to do? Do you want me to stay so we can have this fight again?*

Do whatever you want. Don't worry about it. Go ahead. We'll be fine. I'll be fine.

As Adrian disappeared around the corner in the direction of their house, Renata saw two boys, both a little older than Max, come racing toward the playground. Following them at some distance was a woman, presumably their mother, who was talking loudly into her phone. The woman, in skinny black pants and a bright blue winter coat, lifted her penciled eyebrows in acknowledgment when she caught Renata's smile, then dropped her voice and bent her path to the opposite corner of the playground.

Renata checked her phone for the time and looked up to see the two new boys pummeling each other under the play structure. Max and Luca, who just minutes before had been running up and down the toddler slide, stood outside the steel dome, spectating eagerly.

Renata blew the family whistle, a three-note tune with a trailing glissando, to get their attention. *Five minutes, guys.*

Max looked stricken. *Mama, they just got here!* he said, nodding to the new boys.

I know. But we've got to get home. It's time for lunch.

Ten minutes, Mama, please. Luca panted vigorously to endorse Max's counteroffer.

Five, Max. I'm setting my timer now.

Renata mimicked the motions of setting an alarm on her phone and placed the device back in her coat pocket. She watched her sons as they climbed through the bars of the dome and joined the other boys. Though Adrian had assured her, repeatedly, that Luca's glow was faint outdoors in daylight, she watched him carefully, as she always did when there were other people around. After a reasonable approximation of five minutes had passed, Renata whistled again.

Please, Mama! Max begged.

Now, Max. Come on, Luca. Say goodbye. It's time to go.

Luca turned and ran toward her, doing his usual knock-kneed happy-penguin speed-waddle, while Max shuffled like a sullen chimp, with his shoulders slumped and his back hunched angrily.

Part of the problem she was having, Renata realized—her problem with Adrian, certainly, but also with her life—was that some substantial part of her remained certain that Luca's glow was fake. No, not fake: a mistake. It wasn't that she thought she was being lied to, not exactly. The doubts that plagued her, she'd readily acknowledge, had nothing to do with intentions. It wasn't even so much that she thought her husband was himself deceived: as reluctant as she'd initially been to accept what Adrian and the others were telling her about the glow, as attractive as she'd found the theory of collective hallucination, she also hadn't been able to ignore Max's spontaneous testimony. Renata didn't really doubt anymore that Adrian and Dr.

Krishnamurthi and everyone else were telling the truth about seeing something strange.

Still, by far her most dominant emotion was that the whole episode was just, well, wrong. If she couldn't say how precisely it was wrong, or where exactly it deviated from her own unenlightened reality, her sense that they, and not she, were incorrect nevertheless felt deeply right to her. Whatever they were perceiving was a glitch—a bizarre but hugely consequential glitch.

Of course she'd tried everything that she and Adrian and Dr. Krishnamurthi could think of that might help her see the glow herself: glasses and sunglasses, ophthalmology exams, a dozen different types of film, digital, and infrared cameras. She'd made Luca sit with her in a pitch-black room for an hour straight. She'd had Adrian explain to her over and over again exactly what he was seeing and where he was seeing it. In her desperation she'd even undertaken a twenty-four-hour water-only fast. None of it worked.

Renata's feeling of error, of finding herself jolted into an impossible unreality, was not entirely unfamiliar. She'd experienced versions of it before: when Adrian confessed his affair, of course, and also when she and Adrian realized that Luca's speech was developmentally delayed. Most notably she remembered when Luca was a baby, and his pediatrician found a concerning lump in his abdomen during a routine checkup. A follow-up ultrasound had revealed a dark and concerning mass near his liver that the pediatrician, in a rare lapse into euphemism, suggested was *likely something other than benign.* For two terrifying weeks, one part of Renata's brain had been certain that her son was going to die of cancer, while another part had insisted that such an outcome was simply impossible.

Renata's feeling about the glow was strengthened by that experience: the opaque marble in Luca's belly that his pediatrician and all the oncologists thought was a neuroblastoma turned out to be harmless. This was an important lesson for her. The marble had demonstrated that wrongness could itself go wrong, that denial was not always delusional.

With the nimbus, Renata tried to convince herself, the chances of

a mistake had to be even better. After all, people—even little kids—
got cancer all the time. It was a rare but real event. Something that was
known to happen. The same wasn't true of Luca's glow: boys didn't just
light up without explanation. Which had to mean, she figured, that she
had more than good odds on her side. She had all of history, all of biology,
all of physics. She had—she should have—everything.

A few days later, Renata was slicing grapes for Luca's lunch when she
heard the door of her bedroom click open upstairs. The telltale splash of
an emptying bladder was followed by the telltale hammer of the pipes in
the bathroom sink, and then there was Adrian, in the doorless kitchen
doorway, wearing madras boxers and a gray V-neck T-shirt that hung
loosely, like all his shirts, off the rack of his sharp shoulders. Thanks to
his hummingbird metabolism, Adrian was still as lean as he was long;
though his blood pressure had risen enough lately that his doctor was
threatening pills, his ectomorph outline had barely changed since he was
in high school. Not even their recent tension could keep Renata from slyly
admiring the view.

She always said that she had fallen in love with Adrian for his mind,
and this was true. She had never met a mind like his, never known someone who could talk like he talked. But privately she knew that his body
deserved at least as much credit. She had loved that body, with its sparse
blond fur, its taut and salty skin, all its delectable scoops and ridges, since
it had nearly smothered her the first time they'd made love, and she loved
it still, despite everything.

A prickly wave of warm lust washed over her, and for a moment she
considered putting Luca in front of a movie and coaxing Adrian up to
the bedroom. Instead she stood silently as he moved through the kitchen
behind her, to the spot on the counter where the steel-fronted espresso
machine squatted next to the burr grinder she'd bought him last year for
Father's Day. Renata waited until he'd filled and tamped the portafilter
to ask when he'd gone to sleep.

I watched the sun come up, Adrian said.

Working?

Something like that. I did some reading. Mostly I was thinking, though.

While Adrian made his espresso, Renata recovered a stick of string cheese from the refrigerator and arranged it, along with the halved grapes and some Goldfish crackers, on a plastic plate that had Mater and Lightning McQueen printed on the bottom. *About?*

About what you said the other day. At the playground. About taking care of the boys.

And?

Adrian was quiet long enough that Renata turned around. Leaning with his skinny butt against the counter's edge and his body bent at the hips like a boomerang, he finished the coffee and peered down into the white porcelain cup. His face looked pale and drawn, and the hollows of his cheeks were even steeper than usual.

You know what tasseography is? he said, without looking up.

Something to do with writing.

Almost. It's the art of reading tea leaves. Or coffee grounds.

Fortune-telling.

Mhm.

So what are we in for? How bad is this going to get?

Adrian lifted his cup to eye level and squinted as though he were looking through a monocle. *It says here we're going to be fine. Well, you and the boys will. My future remains resolutely unclear.* He looked up in time to catch Renata offering a weak smile. He smiled back and then looked again into the cup. *It also says we should think about bringing back Mariela.*

Renata's smile dissolved immediately. *Adrian. We talked about this. We can't. It's too risky. For her. For us . . .*

When we made the decision, we still didn't know if this thing was contagious—

And we still don't know . . .

We don't know for sure, that's true. But it's been, what, six weeks now? Almost two months? And it still hasn't happened to anyone else.

It's not just that, though. What if she has the boys out and Luca starts glowing?

I imagine she'd bring them home.

Yeah, but what if someone saw it? What if someone freaked out? He could be in real danger.

So we'll tell her to keep them at home.

And what happens if he starts glowing while she's here and we're not? How's she going to get him to the hospital without anyone seeing?

Adrian glanced down at his feet before looking up again. *Well, I don't think that's going to be an issue. I told Anita last time we were there that we couldn't keep bringing him to the hospital.*

What? You did?

He nodded. *It's too much for Luca. It's too much for us.*

You don't think we should have discussed it first?

You said it yourself. She's not learning anything new. There's nothing she can tell us that we don't already know. Anyway, I didn't think you'd disagree. Do you?

Renata didn't, not really, but she wasn't about to acknowledge that now. *You'd know if we'd discussed it first.*

Adrian turned away from her to make another coffee. Renata called Luca in from the living room and walked his plate over to his place at the small wooden table in their breakfast nook. Luca came in wearing only a diaper under his round belly. He held a toy train car in each hand and was very pleased to show each of his parents in turn how the cars clicked together magnetically. Adrian lifted Luca into his high chair and, over the boy's squirming protests, clipped him into the straps.

When he returned to the counter to collect his second coffee, Adrian said to Renata, *At least consider it, will you? Something needs to change. We need help. You need help. I can't give it to you.*

Renata almost didn't say what she said next. *And why not?*

It's been almost two months. I'm not going to tell you what to do, but I can't keep putting my life on hold for this thing.

I'm sorry if this, this . . . thing is inconvenient for you.

Come on. You know I'd do anything for Luca if I thought it would help. But look at him: he's fine!

He's glowing, Adrian. He's glowing and nobody knows why.

You're really worried about this, aren't you?

To this question that did not sound like a question Renata posed another: *Aren't you?*

Adrian sucked air through his teeth and looked down, as though willing himself not to say something. What the thought might have been Renata couldn't say, but she was certain she watched him subdue it. When he looked up again, she had the sense that a page had turned somewhere in his mind. Adrian put his espresso cup in the sink and answered a question she hadn't asked. *Okay*, he said.

It's empty, Renata said, nodding at the dishwasher.

Without another word, Adrian put the cup in the dishwasher and left the kitchen.

A few months after Adrian's affair, before Renata had announced that she would not be leaving him, not for that single transgression, she'd had an unexpected conversation about her situation with an acquaintance. The acquaintance was a client, a sixtysomething abstract photographer with an attractively cigarette-ravaged voice who had once been the girlfriend and muse of a minor star of the downtown art scene in New York in the seventies and now lived in a yurt on a mostly uninhabited island in Puget Sound. Renata had met the woman through a mutual friend—the photographer was trying to secure a grant to support an exhibition she wanted to stage in Seattle—and got to know her exclusively over the phone.

The photographer liked to describe herself as a recluse by choice and an extrovert by constitution, a combination that made for some very long phone calls that only occasionally touched their putative reason for being. Renata hadn't minded. The woman was bawdy and profane, and her stories about the demimonde she'd left behind, which were precise and hilarious in their skewerings despite being forty years out of date, had done more than a little to help Renata through what had been a very difficult time.

It was in the course of one of these conversations, when the photographer was on one of her tears—this time about the unfairness of human biology in general and the excruciations of weaning in particular—she had two children of her own, both now grown and, in her words, depressingly respectable—that she asked what kind of husband Adrian was. Renata must have hesitated in responding, because the woman answered herself.

Oh, god, she groaned. *Don't tell me you got stuck with a creep.*

He's not a creep, Renata said quickly.

But . . . ?

Renata had never been a kiss-and-tell type—her closest friends had always found her frustratingly opaque on the subject of her sex life— which made it difficult for her to say, even now, what had motivated her to tell this woman, whom she barely knew, that Adrian had slept with a colleague less than a year after Max was born. But she had told the photographer, in considerable detail, along with all the reasons for and against staying that she was then weighing up in her mind.

In the minus column, she said, was the brute fact of Adrian's betrayal, as well as its timing. What kind of man, she'd asked herself, would cheat on a wife while she was still nursing, while her own body was providing life-bearing sustenance, to his first and only child?

Any kind of man, the photographer said. *Every kind of man. Especially one who feels like he's not getting laid enough. Which is not to say it's not a point against him. It's a point against all of them.*

On the other side of the ledger, Renata said, was the fact that the affair seemed to fall squarely in the category of alcohol-enabled blunders. Adrian's colleague, the tenured hussy, was a senior faculty member who had very obviously been after Adrian for some time. While sober he had managed to deflect her heavy insinuations without provoking any ire, but too many margaritas at a conference dinner had apparently convinced him that he couldn't turn down a nightcap in her hotel room without giving fatal offense.

It helped, too, that he'd admitted to his malfeasance almost as soon as it happened: he called her, crying, in the middle of the night, after he'd woken up pantsless on the couch of the hussy's hotel suite. As far as Renata could tell, he'd made no effort to hide or minimize any aspect of the incident. He told Renata everything she wanted to know, he agreed to couples therapy, he donned the spousal equivalent of a hair shirt for several months, and he threw himself on the mercy of Renata's personal court to decide the future of their marriage.

It sounds like you've made up your mind, the photographer said.

It does? Some part of Renata knew she was staying with Adrian already, but she had yet to admit it out loud, and hearing it in the raspy, seductive voice of this woman she'd never met hit her with the force of a surprise.

You still love him, yes?

I do.

And you still like him?

Most days. Especially now, when he's on his best behavior.

You're not leaving, honey. Just promise me two things. First, that you don't think any less of yourself for staying. I've been with plenty of cads in my life, and the unfortunate truth is that some of them are worth keeping. What's important is that you get to make the decision.

Renata murmured appreciatively. *What's the other thing?* she said.

The photographer grunted. *The other thing may sound like it's moot, given the way things look like they're headed. But it's very important. Whatever happens, I want you to remember that you do not need a man to help you raise your child.*

Renata laughed.

I'm serious! the photographer said. *If I were queen of this rattrap of a world I'd have it tattooed on every girl as soon as they hit puberty. Right there on the inside of their eyelids, so that none of them could miss it. One of my kids I raised with his father around, the other on my own. There was absolutely no difference between them, in terms of the work I had to do. If anything, my ex made it that much harder, because he was one more mouth to feed, one more body to clean up after, one more ego to soothe. You do not need a man to do it. You need help. I'm not saying any woman should have to raise a child alone. But that's a very different thing.*

Renata had thought about that conversation many times since Luca started glowing, and she thought about it again as Adrian disappeared down the hallway in his bare feet.

It would not be accurate to say that she'd blown off the photographer's implicit warning. Already by that point she'd begun to wonder obscurely if she would be letting something down (feminism? modernity?) by staying with Adrian, and heavy in her mind was the object lesson of her mother, who throughout Renata's childhood had pickled herself in scorn and martinis while pretending not to notice that her husband was dipping his wick every chance he got. But it was also true, even though she'd never admit such a thing out loud, that Renata couldn't really imagine being single again, or being a single mother ever.

Nor were her reasons for staying purely negative. Of the caddishness of men in general, Renata needed no proof, and she knew better than anyone the long list of her husband's ordinary faults. He was a little too proud of his learning, a little too vain of his looks, covertly competitive, socially myopic, and absolutely certain of himself whenever he wasn't on the brink of neurotic collapse. But he also possessed another, rarer, set of qualities. He was loyal, he was sincere, and when he cared about something he cared intensely about it. He was neither lazy nor cruel. Tenured hussy aside, he'd been a good husband to her already—he listened to her, he laughed with her, he still liked to flatter and flirt—and she had every reason to expect he'd be a good father as well.

In this expectation she was largely vindicated. Adrian might not be a perfect husband and father, but he watched the boys one weekday afternoon a week, and on the weekends he often volunteered without prompting to take them to parks, playgrounds, and birthday parties. He cooked adult dinner at home five nights out of seven, and though he was not particularly handy, he did more than a minimum number of chores around the house. He generally did not need to be asked to take out the trash, or to change Luca's diapers, or to get Max ready for school or ready for bed.

Certainly he was serious about his work, serious to the point of being selfish. But even that selfishness, Renata tried to remind herself, cut both ways. Yes, his sense of his own destiny was extreme. Yes, it was probably unreasonable. But his aspirations had none of the pettiness, none of the pusillanimity, of ordinary striving. Instead they took the form of a mysterious but profound sense of intellectual noblesse oblige, a feeling that he owed the universe some reimbursement for the privilege of his existence, along with a further feeling that this debt could not be repaid with money, or market share, or even a line on his CV. What was wanted from Adrian, Adrian felt strongly, was work: his work, which was to say, the work that only he could do, the work he believed he owed the rest of humanity.

Renata met Adrian before she gave up on writing, at a time when she would have traded just about anything for the ability to credibly conjure his energy of delusion. She'd admired and envied him for his unswerving confidence, and of course she'd resented him for it, too. At first she'd resented it a little, and felt bad about that a lot. Later she'd resented it much more, and felt far less bad, as it became clear that the arrival of Max and then Luca would only accentuate, and not attenuate, Adrian's narcissistic tendencies.

Was her resentment getting the best of her now? Renata forced herself to consider the question. Maybe Adrian was right. Maybe she wasn't being fair. In the first two weeks after Luca started glowing, after all, Adrian had been every bit the husband she could have wished for, the perfect rebuttal to the photographer's universal condemnation of men. He'd spent multiple nights in the hospital with Luca, he'd canceled all his classes without complaint, he'd put in an obvious and visible effort to be more useful around the house. Was it reasonable to expect him to keep that up indefinitely? Was it too much to ask him to put his life on hold just because she felt that's what she needed to do?

Mariela returned to the Bennetts' house a few days later, after the boys had both gone to bed. Though she had her own key, she knocked and waited for Renata and Adrian to let her in. She accepted their hugs and a seat on the plush armchair in the living room, and declined a glass of the Malbec they'd been working on to prepare themselves for the conversation. Renata noticed that she was dressed less casually than usual, in black jeans and a scarlet blouse. Her makeup was more obvious, too: she was wearing a heavy rouge, blue eyeshadow, and purplish lipstick. Renata knew Mariela to be a warm and affable conversationalist, but she could also be shy in the presence of strangers, and tonight she was quiet in the way she'd been when she first started with the Bennetts, the way she sometimes got around Renata's friends.

Adrian and Renata sat together on their gray sectional, him with his legs stretched on the chaise longue, her with her feet on the floor and her knees pressed tightly together. Renata was nervous about saying what they needed to say, and she made no real effort to hide it.

Mariela was far calmer. When Adrian explained what had happened so far, and what little they understood about Luca's condition, she took the news well, which is to say that she took it more or less in stride. She did not flinch or show any other sign of distress. She listened quietly, with her brown hands clasped on her lap in front of her. Her face showed obvious relief when it turned out that the reason for the talk, however odd, had nothing to do with her job performance.

At Adrian's encouragement, she asked a few questions of her own, all of them narrowly circumscribed, almost technical in nature. She wanted to know if the light made Luca uncomfortable (no), whether they had any pictures they could show her (no), whether it gave any forewarning (no), and how long it tended to last (anywhere from two to five hours, usually).

She was curious, too, about how strict Renata and Adrian intended to be about not taking Luca out. (They were prepared for this, and had decided that they could not deny Luca the pleasure of his favorite playground, as long as it wasn't crowded; anywhere else was forbidden without prior permission.)

You don't have to tell us tonight, Renata had rushed to assure her, when it seemed there was no more for any of them to say. Much as she now wanted Mariela to come back, she wanted nearly as badly to feel that she and Adrian had presented the options without bias or pressure. *Take a few days to think it over if you want to. See if you have any other questions we can answer.*

We really just want to be sure that you won't talk to anyone else about it, Adrian added. *For obvious reasons.*

It's okay, Mariela said placidly. *I don't need to think. I don't have more questions. I'll come tomorrow morning.*

It had been Renata's wish (prayer would not be too strong a word, though she counted herself a thoroughgoing atheist) that Mariela would not be able to see the glow. Her reasons, she could admit to herself, were not practical. Adrian was probably right that it would make things easier— for Mariela, for everyone—if she could see that Luca was glowing as soon as it started. At the very least it might help her avoid public spectacle, should the phenomenon decide to show itself when she and Luca were down the street at the playground.

But Renata, for once, couldn't bring herself to care about practicalities. She hoped that Mariela would not be able to see the nimbus for a deeper reason, a simpler reason: she wanted someone on her side. She wanted to share the confidence of someone who could understand what it was like to have her whole life subject to the whims of something whose reality was attested only by hearsay. She'd given up so much already, and if put to the test she couldn't even really say why. (Just last week, she'd had to be obnoxiously vague in trying to explain to one of her college friends why she couldn't make it to her second wedding, in Mexico, an event Renata had been looking forward to for months.) Everyone she knew who knew about the nimbus—Adrian, Max, Dr. Krishnamurthi—knew about it firsthand. Everyone but her.

The chances that Mariela would not be able to see the glow seemed reasonably good. But Renata's wish was not to be. On the third morning of Mariela's return, a Thursday when she and Adrian were both upstairs, she heard a scream from the first floor.

She knew instantly what had happened. She knew, and despite knowing, she let herself hope it was something else, anything else, even an injury, all the brief while that it took her to sprint downstairs. In the kitchen, Renata found Mariela kneeling on the hardwood floor, with her hands pressed so hard against her forehead that her knuckles were pale. Her cheeks were streaked with tears. *Holy Jesus*, she was whispering, over and over. *Holy Jesus, praise your blessed name.*

A few feet away, with a translucent plastic bib around his neck, Luca was bouncing eagerly against the straps of his high chair. In front of him, on the pressed-wood tray, were chopped bits of cucumber and bell pepper. His mouth was painted with a paste of smashed avocado. He looked delighted to see Renata, as if glad to have company for the performance that Mariela arranged for his snack-time enjoyment.

Renata squatted down next to Mariela and put a hand on her rounded upper back. Soon tears came for her, too, and she made no effort to stop them. They sat like that for several minutes, not saying anything, until Adrian arrived in the kitchen.

Luca hooted at his father and made his sign to get down. Adrian walked over to unclip him, tapping Renata gently on the head as he passed. Luca clambered out of his chair and toddled toward Mariela. She recoiled at his approach, and Renata realized that she was trying to avoid contact with the glow. Stepping in quickly, Adrian scooped Luca into his arms.

See? he said. He ran his palm over Luca's head and arms, and bounced the boy lightly to keep him from escaping his grasp. *See?* he said again. *It's fine. It won't hurt you. It doesn't hurt him.*

Luca signaled for Mariela now. Cautiously, she let her hands fall away from her forehead. She reached out to hold the boy's fists in hers. Adrian set him down, and then she wrapped Luca in a hug. On her face, as she touched him, was an expression Renata had never seen before, not in her or anyone.

After a long quiet moment, she looked up at Renata. *He's a special boy*, she said.

He is, Renata said. *But we knew that. You knew that.*

Not like this, Mariela said. *This is a very, very special boy. We are very lucky. We are very blessed. The Lord must be well pleased.*

SIX

Once upon a time, time ruined Warren's life, and not in the ordinary way. Though of course it had done that, too. Time in its regular course of running had hurt Warren, as it hurts everyone. It had roughed him up. It had beaten him down. It had taken his hair, and his health, and his happiness. It had broken his body and bruised his spirit. It had curdled his mind and ransacked his memory. It had robbed him of friends, girlfriends, even his sister, his beloved little sister, who had died of a freak aneurysm at twenty-three. Time was a monster like that: a thief of unimaginable rapacity, a universal saboteur, the perennial enemy of all mankind. No wonder the ancients invented eternity to escape it. For a hundred thousand years and counting, time has had humanity on the run. Could you really blame us for wanting somewhere to hide?

But time, as it turned out, had always had a special thing for Warren. Call it a grudge. Call it an animus. Call it a vendetta, even, even though Warren couldn't guess what he might have done to deserve any of it.

The trouble started when he was eight or nine. To that point his life had been fairly typical for someone with an atypical family like his own:

he was the introverted son of an immigrant doctor from Uganda and a former teacher and Peace Corps volunteer from Cleveland. By that age Warren understood very well that he was not like his schoolmates, and not like them, moreover, in some apparently essential way. To his grade-school mind, however, the difference had everything to do with his father, for Warren was just old enough that his father's strange accent, strange diction, and strange habits were beginning to feel excruciatingly exotic.

Around that age, Warren became convinced he could feel time flowing past him, as most people evidently did not. It was not constant, this feeling, but it was also not especially rare. Sometimes the feeling arrived during the day, but more commonly it came to him after he was in bed: when his room was dark, and his body was still, and the only sounds came from the occasional car driving down the street outside his window, or from the less occasional arguments that his parents tried to save for after they thought he was asleep. The feeling was frictional, almost physical, as though time were a hot wind of the sort that buffeted him when he rode his bike around the neighborhood in mid-August.

The feeling usually came to Warren when he was thinking, as he often did, about the world before he was born. Like most children, he had been baffled to learn that he was expected to believe that his parents—and, by extension, the world—had an existence that predated his own. Unlike most children, however, he never got used to the notion. Sometimes the thought made him feel almost literally dizzy, as though he were being tumbled by an ocean wave or a particularly vicious spell of vertigo. But he was never scared. If anything, in fact, the feeling was exhilarating.

There Warren would be, lying in bed and thinking about something he'd read in the encyclopedia his parents kept in the living room, or one of the issues of *Popular Science* or *National Geographic* that littered their kitchen table. In the dim of his bedroom his mental world would start to whirl. A strange warm breeze would stir, and he would feel it brush his cheeks. The wind-like sensation would gather speed and strength until he could no longer choose to ignore it, until he felt like a figurehead on a ship, or a human hood ornament, as though he were fastened face-first with the kinetic blast of time rushing past him, rushing through him.

Warren knew this was not a common feeling, and already by that age he understood that uncommon feelings were not something people wanted to hear about, especially not from him. Eventually, however, after no one picked up on the many hints he'd dropped about his time-feeling, he came to wonder whether he was not just uncommon but unique. He decided to put the question to his father, who, for all his faults, was generally good in situations like this. A skeptic in most things, he was devout in his belief that knowledge was the only reliable source of power for anyone not born rich. For this reason he never mocked or even laughed at his children's innocent misunderstandings about the world's operation. *You should never be ashamed to want to know more,* he always insisted to Warren and his little sister. *As long as what you know is true, you can never know too much.*

Gently but firmly, Warren's father said that such a feeling as Warren thought he'd been having was imaginary at best. There was no substance to time, he said, no equivalent to the molecules of air in a breeze or the photons that made up a sunbeam. Time was like temperature, time was like heat: a useful abstraction but nothing substantial in itself. The analogy went way over Warren's young head, confusing him several times over. But in a way it didn't matter: Warren was just getting old enough to suppose, shocking thought, that his father was not the impregnable bastion of omniscience he'd always seemed. Maybe he didn't feel time flowing. Fine. That didn't mean Warren didn't.

In high school Warren learned that his father was not alone in his misapprehensions. For his seventeenth birthday, his uncle Mike, his mom's oddball kid brother, gave him a book as a gift. The book was an airport bestseller about contemporary physics, and one of its chapters was about the unreality of time. Not time in general, not time tout court: the book allowed that a certain understanding of time—time as a dimension, time as a variable, time as a vector of entropy—was real enough. Time could be theorized as a component of a strange dimpled fabric called space-time. It could be counted and calculated, and could even be measured, after a fashion, with clocks. But time as we experience it—time as the ever-cresting wave of a present tense that slides inexorably from one moment to the next, time as the great wheel that rolls us relentlessly through our days—that, the book said, is nothing but a psychological illusion. Time is nothing that moves, or passes, or flows. All change is static, and what we perceive as motion is in truth as fixed as the individual frames of a filmstrip.

This was all old hat. McTaggart and Einstein had made the same points decades earlier. Warren knew that now, as he hadn't known it then. Back then, the book's odd ideas about time had confused and astonished him, just as the thought of a Warren-less world had confused and astonished him when he was younger. This is how time got its hooks in Warren. This is how time set its trap.

It would be too much to say that Warren's temporal agitations were entirely responsible for sending him careening toward the catastrophe that awaited him at the Divinity School. But they certainly played a part. In an elective course he took his senior year of college, not long after he got himself baptized as a Catholic, he was assigned Augustine's *Confessions*. He'd read the book before, during his junior year of high school, but the first time around it had succeeded only in making him feel bad about how little sexual experience he'd had by comparison with Christianity's most venerated saint.

On his second reading, however, Warren couldn't fail to notice Augustine's famous meditation on time, or that the author of the introduction to his edition appeared similarly harassed by the obsession that was still haunting him. That author, he read on the back cover, was a professor of theology at the University's Divinity School named Eric Webb. On a whim, Warren wrote him a letter—an actual letter, on paper and everything. He said something about how crazy he'd felt for the questions he had, and how lonely. How was no one else bothered by this, he wondered.

Two months later, Professor Webb responded with a six-page letter of his own. *Mr. Kayita*, it began. *I can't speak to what happens outside the Divinity School, but let me assure you: we're bothered here.*

Time had tricked Warren. Time had tempted him. Time had sold him on the seductive notion that the world he'd grown up in, so routinely described as disenchanted, still held mysteries that awaited someone with the right metaphysical temperament to take them on.

Now time was back on its bullshit again.

After the incident with the car, The Weight gave Warren a New Year's deadline to pay back the whole of his mother's debt. Warren tried earnestly to meet it, he really did. He took a cash advance from his credit-card company and got himself in debt to a handful of payday lenders whose financial terms, while only slightly less onerous than The Weight's, at least did not require his body as collateral. He sold the remains of his car for scrap, and then he sold his bicycle, and then he sold his TV and DVD player. He sold way too many of his books, for way too little money. He skipped his electric and gas bills two months in a row and paid his landlord only half his rent. He even hit up a couple of his coworkers for loans—an act of desperation that proved as unsuccessful as it was humiliating.

It wasn't enough. It wasn't nearly enough. His mother's debt had metastasized like the lymphoma that proved the only thing capable of stopping her disastrous poker career, and now Warren owed nearly as much as he made in a year at the library. Never before had he so desperately wanted to be wrong about time. Never before had he had so much incentive to believe that time didn't move, that minutes didn't pass, that seconds didn't sweep along their appointed course with the fatal implacability of the reaper's swinging scythe.

But of course what Warren believed hadn't mattered in the slightest. Time ignored the theoretical impossibility of its own movement and shoved him ruthlessly forward nonetheless, into new hours, new days, new weeks.

Trapped between money and time, the Scylla and Charybdis of his mortal existence, Warren realized there was no way he'd make the deadline, not with the sum The Weight insisted he was owed. He decided his only real option was to make a run for it—a run, at least, from the marked territory that was his apartment.

Late in the afternoon on December 30, he stuffed his backpack with clothes, a few toiletries, his laptop, and two fifths of Fireball. He surveyed the meager wreckage of his kitchen pantry and packed into a tote bag a few back-of-the-cabinet cans and boxes of food that were probably half a decade old by now. Working on the theory that some combination of the books, the institutional turnstiles, and the brutalist concrete exterior would keep The Weight and his goons at bay, Warren figured he would hole up as long as he could in the sub-sub-basement maintenance room in the Main Library that he used as his unofficial office.

II was winter break at the University, and so Warren had the Main Library building mostly to himself. Even so, he remained almost exclusively in the sub-sub-basement for ninety-six hours straight. He slept in the maintenance room, shaved his face and washed his armpits in the bathroom, and nourished himself on the high-sugar, high-sodium offerings of the vending machines near the elevators. He drank a lot of Fireball and played a lot of Wintermere and watched a lot of porn—drank and played and watched so much, in fact, that he regularly woke up sweaty and cottonmouthed from dreams that involved busty barmaids and half-naked nuns performing unspeakable perversities on a cartoon avatar of a medieval knight. Three times a day, sometimes more, he scanned the websites of local newspapers for obituaries or any other news of his neighbors. He found nothing.

After four days, Warren decided he couldn't take it anymore. He'd had enough of the hypoxic overconditioned air, enough of the penitential fluorescent lighting, enough of the Doritos, granola bars, and Diet Coke that had provided the bulk of his sustenance. He'd had enough of the Adderall stank that floated like a miasma in the library's lower levels, and enough, too, of the ever-less-furtive side glances he caught from the green-skinned weirdos who hung around the sub-sub-basement even though classes were not in session. (*As you are now, so once was I,* Warren wanted to tell the students he saw. *As I am now, so you must be!*) He'd had enough porn and even enough Wintermere. He needed fresh air. He needed clean clothes. He needed a hot bath. He needed an apple, a cucumber, a bottle of beer, a glass of cold buttermilk, another fifth or two of Fireball. He needed, he realized, to leave the library.

Warren couldn't be sure what to expect when he went outside. How much was seventy thousand dollars worth to a man like The Weight? How much attention? How many goon-hours? It was probably best, he figured, to be prepared for the worst. The morning after his fourth night at the library, he went up to the second-floor reading room with the big picture windows that looked out on Fifty-Eighth Street. It was still early, and still fairly dark, though the sky in the southeast was beginning to purple the clouds in anticipation of sunrise. Warren scanned the shadows on the street below him and noticed no obvious warnings. Except for a few students trudging home after all-night study or make-out sessions, the only people he spotted on the sidewalks were service workers headed to their morning shifts at the University's dining halls and dormitories.

Seeing nothing suspicious, sensing nothing untoward, Warren went downstairs. In the bathroom he took a nervous piss and slapped his cheeks with cold water. He watched himself in the mirror as he wrapped his face in a heavy scarf and pulled a scarlet knit beanie down over his ears, until the only skin showing was a narrow band across his eyes and the wide bridge of his nose. Maybe his mother could have picked him out of a lineup like that. Definitely his sister could. But he doubted anyone else. Probably not his father. Certainly not The Weight.

Warren exited the library through a service door in the back of the building. Outside, the air was cold but not Chicago cold: he could breathe without pain and blink without fear of his eyelids freezing together. He fol-lowed a concrete footpath that led north toward a cluster of recently built collegiate dorms. The path was conspicuous in its way—though the sky was lighter now, light enough to make out a bird on a bare-branched tree at fifty feet, the path was still floodlit by a slaloming double picket of LED lamps—but it was also the least obvious way of leaving the library. Warren figured it was worth the risk.

In planning his escape, Warren had spent so much time thinking about how not to get caught—and what he might have to say, do, or promise to The Weight if he did—that he'd left himself almost no mental energy for considering what came next. The possibility that leaving the library would be easy, that it might be as simple as walking out, was not one he'd entertained, even briefly. Yet that's how it went. Head down, heart thumping, feet moving briskly but not fast, he'd walked and kept walking until he looked up to see that he was already four blocks north of campus.

With his heart rate coming down and the adrenaline in his blood beginning to subside, Warren took the minor risk of loosening his scarf until it fell off his nose and settled around his chin. He was hungry—starving even, starving for meat in particular. There was a fried-chicken shack a block away, and a BBQ joint a block beyond that, but he decided to hold out for the see-your-food diner on Fifty-Third instead. (Warren loved a good see-your-food, or at least he loved this one: it was his favorite restaurant in all of Fell Gardens.) He took a table near the back of the restaurant, put his back to the wall like the Mafia guys were said to do, and ordered a hamburger, a salad, a side of bacon, and a cup of coffee.

When Warren was a young boy, a few years before he first began to feel his time-feeling, his father promised him that he would take him to visit Uganda when he was older. Thanks to a pair of civil wars that erupted half a world away from each other—one that started when Yoweri Museveni raided an armory in Kabamba, the other when Warren broke the news to his father that he was giving up on medicine to pursue a master's degree at the Divinity School—the trip never happened. For a long time, however, Warren's father insisted that they would someday travel together to his native country. He wanted to show Warren the village where he grew up, in Wakiso District, and to introduce him to his many relatives. He wanted to show him the seven hills of Kampala, and the Kasubi Tombs, and the palace of the kabaka. He wanted him to eat a proper plate of *posho* and *matoke* (not the distant approximations Warren's mother had attempted), to see the great wonder that was Makerere, and to dip his bare feet in the Nile at its source, near the massive Jinja dam.

And the animals? Warren had asked, one of the first times his father had made the promise. *Will we get to see the animals, too, Taata? Will we get to see the lions?*

Yes, his father had sighed. *We can also see the animals.*

As young as he was, Warren had not missed his father's momentary disappointment at his question. The reaction confused him. At that age, Warren believed that lions were just about the greatest thing the Earth had to offer, now that the dinosaurs were gone, which meant that if Uganda had lions roaming in the wild, then it must be one of the greatest places the Earth had to offer, as well. Not for a long time would he guess how much it probably hurt his father that even his own son could only think of Africa as though he were a *mzungu* tourist planning a safari.

Still, whatever dismay his father felt in that moment did not last long. He was a stern parent, and sometimes a harsh one, but he was not incapable of tenderness. His patients loved him and always swore by his compassion, his humor, and his deep understanding of matters that extended well beyond the medical. It was true that Warren, as a boy, sometimes wished he might come down with some exotic ailment so that he might get a chance to experience that side of his father more fully, but he also could not claim anything like a childhood bereft of paternal affection. (That particular bereavement would have to wait until he was an adult.)

There's something you must know about lions, his father had said that night, after he had let his disappointment drain away. Warren could still remember him sitting there, on the edge of his bed. He could still remember the feel of his weight on the mattress, could still remember the citrus tang of his body odor. *Three things you must know, in fact. The first thing is that the lions in Uganda are very special. They are smarter than the lions anywhere else in the world, for in Uganda the lions have learned to climb trees. When I take you there, you can see them. We will go to Ishasha, and you will see the smartest lions in the entire world, sitting in the branches in the big acacia and fig trees.*

What was the second thing, Taata? Warren remembered asking.

The second thing, my son, is that even though lions are very strong, and very fast, and very deadly—and even though they can be very smart, smart enough to learn to climb trees—most of the time they are very lazy, and very clumsy. They have no natural enemies, and so they have nothing to fear. When we see them you will see what I mean. How heedless they are. How sloppy. How easy they have it, and how careless that lets them be. It's easy to admire a lion: I did it, too, when I was your age. But I will tell you that after I saw them in the wild one or two times, I always found myself more interested in the other animals. All those indistinguishable kob and bushbuck and topi that get neglected so unfairly because they are prey. Every one of them, as far as you can see, always knows exactly where the lions are at every moment. Maybe they are not watching them directly. Maybe they look like they're simply grazing. But they are always aware. They always know. They have an instinct for trouble. They know they cannot afford to be sloppy and careless, not if they want to survive . . .

Warren never did hear the third thing. As much as he loved lions, and as much as he wanted to know what his favorite person in the world wanted to tell him about his favorite animal in the world, even the entire mustered strength of his five-year-old intentions were no match for the soporific power of his father's baritone.

Warren still thought about that conversation with some frequency, not least since it was the first time his father had told him about the instinct for trouble. But he did not happen to remember it while he was eating his burger and his bacon at the diner. What he thought about instead was whether he'd been too strict with himself, too paranoid, in resolving not to visit his apartment or even his neighborhood till after dark. He thought about what Martin Luther had said about solitude: *When we are alone, we leap to conclusions, and we interpret everything in the worst light.*

Warren left the diner under a cold, gray sky that must also have been lonely, for it, too, seemed intent on interpreting everything in the worst light possible. It was starting to snow, and everything in Fell Gardens— the leafless trees, the dirty buildings, the hustling pedestrians—appeared empty of interest or meaningful life. Warren told himself that he still had every intention of sticking to his original plan: he would stay away from his apartment until he was certain he could be safe. But already his determination had weakened to the point that he was able to pretend he didn't notice the plain fact that his feet were carrying him south, across the Midway, into his neighborhood, and onto his street.

It was only when Warren was a block from his building that he recalled the lesson about the lions that he had failed to learn from his father. It was only when he saw the unfamiliar white man leaning against the brick wall of the building's facade that he remembered yet again how comprehensively he'd failed to inherit even a twinge of his father's instinct for trouble. The man was not a lion, but like a lion he'd put no effort into making himself inconspicuous. This far south of the Midway, it wasn't often you saw a white guy who wasn't homeless or a cop just hanging around, and this dude, clearly, was neither of those.

He was big, bigger than Warren, and built like a snowman on stilts: his huge round head sat neckless atop a huge round belly that made a mockery of the athletic pretensions of his triple-striped tracksuit. On his feet, at the far end of his long skinny legs, were black high-tops, and on his face, above his short stubby nose, were sport sunglasses with mirrored red lenses. He was hatless, and gloveless, and though the cold had turned his bald head a bright pink, the falling snowflakes appeared not to bother him at all.

The man was smoking a cigarette with one hand and flicking at something on his phone with the other. Standing there, smoking there, it was obvious he was a lookout. Warren didn't need to wonder what he was supposed to be looking for. He didn't need to wonder who.

With the snow, the streets and the sidewalks were mostly empty, but as best Warren could tell the man had been too distracted by his phone to notice his approach. He turned on his heels and walked back the way he came, toward the intersection at the end of the block. His heart was pounding again and he couldn't get a deep breath, but he did his best to maintain a casual-seeming gait until he reached the corner. He was almost away, almost clear, but like Lot's wife he could not refuse himself one last look back.

This, too, proved a mistake: at just that moment, the man in the track-suit looked over and caught his glance. Probably it was impossible that the man could have identified Warren at that distance. Probably he would have liked nothing more than to return to his cigarette and whatever had captured his glazed attention on his phone. But Warren couldn't help himself. He couldn't convince himself to walk those last few steps until he rounded the corner and got himself securely out of sight. A jolt of something, not the instinct for trouble but some neurochemical distillate of fear, hit him in the base of the skull and forced him to emit a strange little squeak.

Warren started running, and when he reached the intersection he turned right and kept running, as fast as his sore knees and swollen feet would carry him, past a post office, a sandwich shop, and a liquor store. Up the block he saw a group of older people in loose suits and calf-length overcoats filing through the door of what Warren recognized only belatedly as Gabriel's storefront Iglesia Pentecostal. Without much conscious thought—wanting only to escape the man in the tracksuit, whom he was sure would turn the corner any moment—he followed them in.

The church was crowded enough that Warren had to wedge himself through the door to get inside. He was pretty sure he'd escaped the tracksuit guy without being seen, but, not wanting to take any chances, he burrowed through the benign chaos at the back of the church and found a spot away from the door, where he'd be invisible to anyone peering in from the sidewalk. Everyone around him—everyone in the church, as far as he could tell—was old. They smelled of damp wool, lilac perfume, cumin, cigarettes, and cigars, and they carried with them a clattering assortment of canes, walkers, and wet umbrellas.

Warren had walked by Gabriel's church before, hundreds if not thousands of times, but he had never been inside. It was not what he expected. The interior was small and square and very pink. The walls were pink, and the ceiling was pink, and the carpet underfoot was pink. Not just any pink, either: this was not a shy pastel or a chic, tender rose. It was a full-bodied, nearly fluorescent pink of the sort Warren hadn't seen deployed as an implement of interior design since he'd lived in California. A Barbie-doll pink. A bubblegum pink. Where the room wasn't pink, it was gold. The molding and the doors, the radiator covers and the light switches, even the rotors of the ceiling fan overhead had been spray-painted a bright and incongruous metallic yellow.

Surrounded now by a semicircle of elderly men in heavy overcoats and felt hats, Warren heard a surprising but familiar voice come over a loudspeaker. He stood on his toes so that he could see over the shoulders of the men in front of him, and sure enough, up ahead, on a low pink platform in front of a large golden cross, he saw Gabriel standing with his eyes closed. Gabriel was chanting some kind of prayer into the microphone he held in his left hand. The prayer sounded biblical, prophetic, but between the static from the speakers and his own limited Spanish, Warren had no idea what he was saying.

Hands went up all throughout the crowd, a sign of blessings given or blessings received, and a murmur of approval floated up toward the pink ceiling.

Gabriel, eyes still closed, half whispered into his microphone. *Ven acá, Mariela. Trae al chico.*

The church exhaled another loud sigh, and the men in front of Warren, shifting their weight as though to brace themselves for something, moved just enough for him to peer between their elbows. At first what he saw was nothing special: a young woman, thirty years younger than the youngest person in the room, stood from a chair where she'd been sitting. Warren watched her lean over to help somebody else stand up. He gasped when he realized who it was: the little white boy—Adrian's son?—whom he'd last seen in the hospital. Now, as then, the boy was glowing.

After his hospital visit however many months ago, Warren had persuaded himself that the glowing child he remembered had in fact been a drug- or injury-sponsored hallucination. Now, however, he knew that he'd been mistaken to second-guess himself. He'd seen what he'd thought he'd seen. A boy aglow. A lad alight.

Like everyone in the church, Warren couldn't take his eyes off the kid, but it quickly became clear that the boy, for his part, was immune to the concentrated attention of the crowd. His only interest was a pair of toy cars he was zooming all over the platform in front of the altar. When he wasn't racing the cars, he jumped, and clapped, and stomped around. Several times he staged pratfalls for his own amusement, letting himself fall heavily on his diapered behind and then getting up and doing it again. The boy's clumsy good cheer lightened the mood of ponderous solemnity in the church and won him encouraging coos from the crowd of grandparents and great-grandparents. Even Warren, no fan of children in the abstract or in most particulars, found himself smiling as the boy tumbled haphazardly around the dais.

It occurred to Warren to wonder why the boy was here and Adrian was not, but he'd only just formed the question in his mind when he heard a commotion at the back of the room. A small elderly shriek was followed by a large and unhappy murmur. Warren felt a wave of pressure move through the crowd, and he knew without looking what was causing it. He didn't need to see the tracksuit guy pushing through the churchgoers, scanning the room from behind his mirrored sunglasses. Nor did he need to see the identically dressed thugs who were following in the tracksuit's wide wake. He certainly didn't need to see The Weight.

Warren bent his head, hoping to stay out of sight, and moved quickly toward the front of the standing crowd. There was a door up behind the altar—a golden door, of course—and though he had no idea where it would take him, Warren saw no other possible means of escape. Hoping against hope that The Weight and his goons would still be dazzled, as he'd been, by the pink surroundings, he rushed into the aisle that separated two rows of chairs in the center of the church. He was almost at the dais, almost within reach of Gabriel and the young woman, when he heard the goons start shouting from the back of the room.

Warren! Warren heard. The voice was The Weight's—his high, adenoidal whine was unmistakable. *Warren, just stop!*

He should have kept running. If he'd had a moment to think, Warren might have reminded himself that while The Weight was a nasty man, and by all accounts a violent man, he was not the sort to turn a crowded church into a literal bloodbath. The disappearance of the kind of person The Weight usually loaned money to was an occurrence the Chicago PD could reliably be counted on to forget about almost instantly. A massacre at a Mexican church on the South Side was something else entirely: another genre of crime, another district, a whole other denomination. (That, at any rate, is what Warren wanted to believe. The alternative thought—that his instinct for trouble had failed him so spectacularly that he'd visited terror on a church full of pious elders—was too horrible to contemplate.)

Warren should have kept running, but of course he didn't have a moment to think, or so much as a single unhassled neuron to think with. He was all instinct, all adrenaline, and at the sound of his name the instinct and the adrenaline stopped him where he stood in front of the altar. After a few seconds or a few hours—time was up to its old tricks, so Warren couldn't entirely tell—he turned back toward the back of the church. He saw the thugs, shoulder to shoulder, blocking the path to the rear door. In front of them The Weight was stepping forward into the aisle, with his hands up over his head, as though he were trying to calm the agitation of the people who were closest to him. He was trying to smile, too, trying to play it cool for the crowd, but Warren could tell that he was deeply unhappy. *Warren, let's go. Let's get out of here. Let's leave these people be.*

Just then, Warren felt a tug at his pant leg. He looked down and saw the little white boy, who was standing with his arms outstretched. Still running on instinct and adrenaline—he certainly didn't mean to make of the kid a human shield—Warren reached down and scooped the boy into his arms. The boy clapped his ears together and, once aloft, started driving them up the slope of Warren's bald head. Warren looked up and looked down the aisle. The Weight was retreating now, stumbling backward, his fake smile contorted into a terrified rictus.

What the fuck is that, Warren? he shouted. *What the fuck is going on with that little kid?*

WINTER QUARTER

SEVEN

Paul left McGinley, pulled his hood over his head, and descended the icy brick stoop. The sidewalk was covered, like everything else in the neighborhood, with a thick layer of dirty snow. A few days earlier, a dense storm had come down from Canada and deposited a vast white shawl atop the vast Chicagoland sprawl. The snow made a blanket that lay eight inches deep and six million acres wide, covering an area bigger than New Jersey. All of it was swaddled, all of it was smothered: the whole wide wen that stretched from Gary up to Kenosha, from the lake out to Aurora, Elgin, St. Charles, and West Dundee.

The storm had not helped the funk that Paul had found himself in ever since his breakup with Carrie. Nor had the fact that he couldn't even be sure that "breakup" was the right word for what happened. Not that the word really mattered: a sledgehammer by any other name would still split your skull.

It's never been like that, Carrie had said, and she was right. Neither of them had ever asked for, let alone demanded, exclusivity from the other. Their relationship, which they never called a relationship (*cosa nostra* was their private dysphemism) was not made of boundaries and prohibitions. To all outward appearances they were merely friends: good friends, companionable friends, but friends nonetheless. They ate lunch together at least once a week at their favorite Lebanese restaurant. They went to movies together at the art-house cinema. They studied together in the second-floor reading room of the Main Library.

In public, around anyone but their closest friends, the only display of affection they ever allowed themselves was a flirty sarcasm that was easy to pass off as platonic teasing. But when they were home at Carrie's, or "home" at McGinley, or even occasionally when they were both at the library late at night, where they knew all the places no one ever went, it was another story. Sex between them had started as an answer to lust and convenience, a way to pass the time and improve their mood when they were randy or bored or feeling bad about themselves. Eventually, however, it became something more durable and more surprising: not an expression of some underlying feeling but the thing itself. What that feeling was was hard for Paul to articulate. It was not love; even now, as bad as he felt, Paul would not say that. But it was something. It was real. And now it was gone.

In the past they had always understood, without it needing to be said, that when one or the other of them took a new lover it might mean slowing things down between them, or even pausing for a while. Never before had either of them cut things off so definitively. Sure, they'd traded texts a few times since the morning after Paul's birthday, and sure, Carrie had made all the right noises about wanting to stay friends. But he could tell her heart wasn't in it. Her heart was with the lawyer.

Compounding the pain of his quasi-breakup with Carrie was Paul's increasing anguish over his dissertation. For weeks, ever since he visited Adrian's house, he'd been searching for a new subject to take the place of Fra Dolcino. He'd pored over his old class notes, read through the long outlines he'd made to prepare for his qualifying exams, chased down every last lead he could think of. Still he'd found nothing. Nothing suitable, anyway, nothing that didn't have some obvious fatal flaw that told him right away it would be impossible to work up into a proper research project.

Hoping to escape his multiplex despair, at least for a few hours, Paul had decided to take up his friend Billy on the offer of a free lunch at the undergraduate dining hall. Billy was a wild-eyed weirdo from the mountains of North Carolina whom Paul had met on the first day of Div School orientation. The two men had become fast friends, bonding over their rural upbringings, their mutual appreciation for Gram Parsons and Janet Jackson, and their shared sense of having landed in an academic situation for which their previous education had not wholly—on some days it seemed even minimally—prepared them.

Unlike his wife, Salma, a lithe scholar of medieval Islam who was one of the Div School's stars, Billy was no longer a graduate student. He was a huge science-fiction fan, with subsidiary interests in religiously inflected erotica and lucrative utopian cults, and had come to the Div School thinking that he might put these obsessions to productive scholarly use. As it turned out, however, Billy had neither Paul's *Sitzfleisch* nor his wife's talent for the creative close reading of primary sources. After two years of frustration chasing his master's degree—two years, he liked to say, that had taught him everything he needed to know about how he didn't want to spend the rest of his life—he'd decided not to apply to the PhD program.

In the years since, Billy had arranged his life in a manner that made him the envy of not a few of his former peers, Paul occasionally among them. After successfully courting Salma, he'd persuaded her to take a job as a resident fellow in a freshman dorm. The position gave them room and board, a modest stipend, and health insurance in exchange for living with and supervising sixty hyperintelligent, hyper-stressed postadolescents. Most crucially, it took the pressure off Billy to get anything resembling a real job. Twenty hours a week he worked as a manager at the Cup of Salvation, the coffee shop in the basement of Harrison Hall, which left him free to spend the rest of his days—and not a few very late nights—following his true passions: reading and rereading the collected works of Philip K. Dick, playing mahjong for money online, rebuilding damaged guitars, evangelizing for veganism, and catfishing conservative preachers and politicians from his home state.

Paul kicked the snow off his boots before entering the former field house that served as the University's central dining hall. Billy was not hard to find inside: a freckled ox of a man with arms like John Henry and a beard like Karl Marx, he had bright red hair and light brown eyes and tobacco-stained teeth that had never been tortured—his word—by orthodontics.

Paul joined him over at the grill station, where Billy had been chatting up the server who'd just handed him two plates of avocado tacos. Billy was good like that: he talked to everyone, and, possibly in compensation for his imposing appearance, ended up making friends with most of them. Occasionally Paul wondered if that was the real reason he'd quit graduate school. As much as Billy liked to play up his generalized misanthropy, it was plain as day that he liked people—he liked talking to them, liked joking with them, liked hanging around them—far more than he liked even his favorite books.

Billy squinted when he saw Paul, then acted out a pantomime of belated recognition. *Well, well, well!* he said finally, his baritone drawling on the last repetition so long and so loud that half a dozen grazing undergrads ducked at the sound of it. *If it isn't Mister Mystery himself. I wondered if you were going to show.*

When's the last time I missed a free meal?

Billy let out a contented grunt. *That's what I told Salma. She was wondering where you'd run off to and I told her I'd set the perfect trap to find out. Obviously there was always a chance that you'd stowed away on a Vogon constructor ship and were beyond the reach of terrestrial communications. But, failing that, I knew you'd be here today, ready once more to take advantage of my boundless generosity.*

Well, Paul said, *here I am*. He was conscious of being watched by the server behind the grill, who was wearing a black durag and a white chef's smock. *Alas for the Vogons*.

And here, indubitably, Billy boomed again, in the accent that he never tired of reminding people was the nearest cousin of Shakespeare's English that still survived anywhere on the planet, *you are*.

Paul would like to say—he had said, on more than one occasion, to more than one acquaintance who had wondered what exactly Billy's deal was—that this was all a put-on, a burlesque for the sake of the benighted undergraduates who were, in Billy's not-so-humble opinion, far too repressed and uptight for their own good. (He loved quoting A. J. Liebling, who had once called the University's undergraduates "the greatest collection of juvenile neurotics assembled since the Children's Crusade.")

And it was that—a put-on—at least in some respects. But Paul knew Billy well enough by now to know that it was not only that. Born in a Piedmont holler that didn't get electricity until a decade before his birth, Billy had been brought up by an alcoholic father who did a steady trade in ginseng and moonshine and a mother who sounded, to Paul's ears, like a florid manic-depressive. And yet Billy had propelled himself up the Great Pyramid of American social mobility, fueled, as best Paul could tell, pretty much exclusively on his own unshakable self-regard.

With the help of the eccentrics he met on the early Internet—the money he made raising hogs in FFA he spent on a computer he bought off his meth-head cousin and a dial-up AOL account—he'd figured out how to get accepted to a college that was safely out of state and, once there, how to make up for the dismal education he'd received in high school. Despite the fact that he held not one but two postsecondary degrees, he still carried himself with the bristly, unchinkable assurance of an autodidact.

So what's the deal, man? Where you been? Let me guess: It's Carrie, right? Grindin' your goober morning, noon, and twice at night?

Paul winced. He'd seen Billy a couple of times since his thing with Carrie ended, but on none of those occasions was there an opening to tell him what had happened.

Billy misread Paul's expression. He threw up his hands in a defensive gesture. *Hey, I'm not blaming you. She's a catch, man. Whatever it takes to keep her happy. I might could send you some videos if you're running out of ideas.*

Jesus, dude, I'm not going to watch you have sex with your wife.

That's not what I meant. But now that you mention it, I bet we could put something together for you.

Paul laughed, despite himself. *I appreciate the offer, but I don't think Salma would be too happy about that. Anyway, I'm afraid it's no use. Carrie dumped me.*

I told you, man, *that girl ain't worth a pile of spit,* Billy said, after Paul finished telling him about his birthday dinner. He seemed genuinely indignant. *I don't care how much money she's got. I could tell as soon as I saw her she was spoilt like a Siamese cat. Crazy, too, if she thinks she's going to be happy with a goddamned lawyer. It's why I keep saying you gotta date a regular chick, man. All these grad-school girls are nuts.*

You kiss your wife with that mouth?

I kiss her cooter with this mouth, if you must know. Anyway, she's as bad as any of them. She just knows how to keep it under wraps. All these fucking academics are the same. I don't know how you can even handle it. I don't know why you stick around. I only get it through osmosis now—well, I guess there's some venereal transmission, too—but that's already way too much for me. I've been telling you for years: academia ain't right for people who ain't got something wrong with them in the head.

Paul smiled but said nothing. Billy liked to riff like this, and Paul liked to let him.

I'm serious. But tell me, if it's not Carrie taking all your time, where have you been hiding out? Don't tell me you're actually working on your dissertation?

Paul shook his head. *I was. But suddenly I seem to have lost my subject.*

Oh man. Do I want to know? Do you want to tell me?

Not really. It's not exciting.

Has Adrian been around to help?

Paul raised an eyebrow and noticed that Billy was watching for his reaction.

You know Salma TA'ed for him last quarter, right? She said he's been acting weird. For a while there she was half-certain he was in the middle of some kind of breakdown. First he was out for a while, missed a bunch of classes. He got way behind on his grading. Then, all of a sudden, it's like he's never been better. He's wearing clothes that actually fit him, he's taking care of himself, there's no sign of that stoner surfer-bro thing he usually does. You notice anything?

Paul knit his brows as though he were consulting his memory. *No, but to be honest, I haven't seen him much lately.* Technically this was not a lie. Though Paul and Adrian had been in regular contact since their meeting at Adrian's house, nearly all of their conversations since then had happened on the phone or over email.

Salma thinks he's applying for a new job. Apparently a friend of Adrian's just got hired to run the religion center at UCLA. She said he's always talking about how much he misses California.

Paul shook his head. *He just got tenure not that long ago. His family is all set up here. Anyway, if he was going somewhere, I think I'd know. He's chairing my committee, after all.*

I'm just telling you what Salma told me.

No, I know, Paul said, in a softer tone. He hadn't meant to sound so emphatic. *I guess anything's possible.*

After a notable silence, Paul looked up and saw Billy's brown eyes shooting daggers.

Goddamnit. You know, don't you? Billy finally said. *I told Salma I bet you did, but I don't think I really believed my own bullshit.*

Paul didn't say anything.

What the fuck is going on? Billy was looking at Paul with the same determined glare he gave the freshmen boys he caught hitting golf balls off the roof of his dorm.

Paul thought for a long moment. Several times over the past couple of months he'd considered telling Billy about Luca. He knew Billy would love to hear it: like his idol PKD, he was a collector of bizarreries, a connoisseur of the indigenous American berserk. But that was not exactly a point in Billy's favor, for he also happened to be an incorrigible gossip.

Paul looked at his friend with what he hoped was a hard expression. *If I tell you something, could you keep it an absolute secret?*

Billy's freckled face lit up with anticipatory delight. *Yeah, man, of course.*

From everyone, I mean. Even Salma.

Fuck, dude. What happened?

I'm serious. If I tell you, you can't tell anyone else. Even your wife.

Yeah, yeah, okay. Sure.

Promise?

You want me to take a blood oath? 'Cause I'll do it. I promise.

All right, Paul said finally. *But first you're going to have to buy me a coffee, and I'm going to insist you let me put real milk in it. This is going to take a while.*

Later that afternoon, after he'd told Billy what he had to tell him and reiterated his demand for total secrecy, Paul went to the library and climbed the stairs to the second-floor reading room. This was familiar territory, almost as familiar as McGinley House. Paul had spent months here, often working alongside Carrie, to prepare for his qualifying exams. He'd spent months here again, also with Carrie, reading up on Fra Dolcino. More recently, he'd spent several long weeks here trying to find some way to salvage his dissertation proposal.

Paul found an open desk at one of the swastika-shaped study carrels that were situated near the tall windows of the library's second-floor atrium. Through the windows, across Fifty-Eighth Street, he could see the snow stacked up on the crenellations of the Biology Building. He opened his backpack and pulled out a slender book with a mint-green library binding that said, in embossed letters, *The Dictionarius of John de Garlande.*

In the half decade he'd been at the Div School so far, Paul had read his way through two millennia of Christian theology, three centuries of Anglophone literature, and four decades of continental Theory. For just one of his qualifying exams alone, he had made himself fluent in Origen's eschatology, Augustine's soteriology, Aquinas's ontology, and Hume's epistemology. He'd read enough that he could explain how a single syllable split the early Church at the Council of Nicaea and why, ten centuries later, William of Ockham had accused the pope himself of heresy. Sitting in this room, in this library, Paul had squinted his way through Anselm, Husserl, and Marguerite Porete; he'd bruised his brain on Barth, Ockham, and Hegel; he'd fallen hard for Feuerbach, Arendt, and the Pseudo-Dionysius.

One of the favorite books Paul had read in all that time, however, was the small and obscure volume he was now holding in his hand. *The Dictionarius* was a thirteenth-century book that was, as far as anyone knew, the first dictionary to be called by the name. Despite this distinction, neither it nor its author, an English scholar who lived and taught in Paris, were well known. Outside his mention in the OED's most hallowed entry (s.v. "dictionary"), John of Garland's only other claim to any sort of fame was a rude swipe that Erasmus delivered in passing three hundred years after his death.

The *Dictionarius*, as it happened, was very far from the sort of concordance that Noah Webster or Samuel Johnson or James Murray might have recognized as kin to their own. It had no headwords. Nothing was alphabetized. There was no attempt at systematization—no pretense, even, to comprehensiveness. It was, rather, a slim Latin wordbook, a primer for new students at the University of Paris. These students, who were known as "yellow beaks," were often teenagers or younger. They came from all over Europe and were required, for as long as they were enrolled in the university, not just to read Latin but also to speak it, even among themselves. John's *Dictionarius* was intended to help students who were neither wealthy enough to afford tutors nor gifted enough not to need them to avoid the wrath and the cunning of the "wolves": upper-class informers who took it upon themselves to enforce the university's strictures.

The resulting text is a desultory first-person narrative not all that different from the sort of thing you might find in a first-year foreign-language class. After enumerating the parts of the human body—including, "in the cause of education," the male *virga virilis* and its "two pendant brothers," as well as the door-like *vulva*, the incubating *matrix*, and the rearguard *nates*, said to be "displeasing to a religious man"—John leads his reader on a stroll around the Left Bank neighborhood where he lived and taught. Coursing up and down the muddy streets, he introduces cobblers, wine peddlers, tanners, money changers, bakers, goldsmiths, waffle makers, carpenters, apothecaries, the purse merchants lined up along the Grand Pont (now the Pont Notre-Dame), the bowyers at the Gate of Saint Lazarus, and his neighbor William, who sells soap, mirrors, razors, and "steel for striking fire."

Later John takes his reader into his house. There he shows off his clothes rail, where he keeps a coat, a shoulder cape, trousers, tunics, and doublets, and his garden, where he grows sage, parsley, hyssop, fennel, cabbage, spinach, chives, roses, lilies, and violets. He tells us that a worthy man's lodging ought to have hemmed towels, white tablecloths, an armchair, a milk pail, and mousetraps. Clerks, he says, need books, lecterns, a lamp with tallow, an inkhorn and quill, and pumice, while a woman ought to be supplied with scissors, spindle, pestle, and flax. He walks by a field, where he sees ox, sheep, and bulls, and over to the king's forest, where deer, tigers, and otters can be found. At the end of the book, he even recounts a brief vision of heaven—where he has seen virgins, chaste wives, and widows—and hell, where he watched serpents of all types—asps and vipers, seps and basilisks—twist around dancers and whores.

At each of the stops along the tour, John pauses to describe, in Latin, what his reader might expect to find. The *acuarium* is a needle case. Table knives are *mensaculas*. Need peacock feathers for your hat? Ask for *pennis pavonis*. Have a wine goblet that needs fixing? Get yourself to a *reparator ciphorum.* Not all of John's descriptions are dispassionate. He notes that Parisian glove makers are known to "beguile scholars," and not in a good way, with their lamb-, rabbit-, and fox-lined wares. He warns about the hucksters—*auxionarii*—who overcharge students for cherries, plums, and unripe pears; the hawkers—*clamatores*—who repair the fur linings of coats "mostly by thieving"; and the butchers—*carnifices*—who recognize in the young scholars a chance to pawn off their tough and rotten cuts of meat, which serve only to bend the scholars' flimsy *mensaculas.* And then, of course, there are the *desvacuatrices,* or "clean-up women": officially tasked with cleaning up scraps of fabric or gold, they had an unofficial reputation as prostitutes, and were said by John to take special pleasure in cleaning out the purses of university students.

Paul's appreciation for the *Dictionarius* was not complicated. He'd been brought up on the edge of a family, in a farm on the edge of a town, in a part of rural Northern California that might as well have been the edge of Nebraska for how little it resembled most people's idea of the Golden State. He had grown up in the context of no context, without any sense that his life might have some bearing on history, culture, or what his high school teachers insisted on calling current events. The utterly ordinary disaffection he'd experienced as a teenager, a reliable alchemy that turned anything familiar into an object of thoroughgoing contempt, had been compounded in his case by a provincial sense of estrangement. The stuff he saw on TV, and later on the Internet—not just movies, shows, and music but also sports, and politics, and the news—could not have felt more distant if it had been beamed down from another planet.

Unlike the rich kids at his college, unlike Carrie, Paul had not spent afternoons in third grade eating Cheez-Its in the backyards of congressmen, professional athletes, and screenwriters. He had not grown up, as some of his coevals evidently had, thinking it perfectly natural to write for glossy magazines, or run for governor, or win a Grammy. Even the idea that he might someday publish a book, on however narrow and unreadable an academic subject, still occasionally struck him as the height of implausibility.

On top of this feeling (or under it, or sitting uneasily alongside it) was the unorthodox reality of Paul's home life. His mom always swore that she'd never meant to share a roof with her brother's family. But after Steve's wife died in a car accident, when Paul was in elementary school, the inertia of the arrangement proved difficult to disrupt. The setup clearly suited more than a few of everyone's needs, yet it also felt to each of them like a bad decision someone else had made on their behalf.

Uncle Steve was especially conflicted. As much as he appreciated having his sister around to run the house and help raise his daughter, he hated the jokes about incest and sister-wives that he got from his buddies at the bar. As though to prove to his friends, or maybe just to himself, that his was not a nuclear family, he seemed to go out of his way to make Paul feel like an outsider and an interloper.

Paul's feelings of rootlessness were a large part of what had attracted him to religious studies. It had cost his mother no end of agony, even after the sex-abuse scandal had wiped away the last of her allegiance to the Vatican, that she'd failed to convey her faith to her only son. But in raising Paul according to her peculiar interpretation of Catholicism, she'd succeeded in something else: she'd given him a thread, however slender, however fragile, that helped him find his way out of his drifting isolation. It was not too much to say that what the practice of religion had done for his mother, the study of religion had done for Paul. Whatever else it was, after all, religion was culture. Religion was history. And while holding fast to a creed was not the same thing as knowing how that creed came into being, or what theological or political problems it was trying to solve, the one like the other activity gave you a way—gave Paul a way—to reach across continents and centuries, to feel like he was part of something durable.

Of course religion was not special in this respect. Paul recognized that. If his mother had been as devoted to birds as she was to religion, he might easily have ended up across the quad, chasing a PhD in ornithology in the Biology Department. But the contingencies, being what they were, had led him to the Divinity School.

More to the point, they had led him to the *Dictionarius*, whose adolescent yellow beaks, implied though they remained throughout John's narrative, held up a mirror in which Paul couldn't help seeing a dim but discernible image of himself. Even now—five years after starting at the Div School, ten years after hitting the age at which a young scholar might have been palmed a samizdat copy of John's little book at the University of Paris—he still occasionally felt a spurt of the same dizzying disorientation that had convinced him, for much of his first year in Chicago, that enrolling in graduate school was a terrible mistake.

It didn't help Paul to know that his was a common feeling around Harrison Hall. It helped even less to hear people talk about impostor syndrome, which had always struck Paul as a strange sort of self-flattery. The idea behind impostor syndrome, after all, was that you weren't actually an impostor: sure, you might be a recent college graduate who had lucked into the sort of job that a previous generation would have seen as the pinnacle of a career, but, the notion went, that sense of deficiency was only a dirty psychological trick, a self-sabotaging delusion, that kept you from acknowledging that you were in fact always already exquisitely well-qualified for whatever it was you wanted to do.

That was not Paul. He'd always been a diligent student and a serious reader, especially by the standards of his college, where the endowment and the balance sheet were sustained by the families of some truly accomplished fuckups. But it was not until he arrived at the Div School at the start of his master's program, and saw that the syllabus for one of his classes wanted him ready to discuss all eight hundred pages of Kant's First Critique in the second week of class, that he began to appreciate just how unprepared he really was.

For a long time, Paul had been content to keep the *Dictionarius* as a private totem, a secret amulet to help him hold off, or at least to manage, his recurring sense that he was an actual academic impostor. Now, though, more desperate than ever, he was well on the way to convincing himself that he should write about John's little book for his dissertation.

He could admit that it was a little dry as a subject, just as he could acknowledge that the project was unlikely to generate some coruscating insight into the Middle Ages, or modernity, or anything in between. But these drawbacks paled next to the one massive advantage the *Dictionarius* possessed, which was that no one had written about it at any length, let alone with any enthusiasm, since the nineteenth century. Questions as basic as where John was from and how many works he'd actually written were still unanswered, and Paul figured that even if he was not successful in resolving these mysteries, there must be something minimally interesting to say about the man who had given the dictionary its name.

Even the mint-green translation seemed to Paul proof of the project's viability. It was published in 1981, for reasons unknown, by a small press in Kansas. Along with the text it contained an eight-page introduction by an author with no discernible academic affiliation. This was, as far as Paul could tell, the longest dedicated consideration of John of Garland that had been published for more than a century. He guessed, in fact, that you could spend several years trawling the cocktail parties at the annual convention of medievalists in Kalamazoo without coming across anyone who had read three consecutive lines of the *Dictionarius*.

Convinced now that he was onto something, Paul spent the afternoon at the library drafting a memo to Adrian, a proposal for his proposal. He wrote it fast—a good sign—and read it over twice, checking and cross-checking his quotations and filling in some jargon that he hoped would signify at least the possibility of theoretical heft. Feeling better than he had in a long time (telling Billy about Luca had clearly unblocked something), he sent the memo to Adrian with a short note on top. *I think this might be it*, he wrote. *I hope you like it. But let me know what you think.*

Adrian called him the next afternoon. Paul could tell right away that his optimism had led him badly astray.

I don't know, Adrian said. *You could do it. If you really want to do it, you know I'm here to help you. But the thing is, a dissertation isn't just another paper. It's your first book. It's the start of your career. It's a big part of your life. It's going to take, what, three years, five years to write this thing? And then another couple of years to publish it. And all that time you'll be using it to try to get a job. It's going to be the subject of your job talk. We're talking a solid decade at least, and that's the best case, that you're going to be living with this thing. Do you really want to spend all that time with John of Garland?*

The way Adrian pronounced the name obviated any need for Paul to answer the question.

I know you don't want to think of yourself as a gunner. Trust me, I get it. But you're going to have to be, at least a bit. You need something sexy. You need something with some shine on it. Don't assume you're going to slide into a comfortable assistant professorship in a nice little unambitious liberal arts college somewhere out of the way. Everybody's fighting for everything, all up and down the scale. The lower on the ladder you are, the more difficult it is to climb back up. Trust me, I was there. I saw it myself. Used to be you could go to a shitty school and stay for a couple of years before moving on to something better. Now it's like the shitty jobs are designed to keep you stuck. They're just so much work. And, I mean, look, there's another thing, too.

Paul waited.

You're not recording this phone call, right?

No, why?

Good, because I'm going to deny saying this if you ever repeat it. But there's something you need to hear that no one wants to tell you.

I'm listening.

Thing is, it's not easy out there for a white guy right now. I'm not saying that's a good thing or a bad thing—it's probably a good thing—but I am saying it's a thing. Seems like every dean woke up one day and realized that they had too many mediocre white dudes in their departments, and they all set out to fix the problem at the same time. Which is fine and all, except instead of doing what they should be doing, the burden of fixing the problem is falling on guys like you.

Paul, who like most white guys had always had a hard time thinking of himself in demographic terms, felt distinctly uncomfortable. *What should they be doing?*

You want to know how many seventysomething colleagues I have who haven't published a serious book, or even an article, in a decade? All these Distinguished Professors of Such and Such . . . More like Extinguished Professors, if you ask me. If the Dean had any guts, he'd force them to go emeritus, to make room for the next generation. But of course he knows he'd be public enemy number one around Harrison, and he doesn't have the stomach for that.

So, what, Paul said. *I'm back to square zero?*

I had an idea, actually. It might sound a little strange, but bear with me. I think there's something much closer to home that would be just the thing. Remember when I said you needed a project with some shine on it?

Yeah.

And?

I'm sorry. I don't follow.

No, no. It's okay. It took me a while to spot it, too. It's like Heidegger said: It's hard to see something that's too nearby.

Paul was so confused. *You want me to write about Heidegger? I don't think I'm cut out for that . . .*

No, man! Adrian was almost yelling now. *Think! We're sitting here trying to figure out how you can write about someone who died seven hundred years ago. Meanwhile, right downstairs from where I'm sitting now . . .*

Wait, you want me to write about Luca?

Adrian was quick to assure Paul that he didn't want him to write his dissertation about his son. Obviously that wasn't going to fly. Paul was doing a PhD in religious studies, not paranormal pediatrics. But Adrian had been reading around a lot lately, he said. It turned out that there was a whole long history of people glowing. It started with the ancient Zoroastrians, and what they called the *khvarenah*. But that was just the beginning. The glow showed up everywhere, in just about every significant religious tradition you could think of. Everyone seemed to have some version of it. And yet no one seemed to have written about it, at least not with any sort of rigor.

When Adrian finished explaining what he had in mind, he let loose a sigh of obvious self-satisfaction. *What do you think?* he said. *This is virgin soil. This is uncharted territory, but, like, with a map, you know? I'm laying it all out in front of you. It's an incredible opportunity, I'm telling you.*

I don't know, Paul said finally. *It's just so . . . It's so different than what I was thinking. I mean, to be honest, it feels pretty risky. I barely know Latin. How am I going to read all that other stuff?*

Adrian made no effort to hide his exasperation. *Paul, I've known you for what, seven years?*

More like nine.

Even better. Nine years. And you're how old?

Twenty-eight.

Jesus. Twenty-eight. Okay. All right. So here's the thing. We've known each other for nine years so I'm just going to give it to you straight: You've got to get moving. I see you and it's just like . . . I mean, look, before I get up on my high horse, I will freely admit that I was a late bloomer, too. You're younger than I was when I started my PhD, and you're already through your exams. That's not nothing. But I knew how far I was behind when I got here. I knew I was already late. Plus you've got to remember that the game has changed a lot since I was in grad school. Back then there was some flex in the system, especially for guys like us. Now, though? Now there's no room for leisurely dawdling. I'm going to be honest with you, man. I'm going to be harsh: This thing you've got going right now—whatever it is, whatever you think it is—it's not working.

Paul winced. Adrian had never spoken to him this way.

I remember when we met, back when I was adjuncting and you were in college, you were . . . Well, let me just put it this way. I was pretty lost in college, but you, man. You were in the Congo, you know what I mean? You were like Percy Fucking Fawcett in the Amazon. I don't think I knew anything about your family then. Definitely didn't know about your dad. But it was obvious you were someone who was going to need some direction. Some guidance. I was the same way at your age. I needed someone to grab me by the shoulders, to point me in the right direction, and to say: Go there. I knew there was a risk in sending you here. Not because I didn't think you could hack it. You put the time in, you do the assigned reading. That's not everything, but it's a lot. Seventy percent of the ball game, at least. Maybe eighty. Definitely in graduate school.

Paul felt his eyes burning. *Okay,* he managed.

The danger wasn't that you weren't good enough. You absolutely were and you absolutely are. No, the danger was that you'd never get out. This place, the University. It will eat you alive. One gulp, that's all it takes. This only looks like an institution of higher learning. But I'm telling you, it's a predator. It's an apex fucking predator, and it feeds on grad students. You don't realize it, maybe, because one of its tricks is to lull its prey into the sense that they have all the time in the world. There are people, people my age, even a few people from my cohort, probably, who are out there in the world thinking they're still going to finish their PhD any day now. They just need a few more months. They just need to read a few more books, track down a few more obscure and out-of-the-way articles. It's always something. They've outlived their entire committees, some of them. No one at the University knows who they are anymore, but still they're convinced that it's all going to work out for them. This place swallowed them whole, and they have no idea. They're like Jonah in the whale. They're like Pinocchio. They're living, if you can call it that, in the belly of the fucking beast.

Paul put his phone on speaker and covered his head with his hands.

Adrian went on. *And look, I understand why it happens. I know what's holding them back. It's not their research. It's not their professors. It's nothing to do with whether they're smart enough, or anything like that. It's that they get suckered into thinking that their dissertation has to be a perfect reflection of everything they know, everything they are, everything they hope to be. I get that. I really do. God knows I'm not going to sit here and tell you that it's easy for me to remember that my work is not the only thing that counts. But at least when I went through grad school there was still a feeling that there was something waiting for me on the other side of my dissertation. There was some incentive, some negative pressure to help finish the damned thing, you know? I realize it's not like that now. I've seen good people, brilliant people, even, go four, five, six years waiting for a position to open up. For a while I thought that was going to be me. It's terrible. You do all this work, you bust your ass, and when the rejections pile up you realize you wasted the best decade of your life. It's indefensible that we put people through this. It's just insane.*

Anyway, my point is: I am not going to let that be you. You're my first PhD student. I am not going to let that happen on my watch. That's why I'm telling you, this thing I'm proposing, this thing I'm setting before you, this is what you need. Is it risky? Yeah, sure. Of course it is. But that's a good thing, don't you see that? Nothing worth doing is not risky. The whole history of religion teaches that lesson. It's the hero's journey, right? It's why people starve themselves fasting. It's why they take vows of celibacy and poverty. It's why they make themselves martyrs. They know the universe is not a cheap date.

Paul had been waiting to interject. He felt like he needed to say something, but when he opened his mouth only a feeble joke escaped: *I'm already poor. You want me to give up sex now, too?*

Adrian ignored him. *I don't want to give you the wrong idea here. I still don't know what's happening with Luca, none of us do. Maybe it's nothing so exciting as I hope it is. But I can tell you that word is getting out. People are starting to whisper. They're starting to wonder. They're starting to talk. I don't think Renata is ready for this, honestly. She still doesn't want anyone to know. But this thing has been going on for months now. We're not going to be able to keep it secret for much longer. And when they find out, people are going to want to know what's happening. They're gonna need someone to tell them what to think about it. They're gonna need someone to make sense of it for them.*

I still don't understand. What does this have to do with religion? What about the hospital? What about all the tests?

Paul could hear Adrian spit through the phone. *What about them? All that time, all that effort, all that hassle, and what did they tell us? Nothing! They don't fucking know.*

So what, you think this is like some kind of, like a halo or something?

I didn't say that. Honestly I have no idea. But I do know that this is our wheelhouse. At least as much as the doctors'. Just think about it. A kid starts glowing mysteriously. Is that a medical story? No! Maybe it's a fantasy story. Maybe it's a ghost story. Let's hope it's not a horror story. But it very definitely could be a religious story. This is our shit. I want this to be your shit.

Paul couldn't help laughing. He couldn't deny that he was beginning to warm to the idea.

I don't care about Latin or any of the other languages. We'll work that out. Point is, I want you to make yourself an expert on human incandescence. I want you to write a brilliant dissertation, pun very much intended, and when all this stuff with Luca goes big time, you're going to have your pick of jobs. We're going to be a team, man. Okay? You and me. You and me are going to make this happen.

EIGHT

On any other Sunday in any other year, Renata might have said that spending a cold and clear winter morning at the Bouncy Palace in Brighton Park was just one more of the routine indignities of motherhood. By rights she should have been home, warm on the couch under a heavy blanket with a calm blue fire reddening the fake logs in her gas-fed hearth. Adrian would be working in his study, the boys would be ingesting half their weekend dose of animated intellectual property, and she would be left alone with her second latte of the morning to read a month-old magazine, or the print edition of the *Times*, or several consecutive pages of a book she knew she'd never finish. Instead she was here, shivering in a drafty converted warehouse with twenty hyperkinetic kindergartners who seemed determined to test for themselves whether the law of gravity was truly as faultless as every adult in their vicinity seemed to believe.

Before Max turned four, Renata had never been to the Bouncy Palace. She had never heard of it, in fact, never considered that such a place might exist or have reason to exist. It belonged to an aspect of the world that had been hidden to her, as invisible as a folded dimension, for as long as she remained childless. And yet in less than two years it had become as fixed in the landscape of her life as the glittering gray lake or the crossless spire of the University's Memorial Church.

The Palace, of course, was no kind of palace at all. In form and maybe even in function it resembled an old-style asylum, the kind with cushions on the walls and mattresses on the floor and inmates whose eyes flashed with manic incomprehension. Or perhaps, in keeping with its setting—an abandoned freight siding ran alongside its northern perimeter—it was better to think of it as a factory, one whose economic output was not neon bar signs or fake-wood patio furniture or heaps of slaked lime but highly efficient, hassle-free birthday parties for Chicago's "comfortable but not rich" elementary school set. Occupying most of a windowless building in a nondescript industrial compound, it sheltered a psychedelic topography of inflatable play structures. There were stubby street-fair slides and multi-story climbing contraptions, gaudy castles and *American Gladiator*–style obstacle courses, all of them built of brightly colored vinyl and the hurricane exhaust of several air compressors.

In the first of the two big rooms where the inflatable structures were situated, Renata sat on a bench between a water fountain and a box of cubbyholes sized for small shoes. Back and forth in front of her, Max's classmates squealed and screamed as they sprinted from one attraction to the next. Max himself, in green sweatpants and a striped long-sleeve shirt, was across the way, standing atop a tall platform-like construction. A cargo net had gotten him up there, some seven or eight feet above a big soft pit that resembled a pole vaulter's landing pad, but it was already clear that he was having second thoughts. While he clung to a handle sewn into the platform's edge—the bloodless white of his knuckles was visible even across the wide room—a regular procession of his classmates hurtled off the platform beside him, flinging themselves bodily back to Earth.

Renata checked the urge to urge him on. She knew she would not be helping. Max was, as she had been—as she still was, occasionally—nervous, sensitive, and often anxious in his dealings with other people and the world around him. But he was also (also like her) fiercely protective, proud even, of his independence. He was the sort of kid who was always getting hurt, who was frequently sad, angry, or upset, who complained regularly about nearly invisible splinters and nearly imperceptible slights. At the same time, he was also stubbornly resistant to being coddled, and from a very early age had taught his parents that his tear-streaked complaints did not mean he wanted help. (In these respects, as in so many others, Max was the opposite of Luca, who had the pain tolerance of an ox and the equanimity of a house cat but also loved nothing more than to be the beneficiary of his parents' fussing.)

Trying not to be too obvious, Renata watched as Max stood at the edge of the teetering platform. His eyes darted as his classmates came and went like so many paratroopers out the back of a lumbering military plane. Renata could see that Max was steeling himself, psyching himself up to jump, or at least to let himself fall. Twice it seemed he was going to do it. Without letting go of the handle, he shifted his feet a few inches toward the abyss and bounced his knees as though he were testing a diving board. Each time, the effort was thwarted when he made the mistake of looking down.

After the second failed attempt, Max looked up and caught a glimpse of his mother. Renata, feeling her face still tensed in vicarious alarm, forced what she hoped was an encouraging smile. He took it better than she expected, smiling weakly back before deciding, or so it appeared, to depart the platform the way he came. A few steps from the top of the cargo netting, however, a rogue seismic wave rippled through the platform structure, buckling his skinny knees and disrupting his balance. By chance, just then, one of his classmates came wobbling toward him from the other direction and knocked him further out of equilibrium. Before he or Renata could be quite sure what was happening, Max was falling. An instant later he was invisible, a child-sized dent in the semi-inflated pit. Renata held her breath, unsure which way this was going to go. She watched Max climb clumsily to his feet and flash a triumphant grin at his mother. She gave him an awkward double thumbs-up as he clambered toward the exit so that he could do it all again.

The stocky boy with the cornsilk hair who had sent Max flying was Edwærd, the party's newly six-year-old guest of honor and a friend with whom Max had had a handful of playdates. As his name suggested, Edwærd was the son of two self-consciously artistic types. His father, Marcus, was an MFA-credentialed photographer with white hair and a creepy leer who worked in digital advertising, while his mother, Robyn, was tall and lanky with tattoos on her back, arms, and chest. Yet whatever idiosyncrasies Robyn and Marcus had hoped to cultivate in their burly, unfortunately ligatured son had not kept him from demanding the exact same birthday party that all the other kids in his class had demanded from their parents.

For Edwærd, Max, and their friends, a Sunday morning at the Bouncy Palace was the nearest thing they knew to heaven. For Renata, the dank, sticky demesne of King Spring and the Brave Knights of Bouncealot—with its cardboard pizzas, its bored, ironic employees, and the half-chemical, half-fungal odor that suffused its lower atmosphere—was not quite hell. It did, however, stand as a reminder to her of the fleetingness of time, the implacable onrush of mortality, and the gobsmacking sacrifices of self-respect that the mere act of raising a child in the modern world could demand from a woman.

Or at least it usually did. Today, though, things were different. They were different because today Renata was awash in the first genuine spurt of happiness she'd experienced since Luca started glowing. She'd woken up that morning to a message from Paul, Adrian's graduate student. The pith of the note, which he'd sent through her website, was just three lines, but they were three lines that had reoriented her mood entirely: I hope you don't mind too much, but I found your stories in our archive. I thought they were terrific. If you have others, published or unpublished, I'd love to read them.

The pieces were trifles, gewgaws, barely more than sketches or exercises—as insignificant and unambitious as the arpeggios Renata sometimes tapped out on her kids' electronic keyboard to test her muscle memory after twenty-odd years away from the piano. Or at least that's what she'd told herself. In high school, and for more than a decade after-ward, she had wanted to be a writer: not a writer of grant proposals and strategic plans for arts-focused nonprofit organizations but a writer of literature, the sort who might compose haunting quasi-poetic narratives that, as the reviews she'd dared to imagine for herself put it, "crossed and recrossed the boundaries between fact and fiction, biography and fantasy, provocative self-revelation and coy self-effacement." She had sustained this ambition all through her twenties, and had held on to the husk of it much longer, telling herself even after Max was born that there was still time, just as there had been time for Toni Morrison, and Annie Proulx, and Tillie Olsen.

All that felt like a long time ago now. At thirty-eight, with two young boys underwing, Renata was old enough to know what sort of person she was, and what sort she could no longer be. At some point in the past couple of years, not altogether consciously, she'd settled her accounts with her authorial ambitions, shipping them off with a one-way ticket to the realm of counterfactual what-ifs, where they'd joined her former desires to be a killer-whale trainer or an Olympic-caliber swimmer.

Paul's note might have made her sad, or nostalgic, or uneasy. It might have made her all those things at once. Somewhat to her surprise, however, it had merely made her happy. The stories themselves were nothing, certainly nothing she still felt proud of writing. They showcased no special talent, they manifested no particular vision. But they'd been important to her once, as had the *Graduate Review*'s decision to publish them. (She could still remember celebrating with her then-boyfriend at a sushi restaurant the night she got the acceptance.)

Renata liked that Paul had gone home to read them, she liked that he'd liked them, and she liked that he'd taken the trouble to find her on the Internet so that he could let her know. What she liked even more, however, was his suggestion that she might have more fiction in the offing—that her well, such as it was, had not entirely run dry. Though Renata wasn't sure if she could believe that possibility herself, in a way that hardly mattered. It was enough for her, at least in that moment, to know that Paul had believed it.

STILL RIDING THE MORNING'S HIGH, Renata followed Max and the rest of the party into a low-ceilinged room where the pizza and cake would be served. For most of the second bounce session, she'd been trading small talk with another of the parents who had, like her, stayed behind for what was technically a drop-off party. Her interlocutor was the tall, bearded father of a curly-haired little boy who, despite being in Max's kindergarten class, looked like he couldn't be a day over three and a half. Just now, as they settled into the plastic chairs in the Palace Mess, the boy's father was describing, with a suppressed but obvious enthusiasm, his pet theory that the Indiana Jones trilogy ought to be seen as the ultimate Jewish revenge fantasy.

Renata nodded and laughed in all the right moments, and didn't fail to note the effect that her amusement had on the bearded dad. He was plainly charmed by her, and equally plainly spending some significant energy to keep her involved in the conversation. His effort charmed her back, and for a moment she let herself ponder the adult uses to which she might put the inflatable play structures they'd just left behind. The thought made her laugh again.

The dad, whose name she hadn't caught, once again took this as an encouraging sign. *Where do you live? We should get the boys together for a playdate some time*, he said.

Oh, maybe, she said, mentally shaking off the last drifts of her imagined romp. *It's sort of a complicated time for us right now. I'm not sure we could—*

They could do it at our house, the dad said eagerly. *Really, we'd love to have, uh . . .*

Max.

Right, Max. I—

Renata! At the sound of her name, Renata and the bearded dad looked up at the same time to see Courtney Higgenbotham, the mother of a six-year-old named Molly, rushing toward them from the other side of the room. Courtney, it was clear, had just come in from outside: her face was still flush with the cold, she was still wrapped in the cocoon of her calf-length coat, and her brown hair was still smothered in a chunky blue hat she'd knit herself. Though not quite old friends, Courtney and Renata were by now old acquaintances: they'd met in a prenatal group for new mothers before Max and Molly were born, and got together a few times each year over drinks to bitch and reminisce about motherhood. Courtney was a consummate gossip and almost comically excitable; Renata liked her immensely.

Thank god you're here, Courtney said, peeling the hat from her head and shaking her hair free.

Renata stood to give her a hug. The bearded dad stood, too, and, mercifully, didn't wait for Renata to fail to introduce him. *I'm Josh*, he said. *Taylor's dad.*

Courtney flashed a fake smile before asking if she could borrow Renata for a minute.

Seriously, let me know about that playdate, Josh said, offering an awkward parting wave as Renata walked away. *I'm the only Josh on the class email list.*

Out in the hallway, near a row of hooks hung at waist level with the kids' winter coats, Courtney took hold of Renata by the shoulders. *Is everything okay?* she hissed in a loud whisper. *What's going on?*

Renata felt her brow furrow. *I'm fine, I'm fine. He's harmless. Why?*

Courtney looked confused. *No, you and the boys. Juana told me something was happening to Luca. She said she saw him at her church last week.*

Renata felt cold. Courtney tightened her grip on her arms, as if to steady her. *But that's . . . that's impossible.*

She said Mariela brought him. The whole church was there, Juana said. They'd all come to see him. Something about him lighting up? Something about him glowing?

Renata looked steadily into Courtney's brown eyes as her knees went weak. She caught herself before she fell, steadying herself with the help of a coat hook.

What is it, Renata? Tell me what's happening!

Obviously it was a mistake. She knows that.

Adrian.

Adrian was looking at Renata from across their bedroom. It was ten hours after she'd sped home from the birthday party with Max, her head still dizzy with confusion, but this was the first chance she'd had to talk with Adrian since they'd called Mariela to get her side of the story. His face was pale, almost white, and for an instant Renata was certain she could see what he would look like at seventy. He was perched on the upholstered back of the love seat they kept in the window bay—half standing, really, with one foot on the floor and the other barely visible beneath the heaps of toys and the piles of clothes that kept the cushions perennially useless for sitting.

What? She was scared.

Please keep your voice down, Renata said, speaking in a peremptory tone that she knew her husband hated. She truly did not want to wake the boys, but mostly she didn't want Adrian to think for even a second that it was acceptable to take Mariela's side.

She didn't know what to do, Adrian said, pushing on.

She should have called us. She should have called me.

She tried.

She said she tried. I never got any calls. I never got any texts. I never got any voicemail. Did you? In the window behind Adrian, which the tain of the night had turned into a mirror, Renata caught the reflection of her face. Her expression did not exactly please her—the hollow cheeks and empty eyes made her look too ugly for that—but it did satisfy her. Though her stomach was churning and her head felt like she'd been huffing helium, she knew it was best not to let Adrian see anything other than a dispassionate mask. He liked to fight by pretending he wasn't fighting, and too often took an unwarranted delight in provoking Renata under the cover of a feigned rationalism.

You think she's lying? You think Mariela is lying to us?

Renata felt herself wince. *I didn't say that.*

Her phone was on the fritz. It happens. She's got that crappy Korean knockoff. It's always giving her problems.

Why didn't she email?

Adrian threw his hands over his head and then let them fall again to his thighs. *I don't know, Renata. This was the first time this happened to her when one of us wasn't there. She told us she freaked out. She went to the church because her uncle is the pastor there. She didn't know what else to do.*

You're really not bothered? You really think this was all fine?

Not fine, no. I told you it was a mistake. She told you it was a mistake. I'm just saying . . . I'm just saying maybe it's not the worst thing in the world.

Renata glared at Adrian until her eyes burned. *How much worse does it need to get?*

Adrian shook his head and ran his fingers through his hair. He, too, was breathing hard. *It was a lot of pressure to put on her. A lot of weight. Probably too much, to be honest.* He looked down at the floor, and then he looked back up at Renata. *I think we deserve a share of the responsibility here.*

Renata tensed. *Oh, we do, do we? Let's not forget that you were the one who insisted we bring her back.*

Yes, and you agreed with me. Remember? Anyway, you know how she feels about her uncle. You told me about it yourself. She said he's been like a father to her. This much was true. Renata had spoken at considerable length with Mariela about the man she called her uncle, who was actually her grandfather's brother. According to Mariela, he was a good man: humble, kind, sympathetic, and deeply knowledgeable about the Bible.

Can you really blame her? Adrian said.

Renata forced herself to breathe before speaking. *Of course I can blame her.*

She said she bundled him up good. She said you couldn't even tell.

Everyone saw it, Adrian. Not just the pastor. Everyone in her church. Did you miss that part? Juana told Courtney the church was packed by the time she got there. Standing room only.

I meant on the way over. She bundled him up in the stroller so that no one could see the glow.

I know what you meant. What I'm saying is, even if that's true, so what?

Adrian leapt off the love seat. He took two steps toward Renata and then stopped himself. *Well, but right! That's my question, too. So what? Before any of this started, Mariela used to take the boys all over the place. To the playground, to the park, to the lake, even downtown. Usually we didn't even know till after it happened. What's so different here?* His voice had a pleading tone now, and Renata thought she could see in his eyes a glint of real anguish. She felt her guard dropping, and answered him in a quiet voice:

We told her not to take Luca anywhere. That's what's different. We explicitly told her.

I know. That was not good. Mariela knows that, too. She clearly feels very bad about it. Set that aside for now. What was so bad about her taking Luca to church? What are we actually worried about here?

Adrian, be serious. Renata heard a hint of pleading in her own tone and hated herself for it.

I am serious! We can't keep Luca locked up in the house for the rest of his life. He's a little boy. He needs to be with other kids. He needs to be out in the world. Why are you so scared of this thing?

Renata looked at her husband, uncomprehending.

Adrian put a hand up and took a cautious step forward. *I didn't mean that, I'm sorry. I'm just saying . . . I'm just saying, have you considered . . .*

Considered what?

Nothing.

That wasn't nothing. You wanted to say something.

I did, but only if you promise you won't take this the wrong way.

Barely blinking, Renata maintained her gaze.

Adrian took a deep breath. *I just think we have to consider the possibility that we might be seeing this differently because, well, because we're seeing it differently. If you know what I mean.*

You mean because I'm not seeing it at all. That's what you're trying to tell me.

Adrian swallowed and put his head down. For once in his life, he looked like he didn't know what to say.

Mama. Mama. Mama.

Renata turned her head on the pillow and opened her eyes. Max was standing next to her, only a few inches from her face. *Hi, sweetie, it's late. What is it? What's wrong?*

I'm tired. Can I come into your bed with you?

Renata looked back across her bed. Adrian had stayed up, working in his office, when she went to bed, but now he was here, shirtless and asleep. She knew she shouldn't care if she woke him. His insomnia was his problem, just as everything else—the upkeep of his household, the care and midnight consolation of his children, the unyielding minute-to-minute terror that their younger son might be mysteriously combustible—was apparently her problem. Yet not even her considerable talent for passive aggression could persuade her to disturb his sleep. *No, sweetie*, Renata whispered. *We don't want to wake Papa. You can pull out your mattress or you can sleep in your own bed.*

I want to sleep in my own bed. Will you come with me, Mama? Just for a few minutes?

Renata didn't want to get out of bed, but of course she did. She did because she always did, because in this household what she wanted was nugatory. She took her phone from the nightstand and recovered a wadded sweatshirt from under her pillow and followed Max out of her bedroom. When they reached the open doorway of the bathroom, she waved him on to his room. *I've got to pee, sweetie. I'll be right there.*

In the bathroom, a blue square of phosphorescence plugged in over the sink let her avoid switching on the overhead lights. (The night-light was Renata's recurring point of analogy whenever anyone tried to explain to her what Luca's glow looked like.) While she peed, she flipped absentmindedly through her Facebook feed on her phone. She looked up again and was startled to see Max's silhouette in the doorway. He stepped into the dim blue light and she saw that he'd changed out of his pajamas into his Spider-Man costume.

Oh, Spider-Man, hello. You haven't seen Max, have you? He was just here.

It's me, Mama. You don't have to pretend.

Renata frowned. Max always wanted her to pretend. *Okay, buddy. Why don't you go back to bed? I'll be right there.*

I just want to be with you, Max said. *I don't want to be alone.*

In the boys' bedroom, Renata saw Luca lying crosswise at the foot of the bottom bunk. Wearing only a diaper, as usual, he was snoring with a back-of-the-throat rumble. One of his plump, delectable little legs was hooked, in what looked like a horribly uncomfortable position, over a rung of the bunk's pipe ladder. Renata eased his foot back down to the mattress so that Spider-Max could climb up to his bed. She helped him get situated under his comforter and kissed him lightly on the forehead.

Mama?

Yes, sweetie?

Will you lie down with me?

Oh, sweetie. It's so late.

Please, Mama. Just for a little bit. Just until I fall asleep.

Renata was not eager to share a single mattress with her restless five-year-old, but even less did she want to tell him no, especially not tonight. After she and Adrian had finished their fight, or at least put it behind them, Renata had stopped in to check on the boys and had found Max awake in his bed. Clearly he had overheard them talking: he asked her what "Coreen Nockoff" meant, and then whether Mariela was in trouble.

Now Renata climbed the ladder and lay down between Max and the wall. He curled up next to her, with his face in the crook of her neck and his hand resting squarely on top of her right breast.

Mama? he said, once he'd gotten himself settled. His voice sounded heavy. *How do people get superpowers?*

Oh, I don't know, honey. I guess it depends. Do you remember how Spider-Man got his?

Not like that, Mama. That's pretend. I mean a real superpower.

We talked about this, sweetie, remember? The thing about superpowers is that they're not actually real.

Luca has a real one.

What? No, no, honey, that's not—

It's not fair, Mama. How come I can't have a superpower, too?

Renata pulled Max tight against her. *Oh, sweetie, that's not . . . that's not what's happening to your brother.*

Papa said it is.

He did? What? When?

This morning.

Oh, but, honey . . . I'm sure he didn't mean it like that. What did he say?

He said Luca had a superpower.

Is that what he said exactly?

I don't know, Mama. I told him I wanted Luca to stop glowing. I told him I don't like it anymore. He said it was not scary. He said it was like a superpower.

Renata took a deep breath. She and Adrian had a rule about not contradicting each other to the boys, but this was too much. *The truth is, buddy, none of us really know for sure what's making Luca glow. The only thing we know is that it isn't hurting him. And it's not hurting us.* Another thing about parenthood that no one had prepared Renata for: how much lying she'd have to do just to get through the day. *But really, Max. Nobody knows for sure why it's happening.*

Not even Dr. Anita?

Nope.

Not even Papa?

Not even him.

Max rolled over, away from Renata, and after five minutes of watching his tiny shoulders rise and fall in a heavy rhythm, she was certain he was asleep. She wiped the tears from her cheeks with her free hand and began the delicate process of trying to extract herself from the cramped bunk bed without waking him.

Max opened his eyes just as she managed to get both feet on the ladder. *Mama, where are you going?* he said.

I'm going back to bed, sweetie. You should really go to sleep now.

I know, Mama. I'm tired. But how come you can't see Luca?

You mean—

I mean like Daddy and me and Mariela. How come you can't see it?

Well, not everyone can, sweetie. A lot of people can't see it, in fact. And I'm one of them.

But why are you different from the rest of us? We're a family.

I'll tell you a little secret, okay, sweetie? We don't know that, either.

I wish I couldn't see it, too, Mama. I wish none of us could. I wish we were all like you.

Oh, buddy . . . Renata hugged Max close and kissed him on the bridge of his nose. Almost inaudibly, in words that were scarcely louder than an ordinary breath, she said, *I wish that, too.*

Renata had never been a religious person, and despite the impression she had sometimes hoped to convey when she was younger, she had never been all that spiritually inclined. (Like most smart girls of her socioeconomic station, in high school and college she'd been terrified of seeming superficial.) She believed firmly in romantic and maternal love, she was passionate about literature and art, and she'd never found it difficult to be stirred profoundly by a high-altitude hike or a thigh-quivering fuck. But unlike Adrian, who could hardly butter his toast without reference to a multidimensional pleroma of invisible beings, Renata had never sought any extraordinary explanations for any of these emotions. Even Luca's cancer scare had left her untouched by transcendental concern.

In the past, even before Luca started glowing, Renata's metaphysical incuriosity had itself occasionally made her wonder. Was there something deficient about her? Was she blind to the higher truths, deaf to the deeper rhythms? Was she, to put it bluntly, as shallow as she had once feared?

Lying on her back, staring up at the ceiling of glow-in-the-dark stars whose improbable constellations spelled out "MAX" and "LUCA" and "MAMA" and "PAPA," Renata felt a flash of something, some internal heat, wash through her body. In that instant she was sure that the answer to her self-doubts was negative. She'd been wrong to suspect herself, wrong to let herself feel that she was wanting. Maybe Adrian was correct that their different experiences of Luca's condition had caused them to see the broader situation differently. But if this were true, she understood with accumulating confidence, the divergence was a point in her favor.

For it was not merely the case that Adrian was less concerned than she was about what was happening to their son. Renata realized now that he welcomed it.

Of course he hadn't said so openly; Adrian wasn't clumsy enough to make that mistake. But he didn't need to admit it. In the hours since their argument, Renata had come to appreciate that the real dispute, the fight behind the fight, had nothing to do with Mariela. The problem, she'd belatedly recognized, was that her husband simply did not share her conviction that Luca's glow was—and could only be—a threat to everything she held most dear. For Adrian, it was a beckoning light at the end of a long and tortuous tunnel, a beacon he'd been waiting for possibly his entire life.

Renata felt a little ridiculous that she hadn't seen it. As long as she'd known him, Adrian had insisted that the world was fundamentally different than it seemed. The cosmos as he knew it—as he wanted to know it, as he needed to know it—was full of strange beings and mysterious forces. Some of them were locked in sempiternal struggles that would determine the fate of the universe. Others were minutely concerned with human affairs. In the modern attitude toward astrology, he liked to say, there could be found a paradigm for the rationalist suppression of esoteric truth. Just ask any scientist whether celestial bodies could control human activity, and watch how hard their eyes roll. But ask them, then, what makes the crops grow, or the nights fall, or the tides slosh back and forth in their oceanic basins. It is only because we have forgotten how to marvel at an apple falling out of a tree, or a magnet attaching itself to a refrigerator, or a light bulb flickering to life—Adrian would insist to his students, or his in-laws, or his tablemates at a dinner party—that we are able to pretend we aren't living in thrall to invisible forces whose purpose and origin are entirely obscure.

Once upon a time, Renata had been charmed by this little monologue. Though not herself a contrarian—possibly, in fact, because she was not a contrarian—she'd been dazzled by what she saw as Adrian's boldness and intellectual courage. In the years before she got to know him, before she really got to know him, she admired his determination to skewer the pseudoscientific groupthink and high-liberal *bien-pensance* that, in his view, were corrupting everything. Renata herself did not have much of a beef with technology, or sociology, or capitalism. But she liked, or used to like, that Adrian did. Before she'd discerned the alternating current of egoism and insecurity that drove just about everything her husband did, Renata had been able to convince herself that his bizarre metaphysical speculations were the strange but necessary signs of a truly independent mind.

But it was bullshit. She was certain of that now—more certain, possibly, than she'd been of anything in her life. All of it was bullshit. This boy in this bed with her, and his brother in the bunk below: they were not angels or archons. They were not reincarnated souls embarked on their twelve-thousandth cycle of rebirth and purification. To see them truly from the cosmic perspective that Adrian so frequently liked to invoke, they were, to a first approximation, nothing: two animate heaps of oxygen, carbon, and hydrogen that had been sculpted by a billion billion random accidents of evolution, two pinkish primates who would be conscious and alive for a blink of the universe's uncaring eye.

Of course to her they were also everything, the only thing in her life that truly mattered. It was not her problem—it shouldn't be her problem—that Adrian couldn't accept that both things were true. It was his failing, not hers, that he needed overheated cosmogonies and esoteric mythologies to supply some sort of meaning in his life. Obviously Renata didn't like the thought of her own insignificance any more than anyone else did, and the thought that someday she would literally disintegrate did not exactly fill her with joy. Was it unfair? Was it unjust? Was it inconceivable that everything she knew, everything she remembered, everything she was, would someday blip out of existence, never to be seen or heard from again, in any dimension? Maybe. Sure. But that was life. That was the bargain her parents had made for her, and the bargain she, in turn, had made for her boys. It was a cliché to say that the only remaining task was making the most of the time they had together, a cliché to suggest that the only question that remained was how to make it feel like enough. But that was a great thing about not being a writer anymore, maybe the only great thing: Renata no longer had to live in fear of cliché.

Renata was still in Max's bed when she woke the next morning. She didn't need her phone to tell her that it was late, too late. The light in the window behind the bunk beds, a midmorning whiteness that leaked around the edges of the roll-up shade, was proof enough. So, too, was Max's absence: though Luca often got up by himself before everyone else—he contented himself doing puzzles in the living room—his older brother slept late for a boy his age. It was not unusual for Renata to have to wake him on weekdays to make it on time to school. (Weekend mornings, when he was allowed to watch TV, were another story.) There was no sign of him now, though. No sign of anyone, in fact, inside the room or out. Something was wrong.

What was wrong, Renata quickly discovered, was that it was nearly ten o'clock. At least that's what the clock on the boys' wall said. Still foggy, she didn't know whether to trust it. The last time she'd slept past nine was on a business trip to Toronto she'd taken by herself before Luca was born. It couldn't possibly be that late. Max had school today. Adrian had work.

Renata's first thought was that something dire had happened to Luca. Why else would Adrian and the boys be gone? But why, then, wasn't she with them? As the buzz of an incipient anxiety built up in her stomach, she called out for Adrian and the boys. No one responded. Renata picked up her phone from the boys' bookshelf, where she'd left it before climbing into bed with Max. She checked the time, and then her text messages, and then her email, and found nothing to explain what was happening. She texted Adrian: Where are u? Everything ok?

Before he could text back, Renata went to the kitchen and found a note waiting for her on the refrigerator door. *Good morning!* it started, in Adrian's neat handwriting. *I hope you're not panicking, but you were sleeping so soundly that I couldn't bear to risk waking you with a text. I'm taking Max to school and then headed to the office with Luca. Everything is fine, except that I feel bad about last night. Please enjoy your morning so that I can start to forgive myself. L and I are planning to come home by lunch.*

Renata flipped the switch on the electric kettle and sat down at the small table near the kitchen window. This was where art projects happened, where bills got paid, and where the boys slopped Cheerios into their mouths at breakfast while Adrian declaimed at them from the Upanishads or Shakespeare or *The Odyssey*. Sitting here Renata had once spotted a mugging in progress—it was the only time in her life she'd ever called 911—and another time she'd seen several dozen of the neighborhood's green parakeets debauching themselves in a spruce tree. Today, though, the trees and the streets were equally empty. She could see how cold it was, even from inside, and could only wonder which of the boys' assorted outerwear Adrian had forgotten to bring.

While she was waiting for the water to boil, Renata's phone buzzed on the table. She picked it up and saw a text from Adrian. Hi sleepyhead. Did you get my note? I've got Luca at the office. M is at school. All good here! A few seconds later, another message came through. This was a photo, and it took a moment for Renata to understand that what it showed was Adrian's office, packed with people. In the center of it all, standing on Adrian's desk, was Luca.

NINE

In 1756, a British member of Parliament named Soame Jenyns published a book that set out to untangle one of Christianity's most intractable conundrums. Since it was the case, Jenyns wrote, that "happiness is the only thing of real value in existence," and since God was understood to be both omnipotent and supremely benevolent, why "are not all creatures that do exist happy?"

As Jenyns understood well, his question was not new. For millennia, Muslims, Christians, Neoplatonists, Jews, ancient Persians, and practitioners of many other faiths besides had pushed logic to the breaking point trying to resolve what was sometimes known as the Epicurean trilemma: How could a god that was all good and all powerful allow suffering and evil in the universe?

Yet if Jenyns's question was traditional, his answer was not. Though he counted himself a Christian, he did not follow Augustine in defining evil as a privation of goodness, such that sin was characterized as the moral distance that separated a person from God. Nor did he follow Ireneaus in seeing suffering as a necessary part of God's plan for the spiritual development of humanity. Still less did he follow the Spanish Jesuit Luis de Molina, who argued that evil existed because God wanted humans to be truly free, which meant that they had to be allowed to make bad choices.

Jenyns argued instead that we ought to think about human suffering by analogy with animals. It is simply true, he said, that animal suffering contributes to human happiness: we enjoy eating the flesh of dead animals, just as we enjoy wearing their hides as clothes. Might it not also be true, he wondered, that human suffering is the source of happiness for angels and their ilk? Jenyns thought so: "There may be numberless intermediate Beings, who have power to deceive, torment, or destroy us, for the ends only of their own pleasure or utility, who may be veiled with the same privileges over their inferiors, and as much benefited by the use of them, as ourselves."

Warren thought of Soame Jenyns as he glanced up at the angels in the Div School's Old Library. They were oaken, these angels, beings of pure form that were rendered in the same hard and corruptible substance that gave Aristotle his word for pure matter. Carved a hundred years ago with a skill unavailable now at any price, they'd been joined invisibly into the thick rafters that lifted the vault of the Old Library, which occupied most of Harrison's third floor. From below it looked as though the angels were not only hovering but hoisting: the long spans of their oil-stained wings appeared to be supporting the room's high ceiling. Each of the angels was carrying as well a large open book, but none of them were reading. Instead they were watching a crowd of fifty or so people who had gathered for Afternoon Beer, a long-standing Div School tradition that promised cold drinks, warm takeout, and a few hours of awkward postmeridian mingling near the start of each academic quarter.

What were the angels thinking? Warren had pondered that question for the better part of twenty-five years. When he first arrived at the Div School, as a young man full of earnest faith, he'd pictured the angels as tutelary spirits who were silently pleased that in this room and in this building, at least, they were not forgotten. Later, after he'd learned how poorly his sincerity would serve him—in Harrison Hall as everywhere in the University, cleverness was the highest virtue—Warren imagined the angels being annoyed at the inane rumble of show-offy conversations that served no purpose except to distract them from their books.

As he crossed under the rafters toward the center of the room, however, Warren was struck by a different idea. He'd already supposed that he was probably alone in thinking (alone as he was in so much else) that Jenyns deserved better than the scorn he got from his contemporaries. Samuel Johnson had been particularly harsh, ridiculing Jenyns's idea that human lives were playthings for some other, higher order of beings. "As we drown whelps and kittens, they amuse themselves now and then with sinking a ship," Johnson wrote in mocking imitation. "Some of them, perhaps, are virtuosi, and delight in the operations of an asthma, as a human philosopher in the effects of the air pump. To swell a man with a tympany is as good sport as to blow a frog." Johnson was supposed to be a genius, but still Warren couldn't see how Jenyns's suggestion was any less absurd than the orthodox Christian solutions to the trilemma, most of which ended up blaming humanity for its own agonies. Anyway, he thought, who could dispute Jenyns's contention that "the human mind can comprehend but a very small part of the great and astonishing whole"? Or Jenyns's insistence that the perennial urge to find meaning in suffering proved nothing except "the importance of a man to himself"?

Warren even thought it possible to see in Jenyns's hypothesis a kind of consolation. Back when he was a Catholic he'd concluded that the only way to make sense of the world as he knew it—a world in which priests raped children, earthquakes razed cities, aneurysms killed sisters, mothers couldn't stop gambling, and fathers disowned their sons—was to assume that human suffering and evil were literally incomprehensible to a perfect God. (It was for this reason, he'd decided, that Jesus cried out *Eloi, Eloi, lama sabachthani* while hanging on the Cross: only when God stepped out of eternity and subjected Himself to the fatal flow of time was

He finally able to understand why so many people were wracked with mortal terror for so much of their lives.)

Later, after his sister's death and his stint at the Div School cured him of Christianity for good, Warren came around to the view that the best explanation for his many torments was cosmic indifference: in a universe ruled by the second law of thermodynamics, the only mystery about suffering was how any hunk of matter became conscious enough to raise the question in the first place.

Warren made his way to a trio of skirted folding tables in the center of the room, which held flimsy aluminum chafing trays filled with Indian takeout. He decided it was cheering, in a perverse sort of way, to imagine that an angel or other metaphysically superior "intermediate being" might be entertained by his torments and humiliations. The angels had seen so much, after all: the ignition of the sun, the ping-ponging of planetesimals, the molten splash that made the moon, the congealing of the Earth's crust, the crash of continents that raised the mountains. Then there was the freak show of evolution playing itself out over eons: all those manifold monstrosities, all those millions upon billions of genetic dead ends, all those gigatons of pointless organic fecundity. Fish became frogs, dinosaurs became birds, mice became monkeys, all of it before any of it had a chance to be forgotten by a single human being. After so much heavy melodrama, a cosmic choreography of surpassing brutality, surely the angels deserved some divertissement? A little light farce, maybe, enacted by an ensemble cast of eight billion talking apes, to lighten their mood?

Thanks to the overactive radiators, and the windows that had been cracked to compensate for them, the Old Library was too hot where it wasn't too cold. It smelled vaguely of cardamom and coriander, and even more vaguely of long underwear and wet winter coats.

When it was his turn in line at the tables, Warren stepped forward and scooped some curry, rice, and soggy samosas onto a thin plastic plate. He caught a few probing glances that darted away from his own, like baitfish before a boat. He tried to ignore them, tried not to let the unwelcome heat of their interest disturb him. He had more important things to think about than benighted grad students who probably assumed he was a janitor, who were almost surely congratulating themselves privately for their charity toward this unknown Black man, who because Black must be poor, who because poor must be desperate for their condescending generosity.

Warren took the food and the drink over to a corner of the room and lowered himself, painfully, into a stackable metal chair. He ate alone between two oil portraits of former deans and under a window that looked out on the quad. It was barely five o'clock, but the sky on the other side of the mullioned windows was dark already, as purple as a plum.

While he ate, Warren reminded himself that he had not come to Harrison Hall today to solve the problem of suffering. Still less had he come to bark his shin against the enlightened racism that still held sway at the University, despite its recent attempts to refashion itself as the spiritual and intellectual homeland of the country's first Black president. He had come, rather, because he suspected Adrian Bennett would be here.

It was not a given that Warren would come looking for Adrian today. For the better part of a month, he'd tried to put the whole strange episode at Gabriel's church out of his mind. Of course he'd been curious about Adrian's kid, but long experience, dating back to his Div School days, had taught him that his father's favorite maxim was dead wrong: it was absolutely possible to know too much, especially if what you knew was true. Warren told himself that there was nothing to be gained from asking hard questions about the boy or the sudden reversal of fortune he'd enabled. Better to live without a why, as the great mystic Meister Eckhart had recommended.

It almost worked. After a week of no contact from The Weight, Warren had ventured out of his apartment for the first time, though he still made sure to enter and exit his building only under the cover of darkness. After two weeks, he returned to his job at the library and stopped instinctively holding his breath every time he turned onto his street coming home. When a month went by with no indication that The Weight was still after him—nothing was smashed or dented, there were no visits from shadowy goons, there was not so much as a single expletive-laden text message—Warren began to let himself wonder if he was really off the financial hook for good.

It almost worked, but eventually the boy, Adrian's glowing boy, got the better of him. Warren couldn't stop thinking about him. He tried, of course, tried everything: tried to lose himself in a long monograph about quantum gravity, tried to distract himself with The Mace of Wintermere, tried to tranquilize himself with Fireball and Everclear.

Yet even when Warren succeeded for a time in forcing the child out of his waking thoughts, little Luca managed to sneak into his dreams. Sometimes these dreams were merely odd, as when he saw the boy, glowing of course, eating a sandwich on a raft in the middle of a waveless ocean. Other times they were extremely intense. More than once Warren woke up sweating and sore, with a hazy memory of chasing the kid, or following him, through some apocalyptic scenario that involved fires and floods and the airbursts of exploding meteors.

When his conscious and unconscious thoughts about the boy got to be too much to bear, Warren tried at first to calm his mind by walking down his hallway and knocking on Gabriel's door. Gabriel greeted him warmly. He successfully conveyed that Mariela, the young woman Warren had seen at the church, was both his niece and the boy's babysitter. She'd brought the child there because she was unsure, and even frightened, about the strange glow.

Pues? Warren said, momentarily proud that his Spanish, for once, had not failed him. *What did you think about it?*

Gabriel dropped his head and lifted his eyebrows, as though sizing Warren up. Well, he said, at first he thought what Mariela had thought. The *güerito* was blessed, *un milagro de Dios.*

Y ahora? Warren asked. *Todavia piensas?*

Gabriel pursed his lips and shook his head. *No. No más. You see what happen a la iglesia.*

Con los gringos, Warren said. He was wondering if Gabriel would bring it up.

The pastor responded with a somber nod. *Cuidado, amigo. Están peligrosos, esos tipos. Muy peligrosos. Much danger . . .* Here Gabriel said something that Warren could not follow until he returned to English: *No is good. El chico . . . no sé. La luz, pero . . . la luz es mala.*

Mala como el diablo? Warren asked.

Now the old pastor scoffed. *Algunos piensan así. "Lucifer," me dicen. Comprendes? "Luz-i-fer," como la luz, the light. Pero yo no. Yo no sé por qué brilla el chico*—here he made a gesture with his hands, mimicking the glow—*pero creo que es solo un truco. Comprendes? Un truco. Un truck.*

This took Warren a moment. *A trick, you mean? Like a scam.*

Gabriel nodded vigorously. *Sí. Exactamente. Un escam.*

Was it a scam? Was it a trick? Warren had no earthly idea, but eventually he decided that his subconscious was not going to leave him alone until he found out. When he received an email announcing the date and time of the Winter Quarter Afternoon Beer, he spotted his opportunity. He remembered that Adrian had been a mainstay at Afternoon Beers all through Warren's two years in grad school, and he figured the odds of him stopping by were good enough that it was worth taking the chance.

Warren finished his beer and was contemplating a second when he noticed the approach of two guys—in their early thirties, from the looks of them—who were dressed casually even by the generally relaxed sartorial standards of the Div School. One was wearing a black sweater that was visibly tattered around the neck and cuffs. The other was dressed in corduroy pants and a heavy flannel shirt.

You're sure he's coming? the guy in the sweater asked his friend. *You said he'd be here.*

Yeah, dude. Don't worry. I saw him like an hour ago.

Any doubts Warren harbored about who the two men were talking about were dispelled by the sweater guy's next question. *Is he going to bring the boy?*

I doubt it. Why would he?

I don't know, man. The whole thing is so ridiculous.

What do you mean it's ridiculous?

What do you mean, what do I mean? You think it's really happening?

You don't?

Come on.

Come on, nothing. You're the one studying theology.

So?

Aren't you a Christian?

What's that got to do with anything?

You tell me. It's just, I would have thought this sort of thing was par for the course for someone like you.

"Someone like me?" What's that supposed to mean?

It's no insult, dude. I just mean, you know, someone who already believes all that stuff.

Being Christian doesn't mean I'll believe any weird thing that comes my way. It's a religion, it's not magic.

There was a pause, and it took all of Warren's willpower not to look up at the two men to see what had caused it.

What? the guy in the sweater said finally. *What's so funny?*

Nothing, it's just . . . I mean, all religions are magic.

Okay, that's definitely an insult.

It's nothing of the sort. I'm an anthropologist. Of course I think religions are magic. I think science is magic, too, if it makes you feel any better.

Well, it doesn't.

Easy. I really didn't think this would be controversial. Isn't the whole point that Jesus did a bunch of miracles and then rose from the dead? Whatever else that is, it's definitely magic.

And so because that happened, you think I should just believe anything else—

Hold on, I don't think that happened. I'm saying that's what you believe. As a Christian, right?

As a Christian, I believe that faith is the substance of things hoped for, the evidence of things not seen.

That sounds like a cop-out.

It ought to sound like Saint Paul.

Well, as long as we're quoting, remember what Geertz said? "One does not shrug off a toadstool which grows five times as fast as a toadstool has any right to grow."

So you think it's real.

I didn't say that. Geertz didn't say that. He was talking about the Javanese. Anyway, you should know better than to use the r-word around an anthropologist.

What, "real"?

Mmm.

This is why no one likes anthropologists. You realize that, right?

A few minutes later, Warren sensed a small but definite change in the room's atmosphere. Conversations that had been loud and boozy acquired a sibilant edge as they downshifted into a quieter register of murmurs and whispers. The loose congregations of students and faculty drew closer together, puckering like sea anemones into tight conspiratorial clusters. The change was confusing, and for an instant Warren wondered if his earlier assurance had been misplaced. Maybe he would be noticed—maybe he was noticed—after all. But no: after another moment he recognized that the object of everyone's interest lay on the other side of the room.

Warren watched as the crowd in the Old Library reconfigured itself in response to Adrian's arrival. The accommodation was subtle at first, as though Adrian were the star of a trashy, popular TV show, and no one in the room could make up their mind whether to laugh at him or ask for his autograph. A silent wave of stolen glances and knowing nods was followed by a few muted chuckles and the burr of sotto voce commentary. Yet even in the Divinity School, where a century of rarefied scholarship had pressed the case for the sacred dignity of the human spirit—even here the dictates of reason and good taste were no match for the flash of celebrity. This was still America, after all.

Like most of the other middle-aged male professors at the Div School, Adrian dressed like a twenty-five-year-old associate at a management consulting firm. He wore unpleated pants that were skinny but not tight, a crisp checked shirt unbuttoned at the collar, no tie, an expensive-looking sweater, and vaguely fashionable, fashionably scuffed leather shoes.

The two white guys who'd been talking near Warren were the first to approach him. It was clear from their body language that there was some joking going on among the three men, though at whose expense it was impossible for Warren to tell. The jocular mood opened the door for others to join them, and within a few minutes Adrian was ringed by an audience standing three deep.

From across the room Warren could see that Adrian was energized by the attention; the more people who came over to hear him, the more intently he spoke. It was not long before any pretense of conversation evaporated: though at first he seemed to be responding to questions, he looked now to be delivering something like an extemporaneous lecture, or at the very least an extended monologue. The light humor of his affect fell away and his expression grew serious. His arms wheeled in wide orchestral gesticulations, his fingers pinched to emphasize his various points, and his tanned, tenured face began to flush with a ruddy intensity. Still, though, whatever he was talking about was received in good spirits. Even the people who had started out skeptical—there appeared to be a few of them, standing at a distance with sharpened glances—seemed interested now.

Warren couldn't make out what Adrian was actually saying, so he stood and let himself drift into the outer orbit of Adrian's audience. When Adrian spotted him, he gave a friendly nod, locking eyes for a moment, but he did not stop talking.

. . . and what's interesting is that the original Hebrew is ambiguous. Moses comes back after seeing God, and something strange has happened to his face, something that terrifies the Israelites. Whatever it is, this strange thing that's terrifying them, well, that all comes down to this ambiguous verb

qāran. *Typically the word has been taken to mean "to shine," which makes a kind of obvious sense given everything that Moses went through. But the same word can also mean "to sprout horns," which is how Jerome translated it. So there's this question: Is Moses's face shining or did he grow horns? That's, you know, that's where you get the old trope of the horned Jew. You can see why there's a lot of people who want to get rid of the ambiguity entirely. They want to make it all about the shine. They want to blame the anti-Semitic trope on what you might call a motivated mistranslation. And don't get me wrong, I'm interested in that, too, obviously. But we shouldn't forget that hint that the divine is also always already at least a little monstrous, a little demonic, you know? It's that doubleness that interests me. I mean, I know no one reads Lévi-Strauss anymore—he was demolished by Derrida, so what's the point, right? But I think we all let ourselves forget about the importance of binary oppositions a little too quickly. Just to push the point a little further, there's a very interesting paper I just came across, from 2002, I believe, and apparently the shine/horn duality can be found in ancient Sumer as well . . .*

At the end of his impromptu lecture, Adrian answered a few questions from his students and colleagues. Warren hung back, still not sure exactly how he wanted to ask what he'd come here to ask. Eventually Adrian made his way over.

Hey, man, he said in a friendly tone. *What are you doing here?*

Oh, you know. Warren lifted his beer bottle in the weak hope that it would deflect the question.

The gesture seemed to work. *I've been meaning to come to one of these things since I got hired,* Adrian said. *I used to love them so much. But I'm ashamed to say this is my first one since . . . well, since my last one in grad school, back when I was still dissertating. How about you? You a regular?*

Yeah, no, not at all, Warren said. *This is my first time back, too. It's been a while.*

Cheers to coincidence, then. Adrian winked and lifted his own beer bottle in Warren's direction. *Hey, I should have asked you at the hospital, but: What are you doing these days? I guess you live around here. You teaching?*

Warren's voice deserted him. *No,* he managed hoarsely. *I'm working at the library. I do catalog maintenance, mostly, which mostly means a lot of database work.*

Oh, for real? That's cool, man. That's great. It's good? You're enjoying it?

It's all right. All these *mans* were starting to get on Warren's nerves.

And remind me, what did you end up writing on?

Writing?

Your dissertation. I remember seeing you around the Div School but I don't recall what you were studying.

Oh. Warren's mouth went dry again. *I didn't write a dissertation.*

Oh, really? God, good for you. I tell my students, you know, do a PhD if you really have to. If you really think there's nothing else in the world that will satisfy you. But only if. If there's anything else in the world that will make you happy, do that instead. It's not for everyone. A lot of people don't get that until it's too late. I'm glad you realized in time.

Well. It wasn't really my choice.

What do you mean?

I applied to the PhD program. I didn't get in.

Wait, seriously? Oh, shit. That's absurd. I would have thought some-one like you—Warren looked up at the phrase and saw Adrian's eyes widen for a moment before he regained his composure—*I mean, you always seemed like one of the people everyone liked. What happened? Do you know?*

Only what I heard secondhand. I guess I was not one of the people every-one liked. One of my professors apparently blocked my admission.

You got blackballed? That's awful. Do you know who it was?

Warren was quiet for a moment. He had not come here to talk about his academic history, certainly not to Adrian, and already he'd divulged more than he might have preferred. But something—the beer, the oily Indian food, the abundant trauma triggers scattered throughout Harrison Hall—compelled him to keep talking. *You remember Willard McGrath?*

Fuck, seriously? Sure I remember him. I was his TA for a quarter. I wish I could say I was surprised, but he was pretty touchy. I'm sorry. That's awful.

It is. It was. But it was also a long time ago.

Honestly grad school still feels like yesterday to me, but I guess you're right. I'm glad you have some perspective on it. Really glad you landed on your feet.

Warren almost spit out his beer at the thought. He repressed a bitter smile. *Seems like you did all right for yourself.*

Oh. Well. You know how it is. Adrian glanced up again, with an expression that said he was also relieved to change the subject. *With the way things are right now, it's all luck. It could of been me, could of been anyone.*

Warren grunted. *I don't know about that.*

Adrian mistook Warren's meaning and ran a hand through his hair. *Sure, sure. Obviously it's not totally random. That's one thing I've learned. Things never work out as fast as anyone wants, but I'm going to tell you, having seen what I've seen, I do have to believe that water finds its level eventually.*

That's what I've been told.

Adrian sucked air between his teeth. *Oh, no, man, come on. I didn't mean that. That's not what I meant at all. I know it's not that simple. Hell, if any of about a dozen different things hadn't broken my way, I'd probably be working at a library somewhere, too.*

Warren tried not to show his annoyance at the slight. *Well*, he said. *It's not so bad.*

Adrian dropped his head. *I'm going to stop talking now. I'm sorry. That's not what I meant, either. I hope you know that. I love libraries. I love librarians. It's a sacred task.*

Warren saw Adrian start to fidget uncomfortably. Not wanting the conversation to end just yet, he put up a hand in a consolatory gesture. *Don't worry about it. But listen, I'll be honest with you, it wasn't a coincidence I found you here today.*

Adrian looked puzzled. *No?*

I was hoping you would come. I wanted to ask you something. About your son.

Adrian nodded and offered a wary smile. *Oh right. Of course.*

You know I saw him.

Yeah. Sure, man.

Now Warren was confused. *You do?*

It was pretty obvious. You looked like you saw a ghost. I'm sorry I didn't stick around to explain what was happening. It was a pretty crazy time, as you might imagine.

Oh, you mean at the hospital. That's not—

Anyway, what can I tell you? There's a lot we don't know. But it's not dangerous, if that's what you were worried about. At least it doesn't seem to be.

Warren considered for a moment whether to clear up Adrian's misunderstanding. Before coming to Afternoon Beer, he'd assumed he'd at least mention seeing the boy at Gabriel's church, even if the story he told was Weight-less and substantially sanitized. But now he decided against it. He'd come to get information from Adrian, not to dispense it.

It wasn't that, Warren said. *Mostly I was just curious what it was. What it is, assuming it's still happening.*

Oh yeah, it's still happening, Adrian said. *As far as what it is, or what's causing it, I wish I could tell you. I wish I knew.*

Your boy is okay, though? Luca? Is that his name?

Luca, yeah. And yeah, he's okay. Better than okay, if you ask me. My wife might tell you otherwise. But the nimbus doesn't seem to bother him at all.

The nimbus? That what it's called?

That's what we're calling it. But only because we got tired of calling it "it." I wanted to name it something else but my wife thought my idea was dumb. She liked "nimbus" better, said it sounded less threatening.

What did you want to call it?

Oh, it doesn't matter.

Still I'd like to hear it.

Adrian's face brightened. *So, there's this thing you find in the Zoroastrian scriptures. It's a supernatural glow that proves the divinity of kings. It's called a* khvarenah.

    Varena?

    Khvarenah, *yeah. With that sort of guttural aitch sound in front.*

    Warren was quiet again.

    What do you think?

    I think your wife knows what she's talking about.

    Adrian laughed. *You're probably right. She usually does.*

TEN

Paul was sitting in a study carrel in the basement of the Main Library, working his way through Gershom Scholem's *Major Trends in Jewish Mysticism*, when he heard his phone buzz in the front pocket of his backpack. He closed the Scholem over his pen, marking the chapter where he'd been reading about the Hasidic *kavod*, and took his phone from his bag. It was Adrian.

Paul, hey.

Hey.

I got a question for you. Sorry, are you busy?

Not really. Just working on my proposal.

Right. How's it going?

It's . . . Paul hesitated while he decided how honest to be. *It's going okay. There's a lot of material here, that's for sure.*

See! Adrian sounded jubilant. *I told you. This is a gold mine.*

Yeah, it's just, it's a lot, you know? I'm not quite sure how I'm going to pull it all together.

Listen, don't worry. That's a good problem to have. The best problem to have, really. Way better than the opposite, right?

No, I know. To be honest, I'm just a little overwhelmed.

That's okay. I get it. I do. But really, I promise you it's going to be fine. Everybody feels that way when they're just getting started. Or at least, I do. It's how you know you're onto something worthy of your time and intelligence. But I want you to remember something, okay? You're going to crush it. Do you hear me?

Somewhat to Paul's surprise, the reassurance helped. *Yeah, okay.*

I'm serious. I even had an idea for a title for you. Ready? "The Luminous Numinous." Or maybe "The Numinous Luminous." It works either way. What do you think? Pretty good, right?

Sure, Paul said, not at all sure.

But listen, if you want to talk things over, we can do that, okay? Not now, I mean, but soon. Maybe we should get together, have ourselves a proper meeting. You know, like a real adviser/advisee thing?

That might be useful, thanks.

Absolutely. I want you to hold me to it. And I still want to have you over for dinner. But look, that's not why I'm calling. I was hoping to ask you a favor. You're coming to my talk today, right?

Paul had not in fact been planning on going to Adrian's talk. He had not in fact known that Adrian was giving a talk. *Yeah, totally. Of course. What time was it again?*

One thirty. At the chapel. It's going to be good, I think. I mean, who knows. We'll see. Anyway, I could use some help with something.

Sure, of course. What's up?

Do you think you could come by the chapel a few minutes before I get started? I've got a little surprise planned. You can probably guess what it is, but it's all come together kind of quickly, and I could use your help.

Paul left the library after lunch. The sky was dull and gray. The streets were wet enough to sizzle under passing cars. All up and down the sidewalks ran islets and peninsulas of frozen slush—a late reminder from the City of Big Shoulders that it was not giving up winter because it had to, only because it wanted to; it could still mess you up whenever it felt like it.

Paul crossed Fifty-Eighth Street, barely dodging a shuttle bus that didn't bother to slow down for him or any other pedestrian, and passed under the arched stone siege gate that defended the northern edge of the Main Quad.

Despite the weather, it was a hopeful time on campus. It was early March, and with the vernal equinox just a few weeks away, the days had begun to act like real days again. They had a heft and a duration, a breadth and a density. By the California standards that Paul had grown up with, it was nowhere near warm enough to feel like spring, but unlike even a few weeks earlier it was no longer impossible to imagine that spring was coming—that even summer might someday arrive.

For the first time in a long time, Paul was feeling hopeful, too, not about the weather but about his PhD. For the first time maybe ever, he was beginning to think he could see his way out of grad school. The thought was both thrilling and frightening, and Paul tried to protect himself from the latter aspect by reminding himself that he still had a long way to go. A lot of work remained ahead of him, and none of it would be easy.

For one thing, he still felt entirely unprepared for his colloquium, which was scheduled for Spring Quarter. He understood, too, that getting his proposal approved was just the beginning of the very long slog that would be his dissertation.

Nor had he exaggerated when he told Adrian that he was already feeling overwhelmed. In the six or so weeks that he'd been working on his proposal, he'd accumulated almost too many examples of nimbus-like phenomena. There were auras and glories, prabhamandalas and flaming halos, hilot and aureolas. Most of them showed up in languages he couldn't read and religious traditions he knew nothing about. Back at the study carrel, he'd collected a pile of books nearly three feet tall, which together covered six continents and twice as many centuries.

To read at such a scale, to work at such a scale, to think at such a scale, did not come naturally to Paul. His one pertinent academic talent, the thing that had let him survive far beyond what his talents should have allowed, had always been his intellectual modesty. Lacking capital of every kind—money, experience, illustrious relatives, meaningful social connections—he'd understood intuitively to stay away from the big topics, and never made the mistake of trying to solve life's mysteries in a term paper. He'd gotten as far as he had not by standing out but by slipping in. On the rare occasions when he was able to imagine what his ideal academic career might look like, he had always pictured it as a business of seams and creases, of roundabout paths and forgotten obscurities that would not make him famous but might keep him employed.

Yet for all the difficulties that he knew were waiting for him, Paul couldn't help but feel that Adrian was correct: the problems he was facing were good problems to have. Maybe he had been too hard on himself. Maybe he'd sold himself short. Maybe he wasn't an impostor after all.

Feeling better about his life than he had in a long time, Paul walked to Campbell Chapel by way of a long curving path that cut across the Main Quad. Outside the chapel's heavy wooden doors he was surprised to see a small group of people who appeared to be waiting for something. Campbell was not exactly inconspicuous: along with Harrison, to which it was connected by a photogenic stone cloister, it was one of the few freestanding buildings inside the quad. But it was, by now, almost entirely obsolete. Anachronistic even before it was built, a relic of a relict, the tidy little chapel had been the gift of the widow of one of the robber barons who founded the University—a devout woman who was all too happy to believe her minister's insistence that when Jesus preached poverty he actually meant philanthropy. These days the chapel was used occasionally by ministers-in-training from the Div School to practice their sermonizing or by campus chamber ensembles to rehearse their recitals. But mostly it was not used at all.

Paul noticed that quite a few of the people outside the chapel were pretty obviously not students, or faculty, or University staff. Standing by themselves or in small groups, they looked tentative and uncertain, as though intimidated by their surroundings. They looked different, too, physically and fashion-wise. They were rounder, older, and heavier, and their clothes and accessories were less casual than the usual undergraduate uniform of jeans, T-shirts, flannel pajama bottoms, and cotton sweats.

Seeing them gave Paul an idea. He fished his phone from his pocket and texted Billy a short message. The response came immediately, and Paul answered it with one word: Cool.

He stepped through the small crowd and pulled open one of the chapel's medieval-looking doors. Not wanting to send the wrong signal to the waiting crowd, he closed the heavy door behind him after he stepped over the threshold. Though not a Catholic anymore, he felt compelled to dip a finger in the stoup of holy water and daub himself with a shape that he'd never not been able to think of as an upside-down "4." He walked quickly through the vestibule, passing its buffet of beseeching pamphlets and its squadron of off-duty stanchions, and pushed through a swinging door into the nave of the chapel.

Paul had read one of those pamphlets on a previous visit, and had learned from it that Campbell's namesake and benefactress had intended to build a chapel on the University grounds that would rival the glories of Louis IX's Sainte-Chapelle. The widow died before building began, however, and her son, with the assistance of his many lawyers, succeeded in reducing the scale of the project to preserve as much as possible of his already obscene inheritance.

The result was a small stone church with a high hammer-beam roof and narrow pews that lined each side of a carpeted aisle. Overhead ran a frieze of shellacked walnut, and above that was the clerestory: a parade of vivid stained glass that depicted not just Christian saints and Jewish patriarchs but also scenes from other religions, including Siddhartha under the fig tree in Bodh Gaya, the Hindu Trimurti, Confucius and Lao-tzu meeting at the court of the Zhou dynasty, the Jain Samavasarana, Mohammed's night journey on the back of the Buraq, and a glassine copy of a Mondrian triptych that was influenced by the Theosophical teachings of Madame Blavatsky and Rudolf Steiner.

The windows, too, were apparently the result of the widow's son's meddling. Though the brochure tried to present the interfaith pantheon as a tribute of sorts to the Parliament of the World's Religions, which came to Chicago in 1893, reading between the lines it seemed clear to Paul that the son intended it as a permanent act of revenge against his mother. Paul didn't much like churches, and if asked to rank the world's evils, he would put inherited wealth near the top of his list. Still, he had to respect the widow's son's monstrous pettiness: by taking one last swipe at his mother's Christian piety, he'd ensured that the chapel that bore her name would be haram for any serious Muslim and openly idolatrous for everyone else.

Paul stepped into the nave and texted Adrian to let him know he'd arrived. A minute later, at the other end of the chapel, a door opened in the wooden wainscoting. Adrian stepped through, holding Luca in his arms. As Paul expected, the boy was glowing.

So here's what I'm thinking. I went to all the trouble to prepare this talk, so I might as well give it, right? Adrian said, once he'd led Paul back to the narrow room that served as the chapel's sacristy. He was sitting in a metal chair with Luca, who looked like he was almost asleep. His head lay heavily on his father's shoulder, and though his eyes were open, his gaze was distant and unfocused. *And this guy could probably use a rest before I bring him out. This whole idea came together so fast that I kind of forgot I was going to end up right in the middle of his nap time. Actually I guess it's not the worst thing in the world if he just sleeps through it, so long as the nimbus sticks around.* Adrian looked at his watch. *It's only been a couple of hours so far. I think we'll be fine. My talk is only about twenty minutes long.*

So you just want me to watch him back here?

Pretty much. If he wakes up and starts to fuss, you can just play with him until it's time. Adrian toed a backpack that was leaning against the wall near his chair. *I brought a couple of toys he likes. They're in here. I brought some cheese sticks, too, if he gets hungry. And a couple of pouches.*

Pouches?

Yeah, pouches. Adrian looked at Paul for a long couple of seconds before shaking his head and laughing silently. *Oh Jesus, you don't know what I'm talking about, do you? My god, you have no idea what sort of bliss you're living. What do the Catholics call it? Happy ignorance? Blessed ignorance?*

From somewhere deep in his memory Paul recovered the word. *Invincible.*

No, that's not what I mean. Blessed is better. Such blessed ignorance not to know what a pouch is. Adrian looked down at Luca and stroked his head, running his fingers over his thin blond hair and through the gently wafting aura of the nimbus.

Adrian went on. *I can almost remember what that's like. Almost. You can't imagine how many brain cells you have to give over to all this crap. I used to have a good fucking memory, man. At one point I'd memorized the first hundred lines of like six different epics. The* Iliad, *the* Aeneid, *the* Mahabharata, Gilgamesh, *the* Divine Comedy. *That's five. Jesus, see what I mean? I can't even remember what the sixth one was. Hold on, this is actually distressing. Give me a minute.* Beowulf! *Right, fuck.* Beowulf. Hwæt! We Gardena in geardagum, þeodcyninga, þrym gefrunon, hu ða æþelingas ellen fremedon. *See, this is what they don't tell you about parenthood. You know it's going to be hard. You know you're not going to sleep. But they don't tell you you're going to trade in* Beowulf *for* The Little Blue Truck, *you know?* Adrian looked at Paul and shook his head again. *You've never heard of* The Little Blue Truck, *have you?*

I assume it's a vehicle of some kind.

Fucking hell. Okay, this is depressing me. Point is, don't worry about the pouches. They're these fruit and veggie things. Baby food, basically, but it comes in these pouches that look like Capri-Suns instead of glass jars.

Capri-Suns?

Adrian leveled another hard glare at Paul. *Now you're messing with me.*

Paul smiled.

You actually scared me there.

My mom used to tell me stories about Capri-Sun when I was a kid. Some kind of primitive fruit juice, right? Something you drank while you were watching VHS tapes, if I recall? Or what was the other one? Beta something? My mom thought it was important that I learn the ancient ways.

Adrian laughed. *Nope. Nuh-uh. You're young, but you're not that young. You don't get to sound like one of my undergrads.*

I was one of your undergrads, remember?

That was a long time ago. You're over the hill now.

I'm twenty-eight!

Eh. Twenty-eight is the new forty. It's all downhill from here.

Luca stirred. He lifted his head and looked around, as though he were searching for something, or for someone. He made a sound like a mourning dove's cooing and let his head fall again against his father's lean shoulder.

Let's see. What else do you need to know?

It was pretty obviously a rhetorical question, but Paul took the opportunity of Adrian's good mood to ask something that had been niggling at him since he left the library.

Can I just ask, what changed?

Adrian squinted. *Changed how?*

Paul nodded at Luca. *I thought you were trying to keep this, all this, kind of quiet.*

I was. We were. Renata especially. But it didn't seem right, you know? Don't hide your light under a bushel, right? I brought Luca into my office once and people keep asking me to bring him in again. They want to see him. They want to see it. Anyway, it's not like we're dropping him in the middle of Millennium Park. It's just the Div School. People we know. I trust them to handle themselves.

I'm pretty sure I saw other people waiting out front? I don't think they're from the Div School.

Adrian scowled. *Out front where? Here?*

Paul nodded.

Hmm. Okay. Well, let's see how it goes. If something seems off, I'll pull the plug. I'm sure it will be fine, though. Right?

Yeah, I guess. Sure.

Don't worry. It's going to be great.

Before he went out to deliver the lecture, Adrian raided a closet and discovered a cache of folded towels and spare vestments. (A half-empty fifth of whiskey, too, which he held up for Paul's amusement.) The sacristy was not much bigger than an elevator cab, but still he found space on the floor to assemble a sort of nest for Luca. Once Adrian had set him on top of the cushioned pile and draped him with a white cassock, the boy closed his eyes. He was snoring already, and not quietly, by the time his father gave Paul an encouraging thumbs-up and slipped out of the sacristy.

Paul found a switch on the wall that piped into the small room a tinny transmission of the sound from the microphone in the chapel's pulpit. He listened for a while as Adrian did the thing he always did so well in his lectures, hopscotching across time and space to demonstrate the ubiquity of sacred illumination. From ancient Persia he jumped to Israel and Babylon, and from there bounced through Christianity, Islam, Hinduism, Tibetan Buddhism, and even nineteenth-century Spiritualism, where he dwelled for a time on the "countermyth" of Lucifer the Light-Bringer.

Paul tried not to be bothered that the lecture was getting uncomfortably close to the territory he was supposed to be covering in the dissertation Adrian had asked him to write. He tried to focus, instead, on how Adrian choreographed his intellectual acrobatics: where he leapt and where he landed, where he skipped and where he settled, where he rushed forward, chasing a novel insight, and where he held back, recuperating his rhetorical energy on the way to a grand sweeping conclusion.

It was all impressive enough in its way, but it didn't take long before Paul admitted to himself that he was far more interested in Luca—which was to say, in the nimbus, which showed itself even through the heavy cloth of the cassock. This was, he realized, the first time he'd seen the glow since the first time he saw it.

In the religious texts Paul had lately been reading, the glowing of saints and holy men and women was almost uniformly described as overwhelming. The refraction of divine glory through a human face or a human figure was so powerful that it often blinded anyone who looked upon it. Luca's glow was nothing like that. In the dim light of the sacristy, the glow was bright enough to be distinct, but there was nothing dramatic about it, or even all that intense. The lazy motion of the wisps and tendrils suggested no sort of power or force, certainly nothing frightening, in the way Moses's face was said to appear to the Israelites on his return from Mount Sinai. The nimbus's light reminded Paul, instead, of the whorling of candle smoke in a stilled room or the swirls of heat rising off a toaster.

Though the glow was oddly pacific, Paul began to feel increasingly unsettled. It was not the nimbus that caused his unease, or not the nimbus alone. As strange as it was to see, as weird as it was to feel nothing when he let his hand hover over Luca's sleeping forehead, Paul found himself far more troubled by the words of Adrian's talk drifting down out of the ancient sacristy loudspeaker. Paul had always admired and envied his adviser's talent for making far-flung connections. But watching the nimbus rustle and waver across Luca's cassocked body, what had appeared to him even a few minutes earlier as Adrian's high-flying virtuosity now started to seem more dizzying than dazzling.

Of course Paul understood what Adrian was trying to do with his talk, and he thought he understood why. Though Adrian couldn't have prepared his lecture knowing that Luca would be glowing today, he could easily have prepared it expecting that the nimbus was not going to stay a secret for long. As a scholar of comparative mythology, he was a firm believer in the Gospel of Saint Saussure, who preached that meaning was nothing fixed or inherent. Knowing that the nimbus could not signify anything in isolation, Adrian would be aware that if he wasn't the person to provide the context that could give the nimbus meaning, then someone else would almost certainly come along to do it in his stead.

Nothing about this had ever bothered Paul before. Though intellectual history had a bad reputation in most academic departments, he'd always found the endeavor, particularly when applied to religion, intensely appealing. He especially liked what he saw as the ironic cast of its central lesson: that while ideas mattered very much in history, they almost never mattered in the way the people who held those ideas hoped or expected. Paul liked this lesson not least because it reinforced his long-standing allergy to ambition. After all, if irony was the only way to find meaning in history, if everything signified but signified differently than intended, then what was the use trying to achieve anything permanent? What point could there possibly be in trying to build or discover some landmark that would allow you to orient yourself among the immensities? Or if you must have ambition, why pretend that what you were after was anything other than self-serving? If meaning was always up for grabs, if intentions were always overdetermined, why not do what Adrian was doing? Why not use whatever was ready to hand, including your own son, to get what you wanted out of life?

Yet as he sat in the sacristy, with Luca on the floor in front of him, Paul felt himself seized by a strange and sudden allegiance to the nimbus. Obviously it was in its way a neat vehicle for Adrian's hermeneutical explorations. It showed no signs of being partial to any extant faith tradition. It made no claims about the coming apocalypse, or the divine favor enjoyed by this or that slice of humanity, or the eternal peril that awaited everyone else. The nimbus asked for no offerings. It demanded no hecatombs. Unlike the glowing torso of Apollo that enthralled Rilke, it did not insist, *You must change your life.* In fact it did nothing, as far as anyone could tell. Nothing except to hint, perhaps, that our justified true beliefs about human luminescence were still woefully incomplete.

But still: the boy was glowing! The light was not a myth. It was not a metaphor. It was not a legend or parable passed down through twenty generations before it was scribbled on a scrap of papyrus. It was not a story people told themselves to feel better, or at least to feel less bad, about their place in the universe. Maybe the nimbus was a fake, a hoax, an illusion. Maybe it was an unknown natural phenomenon, or maybe it was something truly supernatural. Maybe the nimbus was real, or maybe it wasn't. Either way, though, shouldn't that fact matter? Didn't it deserve something better, Paul wondered, than one of Adrian's ostentatious performances of "historical phenomenology"?

PAUL WAS STILL PONDERING what this all meant, especially for his dissertation, when Adrian wrapped up his talk and came back to the sacristy to get Luca. The boy woke up fast, blinking into full consciousness immediately. He hooted at the sight of his father, and hooted again at Paul, whom he appeared to recognize, as he had not before. Adrian was worried that the nimbus might start dimming, so he took a toy car from his backpack, handed it to a delighted Luca, and carried the boy quickly out into the nave. Through a peephole in the wall, Paul watched them go, and then he left the sacristy himself through an exterior door and looped around, the long way, to the main entrance of the chapel. He went inside, found Billy near the back, and took a seat beside him.

Paul had been curious about how other people would react to the nimbus, and he was not disappointed. One portion of the crowd—the smallest but most obvious—comprised those who were seeing the nimbus for the first time. A few of this number appeared to be taking it hard: there was an older woman near the front, wearing a scarf like a babushka, whose mouth was literally agape. A woman in the same pew was crying vigorously. Others seemed anxious and unsure about what they were witnessing. They rubbed their eyes, they cleaned their glasses, they looked away and looked back again as though trying to catch in the act whoever was pulling the trick. Still others—including Professor Richardson, who taught anthropology at the Div School—refused to look, covering their faces with their hands or dropping to their knees on the kneelers and lowering their heads. There was a lot of praying going on, that much was clear. There was even some singing. From somewhere up front, Paul heard a woman's voice, hoarse and not especially tuneful, start humming "This Little Light of Mine."

Another part of the crowd, made up mostly of Div School students and faculty, pretty obviously couldn't see anything out of the ordinary.

They squinted and stared, craned their necks and shifted in their seats, and inevitably gave themselves away by leaning over to their neighbor for some hint or clue that might help them see what they were missing.

Billy, unfortunately, was one of these. Ever since Paul had told him what was going on with Luca, he'd been needling Paul, urging him to find some excuse, however clunky, that would give him a chance to see the nimbus. (His fascination was so intense that he'd missed the joke when Paul suggested that maybe Billy should be the one writing the dissertation Adrian wanted. Billy considered the possibility for a long minute before shaking his head and drawling a long *Nahhhh* and adding, *I made Salma promise to kill me if I ever seriously thought about going back to grad school.*) But now he was here and he couldn't see anything unusual.

You're sure he's still glowing? he whispered to Paul. *It must be faint, right? Kinda hard to see? It's not like crazy bright, right? You said it was more like a subtle thing? Maybe I'm just too far away. Can you see it from here? You're sure?*

Yes. No. No. Not really. Yes. No. Yes. Yes. It gave Paul no pleasure to let his best friend down.

The remaining members of the crowd, Paul guessed, had seen the nimbus before. He'd known such people were out there: Luca's impromptu visit to Harrison, after all, was well on its way to becoming a minor legend around the Div School. Paul figured he could spot the others from their expressions. Their faces showed no signs of straining or agitation. That Latina woman with the mole on her cheek, for instance, or that older white man with the pinched features, or even that balding brown-skinned man a few pews ahead, whom Paul recognized but couldn't place. What he saw in all of them was the satisfaction of a doubt relieved, the reassurance of a question resolved. He wondered if he looked the same way to them.

It became clear pretty quickly that Adrian hadn't given much thought to how this second part of his presentation was going to go. For the first couple of minutes, he stood in front of the altar with Luca in his arms. The arrangement was stilted and awkward, and reminded Paul of nothing so much as the 4-H auctions where his cousin sold lambs when they were kids.

As though sensing this, Adrian eventually set Luca down on the dais and sat next to him. Without the aid of a microphone he narrated the history of the nimbus—Paul counted it a grace that Adrian only alluded to him in passing, and did not name him or point him out—and what was known about it so far. There was a strong undercurrent of hushed conversation as Adrian wheeled his rambling story across the uncharted grounds of his family's recent history. Luca did not seem aware of the chatter. Still less did he seem aware of all the attention directed his way. His only care in the world right now was the tiny car he repeatedly sent skidding across the smooth floor of the chapel.

Adrian had only been speaking for about ten minutes when, without any obvious coordination, several people in the pews stood up and moved to the center aisle. There was some confusion at first at what was happening and why, enough that Adrian stopped speaking for a moment and pulled Luca onto his lap. But the commotion resolved itself quickly as the people in the aisle sifted themselves into a single-file line and began shuffling toward the front of the chapel, like they were waiting for Communion.

Paul saw Adrian tense at their initial approach, and he saw Luca echo his father's alarm. Father and child relaxed again when the first person in the line, a reed-thin Black woman in a gray skirt suit, kneeled a few feet in front of them, crossed herself, and kissed her thumb. She stood again and walked back to her seat. The second person in the line, a heavy East Asian man, bowed his head for a few silent seconds before departing. The third person, a white Div School student, smiled at Adrian and blew Luca a kiss. (Luca, to everyone's delight, pretended to grab the kiss out of the air and smack himself with it in the cheek.) So it went, for another ten minutes at least, as more and more people joined the line.

Before he knew quite what he was doing, Paul, too, was standing in the central aisle. Soon he was standing in front of Adrian and Luca at the front of the chapel. Adrian looked at him, shook his head, and let fly a disbelieving laugh. Luca looked, too, and when he recognized Paul he smiled and hooted, as though to say hello.

ELEVEN

Renata was in her kitchen, feeding Luca a midmorning snack of apple slices, corn puffs, and milk, when she heard the doorbell ring innocently for the last time. It was a Tuesday, and she was not expecting anyone, not even a UPS driver. But this, in itself, was no reason for concern. Nor was the fact that Adrian wasn't home. Though not reckless about her and the boys' safety, especially not lately, it was a sign of the kind of life Renata had lived that she'd never considered her doorstep a zone of particular danger. She'd never needed to barricade herself against a would-be rapist or burglar. She'd never been asked by a cop to step outside. She'd never been served a subpoena or an eviction notice. To that point in her life, in fact, the most distressing experience she'd had with a stranger at the door had arrived with a pizza deliveryman who tripped on his way up the stairs and cut his head bad enough to need an ambulance.

At first there was nothing obvious to suggest that this time would be any different. When the doorbell rang, Renata left Luca in his chair with his food and told him not to eat too fast. She answered the door and saw on her stoop a young man in a blue oxford shirt with a tie.

He had a mop of thick brown hair on his head, glasses on his face, and a distinctive oblong notebook in his right hand. He looked so much like a University undergraduate that even the latter object prompted no immediate alarm: rare as it was for Adrian's students to come by the house, it was hardly unprecedented. Her impression of who the young man probably was, and what he'd probably come for, was only strengthened when he asked, in a nervous voice, whether Professor Bennett was at home.

I'm sorry, he's not. He's teaching now.

Oh, oh. Okay. The student looked off to the side, as though making up his mind about something. *Are you . . . Do you mind if I ask if you're his wife?*

Renata smiled, hoping to put the boy—he was definitely a boy—at ease. *I am, yes. Renata.* She put out her hand, and the boy, still visibly unsure of himself, grasped it weakly and gave it a quick shake. *Are you one of his students? He should be on campus if you're trying to find him.*

Actually, the boy said, *I'm a reporter for the* Chicago Daily. *It's the University's college newspaper.*

It was at this point, Renata would reproach herself later, that she should have understood what was happening. It was at this point that all the anxieties and worries she'd accumulated over the previous six months should have done something useful for once by warning her that the boy on her doorstep was not a boy at all. That he was not a college student, or even a man. They should have warned her that he was the enemy: the scrawny, over-acned advance guard of an army that was coming to lay siege to her and her family's home. Renata should have been ready for this. She should have known exactly what to do, exactly what needed to be done. Instead she just stood there, a little confused but still smiling, oblivious to what she was confronting at her front door.

I'm doing a story about your husband, about Professor Bennett, the boy went on. *About a talk he gave on campus the other day . . .* The boy trailed off, as though uncertain if anything else needed to be said.

A talk? Renata said, still not getting it. *I'm sorry, like I said, my husband isn't home right now. Maybe you can email him.*

Actually the story is not just about him. It's about your son, too. The one your husband brought to Campbell Chapel. As you might imagine, a lot of people are talking about what they saw there. What they thought they saw . . .

Now, in a sudden rush, Renata understood why the boy was here. Her body froze, and so did her mind. For a moment she couldn't hear anything else the boy was saying. *I, I'm sorry*, she stuttered.

Do you think I could just see him, maybe? Your son? Renata saw the boy reaching for something in his back pocket, and in the space of an instant she convinced herself that the pimpled college student on her stoop was about to pull out a gun. Before she could act on this suspicion, he brought his hand back around and held up his phone. *Do you think I could just get a picture?*

Finally Renata summoned the wherewithal to do what she should have done before. She shut the door in the boy's face. She flipped the dead bolt, and latched the security chain, and tried to ignore his shouting. (*People are talking, ma'am. I have four people on the record who say they saw your boy glowing.*) She ran to the kitchen, checked the locks on the door to the backyard, unclipped Luca, and carried him upstairs. She waited up there, in her bedroom, with her door closed, and didn't come out until Adrian came home.

The first photographers showed up the next morning before Max went to school. There were two of them, originally. They appeared within an hour of each other outside the Bennetts' house, not bothering to knock or introduce themselves. They parked their cars down the block and set up their gear—tripods, cases, cameras, zoom lenses the size of construction cones—on the sidewalk across the street. Public land: they knew what they were doing.

Max spotted them first. His toothless smile, which would eventually end up on a few low-rent websites before the photographers realized

they had the wrong kid, was captured in the two minutes it took Renata
to figure out why he kept saying *Cheese!* to the front windowpane. She
slammed the curtains closed and yelled upstairs for Adrian, who was still
in bed.

The previous night, Adrian had tried to insist that her confrontation
with the young reporter was no big deal. *He had no business coming here,*
he allowed. *But look, it's just the college paper. I'll call their adviser. I'll get
it straightened out.*

Now, though, even in his groggy state, Adrian seemed to appreciate
that Renata's anxiety was not unwarranted. *Okay, okay, you're right,* he
said, after she showed him the photographers through a slit in the curtains. *Yesterday was whatever it was, but this is not cool.*

Adrian went upstairs and came back down a few minutes later. He
had changed out of his pajamas and was now wearing jeans and a sweatshirt.

Where are you going? Renata asked him.

I'm going to go talk to them.

Adrian!

What?

You can't just go talk to them.

Why not?

What are you going to say?

I'm going to tell them the truth.

What?!

*Relax. I'm going to tell them that there's nothing to see. I'm going to tell
them there's no point in staking us out.*

*Adrian, don't be naive. Those are paparazzi out there. They're not going
to listen to you.*

*Renata, please. This is Chicago. This isn't Hollywood. Those aren't
paparazzi. I'm sure they're just freelancers trying to make a buck. I'm going to
tell them they're wasting valuable time here.*

Renata watched him go. Through the slit in the curtains she watched
the two photographers jump up in unison when they saw Adrian come

through the door. She watched them shoot photos of Adrian during the whole long minute it took him to cross the street. She watched them keep shooting while he spoke to them, while he gestured at them, while he pointed down the street and pounded his hand in his fist. And she watched him return, defeated, as the cameras captured every slinking step until the door slammed closed behind him.

The local reporters arrived later that day. These were, as a class, far more civil (if no less determined) than the twin paparazzi, whom Renata had already begun to think of as Tweedledumb and Tweedledumber, and came in various flavors, which Adrian and Renata learned to distinguish by their appearance. The chirpy television correspondents wore suits and slim dresses under tailored winter coats, along with lots of makeup. They never strayed out of sight of the massive cameras that were lugged around by heavy white guys in black jeans and thick flannel. The newspaper journalists, who were uniformly middle-aged and a little too obviously hanging on till the next buyout rolled around, wore sagging suits with white undershirts visible in the open space where a tie should have been. The public-radio reporter looked barely twenty; she wore bright leggings under a corduroy skirt and a sweater that even Renata had to admit was kind of cute.

One after another they climbed up to the porch and rang the door-bell and smiled apologetically while pleading their case. They asked if they could just come inside for a minute, unless maybe Luca and one of his parents wanted to come out? They had heard things, they said. People were talking about a boy on the South Side who was glowing mysteriously. Some of those people were willing to go on the record with what they'd witnessed. But being the responsible journalists they were, the reporters wanted to hear it straight from the Bennetts. They wanted to see for themselves. The sweet talk and sympathetic nodding continued right up until the moment it became clear that they were not going to get the exclusive they'd promised themselves—or, worse, their editors. The public-radio reporter alone seemed undimmed when she handed over her business card and said, *Only when you're ready, but, please, as soon as you're ready.*

Renata could tell that Adrian was tempted to invite them in, even after his frustrating experience with Tweedledumb and Tweedledumber. Left to his own devices, she suspected, he would have made them coffee, offered them a beer, let them hang out in the house as long as it took for the nimbus to show itself again.

Renata wanted none of it. She shut down even the slightest suggestion that one or both of them should consider engaging with the media. Part of this, no doubt, was that she was still pissed that not once but twice—first at his office and then at the chapel—Adrian had let people gawk at Luca like he was some sort of freak-show spectacle. But she also had a practical rationale: she'd absorbed enough crisis PR in the course of her consulting work that she knew there was nothing to be gained from publicity, and very much to lose. A few interviews would inevitably lead to a lot more. The early excitement and hype would curdle into bitterness and rancor. Before they knew it a locust swarm would devour their lives and leave them ravaged.

Renata's policy was firm, and, to his credit, Adrian stuck to it: until she said so, there would be no interviews or posed photographs, no outdoor excursions for Luca, no one allowed in the house they didn't know already—essentially nothing that would feed the story or give it oxygen to grow. All they would allow by way of public comment was a single sentence that no one could prove was a lie: "We are dealing with a family medical issue, and we ask for privacy for ourselves and our children."

Renata's precautions appeared to have little effect at first. The reporters from the more respectable news organizations couldn't run a story about a glowing boy on the strength of a rumor, of course. But the Internet and the tabloids were happy to step in where the more respectable news organizations feared to tread. By the end of the first week after Adrian's chapel stunt, pictures of Max with a photoshopped halo began to circulate in the less reputable corners of the digital mediasphere. There the pseudo-story might have remained, alongside the accounts of extraterrestrial love hotels and sightings of a grizzled and grinning ninety-five-year-old JFK, were it not for a report in the college newspaper that quoted the insistent claims of an anonymous Div School student who said he saw the nimbus at Campbell Chapel, as well as the testimony of an elderly couple who swore they saw a glowing boy at their church on the South Side.

These accounts provided the necessary prompt for a media siege to begin in earnest. Tweedledumb and Tweedledumber were joined by a dozen other photographers whose clicks and flashes assaulted the Bennetts every time one of them stepped foot outside their house. The TV reporters came back, on a hostile footing now, and made no pretense of empathy or politeness. With the help of their antenna trucks and camera-men, they established an encampment of sorts that made it impossible for anything wider than a motorcycle to fit down the Bennetts' street. The public-radio reporter came around again, as did the gray-skinned survivors of the bankrupt dailies, and with them a new crop of journalists—from college newspapers, local blogs, Spanish-language outlets—there was even a stringer from the *New York Times*—who'd convinced their editors that it was worth spending a few days down in Fell Gardens to see what all the fuss was about.

The journalists and gawkers and hangers-on were not content to wait outside the Bennetts' house. They called and texted Renata and Adrian at all hours, rendering their phones essentially useless. They emailed constantly. The more obnoxious among them stood on the stoop and shouted questions or slipped papers pleading for interviews through their mail drop. Twice Adrian caught people snooping in their backyard, and it was not exactly reassuring that the cops who answered the 911 calls both times seemed more interested in checking out what they'd heard about the nimbus than in apprehending the trespassers.

The frenzy inside and outside their house was bad enough that Renata and Adrian seriously considered leaving town. Renata could take Luca to her mother's apartment in Manhattan, or maybe all of them could stay in a hotel or a rental in a random town where no one could find them. The appeal of this plan was seriously diminished, however, when they realized that the boys would not take it well. Max in particular: though Renata had been rigorous about keeping Luca indoors, for the first couple of days she'd let Adrian convince her that it was okay for Max to keep going to school. Of course Max had noticed the strange doings on his street, and of course he had not been pleased to see so much interest in his little brother. Soon he demanded to stay home with the family—Renata was about to pull him out anyway—and now he was spending most of his time playing alone or reading in his bedroom.

Luca, too—bubbly Luca, who never met a vehicle he didn't adore, who'd made fast friends with all the dogs and cats on their block—was also showing the strain. People pleaser that he was, he appeared to sense, obscurely, that his glowing was somehow responsible for the unhappiness of everyone around him. Before the media uproar began, he had almost stopped noticing the nimbus; for him, Adrian had surmised, it must be no different than steam or rabbits or any of a hundred other unfamiliar phenomena that a two-year-old has to assimilate into their experience of the world.

Once the furor began, however, Luca began to react strongly against the nimbus whenever it appeared. He scratched at it and growled at it. A few times Renata even caught him biting his arm to get rid of it.

Adrian's commitment to Renata's media strategy was tested severely when he realized that the story the reporters were chasing was not really a story about a glowing boy. It could not be a story about a glowing boy, for the simple reason that boys don't glow. Instead it was, it had to be, a story about something else: some sort of fraud, most likely, unless it was a psychological sickness, or a strange and perverse instance of child abuse. The most generous interpretation—the one, Renata realized, that the public-radio reporter was pursuing, which made her like the girl even more— was that the whole thing was an honest mix-up, a sincere delusion of sorts that had something to do with the persistence of irrational beliefs in a rationalist age. No one actually thought the nimbus was real.

This journalistic skepticism was bad enough, as far as Adrian was concerned, but what got Renata bothered was the jokes. She couldn't care less what people did or did not believe, especially since she barely believed any of it herself. But she really didn't like watching her son become grist for the social-media snarkmongers. She especially resented the suggestion—which sometimes came packaged as an insinuation, and other times as an outright accusation—that she and Adrian were doing this all for clout and publicity.

Spotting an opening, Adrian suggested to Renata that it was not fair to let the accusation stand. Not fair to Luca. Not fair to them. Wouldn't it make sense, he said, to go out and talk to the reporters? What was so wrong with letting them see the nimbus for themselves? Maybe they could even hit the story head-on. They could take Luca onto a cable-news program or a late-night talk show—they could bring Anita Krishnamurthi with them as well—to explain patiently but firmly that while no one could say what was causing the nimbus, no one could equally say that it was a mere mirage.

Yet even through the worst of it, even when a popular comedy website ran a fake advertisement for a rent-to-own service hawking glowing children who could be used for party decorations or subterranean mining operations, Renata held her ground. She beat back Adrian's resistance the same way she usually won fights: by telling him exactly what he was thinking, and exactly why he was wrong, and waiting patiently for him to acknowledge that she had his number. They had the fight over cappuccinos one morning, after another fitful night of occasional dozing, while the boys watched *Paw Patrol* in the curtained living room.

You think this will go like one of your classes, she said. *You think those people out there are like your students. You think they're waiting to hear what you think. You think they want to hear what you think.*

Come on, Adrian protested. *I'm not so naive as that. I don't even think my students—*

You don't even think your students are that interested in what you're say-ing? Fine. But the difference is this: maybe they aren't interested, but they need to listen to you at least a little. They need to know what you want them to know, because that's the only way they're going to get out of your class with a decent grade. This isn't like that. I know that you think you can walk out onto the porch and give a brilliant lecture. You think you can dazzle them with your charm and your erudition . . .

Adrian gave a little snort-laugh. *I'm hurt that you think there are people I can't dazzle with my charm and erudition.*

Renata didn't smile. Instead she pointed toward the front door. *All those people out there think you're crazy.*

I know! I'd think I was crazy, if I were them. But the difference is, I've seen the nimbus, and they haven't. So we'll show them Luca—

So we'll show them Luca, and then what? Most of them will be like me. They won't be able to see anything, and then they'll really know we're full of shit.

But the others—

But the others will see something, sure. Something they can't photograph or film. Something that not even you or Anita or anyone will be able to explain. Do you think those journalists out there will just take it at face value and type up a happy story about the glowing boy and call it a day? Of course not. Most likely they'll think it's a trick, and then they'll really come after us. But even the other ones, the ones who think it's real somehow, whatever real is supposed to mean, what exactly do you think they're going to do with that conviction? Whatever they do, do you think it's going to help us? Do you think it's going to help Luca?

For the period that comprised the most intense phase of their involuntary lockdown, the Bennetts relied on neighbors, friends, and Adrian's colleagues to help them manage the mundanities of life. They relied especially on Paul, who texted Adrian after he saw the first news reports and announced himself eager to help however he could.

Renata was initially reluctant to take him up on the offer, not least because Adrian had always been scathing about professors who used their grad students to run their lives. The clichéd stuff—dropping off dry cleaning, picking up takeout, buying cigarettes or Starbucks—was bad (and common) enough. But Adrian also had colleagues who put their grad students to work washing their cars, cleaning their apartments, and sorting their medications. (One student of Adrian's acquaintance had drawn the line at biting pills in half, but this didn't stop her professor from complaining about her to the Dean. *I don't see the problem*, the professor had apparently said. *If she's doing something I'd otherwise have to do myself, then I'll have more time to think and more time to read and more time to write. Isn't that the point of a research assistant?*)

When Adrian caught wind of Renata's stalling, he told her to stop being so scrupulous. *Obviously this isn't the same thing*, he said one evening, after suggesting that they should ask Paul to pick up some household supplies they needed from the drugstore. *This is hardly an ordinary situation.*

Renata couldn't disagree with the last part; the situation had gotten bad enough that Adrian was canceling classes again. Still, something didn't sit well with her about the suggestion. *I wouldn't care if it was just your books or something from your office*, she said. *But this is personal stuff. It just doesn't feel right to ask him to pick up toilet paper and pinworm medicine for us.*

He's asked me like ten times how he can be useful. Not "if." "How." He wants to help.

It's very nice of him. I hope you've told him that.

I have, many times. I told you he's a good guy. A little lost, a little naive, but profoundly decent. Of course I'm sure it doesn't hurt that he has his dissertation colloquium coming up. But I've known Paul long enough that I think we can take him at his word. He wants to help. We need help. Why are we making this hard?

Renata discovered that she could accept this line of logic. She knew she was in dire straits. Her family was living in a bubble. No: they were living in a city, a walled and beleaguered city. Outside was a huge army, quartered in tents as far as you could see. They were flinging boulders, arrows, dead cows in over the walls. Inside, the Bennetts had maybe five days of food. She could feel the pressure. Adrian was right: they needed help.

With the consent of the Bennetts' backyard neighbors, and the energy and agility of a twenty-eight-year-old body, Paul figured out how to snake his way up to the back deck without being noticed. Twice a day, once in the morning and again in the late afternoon, he texted to see if Renata or Adrian needed anything. Slowly at first, and then with increasing frequency, Renata answered with suggestions of small errands that might be helpful, but only if he had time. He handled every one, promptly and with no hint of annoyance or hesitation. Pretty soon he was buying the Bennetts' groceries. He was taking their car in for its annual inspection. He even bought them diapers.

He was helping in other ways, too. When the nimbus hit the news, Adrian had been flooded with so many email messages that he could barely stand to look at his inbox. (Renata got some mail, too, but nothing like Adrian, whose address, it took him far too long to remember, was posted on his Div School faculty page.) The media requests were only the start of it. Messages came in from friends, colleagues, and students, from childhood acquaintances and former classmates, from strangers, spammers, and scammers. Not all of the emails were about the nimbus, at least not explicitly. There was a lot of checking in to see how Adrian was doing and hoping everything was okay. There was also a sizable stream of notes that justified themselves with oblique or straightforward allusions to this or that mention of Adrian and/or Luca that the sender had recently encountered. And in the midst of all that, there was, still, the lesser flood of ordinary email—from students, colleagues, administrators—that had already been overwhelming before news of the nimbus went public.

Paul volunteered to help Adrian triage his inbox, and though he could mostly do this on his own, he sometimes came by the house to make sure Adrian wasn't missing anything important. The more he visited, the more the boys got used to having him around, and it wasn't long before Renata caught Paul in the living room helping the boys build a Lego version of what Max, aping Adrian, insisted they call the Sears Tower. Paul seemed to be enjoying himself (Max and Luca, she could tell, were in heaven) and, sure enough, he made a point before he left the house that day to mention that he'd be glad to watch the boys from time to time.

For three weeks the hurricane raged. For three weeks the maelstrom blew. For three weeks the journalists rotated in and out of their streetside encampment. Eventually, though, they got bored, just as Renata predicted they would.

Probably it helped that from Lakeview there came word of a couple who, after fifty years of marriage, acknowledged to their children and the world that they were not just spouses but siblings, and had the temerity to insist that they regretted nothing about their scandalous happiness. Probably it helped, too, that around the same time a man from Elmwood Park claimed he'd found a cache of buried treasure in his backyard. Probably it helped most of all that the same half dozen witnesses narrating the same half dozen accounts of the nimbus could not provide enough fuel to push the story out of the odd-news sections and into a more respectable journalistic register.

Whatever their reasons, by the fourth week after Luca's visit to the chapel, the reporters had all gone home. The TV trucks folded down their antennas and drove away. The cable bookers stopped calling. The late-night comedians turned their smug attention elsewhere. A handful of magazine writers, skilled in the dark arts of long-form persuasion, kept emailing pseudo-sincere pleas for just a few minutes with you and Luca so that we can get your side of the story and try to help our readers understand what's actually going on. But they were either too poor or too lazy to show up at the Bennetts' house without a commitment, and so it was easy enough to blow them off.

So long as the enemy army was waiting outside, Renata hadn't left the house unless it was absolutely necessary. It wasn't worth the hassle. It wasn't worth the harassment.

After the journalists drifted away, however, Renata and Adrian slowly became reacquainted with the outside world. They started doing their own errands again. They took Max down to the lake and let him play at the playground, let him glory without admonishment in the temporary illusion that he was a single child. After the street-clogging encampment came down and even Tweedledumb and Tweedledumber stopped their stalking, they managed to get the boys out of the house and into the car early one Saturday morning for a day trip up to Madison. Feeling safe in their out-of-state anonymity, they ate pale-skinned brats and checked out the capitol and marveled at their freedom in the open air.

Only after she escaped did Renata realize how much damage her impromptu lockdown had done. The experience reminded her of a trans-pacific flight to Vietnam that she and Adrian had taken before they had kids. When she got on the plane she was happy, healthy, and eager about the trip; when she got off, she was a wheezing, snotty, mewling mess. Between those two endpoints she'd felt herself fall into a gray, gauzy dreamland in which she was too tired, too enervated, to do anything but watch seatback movies with half-dozing eyes and chomp mindlessly on foil-wrapped car-bohydrates. The lockdown had been like that, too: alone or with Adrian or with the boys, she'd probably watched close to six hours of TV a day, something she hadn't done since she was a teenager. Not coincidentally, she'd gained eight pounds over the same brutal three weeks.

The enforced time together was hard for other reasons, too. Renata was not able to forget that all that suffering was Adrian's doing, and she was not able to forgive how uncontrite about the chapel episode he continued to be. Yes, he'd offered a few apologies at the outset. Yes, he agreed that he should have talked it over with her before dragging Luca out into public. She could tell, though, that he wasn't actually all that regretful. If anything, he seemed to feel (though he never quite said so; he was too smart for that) that Renata's strict rules about the circus outside meant that he was the one making the greater sacrifice.

With the lockdown ended, Renata decided there was no reason to postpone her annual dermatology appointment. It would not take long: her doctor's

office was just on the other side of campus. Still, she'd have to find something to do with the boys. It was tempting to leave them in front of the
TV and let them go full zombie while Adrian worked in his office, but
she knew that Max would not be able to handle it. Inevitably he would
bother Adrian, and then Adrian would get upset at Renata, and then
Renata would get upset at him, and then no one would be happy, except
maybe the dermatologist.

For a few long moments, Renata considered calling Mariela to see if
she wanted to return. She decided against it, largely out of guilt: she still
felt bad about the firing, even as she still felt it was eminently justified.
Instead, almost on a whim, she decided to text Paul. He answered her
message immediately and said he'd be glad to come.

When she got home after her appointment, Renata found her sons in
the living room. They were playing a game that Max had just invented,
which involved a chessboard, checkers, raisins, and Monopoly money.
It did not yet have a name but apparently already had a reigning world
champion. From all appearances, Luca had been reminded of this latter
fact every three minutes or so by his brother, said titleholder, but it did not
appear to bother him in the slightest. The sweet boy was happy to lose,
happy to lose forever and always, so long as it meant that he was allowed
to play.

Paul and Adrian were in the kitchen, talking over open beers. Renata
was surprised and not altogether pleased to see this. It was only three o'clock
in the afternoon. For weeks now, for months now, her husband had been
complaining about how far behind he was in his work, how even locking
himself up for twelve hours a day would likely not allow him to make up
for the time he'd lost dealing with the furor around the nimbus. Renata
had tried to be sympathetic. She'd given him the space he needed. She'd
kept the boys away from his door for long hours each day. Only a few times
had her frustration gotten the better of her best intentions. Only once had
she let herself remind him that he was the reason they'd had to turn their
lives upside down.

And now he was drinking? In the middle of the afternoon? After
telling Renata there was no way he could afford a break to watch the boys

while she went to her appointment? Renata set her teeth and forced her face into a fake smile. *What are we celebrating?* she said, in what she hoped was an upbeat tone.

Adrian either missed or misread her annoyance. With an overwarm expression he came over to her and took her hand and spun her around, like they were dancing. He kissed her sloppily on the mouth, his breath thick and hoppy, and then he stepped back and held up his beer. *So much good news. I'm not sure where I should start. You want one?*

I think I'd rather hear this good news first.

Adrian tilted his head and lifted his eyebrows, as if to say, Your loss. *I just got an email from the head of the Olson Foundation. John Olson wants to meet me.*

Who is John Olson?

I thought you might have heard of him. He's a billionaire, a big philanthropist. He's very interested in religion—not the crazy kind, it's not like he's trying to find Noah's ark or turn everyone into a Christian fundamentalist. His big obsession is religion and secularism, science and religion, that kind of thing. In my world, our world—Adrian looked at Paul—*he's a huge deal. He funds all kinds of prizes and fellowships and centers.*

Renata let her face fall. *And why does he want to talk to you?* she said carefully, with as little inflection as she could manage.

This time Adrian got the point. He put his hands up to pacify her. *Hold on. I haven't even written him back yet.*

Adrian, we just got through a month of hell, we finally got everything quieted back down, and you want to open up that box all over again? Renata felt her forehead getting warm.

Like I said, I haven't written him back. I knew I needed to talk to you first.

Renata looked at Paul, who glanced away as soon as her eyes met his. She did not want to have this fight in front of him. He'd been so good to the Bennetts. He deserved better than that. *That's probably a good idea. We can talk about it later. But you know I'm not going to change my mind. Dare I ask what the rest of the good news is?*

Adrian pursed his lips, took a drink of his beer, and thought for a moment. He turned to Paul, who looked like he wanted to climb into one of the kitchen cabinets. Renata watched Adrian and forced herself to take several long slow breaths.

I told you, Paul said to Adrian. He was still conspicuously avoiding Renata's gaze. *I appreciate the offer but it's really not necessary . . .*

What's not necessary? Renata said coldly.

Paul turned to her. *Really, it's nothing. Don't worry about it. I mean, it's not nothing. Adrian was trying to help me out. I already told him I was fine.*

Adrian, what are you not telling me? she said, drawing out the words slowly.

Adrian exhaled. *You know where Paul's been living? In his office, at the Graduate Review.*

Renata felt a thaw in the sternness that had frozen her body. *Wait, what?*

Yeah. For months now. All this time he's been helping us, he's been sleeping on a couch in his office.

Renata was genuinely surprised. *Jesus, Paul, why didn't you say something?*

Adrian nodded and kept talking. *Of course I was going to talk to you about it, but, you know, I just thought, he might as well sleep in my office. We have a perfectly good fold-out bed in there.*

This suggestion surprised Renata even more than the original proposal. Even though he had an office at the Div School, barely half a mile away, Adrian always made it clear how disruptive he found it whenever Renata's mom or another guest stayed in his office.

Obviously it wouldn't be permanent, Adrian said. *Just until he finds something. It just seems like such a waste of good square footage.*

No, I can't, really, Paul said. *It's very nice of you, but I promise I'll be okay.*

Renata looked at Adrian, and then at Paul, and back at Adrian again. *Okay*, she said at last. *I think I'm ready for that beer.*

TWELVE

In Brooklyn, they received crisp dollar bills from the Messiah on Sundays. In Uttar Pradesh, they drank from skulls and smeared themselves with ashy cremains. In Wollongbar, they shunned the music of J. S. Bach and relied on breast massage to prevent cancer. In Niterói, they courted possession by the long-dead spirits of wise slaves and feisty gauchos. In Jackson County, they awaited the end of the world, when the saints from these latter days would build a New Jerusalem on the two-acre plot where the Garden of Eden had once grown. In Umuahia, they learned that cleanliness was godliness. In Rabwah, they preached that Jesus survived his crucifixion and died an old man in Kashmir, while looking for the lost tribes of Israel. In Kostroma, they read Pushkin as prophecy and blamed the corruption of the world on the degradation of the world's alphabets (and also, obviously, on the Jews). In Tokyo, they said that the Earth's magnetic poles would flip and cause planetary catastrophe, unless a bearded Arctic seal that went missing from its habitat was rescued from the electromagnetic waves that had sent it astray. In Calcata, they venerated the holy foreskin snipped from the eight-day-old penis of their incarnated God.

And on the Internet, for a while, they met on a nearly defunct Web forum to share stories about a glowing boy who lived in Chicago.

Warren couldn't say how he'd first discovered the forum, except that he'd probably found it the way he found everything online. The Internet, to him, was an ocean: an immense, infinite sea with discernible tides and currents but no firm boundaries or divisions. Warren knew when he was playing Wintermere or answering his boss's emails or working in the library's catalog database, but to ask him where he spent most of his time online was like asking a fish if it lived in Monterey Bay.

What he could say was that he'd found the site shortly after he'd seen Adrian's boy at Campbell Chapel. Warren hadn't known for sure that Luca was going to be there, but when he received notice of Adrian's talk on the same Div School listserv that had told him about Afternoon Beer, he figured Adrian would find a way to involve his boy.

At the chapel, Warren saw Luca glow for a third time. He saw, too, as he had at the church, how what Adrian called the nimbus had affected other people. The effect was neither magical nor miraculous: the blind were not made to see, the lame were not made to walk, no one else spontaneously started glowing. But there was an effect nonetheless, and astonishment, a general astonishment, was the only word he could summon to describe it.

In life, in general, Warren was not so presumptuous to imagine that he could guess what other people were thinking. He'd been wrong too many times—more to the point, he'd been wronged too many times, both misunderstood and misinterpreted by wannabe thought-readers—to allow himself the impertinence that busybodies liked to call empathy. Still, the individual dramas that played out on the faces of the people around him in the chapel were hardly private. Some of the faces were weeping, some of them were smiling, some were weeping while they were smiling. Warren saw relief, exultation, fear, wonder, and a dozen other emotions ripple through the pews like so many wavelets.

Almost everyone stayed in the chapel until Adrian took Luca away. (The only people who left early were those who had seemed unmoved by the nimbus; Warren did not yet know that some people—the majority of people, in fact, though not the majority in the chapel—couldn't see it.) After the impromptu service was over, they stumbled and staggered out into the bright gray sunlight. Some of them looked dizzy. Some of them looked lost. Still others of them looked as though they were gazing upon the University's Main Quad for the first time, and saw in it a scene of indescribable fascination.

When the nimbus hit the news, Warren followed it obsessively online. No one really knew anything, that much became clear. Or at least no one knew anything that Warren didn't know better. At some point he realized that outside of Adrian and his family, he could probably lay claim to having seen the nimbus more times than anyone else on Earth.

He didn't know what to do with this knowledge until he found the forum, a relic of Web 2.0 that was neither popular nor anywhere close to cool. It was the sort of place where you could find small, vigorous communities who liked to argue about pencils, or offer advice for cross-country hitchhikers, or trade stories about life in the merchant marines.

The subforum about the nimbus grew out of a long thread on another subforum that called itself the Durable Improvement Project. This turned out to be a not-so-secret code for technology-enabled eugenics. DIPpers believed that what they called "random breeding" would someday be seen as a practice as primitive as human sacrifice. Between IVF and gene editing—they were especially excited about new research on something called CRISPR/Cas9—there was no reason, they thought, why humans could not be smarter, stronger, taller, and more conventionally attractive than they are now. It was perhaps telling that baldness, shortness, sweatiness, and lackluster genital development were high on the list of scourges the DIPpers hoped to flush from the human gene pool, but nothing interested them more than longevity. It was an article of faith on the subforum that humans should routinely live five hundred years or longer.

The earliest posts about the nimbus on the DIP thread converged on an agreement that the phenomenon must be some kind of heretofore unknown human bioluminescence. From there they spun off into speculations about whether and how what they assumed to be Luca's extraordinary genetic material might be harvested and exploited. When someone else suggested, not altogether politely, that the DIPpers' interpretation was not well supported by the reports out of Chicago, a long and occasionally vicious argument commenced that resulted, finally, in several people being banned from the DIP subforum for life. It was these exiles who started the new subforum dedicated exclusively to the nimbus. It was this subforum Warren found, a week or so after the discussion had already gotten underway. And it was this subforum where, far faster than he would have thought possible, something that started to look very much like a religion began to cohere.

Warren never intended to get involved. By nature in life, online and off, he was a lurker, not a poster. Though he felt his Internet addiction to be as severe as anyone's—even his patience for reading books was lately crumpling under the vacuum-force attraction of his phone—he was immune to the dopamine rush that turned social-media users into fiends. Part of it, certainly, was that he didn't need people to know what he was thinking. Part of it, too, was that he didn't particularly *want* people to know what he was thinking.

One day, however, about a week after he discovered the subforum, Warren was reading through the latest posts about the nimbus when he came across one that caused him to abandon his usual approach. The post was by someone who called himself DaBearz. He purported to be a close friend and neighbor of Adrian's, and he said that he'd seen the phenomenon many times. Everyone else was getting it wrong, he wrote. The glow was not, as the DIPpers had assumed, anything biochemical. But it was also not supernatural or paranormal. In fact, it was nothing like the radiant haze described by the fame chasers whom the know-nothings in the media kept putting on local TV.

What people were inaccurately calling a glow, he insisted, was nothing more than a weirdly persistent and visible form of static electricity. In the right weather, the very fine hairs on Luca's skin would crackle and pop with tiny sparks. It was undoubtedly odd, DaBearz said, but it was odd in the way St. Elmo's fire was odd. Odd in the way ball lightning was odd.

This was ridiculous, of course. Everything DaBearz had written except the part about the supernatural character of the nimbus (about which Warren had no more idea than anyone) was absurd. The people who had seen Luca in Campbell Chapel had not cried till they were gasping because they'd gotten confused about some static electricity. They hadn't come out of the chapel staggering like they were drunk because they'd tricked themselves into seeing a full-body halo.

The post was so ludicrous that initially Warren hardly gave it a second thought. Every day, in every house in every town in every province in every country on Earth, people pulled out their phones or logged into their computers and wrote nonsense on the Internet. This was nothing to marvel at. What got Warren's attention, though, what persuaded him finally to climb two flights of stairs up to the computer lab in the basement and register for an account on the forgotten website, was that some of the subforum members seemed to be taking the impostor seriously. DaBearz's post was received as both disappointing and a relief, for if the nimbus was only a natural phenomenon transmogrified by rumor into something bizarre and fantastical—the same old alchemy that made werewolves out of rabies and zombies out of catatonic schizophrenia— then no one had to change their minds about anything. The world was what they'd always thought it was, and the whole fuss was much ado about nothing. Maybe it was time, some of the posters suggested, to shut the subforum down.

Warren's first response to DaBearz was brief and direct. This is not right, he wrote. I've seen the boy in question myself, and while I can't say anything with any assurance about what has been happening to him, and definitely can't say anything about why, I can guarantee you that it is nothing like what DaBearz has described. I don't know why he's trying to mislead everyone here, but I would advise you all to take his report with a hefty grain of salt.

Warren's response kicked off a flame war that rivaled the intensity of the debate that had given the subforum its original reason for being. Warren mostly stayed out of it, but such were the emotions on the matter that at one point a moderator of the subforum went rogue and revealed that DaBearz had been posting via an Internet provider in Birmingham, England, while Warren's IP address was traceable to the University. This breach of subforum ethics horrified everyone. (Including Warren, who was more grateful than ever that he'd taken the trouble to use a computer other than his own when submitting his posts.) But it also gave Warren an instant credibility. People asked him to say more about what he'd seen. They pleaded with him to verify this or that rumor, to provide whatever data he had that might confirm or scuttle whatever pet theory they'd come up with.

For reasons he couldn't fully explain to himself—his general sense of responsibility to the world had mostly died with his sister—Warren felt compelled to help. He did not write a lot, and risked nothing in writing that offered even a hint of his real-life identity. But what he wrote was taken seriously, and this encouraged him to keep posting.

It soon became evident that Warren was not the only member of the subforum who had seen the nimbus firsthand. Eventually two people who had seen Luca at the chapel found their way to the website, as did someone who claimed to be a student at the Div School. Their accounts of what they'd seen largely aligned with what Warren had reported, thereby reinforcing the weight of his authority, but in one respect they were substantially different. Each of the other people reported that their encounter with the nimbus had resulted, days or weeks after the fact, in a significant improvement in some aspect of their life. One of the people from the chapel, who confessed that she'd been terrified at first to see Luca glow, found a new job within three days of the incident that got her away from a terrible boss. The other person from the chapel said that a chronic and extreme case of psoriasis that he'd suffered since childhood cleared up within a week and had not returned. And the student, who said that she'd been on the brink of dropping out of grad school for lack of money, said that just a day after her sighting of the nimbus at Campbell she'd been granted a long-shot fellowship that she was certain she had no chance of winning.

None of these cases were dispositive, of course, and when others on the subforum asked Warren if he'd noticed anything similar, he'd initially answered in the negative. He believed this to be true when he wrote it. His back and knees and the soles of his feet still hurt as much as they had before he saw the nimbus for the first time. His job was still only bearable, and his boss and his colleagues were still a source of frequent annoyance. His social life, with the exception of the subforum, was still as empty as it had ever been. He had no close friends, no congenial acquaintances, no one from past phases of his life with whom he'd kept up even minimal contact. Love still seemed entirely out of the question for him, and sex . . . Well, actual sex with other humans had somehow fallen by the wayside, like so much else in his life.

Warren continued to believe himself unaffected by the nimbus until one warm early evening in late April. It was the time of year when you could almost feel the days expand from one diurnal roll to the next. The western half of the sky was pink and yellow with long smudged lines of blue clouds, while the east bled indigo up from the invisible lake. Warren must have been thinking about something—he would not remember what even a few minutes later—because he did not see, until it was too late, that two white men in tracksuits, one skinny as a pike and the other square as a concrete block, were standing, smoking, just outside his apartment building.

The Weight looked up at Warren just as Warren realized that he was looking at The Weight. It was not a happy recognition. His first urge was to turn and run, but he was close enough that escaping was already out of the question. Fortunately another feeling—a wiser, more realistic

emotion, which expressed itself as a paralyzing flash of cold terror—
seized his legs and locked him in place.

I'll get you the money, Warren heard himself saying. He felt a pressure
in his bowels and clenched hard to keep it at bay. *Just please, let me be, I
promise I'll get you the money.*

Oh, it's too late for that, The Weight said ominously. *It's far too late for that.*

The concrete block rumbled with what Warren took to be a laugh.

The Weight looked at his henchman and nodded off to his left. *Go
keep an eye on the car. I don't want the cogs around here to run off with it
while we're not watching.*

The block looked confused. *You ain't gonna need my help?* He pounded
his fist, as big as a softball, into the palm of his other hand. *I'd really like
to give you some help, boss.*

The Weight spit on the street. *I said go watch the car.* When the block
was out of earshot, The Weight looked hard at Warren. *You live here,
right? This is your place?*

Warren nodded. It was pointless to dissemble.

*Take me up to your apartment. Come on, let's go. We've got some business
to discuss.*

So this is it, Warren told himself, as he climbed the stairs to his floor.
This is how the curtain is going to drop. His legs felt simultaneously
heavy and weak as he walked down the long hall to his apartment. He
took longer than he needed to withdraw his key ring from his pocket.
He exhaled hard and intentionally to steady his hand as he slotted the
key in the lock. His heart felt like it was about to erupt out of his chest.
He put his hand on the doorknob, and as he stepped over the threshold
he waited for the cold circle of steel on the back of his skull. His mind
was mostly static now, a radio on the fritz. For a single moment of clarity
he wondered if he'd hear anything, see anything, feel anything, before
everything ended for good.

Fucking go on, what are you waiting for? The Weight said. He was still behind Warren, who was still halted in the open door. His legs were locked again and refused to move until The Weight pushed on Warren's back with his fingertips. *Let's go. Let's go.*

Out of habit, Warren slipped off his shoes as he entered his apartment. He only belatedly appreciated the absurdity of the act. In a few seconds or a few minutes he would be a shit-stained carcass, blood and meat on the floor. No one was going to care about the dirt he tracked in from outside.

Where do you want me to go? Warren said, when he reached his kitchen.

Why are your hands up? The Weight said behind him. Warren hadn't realized they were. *I'm not the fucking cops. Just go somewhere we can talk. Don't you have a couch? A living room?*

Warren nodded and shuffled forward.

You know I'm not going to hurt you, right? The Weight said with an audible scoff, as though he'd just realized what Warren was thinking. *I mean, I appreciate the concern. But if I wanted you hurt, it would be Shrek in here and not me.* Warren was even more confused now than he had been before. What The Weight said next didn't make the situation any clearer. *This is not about the money. Second thought, let me put it this way. It's not only about the money.*

I don't understand, Warren said slowly. He wanted to believe what he'd just heard, but he still couldn't trust the words or their speaker. He led The Weight into the living room.

I just want to talk, The Weight said. He nodded at Warren's reading chair. *Come on, sit down. I promise I'm not going to hurt you. Not today.*

Warren remained standing. *What do you want to talk about?*

The boy. I want you to tell me where he is. I want you to tell me how I can see him again.

The Weight had loomed so ominously for so long in Warren's imagination that despite their previous encounters it was only now, standing a few feet from him in his own apartment, that Warren appreciated how unmenacing he actually appeared. He was tall, certainly, but he was not big enough, not broad enough, to be physically imposing. His arms and legs were long and lean; his pencil-eraser head sat atop a skinny pencil neck with a bulging Adam's apple. He did not look fragile, not exactly, but he also did not look anywhere near sturdy. Maybe he wouldn't topple in a breeze, but it was not hard to imagine him being knocked around by a decently gusty storm.

And then there was his face. Warren wasn't good with faces. He didn't usually notice them, didn't often remember them. He was no connoisseur of features, had no running catalog of eyes, noses, hairlines, jawlines, cheeks, and jowls. He could only tell you the color of his mother's eyes because he decided it was ridiculous that he couldn't remember spontaneously, and so chose to memorize the datum (hazel) as though it were any other ordinary fact.

In keeping with that general tendency, Warren hadn't recalled anything about The Weight's appearance from their previous run-ins. Yet even though he was, now, in at least as much danger as he had been before, Warren couldn't help marveling at the disjunction between the blond terror-jockey he'd pinned up on a wall of his imagination and the utterly ordinary pink face in front of him.

Like the rest of The Weight's body, his long, narrow face appeared as though it had been stretched by someone pulling at each end. This impression was enhanced by a thin, delicate nose that looked like it had been borrowed from a portrait of a brooding nineteenth-century authoress. His off-kilter blue eyes, which fell away from the centerline of his face at surprisingly steep angles, appeared as though they were frozen mid-sigh, just as his long cheeks, whose reddish-blond stubble could not hide their underlying pink tinge, seemed caught in a permanent blush. The face had nothing special about it: no spark of physical charisma, no aura of physiognomic authority. It was the kind of face you might expect to find on a rural mail carrier, not a criminal mastermind.

The Weight dropped his narrow frame onto Warren's sofa. *You're*

really just going to stand there, huh? Okay, so you know what happened at
that enchilada church. You don't know what happened after . . .

As The Weight launched into a rambling story, Warren found it
possible, finally, to believe that he might survive this day after all. The
Weight hadn't been lying about wanting to talk, so perhaps he wasn't
lying about not wanting to hurt Warren, either. He spoke without
pause or interruption for nearly twenty minutes, beginning with the
episode at the church (despite himself, he told Warren that story all
over again) and then moving on to a series of events that happened to
him in the aftermath of seeing the nimbus—none of which, he was
certain, were accidents.

In the course of The Weight's long monologue, Warren discovered
that one of his assumptions had been correct: the nimbus had scared The
Weight, badly. He was, by his own description, a believer. He declared
his belief not in the all-powerful, immaculately benevolent god of the
Christians, Muslims, and Jews—a dime-store Nietzsche, he said at one
point that churches were for fools and only the weak got on their knees
to pray—but in what he called "spooky shit." From the time he was very
young, he said, he'd been aware of many strange and inexplicable hap-
penings. He knew that ghosts were real, for instance; he'd been haunted
by a few of them himself. He'd had prophetic dreams that had saved his
life and kept him out of prison more than once. He'd also come to the
conclusion that there were powerful hidden forces in the world that were
usually chaotic and often working at cross purposes, but which occasionally people could learn to influence, and even control. Luca, he was sure,
was one of these people—though he guessed that the boy would need to
grow up before he could make proper use of his gift.

And the nimbus was a gift: The Weight had no doubt. The glow had
frightened him, he said, because he understood immediately that he was
in the presence of spooky shit . . . *and spooky shit, you don't fuck around*
with it. I seen guys who thought they were better or stronger than that stuff.
They all ended up the same way. He made his finger a blade and drew it
across his neck. *That's how my brother ate it. He got tangled up with these*

Haitian cogs who were into all that voodoo shit, and he thought he could out-smart them. Tried to get me to help him run a shuffle on them. I warned him, told him he was messing with stuff he didn't want to be messing with. But do you think that fucker was suddenly going to up and decide to listen to his baby brother? The Weight closed his eyes and shook his head. *Anyway, I saw that glowing kid and right away I knew I was dealing with something, what do they call it, paranatural. At first I thought you were lucky that kid liked you so much. It took me a while to realize, no, that wasn't luck. That was the spooky shit working. That was the spooky shit doing its thing.*

Up to this point, Warren had not said three words in response to The Weight's story. But now he felt compelled to interrupt him. *What do you mean doing its thing? What thing?*

The Weight looked surprised, and then, after a few seconds, he smiled broadly. *You don't know? You ain't figured it out yet?*

I'm not sure I know what you're talking about.

The Weight bit his knuckle and looked over his shoulder, out the window. *Fucking A, man. Ain't you supposed to be the smart one? Ain't you the guy with all the degrees? I'm pretty sure your mama even told me you were some kind of religious expert.*

Warren winced at the mention of his mother. *That was a long time ago. And it had nothing to do with this,* he said. *It had nothing to do with the nimbus.*

What's the nimbus? Oh, that's what it's called? See, I knew you were an expert.

It's not called anything, Warren said, his tone now edgier than he would have allowed himself even a half hour earlier. *That's just what they're calling it.*

So what else do you know, huh? What else have they told you?

It appears I know somewhat less than you do, Warren said.

The Weight heard the comment as a joke and laughed. *And you ain't figured out that this, this nimbus thing is kinda like a good-luck charm? Except it's not luck, like I said. It's the glow. It's whatever the glow is that's doing it.*

That is something I've heard, Warren said. *But I'm not so sure. I've seen the thing three times and I certainly haven't seen any luck come my way.*

The Weight leaned forward and put his skinny elbows on his skinny knees. *You've seen it three times? Where else?*

Warren winced; he'd said too much. *I know the boy's father a little. I see them around sometimes.*

The Weight sat up, clapped his hands, and rubbed his palms together. *Goddamnit! I knew it. I knew you'd know something.*

Warren did not like that response. He sat in silence until The Weight spoke again.

You still don't get it, do you? The Weight said. *Let me help you here, smarty-pants. When's the last time you seen me? Before now, I mean.*

At the church.

And why'd I want to see you at the church?

Presumably it had to do something with the money my mother owed you.

Close enough. It had to do with the money you owed me. And what happened after that?

What do you mean?

After the church. What happened with the money?

I don't know. I didn't really hear from you. Until today.

The Weight sat up and clapped his hands again. *Exactly! You think that was just a coincidence? You think I just forgot about you? I had someone watching you all this time. You think you just got lucky? Come on. That was it. That was the kid. That was the nimbus working.*

Warren let his thoughts drill along on The Weight's quasi-logic for a moment. It was nice to think the world worked that way: nice to think that there was something else out there for which or for whom the adamantine laws of physical nature and the chaos of human history were something less than obligatory. Warren knew this from personal experience.

In high school, he had talked himself into believing that the omnipotent, omniscient, and immaculately merciful Creator of the universe had made human beings just intelligent enough, and just free enough, that they were responsible for the sin that condemned them to an eternity of terrible torture, unless the same immaculately benevolent Creator had for inscrutable reasons decided in advance that they should not suffer such a fate, in which case they would receive the grace to enroll, as Warren had, in a Church that loudly proclaimed itself the only reliable arbiter of ethics, the only faithful steward of the sacraments, and the only trustworthy road to salvation.

As he got older and read more deeply into Catholic history, Warren had immersed himself in the writings of apophatics like Pseudo-Dionysius and Meister Eckhart and Angela of Foligno and Simone Weil. They helped him convince himself that Christianity was not about power. True faith was about abnegation. It was about emptiness. It was about rejecting any idea that God was a tidy transcendental signifier that made metaphysics susceptible to rational investigation. Still less was God the Big Daddy in the sky who existed to flatter our desires for safety and significance. On this point, Warren came to believe, the mystics fleeing the egotistical sublime and the nominalists like William of Ockham had it exactly right: God in God's infinity lay infinitely beyond all human categories of comprehension. To accept that fact was to understand that theology as such, the reasoned pursuit of truth about divinity, was strictly impossible. God was beyond being and beyond knowledge—or at least any knowledge that He did not disclose to humans directly.

All of this was very convincing to Warren, right up until it wasn't. What precipitated his departure from Catholicism was not a loss of faith in God so much as his loss of faith that we might have any idea what or whom God might be. It was not science that challenged his beliefs but history: the same study of history that had initially deepened his religious feeling now turned against it, fatally. History proved to Warren's disappointed satisfaction that the Bible and the Church, traditionally understood to be the two guarantors of the veracity of Christian doctrine, were almost laughably unsuited to that task. The Gospels couldn't even agree on Jesus's genealogy! And a Church that encouraged Crusades and cozied up to Fascists and did everything it could to hide the sexual abuse that was well-nigh endemic in its institutional ranks was not one he could trust to point sinners like him to heaven.

When the break finally came—when he decided that he could no longer call himself Catholic, or even a Christian—Warren was able to appreciate, in retrospect, what Freud, and Marx, and Nietzsche had all been trying to tell him: the religious refinement he'd sought in Divinity School was merely a sophisticated cover for unsophisticated psychological urges. He saw that Christianity's obligation to pray without ceasing, its promise of immortality, its high moral theatrics (in which every word, every deed, every thought was a skirmish in the cosmic war between God and Satan) had obscured the same ground-level existential insecurity that compelled The Weight to believe in ghosts and lucky charms.

But all of that was in the past. Warren was not like The Weight, not any longer. Whether God existed was still an open question for him, but he harbored no doubts about his own significance in the world. This was the great and terrible lesson that time had taught him, for what was seventy or so years set against the billions that preceded him, and the billions without him yet to come? The Christians, thinking themselves humble, liked to read out the words of Ecclesiastes at funerals: "We are dust, and to dust we shall return." But Warren knew that the situation was even more dismal than that. The same sun that fed the plants that fed the animals that fed him and all his ancestors and everyone else on Earth would someday expand and destroy even the dust that their bodies had once been. Not even the atoms would remain intact, for the sun would eat these, too, and split them, and fuse them into elements unrecognizable.

The luck is going on with you, man? You look like you just had a stroke. You still with me?

Yeah, I'm okay, Warren said, snapping himself back from his vision of solar annihilation. He adjusted his posture in his chair and brushed off the top of his pants. *I'm all right. I still don't know what this is all about, though. What do you want from me?*

The Weight smiled and rubbed his hands together. *Good question, good question. I like a man who knows how to get down to business. I told you I had a proposition for you. I want to make a deal. It'll be good for the both of us.*

Okay, Warren said dully. As relieved as he was that he was not about to be murdered, he felt himself in the heavy thrall of a post-adrenaline exhaustion spell. He wanted The Weight out of here. He wanted to take a nap.

I want you to take me to the boy again. I need to see him. I'm pretty sure whatever he did for me is wearing off. I need to get some more of that nimbus thing. I don't want my guys to come, though. Just me.

Warren thought for a moment before speaking. *I don't know where the boy is.*

The Weight looked at Warren skeptically. His tone turned sarcastic. *You said you knew his dad. Don't you think the chances are pretty good he's gonna be wherever his parents are?*

I don't . . . Warren stopped himself and thought again. *I don't know him like that. I met him a long time ago, like two decades back. We're not friends.*

I don't care what the fuck you are. Make up something. Tell him it's been a long time, you want to get a beer, play fucking Ping-Pong. I don't know. Just figure it out.

How is this good for me?

What?

You said this was going to be good for me. I'm not exactly seeing what you mean.

The Weight leaned forward on the sofa. His face puckered into a sour expression. *Oh, I get it now. You think you're better than me. You think I'm not good enough to see the kid. You think I'm not going to be good on my word.*

I didn't say that, Warren said. *I didn't even think that. I'm just asking you what's in this for me.*

What's in this for you is that when it's all done, I leave you the fuck alone. You do this for me and we're even. We're square. You never have to see me again, and I finally get to fucking forget about you.

What are you going to do to him? To the boy?

The Weight stared hard at Warren. *Jesus Christ, man, you must think I'm a real piece of shit. You think I'm going to fucking hurt the kid? What kind of monster do you think I am? Ain't you never heard of the goose who laid the golden egg? He's the fucking goose, man!*

You promise you're not going to hurt the boy?

The Weight put his hand on his heart. *I told you. I don't fuck around with spooky shit. I'm not gonna make the same mistake my brother did.*

And you promise you're not going to kidnap him or something?

Jesus, Jesus, Jesus. Come the fuck on. You think I want to deal with a fucking toddler? I had three of my own. Made that mistake too many times already. I just want to see the kid glow again. That's it. Meet his dad maybe, maybe work something out so I can get a little recharge from time to time. But that's between him and me. You just need to get me in the room. Do that, and you're off the hook. At least as far as the two of us are concerned.

Warren took a long, deep breath. *Okay*, he said finally. *Okay. I'll help you.*

SPRING QUARTER

THIRTEEN

The day before Paul's colloquium started benignly enough: Billy and Salma, sensing his nerves, treated him to lunch at the lacquered-wood pizza-and-hamburger joint on Fifty-Seventh Street, the same spot where the Chicago Seven planned the presidential campaign of Pigasus J. Pig back in 1968. Salma, bless her, spent most of the meal in reassurance mode. Mostly she confirmed what Adrian had told Paul earlier. Salma couldn't be certain that Paul was wrong to fear Marcus Doran—according to Adrian, he'd written a few days ago to say he still had some questions he was hoping to resolve at the colloquium—but even if Paul wasn't wrong, Salma was sure that Doran would not use this occasion to make his move. The colloquium was supposed to be little more than a formality. It was not the right setting for a ritual humiliation.

Besides, she said, word had it that Doran himself was on shaky ground. Though elsewhere in the University you could find departments where open combat was the preferred mode of academic politics, the Div School was not one of them. The centrifugal forces generated by so many scholars working at methodological cross-purposes (confessional theologians and atheist anthropologists, historians and philosophers, scriptural critics and structuralist mythographers) made it too fragile for spittle-flecked hostility, and so a norm of pseudo-civil passive aggression had taken hold. Doran might be an asshole—he was an asshole, Salma corrected herself—but he'd rubbed enough faculty the wrong way that there was already open talk of rescinding his joint appointment. He was smart enough to know that he had to be careful.

After lunch ended, Salma paid the bill and said goodbye. She had an afternoon section to teach for her Islam in European Literature class. Paul had planned to go back to the library to look over his proposal and his research notes one more time, but Billy wouldn't hear it.

You're ready for this thing. If I know you like I know you, you've read everything you were supposed to read five times through, and everything else at least twice.

I promise I have not—

Anyway, it's like a marathon, man. You've got to give your brain a chance to rest before the big day. Today's your day to taper.

Paul shot an incredulous look at Billy, who almost certainly had never run three consecutive miles in his life. *What do you know about marathons?*

Billy laughed. *I know as much about them as I do about dissertation colloquiums, which is to say that I know what my dear wife has told me. She's run six. Come on, let's go shoot some pool over at Dylan's.*

Paul thought for a moment and decided Billy wasn't wrong about the mental break. Doran was going to do what Doran was going to do. Paul wasn't going to change that now. *Okay, but I'm not drinking. No shots, no cocktails, no beer.*

One beer, you can have one beer.

I'm not going if you're going to force me to drink.

Okay, okay.

And we need to stop by the Review *first. I've got to drop off a few things.*

When they got to McGinley, Paul saw two men, both middle-aged, both wearing dark suits that pulled tight on their heavy frames. They were standing on the front stoop. In itself this was not unusual; every once in a while someone got lost or confused and ended up knocking on the door thinking they'd found the Student Research Office or the Hillel Center. Paul was slightly alarmed, however, to see that the front door to the house was open. Maybe a staffer at the *Review* had opened it to greet them, but if that was the case, he or she was nowhere to be seen.

Hi, can I help you? Paul said as he approached the stoop.

One of the guys, bald with a goatee, looked up from a clipboard. *You live here?*

I work here, Paul said. *This is the office of the* Graduate Review. *What can I do for you?*

The bald guy looked at his companion, who was taller and tanner and had a full head of jet-black hair. *It's just you in there?*

Paul didn't like where this was going. *Well, no, we've got a staff. About nine of us.*

About?

Depends on whether you count the intern.

Do you?

Paul couldn't tell if the guy was joking. *Depends on the day.*

I see. We're from Buildings and Facilities. We're doing a building audit.

Oh, yeah. It's just us. We mostly use the second floor.

The black-haired guy smirked and looked back over his shoulder at the open door. *I would hope so, given what we saw in there. You know this facility is a massive liability, right? Broken glass, busted-up furniture, exposed nails—it looked like someone even tried to start a fire in the fireplace?*

Oh, we didn't do that, Paul said quickly. *We didn't do any of it. That whole mess has been there longer than I have, and I've been working here for four years.*

That's not exactly what we want to hear, the bald guy said. *Look, we're going to need to get that cleaned up, and until we do, we can't have people going back and forth through the building. We've got someone coming over right now to change the locks and put in a key card system. I don't know why you don't have one already.*

You're going to lock us out? But what about the Review? *We've got a new issue going to press in a couple of weeks. Our computers, everything is all up there.* Paul felt the air go thin in his lungs.

I don't know about any of that. You'll have to talk to your supervisor.

What do you mean my supervisor? Like, the editor? He'd ask you the same question.

Is he like you?

What does that mean?

I mean, is he like you? You know, young.

He's in charge of the magazine.

He's on faculty?

No, he's a graduate student.

And who's his supervisor?

Paul scoffed. *You guys got some ID? I know you said you're from Buildings and Facilities, but I think I'd better be sure.*

Listen, kid—the bald guy started to say. The black-haired guy stopped him with a hand.

No, it's okay. It's a good question. He has every right and every reason to ask it.

The guy opened his wallet and showed Paul his staff ID. *Now it's your turn*, he said.

Paul was annoyed at himself for not expecting the turnabout. He showed the man his student ID.

Okay, Paul, thank you. So, I don't know what to tell you about your computers and all the rest. I do know that I can't let anyone in here with the first floor in the state it's in. The second floor we couldn't see, except for the bathroom and a conference room, because all those doors were locked and don't seem to work with any of our master keys. We're going to have to change those, as well, but assuming your offices are in better shape than the first floor, then you can have your editor talk to his supervisor, and they can talk to our office about what to do next.

Paul tried not to let his panic slip into his voice. *You guys can't do this. You don't understand*—

I can do this, and I am doing this, the black-haired guy said. *And for what it's worth, I do understand the most important thing, which is that I can't have people walking through this building when it looks like a demolition zone.*

Billy stepped forward. *Can he at least go and get some of the stuff he's going to need from his office? Pull some files off the computers?* He turned to Paul. *You've got books up there, right? And thumb drives. And probably some manuscripts or something.*

Paul nodded somberly, and said a silent prayer of gratitude to his best friend.

The bald guy looked at the black-haired guy and then back at Paul. *I'll give you five minutes. But be careful. I don't want an accident while I'm standing here.*

Paul walked past the men and then raced up the stairs, taking them two at a time. He unlocked his office, waited for Billy to come huffing up behind, and then locked it again once they were both inside.

Jesus fucking Christ. I'm fucked. We're fucked. This is the worst possible thing that could happen to me.

Breathe. It's going to be okay, Billy said. *But we've got to get you packed up.* He looked around. *It's way too obvious you've been staying here. Get those clothes. I'll get the sheets. The other stuff I think we can make look like a plausible office.*

Fuck. Fuck. Fuck. I've got to text Ross. This is a disaster.

Do you have any extra backpacks? Any bags with zippers?

The best Paul could do was a stack of tote bags the *Review* had printed for its sixtieth anniversary. Fast as they could, the two men emptied the filing cabinets that Paul had used for dressers and knotted the totes closed with the shoulder straps. Paul stuffed his bedsheet into his backpack and draped his fleece blanket across the back of his couch, like it was a lap rug. They were nearly finished when they heard heavy steps coming up the stairs. Paul and Billy stopped and looked at each other, and then at the eight or so bulging tote bags on the floor. Without a word, Billy opened the window next to Paul's desk and started dropping the totes to the sidewalk below.

Paul put on his backpack and unlocked the door. The bald man stood outside, less than a foot away. *I figured I'd check it out up here, since you have keys*, he said. *Mind unlocking the other rooms for us?*

Paul offered no more resistance; it bothered him not at all that the man might see Ross's well-used ashtray. After the man satisfied himself that the situation was as Paul had said it was, Paul locked up and led Billy down the stairs.

Want your toothbrush? the man called from overhead.

Paul looked up, and his heart sank. *My what?*

The man held up Paul's blue toothbrush. Paul bit his lips and said nothing.

You might want to grab it before you go. Wouldn't want to give anyone the wrong idea, like someone was living here.

Billy and Paul took the tote bags back to Billy's dorm. Billy said that Paul should just stay there for the night. He could sleep, as he usually did, on the fake-leather couch in the common room. Paul had done that before, usually after drinking too much wine or whiskey or moonshine on the roof of the building with his best friend and a few select freshmen. But precisely because he'd done it before, he knew it would not be a good option, not for tonight. Though Billy's freshmen all knew Paul by now, and though they seemed to have no problem with him camping out in their midst, they also saw no need (and why should they?) to adjust their habits for his sake. The last time Paul had stayed in the common room, during a blizzard that made Salma worry he was going to freeze to death if he stayed in McGinley, Paul had been kept awake past three in the morning by the popcorn-munching all-nighters. He was woken again, before six, by the early-bird athletes. He couldn't risk that the night before his colloquium.

With the dorm off the table, Paul swallowed his pride and called Carrie. She was surprised to hear from him. It was, as she didn't fail to mention, not just the first time they'd talked in nearly two months; it was also the first time they'd talked since she'd written a long and intense email practically begging him to be friends again. It was clear to Paul that Carrie had interpreted his lack of response as a reproach, and for this he could hardly blame her. He'd been a little irked by her note, and a little hurt by it, and also a lot busy helping the Bennetts during their crazy spell with the media. He told himself that when it was all over he would sit down and write Carrie back, but one thing and then another had kept him busy until it felt like it was too late.

In any case, Paul could tell almost instantly that staying at Carrie's apartment was as much of a nonstarter as staying at the dorm. She would let him, no question, if he asked her outright. But to ask her outright was a bridge too far. She was still angry with him: this much became obvious when she mentioned, early and unprompted, that she was still seeing the lawyer, and that she was happier than she'd been in a long time. Paul knew this was bait for a conversation he didn't want to have, not now and maybe not ever.

He was running out of options, but still it was with no small trepidation that Paul texted Adrian to see if he might, after all, take the Bennetts up on the offer of their guest room, just for one night. He had turned them down previously: though Adrian told him that Renata was fully on board, Paul had not been able to forget her expression when Adrian first suggested that Paul stay with them. He hated little more in life than feeling obnoxious or in the way, and anyway his situation at McGinley had been perfectly adequate as long as it lasted. He didn't need to insert himself into someone else's family, and he especially didn't need to insert himself into Adrian's. Now, though . . . well, now was another story.

Adrian texted Paul back right away, a series of rapid one-liners in his usual style:

Paul so glad you wrote.

Was just about to call.

Two things:

1/ Yes absolutely you can stay with us.

I insist on it, in fact.

Demand it haha!

But 2/ I'm not home right now.

Which actually makes it easier. My office is totally empty. It's all yours.

I flew down to Dallas last-minute to meet John Olson.

Really good stuff happening here.

Can't wait to tell you.

DON'T WORRY I'll be back for your colloq.

Have a flight out first thing tomorrow AM.

Will go straight to Harrison from Midway.

I'll call Renata right now and tell her you're coming.

I know you'll be worried because you're always worried.

But she'll be thrilled, trust me.

She thinks you're great.

A few minutes after his initial flurry of texts, Adrian wrote again:

Told you.

Renata says you definitely should come.

She's home so go over whenever.

Maybe just text her a five-minute warning on your way.

I'm sorry I can't be there.

But everything's going to be fine, trust me.

No, after what I heard today I think I can do that one better.

Everything's going to be great.

That evening, Paul brought a backpack with some clothes, his computer, and his toiletries over to the Bennetts'. Renata welcomed him and immediately filled half a fat goblet with red wine. (*Adrian said you'd need this*, she said.) The boys were already asleep, so Renata and Paul stayed up talking awhile over the wine, and then Renata took him to get settled in Adrian's office.

There was one other thing Adrian told me to tell you, she said before leaving. *He says the same thing to me, and it drives me up the wall, so I'll spare you. But I will say that I hope you sleep well tonight. I'm sure this colloquium thing is going to be fine.*

Paul laughed. *You can tell me what he said.*

Renata lifted her eyebrows. *You sure?*

Yeah.

He said you should just relax.

The next morning, Paul put on clothes and went downstairs. In the Bennetts' kitchen, at the table by the window, Luca and Max were eating cereal. Luca started hooting as soon as he saw Paul, and Max gave him a broad, shy smile.

Renata, who was standing at the counter with a knife in her hand, smiled, too, not shy at all. *Hey, there he is*, she said. She was wearing faded jeans and a white T-shirt and had her hair pulled back in a ponytail. She looked cute in a fit-mom sort of way. In front of her on the counter was a cucumber cut the long way, as well as a spread of baggied food and two open lunch boxes. *The boys have been waiting. Haven't you guys?*

Both boys nodded vigorously, like bobbleheads.

I told them they couldn't wake you up. They were very excited to hear you were here.

Paul, Paul, Paul, Max said. *Can I show you something?*

Let's give him a chance to eat some breakfast, Max.

But Mama, I want to show him before school!

Luca bounced in his seat and clapped his hands.

Not you! Max said sternly. *It's mine to show him.*

Renata stopped chopping. *Max, it's okay. You'll have enough time. Let Paul get some breakfast.* She turned to Paul. *I made you some coffee. It's usually Adrian's job so I'm not very good at it. But it ought to be drinkable.*

That's amazing, Paul said. *The only bad coffee is no coffee at all.*

Renata snorted. *You'd better not say that in front of your adviser. He just might change his mind about you.*

Paul took the coffee and tried a sip. *Well, it's excellent*, he said. *Best coffee I've had all morning.*

Renata smiled. *I hope you got some rest. Feeling okay about everything?*

Honestly, you saved my life, Paul said. He was only exaggerating a little. *I was just about ready to pack up my stuff and go sleep in the library.*

I'm glad it didn't come to that.

After finishing breakfast—he announced himself happy with Cheerios, much to the boys' delight—Max took him into the living room to show off a contraption he'd built out of colored plastic. He handed Paul three metal marbles, showed him where to drop them, and watched eagerly as they clacked down the chutes. *Here, let's do it again!* he said when the marbles were at the bottom. So they did. And then they did it again. And again. Luca waddled in to watch them do it a fifth time. Max refused to let him drop the marbles in the contraption himself, but a precocious spurt of demonstrative generosity prompted him to allow Luca to remain in his proximity for the sixth, seventh, and eighth runs.

Paul was mentally reviewing the main points of his dissertation proposal when he heard Renata talking quietly on the phone in the kitchen. It was Adrian, he realized. Paul couldn't make out what Renata was saying, but her tone, hissed and angry, only confirmed for him what the bare fact of the call had already revealed. Adrian should have been somewhere over Missouri by now. Definitely not in cellphone range.

Renata entered the living room and held her phone out to Paul with an outstretched arm. Her face remained blank even when Luca ran over to her and hooted to be picked up. *He wants to talk to you*, she said. Her voice was hoarse in a way it hadn't been five minutes earlier.

Paul got up off the floor and took the phone. *I'm sorry*, Renata said before she released it. *I'm really sorry.*

Four hours later, Paul was sitting at a round wooden table in Marcus Doran's office, staring despondently at the starfish-shaped speakerphone in front of him. The office was enormous: it occupied half the square footage of an upper floor in the stone tower of the University's ancient-looking History Building. To Paul it seemed nearly as large as the Dean's suite in Harrison Hall. Between the two long walls—one lined with enough books to constitute a private library in miniature, the other with five Gothic-arch windows lined up like boats in a marina—there was more than enough room for the table, two couches, three massive rugs, and an oak desk large enough to accommodate an uncut sheet of plywood. Through the windows Paul could see out to the far side of the Midway, where the University, having successfully driven down housing prices over several decades through a campaign of systematic impoverishment, had bought up all the land and was now in the midst of a new phase of quasi-colonial expansion.

On Paul's left sat Thomas Hart, the genial former priest who taught theology at the Div School. Hart was widely beloved at the Div School, which probably explained how he had so successfully resisted going emeritus despite being a year shy of eighty. His large head, mostly bald, was disfigured by old-mannish skin tags, brown liver spots, and what appeared to be a fairly severe case of keratosis. He had a long face that sagged as though it were made of wax left out in the sun too long. His eyes were fogged and rheumy, and his nose wore the telltale purple of a man who'd found no good reason among the laws of God or men to stop drinking after a third whiskey each night. Yet despite the obvious effects of age on his body, Hart's mind, especially his memory, was said to be as powerful as ever. He had once memorized the whole of the first part of Aquinas's *Summa Theologica* as the priestly equivalent of a party trick, and Paul himself had seen him quote from memory a whole impressive run of objections and *sed contras*.

Doran sat exactly across the table from Paul. Though he was a tall man, as Hart was, the appearance of the two could not be more different. Hart looked like he might stroke out if he made the mistake of drinking from a particularly strong cup of herbal tea. Doran, meanwhile, looked at least a decade younger than his fifty-eight years. His face was taut and lean, his eyes were small and black, and his chin came to such a sharp point that it would not surprise Paul to learn it had been used as a weapon in a street fight.

Doran was not, as far as Paul knew, a Catholic or even a Christian himself. But he shared with the zealots of that faith a belief that the mass of humanity, his students very much included, could not be trusted with its own judgment. You could see that conviction even in his scholarship: though he was savvy enough to make all the right noises about Urban's atrocities, it was impossible to ignore an underlying current of admiration for the pope's ruthlessness. To his mind, people in general (as well as in most specifics) were weak, stupid, and fickle: what they needed was a firm hand to point them in the right direction, and a steel-toed jackboot to get them moving that way.

Doran looked at his watch, and then he looked at Paul, and then he looked at his phone, and then he looked back at Paul. His expression did nothing to alleviate Paul's sense that he was in deep shit. It was now nearly fifteen minutes past the time when the colloquium was supposed to begin, and Adrian had not responded to any of Paul's or Doran's many attempts to get in touch.

He knows the time, right? Doran asked Paul for the third time. For the third time the question sounded more like an accusation than a query. *I can't sit here all day.*

He told me over the phone this morning, and he texted me, too, Paul said, as he had both of the other times.

Hart, who seemed not to notice Doran's crackling hostility, lifted his large head. *Perhaps we should reconvene another time, once Professor Bennett returns. It seems something must have come up that prevented him from joining us.*

Paul, who was at the point of having to remind himself to breathe, stopped mid-exhalation when he saw Doran's face and the upper halves of his ears turn a bright angry pink.

Absolutely not. I prepared for today. I set aside time for today. I cannot afford to postpone this. Doran's head was vibrating as he said this. Paul was suddenly glad to have the table between them.

Well then, Hart drawled. *What do you propose we do, Professor Doran? Surely we can't have a colloquium without Paul's adviser here.*

And why not? Doran said. *I'm here. You're here. Paul's here. We can do our part. Adrian can do his later. I don't especially need to hear what he has to say.*

That's fine, Hart said. *But as Paul's adviser, perhaps he might care what you have to say.*

Paul concentrated on taking another breath. He had not known that Hart was capable of even this much resistance. For a moment, he let go of his agnosticism and offered a prayer to the God Hart had once served as a priest. Please, Lord, he prayed, give him strength.

Fine, Doran said, still shaking. *We can record it.* He looked at Paul with a ferocious expression. *Do you want to do it on your phone? Or shall I do it on mine?*

Paul's mouth was too dry to answer. He took his phone out of his pocket, quickly checked his messages for any last sign of Adrian, and flipped to the voice memo app.

Very good, Doran said. *Let's get started.*

When Paul saw Adrian's name flash across his phone, he was walking over a freeway overpass in a part of Chicago he'd never visited before. It was several hours after the worst hour of his life, and he declined the call without a second's hesitation. If he never spoke to Adrian again, it would be too soon.

What Paul was doing on the overpass was a question he could not answer for himself with any precision. Not that he was thinking precisely on any subject right now. As soon as the colloquium had ended, he'd taken a bus, and then a train, to get himself far away from the University in a hurry. He'd gotten off the Red Line at Addison for no particular reason and had walked several miles west to get to where he was now.

Still in a daze, he kept walking until his phone buzzed to signal a new voicemail. Paul decided he had to hear Adrian's excuse once: once and once only. He had to know whether the betrayal was as pure and untainted as he assumed. If Adrian had been struck down in the street by a tank-sized pickup truck, or maimed to within an inch of his life by an errant shotgun blast, or if he'd fallen victim to some other extenuating circumstance that resulted in gross bodily injury, those facts would have done nothing to ameliorate the drubbing that Paul received from Doran during his colloquium. But the added pain—the additional pain, in some ways the deeper pain—of Adrian's absence might have hurt a little less.

He pressed a button and held the phone to his ear. He listened to as much as he was able, but before Adrian stopped talking Paul was vomiting into a storm drain at the far end of the overpass.

The colloquium had gone about as badly as it could have, which was far worse than the worst Paul had let himself imagine ahead of time. Doran had simply destroyed him. He had validated every one of Paul's doubts about his proposal, and then added on top of them a dozen new ones. He had objected to the project on theoretical, methodological, epistemological, practical, moral, and metaphysical grounds, and had suggested, more-over, that Paul's willingness to contemplate such a dissertation suggested a lack of scholarly judgment so dire that it was a wonder someone had let him into graduate school in the first place. He had accused Paul—fairly enough—of being addled by an abiding intellectual confusion, but then he'd gone on to level the further accusation—entirely unfair—that this confusion must be the result of too much coffee, alcohol, marijuana, and/or speed.

Paul had sat through it all, saying little except when prompted by a direct question from Doran. There were not many of those: Doran was clearly there to talk, not to listen, and Paul understood that there was no point trying to interrupt his diatribe. Nor had Hart been much help, even after he recognized that Doran appeared determined to end Paul's academic career on the spot. Hart had interjected where he could, he had contradicted Doran where he was able, and he had tried, more generally, to be a voice of steady conciliation. More than once he offered the reminder (ostensibly to Paul, though it was pretty clearly directed at Doran) that the colloquium marked the beginning of something, not the end, and that there was more than enough time to address everyone's concerns. Doran quite obviously did not want to hear this, but he respected Hart's seniority enough to let the comment dissipate in the dead air of his office before continuing his harangue.

At the end of the colloquium, eyes burning but not yet filling with tears, Paul had rushed out of Doran's office and into the hallway. The elevator didn't come until Hart had caught up to him. Once the doors were closed, the genial old cleric had turned to Paul with a look of sympathy. *I've been a professor for nearly forty years, Paul. I've probably supervised or sat in on upwards of two hundred dissertations. I'm sure you've heard a lot of people tell you how agonizing this process can be. It's true. Some of my colleagues, past and present, are quite awful to their students, and I personally have seen things in my time that I can hardly believe. We're going to get you through this. Professor Bennett and I will. But I want you to promise me one thing: if anyone ever suggests that you didn't have it that bad, that what that man put you through was just your run-of-the-mill academic hazing, I want you to promise me that, mentally at least, you'll tell them to fuck right off. Okay? I've never seen something like that. It was unacceptable, and I'm very sorry it happened to you.*

Paul wandered around north Chicago until nightfall. Eventually he decided he'd better get back to the South Side, to recover his things from the Bennetts before it got too late. Tonight and probably for the next week he'd have to sleep at Billy's dorm, but he understood already that it was time to leave Fell Gardens, and the University, for good. He had no idea what he was going to do next, or where he was going to go. He couldn't say if he was going to stay in Chicago, or whether he wanted to. On one point, however, he was clear. He was done: done with Doran, done with Adrian, done with his doctorate, done with the Div School.

He texted Renata when he was a couple of blocks from her house to let her know he was on his way. She wrote back right away. *Paul, I'm so sorry. Adrian told me. He's such an asshole. Anyway, I'm here, he's not. Feel free to come by.*

A few minutes later, she opened the door wide and said nothing. She was wearing a white blouse over jeans and had her hair twisted up in a bun behind her head. When she stepped back to let Paul inside, he saw that she'd set out a bottle of wine and two wineglasses on the table. *I know you probably don't want to hang around here*, she said. *But have a drink with me at least before you go. The boys are down. Come on, we can commiserate.*

It was a bad idea. Paul knew that. But so what? Evidently this was a good day for bad ideas. Paul understood that he was going to have to narrate the whole awful experience of the colloquium as soon as he got to Billy's—Salma especially would want to hear every detail—and that was not a task he was eager to undertake sober. Anyway, he'd always liked Renata; he'd gotten the sense she was interesting in ways her public presentation did not easily reveal.

He liked her even more for saying her husband was an asshole. As recently as yesterday Paul would have told anyone who asked that he owed his entire academic career, such as it was, to Adrian. Now, though, the liquidation of said career at the hands of Marcus Doran had wiped away every last iota of indebtedness. Paul was mostly feeling bad about his own failings—shame, disappointment, embarrassment, and grief were all churning inside him—but he did not find it difficult to dislike his adviser at the same time, and he was glad for Renata's validation.

Over the course of the next hour, Paul and Renata talked about the colloquium but not in detail. Renata seemed content to hear as much as Paul wanted to tell her without prompting, and what Paul wanted to tell her was not much. It was enough to convey that the occasion had been a disaster. Pretty quickly they moved on to other subjects: to the nimbus, of course, and the aftershocks of the media earthquake that had rocked their lives for nearly a month, but also to their parents, to their childhoods, and to poetry. They discovered a shared love of Wallace Stevens and George Oppen, and disagreed volubly about Ezra Pound. (Paul couldn't get "And then went down to the ship" out of his head; Renata felt the same about the anti-Semitic letters and the Fascist radio speeches.) The talk and the wine helped Paul to repress his agony. Once or twice, he even caught himself laughing.

By the time they finished a second bottle of wine, Renata had convinced Paul that there was no reason to sleep at Billy's dorm. Adrian was still in Dallas. His office was still unoccupied. The boys would be thrilled for another morning with Paul. Why compound a shitty day with a shitty night of shitty sleep on a shitty institutional couch?

Renata went to the kitchen and filled tall glasses of water for each of them. She brought the water back to the table and disappeared again into the kitchen. When she came back again, carrying a pint of raspberry sorbet and two spoons, she pulled her chair up tight next to Paul's and sat

down. She was sitting close enough that he could smell the wine on her
breath. He watched her open the pint, scoop a curl of sorbet, and hold her
spoon out. He leaned in and took the bite, and then he leaned farther and
kissed her with cold closed lips.

Until that moment Paul had wondered if he was misreading a shift in
the mood between them. There'd been hints all night—her insistence on
him staying over chief among them—but nothing unambiguous enough
for him to venture a move. It wasn't that he had any hesitation on Adrian's account; if anything, hooking up with Renata would be just the start
of the punishment his erstwhile adviser deserved. But the day had seen
enough humiliation already. Paul didn't think he could handle any more.

The thing with the spoon and the sorbet seemed a clear enough invitation that Paul was surprised to register Renata's surprise at his kiss. She
pulled back at first—not a lot and not far, but enough to suggest something other than eagerness. She looked at him while he waited for her
to make up her mind. Her gaze was nearly too intense to meet, a pair of
spotlights searching for something in the darkest night. After a few seconds she took Paul's chin in her hand and pulled him back to her. She let
him kiss her again, this time with open lips, and Paul felt her pull some
of the melted sorbet from his mouth.

They went on like that for a while, making out as though they were
new to the whole business of kissing, as though making out were enough
to satisfy them. But of course it was not enough to satisfy Paul, and after
enough time had passed that he felt his patience could not be called into
question, he reached down and put his palm on the inside of Renata's
jeaned thigh. She allowed this, but when he attempted to advance farther
up the seam, she reached down herself and seized him by the wrist. She
stopped kissing Paul and peered deep into his eyes again. She let her head
tip forward until her hairline touched his and took a heavy breath. They
sat like that for several long seconds, and then Renata leaned back and
pulled Paul's hand to her mouth. She gave him a long, light kiss on the
back of his knuckles, pushed her chair back, and stood up.

Paul watched her collect the empty wine bottles in one hand and the empty wineglasses in the other. He was certain it was over, finished no sooner than it had begun, but then she looked down at him with an expression somewhere between sadness and pity.

Are you coming? she said hoarsely. *If we're going to do this, we're not going to do it here.*

FOURTEEN

Renata was laughing. She was laughing even though she didn't want to be laughing, even though she'd tried, with whatever reserves of willpower the wine had not eroded, to stop herself from laughing. For a moment she'd allowed herself the illusion that a brief, heroic exercise of self-control might subdue the impulse. She and Paul were spooning on the sleeper couch—she could cheat on Adrian in his office, apparently, but she wasn't prepared to make him a cuckold in his marital bed—with her back to his belly and his rapidly deflating dick still smushed, a little uncomfortably, in the slickened crease it had made at the top of her buttocks. She bit her cheek and took a few careful breaths, counting silently to ten. It was hopeless. The urge to laugh was tectonic, the upthrust of hilarity irrepressible.

When the laughter broke through, causing her body to shake, Renata felt Paul press himself more firmly against her. His hand stroked her head just above her exposed temple, and his lips grazed the dimple of her nape. His breath was hot against her skin and carried the unmistakable tang of the foreplay he'd insisted on. *Are you okay?* he whispered.

It took Renata a moment to understand what accounted for this tenderness: Paul thought she was crying. The recognition made her laugh even more. Working herself free from the crook of his sideways lap, she rolled over so that he could appreciate his mistake. He tried to hide his surprise under a quick grin, but Renata could see that he was confused, and possibly even hurt. *I'm sorry*, she said, not at all convincingly. She leaned over to kiss him, as if to make amends. It almost worked, but he took her up on the offer a little too eagerly, and the enforced solemnity of the moment caused her to nearly bite Paul's tongue in half when she erupted again. She was still convulsed and quaking when another uncontrollable instinct made itself known. *I'm really sorry*, she said. She laid a hand on Paul's arm, an offering of contrition, and found her underwear among the sheets. *Give me a minute, all right? I've got to pee.*

Was she okay? It was only when she was seated on the toilet, depositing what felt like a jeroboam of red wine into the bowl beneath her, that Renata fully grasped the absurdity of the question. She was still pretty drunk and had just thrown away a decade of unilateral monogamy for a louche affair with her lousy husband's grad student. Of course she wasn't okay. She was *fantastic*.

The sex itself had been clumsy, vigorous, and fun. Renata had forgotten what it was like to sleep with someone when the moves were not all choreographed in advance. Paul didn't know what she liked. He didn't know where she was ticklish or sensitive. Fortunately it hardly mattered: after a few tactical gropings, she very quickly found herself flat on her back on the edge of the bed, with her jeans on the floor and Paul lapping energetically between her thighs. Their drunken pace was tempered only by their drunken unfamiliarity. Yet even the missteps (the clicked teeth, the awkward angles, the painful blasts of premature intensity) gave the whole business an air of enticing inefficiency. Everything between them was new and unpredictable. Everything was exciting.

Renata was not surprised to come before Paul did; her body knew what it needed and knew how to get it. She was, however, confused to feel Paul withdraw himself just before releasing a warm spurt onto her belly. A little recklessly, but only a little—she trusted her IUD, and trusted Paul's epidemiological assurances—she had told him not to worry that he didn't have a condom, and might have figured that settled the question. But as Paul would explain to her later, with no small amount of amusement, that assumption betrayed her long absence from the open market: how, or at least where, a coupling was to meet its final conclusion was the subject of a new scruple, an additional link in the chain of consent that well-meaning men like Paul were now expected to obtain.

Renata flushed the toilet and cleaned herself up. Before returning to Adrian's office she stopped off in her own bedroom to get the blue T-shirt she wore most nights to bed. Paul was naked under the sheet, scrolling through his phone, when she returned. He put the phone down, and tried to pull her back to horizontal when she sat on the edge of the mattress. *Stay*, he said.

Mm-mmm. Not a chance, Renata said, resisting his tug. *As soon as I lie down I'm going to pass out. I can guarantee you I'm going to have one or both of the boys crawling into my bed tonight. It's not going to go well for any of us if they can't find me.*

Okay, okay, Paul said. *Will it be a problem? That I'll be here in the morning?*

Renata laughed. *That's what you're worried about?*

Paul laughed, too. *I'm not worried about anything. Not for my sake. But I don't want to make any trouble for you.*

Renata couldn't keep herself from smiling. *Well, that's very sweet of you, but if that's the issue, perhaps you should have considered that half an hour ago.*

Paul gave an exaggerated pout. *You know what I mean.*

I do. Renata put her hand on Paul's hairy thigh. *And I appreciate your concern. But this is my problem to deal with, not yours.*

It's a little bit my problem. He is my adviser.

Renata scoffed. *You're going to keep him as your adviser after all of this?*

Well, no. No, obviously I can't do that.

Exactly. So then you don't need to worry about it. I'll tell Adrian that letting you stay over was the least I could do, after what happened today. Technically it won't even be a lie.

That's it? That's all you'll say?

Renata searched Paul's face. She couldn't tell from his tone whether he was disappointed or merely curious. *For now,* she said. *But that's going to be up to me.*

Paul took her hand in his. *Okay,* he said finally. *That's fair. I just don't want you to suffer for this. I like you a lot. Obviously. I mean, I wouldn't be here if I didn't. And the last thing I'd want is for you to get hurt.*

Renata moved her hand up to Paul's face and stroked him just above the ear. He looked so young, and he sounded so lost. She wondered what he would do now. Where he would go. Who would help him. Did she really just have sex with this poor confused boy? Renata felt a frisson of scandal at the thought, and she couldn't honestly say she disliked it. She felt another surge of the maternal feeling she'd felt for him earlier in the night, the same warm instinct that had prompted her, somewhat ridiculously, to offer him sorbet from her spoon. At Paul's age she would have found his reaction bizarre and confusing. You feed a man like a child and he thinks it's a turn-on? Not until she married Adrian had Renata understood how right Freud had been.

I appreciate that, Paul, she said. *And I don't regret a second of what just happened. Not yet, anyway. That was very nice, and if my head wasn't pounding already with the wine I might even say we should do it again. But you can't be the good guy here. None of us get to be the good guy here.*

He frowned. *What do you mean?*

I mean we did what we did. I know you didn't want to hurt me, but you did want to hurt Adrian. So did I. I'm not saying that's the only reason I just had to wash your semen off my stomach. But let's be adults about this. It's definitely one of the reasons. Probably one of the big ones.

Paul thought for a moment. *Okay,* he said. *I can live with that.* He took her hand again and squeezed it, then tried pulling her down close to him again. *You're sure you don't want to go again? One more for the road?*

Once again Renata resisted his pull. She stood up, and only once she was secure on her feet did she lean down to kiss him on the cheek. *I'm sure. Thank you for tonight. Sleep tight.*

He was gone the next morning when she got up. He'd left, apparently, even before the boys were awake, for when Renata asked Max if he'd seen Paul, Max looked at her like she was crazy. *Uh-huh, Mama. Yesterday, remember? He stayed with us.*

It was a long day waiting for Adrian to get home from Dallas, and Renata spent most of it trying to crawl out from under the nauseating thumb of her hangover. This effort was helped not at all by the fact that Luca started glowing just before lunch. (The appearance of the nimbus was duly reported by an aggrieved Max, who understood that it meant he'd be trapped in the house all afternoon with his brother.) She was surprised, however, to discover that her regrets about the wine were not matched by similar regrets about Paul. Renata was no stranger to shame; she was the kind of person, Adrian liked to joke, who could find a way to feel guilty for breathing someone else's oxygen.

Cheating on her husband was indisputably a fault, however boringly bourgeois it might seem. And yet Renata felt not even a twinge of remorse about sleeping with Paul. What she'd said to him the night before was true enough: pretty obviously they had both wanted to hurt Adrian, and for good reason. She was certainly angry at him for the Dallas fiasco. (On Paul's behalf, yes, but also her own: she'd been on a nonstop jag of caring for the boys, and Adrian hadn't even bothered to ask if he could extend the trip that she hadn't wanted him to take in the first place.) She understood now, though, that she'd been angry at a deeper level, too, a level she could only appreciate in retrospect.

At the same time, as real as Renata's anger was—as insistent as the demand for justice it contained—Renata felt that these alone could not wholly account for her weird absence of recrimination. It was too neat, too tidy to say that Adrian had fucked her and Paul over, and so therefore they had fucked each other. She began to wonder if, and pretty quickly began to suspect that, her equanimity might have something to do with Adrian's own affair, five years earlier. Renata had never consciously thought of herself as holding a get-out-of-jail-free card after Adrian let himself get seduced by the tenured hussy, but maybe her subconscious had other ideas? This wouldn't be the first time.

It was probably too much to say that sleeping with Paul had quenched her resentment toward her husband. Yet as she played with the boys, and fed the boys, and put the boys down for their naps, and played with the boys again, Renata couldn't help noticing a strange lack of anger that seemed to be the flip side of her strange lack of guilt. At regular intervals she reminded herself that at least a little demonstrative annoyance would probably serve her well. Adrian would expect her to be upset; he'd heard her frustration on the phone the day before, and had already begun brewing the mix of excuses and justifications that he would offer up in place of an apology. Renata wasn't sure yet whether she was going to tell him about Paul, but until she decided, she didn't want him to have any reason to wonder about her complacency.

Renata's reminders to herself turned out to be unnecessary. Adrian came home that night in a boisterous, almost obnoxiously ebullient mood. He swept in through the front door and belted a *Hello* that was loud enough to startle Max out of his fragile sleep. When Renata rushed out from the boys' bedroom to quiet him—she'd nearly passed out herself while lying with Max on his mattress—Adrian swept her up into a hug, grabbed her butt with both hands, and gave her a forceful, overdramatic kiss. He stepped back to show her his new clothes: stiff black Wranglers, a Garth Brooks–looking Western shirt with blue and black panels, and a pair of shiny black-leather cowboy boots.

What in the world are you wearing? Renata said. He looked far too absurd for her to muster any anger. She didn't even try to keep herself from laughing.

A gift from John Olson, Adrian said, his eyes twinkling.

He bought all that? He gave it to you?

Adrian put his hands on his hips and cocked a heel. *Pretty great, huh? He said if I was going to be coming down to Texas with any regularity then I should learn to dress like a Texan. Plus I think one of his minions heard me mention that I hadn't packed enough clothes for a four-day trip. Honestly, I think this trip changed my life—our life, hon. This guy, my god. I can't wait till you meet him. You're going to love him. He's seventy-eight and he has more energy than most of my students. He's richer than shit, he's smart in this charming kind of amateur way, he's a huge reader—you wouldn't believe how much he's read—and you want to know the best thing about him?*

He farts rainbows?

Wouldn't surprise me in the least. But no, this guy, I'm telling you, he's unlike anyone I've ever met. He's just got this tremendously open mind. The way he thinks about the world, it's like, he really seems to think anything is possible. I guess it's the money, I don't know. It seems clear that has something to do with it. You tell him you can't do something because of X, Y, or Z reason and he just laughs. I told you he wants to endow a research center at the Div School, right? Not a small one, either. We're not talking the kind of piddly little pissant thing the Dean likes to make up to flatter his senior faculty. Olson wants the real deal. We came up with a name—well, I kind of came up with a name: The Olson Center for Religion in a Secular Age. I told him everyone would end up calling it the Olson Center, and he loved that. He's going to donate ten million dollars to start it up. Ten million dollars, hon! Do you know what that will get us? And he said that was just for starters, to get us off the ground. At one point I said—I mean, I was trying not to let us get too far ahead of ourselves—I said to him, "So what happens if the University doesn't want to do all this? Or if they don't want to do it this way?" And he said to me, "You ever seen a university turn down ten million dollars? And if they do, then to hell with them—we'll go somewhere else."

Easy for him to say.

Yeah, but that's the thing. I told him that. Well, not exactly that. But I told him it wouldn't be so easy to move to another school, not with me just getting tenure and everything. He laughed. He said, "Adrian, I'll get you a tenured professorship anywhere you want. Harvard, Yale, Oxford, you name it." Which, you know, obviously was nice to hear. But the thing is, hon, it went so much more beyond that. He sees the whole world that way. It's like what you and I are used to thinking of as the limitations of reality are for him at best suggestions, or maybe the starting point for a negotiation. The guy, I'm telling you. He's raunchy as hell, got this big Texas attitude and this big billionaire ego, but he's a real seeker, I could tell. He's got enough money to buy anything he wants. He could probably buy a country. But he knows it's not enough. He knows there's something else out there, something that's hovering there just outside our grasp. That's why he's so into the nimbus. He has this theory, it's kind of crazy but no crazier than anything else we've come up with. He's a Christian. He believes in God, he believes in Jesus. But he told me he's convinced that there are spirits out there trying to tell us something before it's too late.

Spirits.

Yeah, you know, like angels or something. He said he's been collecting evidence of things like this for a while. Things like the nimbus. He thinks they're a kind of message.

And what exactly is this message supposed to be saying?

I'm not sure. He wasn't totally clear on that.

No, of course not. Why be clear when you've got ten million dollars to spend on vague insinuations?

Renata, come on. Don't you see what this is? Don't you see the opportunity?

Adrian, have you forgotten that this is Luca you're talking about? Your son? I understand exactly what you think this is. That's what worries me. A loopy billionaire believes our little boy is channeling messages from the great beyond. How is that supposed to end well for any of us?

Renata. It's not like that. He's not like that.

You just met him, Adrian. How do you know?

I think I'm a pretty good judge of people. I was smart enough to marry you, wasn't I? Adrian offered a conciliatory smile and reached with both hands for Renata's waist. She backed away from him before he could pull her into a hug. *I don't think I explained it well. It's not that Olson thinks Luca is carrying a specific message. He's not one of these nuts who thinks the end of the world is coming next week or anything like that. He just thinks that these higher beings, these angels or whatever, are trying to remind the world that they exist. That there's something else out there.*

And you think that sounds just dandy.

I already said I thought it was kind of crazy.

And yet still you're eager to take his money and let him do whatever he wants to do with Luca.

Come on. You know I wouldn't—

You think this guy is going to give you ten million dollars for a center with his name on it, and he's not going to expect anything in return?

Honestly? I do! I know you're not going to believe this, but I actually asked him a version of that question. And you know what he said? He told me the same thing that I'm always trying to remind my students. He said nothing worth doing is worth doing if it's not risky. He said his whole career he's had people telling him he was going to lose everything if he took this, that, or the other chance. Anyway it's not like ten million dollars is a lot for him. He probably spends that on cowboy boots in a year. Plus he swore to me up and down that he has neither the inclination nor the time to microman-age. He said over and over again that he wants to do things right. He wants serious scholarship, and he knows that means he needs a serious scholar in charge. He wants me to run this thing. Not him. I'm going to have final say over anything we do or don't do. He's not going to meddle. He really doesn't want to half-ass it.

Adrian, please. You're too smart to be this dumb. This guy is just doing the thing rich guys always do. He can't get the world to pay attention to his nutty ideas on the merits, so he decides to throw money around until people start listening, or pretending to.

And what if they're not all nutty?

Renata looked at her husband and let out a long sigh.

Not the Christianity stuff. Obviously I don't go in for all that. But the fact remains that our son is still glowing, and nobody knows why. You keep talking like that fact isn't a fact. It's like you cannot accept that this is all actually happening.

Renata looked down at her bare feet and felt tears welling in her eyes. *Yeah, well*, she said quietly. *Can you really blame me?*

The next morning. Renata was sitting at the table in their kitchen while Adrian made lattes for each of them. They hadn't talked much before going to bed, and had barely said three words to each other after they woke up. Now, though, as he brought her coffee over to the table, twisting the cup so the stem of the tulip-like design in the foam was properly oriented, he told her that he'd stayed up late thinking about their conversation. He still thought Renata had the wrong idea about Olson, he said, but after thinking about it over the course of a long and sleepless night he could appreciate better why she might be suspicious. She hadn't met the man. She hadn't looked into his eyes and seen the sincerity that Adrian had personally witnessed, and so it was understandable that she'd still have some doubts. A lot was happening, and it was happening very fast, and Adrian said he'd realized he hadn't done enough to bring her along. He felt bad about that, and he was sorry.

This is a strange sort of apology, Renata almost said. But she, too, had slept badly the night before—Max woke her twice, and she'd had to get up a third time to pee—and her appetite for a fight, or even another spat, was at a low ebb. Instead she accepted her coffee from Adrian in silence, hoping that a display of quiet acquiescence would encourage him to postpone the conversation he clearly wanted to have.

She was not so lucky. Adrian brought his own coffee over to the kitchen table and sat across from her. He reached across the table and took her hand in one of his. He looked at her significantly. That wasn't all, he said. He'd realized there was something else going on, something for which he also owed her an apology. What she'd said about the nimbus the night before had helped remind him that it was far too easy for him to forget that she couldn't see it. For him it was totally natural that their family's little world had been turned upside down by what was happening to Luca. But he could only imagine how it all felt to Renata. Her life had been thrown into total upheaval for something she couldn't see for herself. Adrian said he hadn't fully appreciated how much she was being asked to take on faith.

Even very recently Renata would have been gratified to hear Adrian say exactly those words in exactly that order. Not that they would have helped everything, but they might have helped something. This morning, however, Adrian's belated awareness only added to her aggravation. She wasn't thinking about divorce (she couldn't begin to contemplate dealing with the logistics of a separation), but she felt done with her husband in some deep sense that was just beginning to make itself clear.

I think I need some time, she said, answering Adrian's stare with a hard look of her own. She wasn't quite sure what she meant, but whatever it was was different than what Adrian heard.

Of course! he said brightly. His tone sounded as though they were negotiating the terms of a deal and he'd just heard a first offer that was far lower than he'd expected to pay. *Of course you do. I actually was going to suggest that. You should take the day. Take the car. Go get a massage. Get your nails done. I'll watch the boys. Really, anything you want, I want you to go do it. Don't worry about us. We'll be fine.*

It did occur to Renata, on her way up to Ukrainian Village the next day, that if she wanted to be especially perverse about it, she could interpret Adrian's last remark as permission to see Paul again. But that would suggest that she wanted to see Paul again, which in turn would suggest that she wanted seeing Paul to mean something other than it did. And she didn't want that. She didn't want any of it. What happened with Paul was pleasant to think about—her body enjoyed the memory even more than her mind did—and she was coming around to the opinion that it or something like it might have been necessary, might even have been inevitable.

But it was also, clearly, a one-off. Renata had no doubts about that. It was easy enough to say that she liked Paul: she liked talking with him, liked drinking with him, liked watching him play with the boys, liked being naked with him in bed, even if his eagerness had reminded her how well she'd trained Adrian over the years to respond to her needs before his. She also felt bad for him. She felt bad about what Adrian had done to him, and felt bad, too, that Adrian seemed not to feel bad about it at all. When he got home from Dallas, he'd apologized to her but said nothing about flaking on Paul. Nothing in his demeanor suggested he had any idea how much anguish he'd caused.

Renata liked Paul and she felt bad for him, but she counted it one of the hard-won lessons of her life that these were not enough, either separately or together, to even begin to make her think she had any kind of future with him. Though she couldn't honestly say whether she still wanted a husband, she was certain she didn't want a boyfriend. And if she was going to have a boyfriend, it wasn't going to be a twenty-eight-year-old grad student in the midst of a quarterlife crisis.

Renata drove north until she found a parking spot on a side street near the Double Door. She walked back south to Division. It was a bright and clear May weekday, temperate in every dimension. Adrian had misunderstood what she was telling him, but she was not sorry about taking him up on his offer for a day away from the boys. And while she had cringed a little when he told her to get a massage and get her nails done—cringed not because he was wrong about how she wanted to spend her free time but because he was right—she was glad that she hadn't let that stop her.

Renata arrived at her favorite massage parlor, said hello to Marlene, a green-haired pixie with tattoos from her wrists to her ankles, and made her way to one of the back rooms. She undressed and lay prone on the draped table. Marlene came in, pushed play on an old-style iPod, washed her hands, and started working the knots in Renata's upper back. As Renata lay with her face in the cushioned doughnut, she started thinking again about Paul. While they were drinking wine before they'd hooked up, he'd told her that he was probably done with graduate school. Renata had pressed him gently on this point, wondering if perhaps it was too early to make a decision that monumental, but he was certain. While he did not seem eager to divulge too much of what was actually said in the colloquium, he alluded to it in a low tone of terrified awe, like someone who had witnessed something horrific, something unspeakable.

The day after the affair, Renata had told herself that Paul's insistence about the end of his academic career was one of the reasons she had not stopped herself from sleeping with him. Practically if not technically, she could let herself believe, by the time they'd hooked up he was no longer Adrian's graduate student, and this in her mind somehow made it better for all three of them. Maybe that was even a little bit true, but now that she was past the point of needing to justify herself to herself—the dizzying, not entirely unpleasant confusion of sifting through how she'd become *that kind of woman* had lasted all of about twenty-four hours—something else struck her about Paul's snap decision. He was right. Of course he was right. Leaving was absolutely the correct decision.

Renata and Adrian had started dating when he was in the middle of his own academic crisis, back when he was an adjunct and beginning to wonder if he'd ever find his way to a tenure-track position. Back then Renata had understood what being a professor meant to Adrian, and because she loved him she wanted him to succeed. She was a modern woman. She was a feminist. She did not intend to let his ambitions trump hers; stated as baldly as that, she would have rejected the suggestion out of hand. Yet that's what happened. Somehow, without meaning to, without even really noticing, she'd slipped into a stereotype. She'd pushed Adrian to follow his dreams even as she was in the process of abandoning hers. She'd worked for money so that he could chase his intellectual destiny. He'd kept at it and so had she—running her business, raising their kids, forgetting that she'd ever wanted to do anything else—until eventually he got nearly everything he wanted: a good job, two books with his name on the cover, tenure. And now he was on the verge of founding an academic center with millions of dollars at his disposal. And for what? All so that he could treat the kid he routinely described as his first and favorite grad student as shittily as Adrian's professors had treated him? All so that he could exploit his own son to secure himself a spot in history?

Renata knew that it was grotesque to envy Paul anything after what he'd been through. Clearly he was devastated, and as bad as Renata had been feeling of late, she was not that. Still, he was a smart guy, handsome if not particularly her type, and he seemed to possess none of the off-putting social peculiarities that afflicted so many of Adrian's colleagues. Plus he was not even thirty, with no kids and no family. No job but also no obligations. He had a whole fresh life ahead of him if he wanted it. A clean break. A blank slate. Maybe Renata didn't really want to leave Adrian. Definitely she didn't want to leave her boys. But she could be forgiven—couldn't she?—for indulging the fantasy of that kind of freedom.

Renata stayed away from the house all afternoon and into the evening. After the massage she went for lunch at a sushi place on Milwaukee, and then she scored a walk-in appointment at a hair salon she'd heard good things about from a friend. The haircut was nothing complicated—a tryout disguised as a trim—and when it was finished she walked back down to Division, to a bar with sidewalk tables that she'd spotted on her drive into the neighborhood. Kicking herself for forgetting a book, she pulled a *Reader* off the rack and ordered a draft IPA. She drank the beer and read the paper at a wire table on the sidewalk, and let herself be delighted when a shag-bellied golden retriever ambled over from a couple with a baby stroller and nuzzled her legs.

When she got home, after eating a slice at a Roman-style pizza place near the sidewalk bar, the sky in the west was a deep orange and the moon was up over the lake. The house was quiet: the boys were asleep, the kitchen was clean, and Adrian was nowhere visible. Renata went upstairs and saw a line of light under the door of his office. An errant thought made her pause before knocking: Had she and Paul been found out? She couldn't imagine how it would have happened—she'd washed the sheets, erased the texts she and Paul had sent each other before he came over, checked and rechecked the room for incriminating evidence—but it was easy to imagine that this is what getting caught would look like. Adrian would be sitting inside, waiting for her, stewing in his rage.

Stop being crazy, Renata told herself. She knocked quietly on the door.

Yeah, I'm in here, Adrian said. Renata heard nothing angry in his muffled voice, but still she took a deep breath to steady herself before turning the doorknob.

Adrian looked up from his computer and smiled when she entered. He looked genuinely happy to see her, and for the first time in nearly a week she was not unhappy to see him.

Come here, he said, *you've got to see this.*

Renata walked over and stood behind him. She let him take her hand in one of his, let him absentmindedly tangle his fingers in hers while he scrolled through something on his screen.

Check this out. This is really unbelievable. The screen's contents wheeled upward as he flicked the dial on his mouse.

I don't know what I'm looking at, Renata said.

Someone I know from a long time ago just sent it to me. It's a whole forum of people talking about Luca. Talking about the nimbus.

Renata felt her stomach drop. *Oh no, Adrian. Not again.*

No, hon. It's not like that. This is not like the other time. This is just ordinary people. Some of them have seen it. Some of them want to. They've got all kinds of theories about what's causing it, but that's not even the best part.

I'm waiting.

The people who have seen it, they say it's been helping them.

What do you mean?

I'm going to send you some of these posts. You've got to read them. Some of these stories are heartbreaking. People are sick, they're broke, they're abused, they're depressed. It just goes on and on. But then they saw the nimbus and their lives started to get better. It's not like a miracle, not an acute miracle anyway, but they're convinced there's a cause and effect situation here.

Renata pulled her hand back. Whatever slight good feeling she was beginning to feel for her husband was gone again. Adrian, still scrolling, didn't seem to notice.

It's not the craziest thing in the world. I mean, I never thought of it this way. But look what happened with Olson. Think about what's happened to us.

Yes, Renata thought, already stepping back toward the office door. Just think about what's happened to us.

FIFTEEN

You want another one of those, honey? A big-haired, broad-bosomed waitress stood over Warren's table, near the front window of the Greek diner on Fifty-Seventh Street, and nodded down at his nearly empty Diet Coke. Warren knew the waitress well but not by name: she'd been working at the diner at least as long as he'd been coming to eat there. Over two decades he'd watched her hair go gray and her skin get loose and her eyes turn yellow, and he was certain that the report from her side of the order pad was at least as depressing.

Sure, Warren said, even though his bladder was warning him against it. *Sure. Thank you.*

When the waitress left, Warren looked over at the front door, with its dangle of sleigh bells, and then out the big gold-lettered window. Seeing no sign of Adrian, he checked the time on his phone, and then his messages, and then his email, to confirm, as he had several times already, that he was not mistaken about the time and place Adrian had chosen for their appointment. As he knew already, the email said twelve thirty, which meant that Adrian was nearly twenty minutes late.

Technically, the meeting at the diner was Adrian's idea, even if it also happened to be the idea (or something very much like the idea) that Warren hoped he would have. *We should talk,* Adrian had written, after Warren emailed him a link to a long thread on the subforum in which several of the members said they wanted to see Luca again in real life. *Just you and me. Not the others, not yet. We can get lunch. My treat.*

Warren had initially interpreted the brief note as a sign that the scheme he'd set in motion had a chance of success. Now he wondered, though, if he'd misread Adrian's tone. His first assumption was that Adrian's request to meet one-on-one was as straightforward as it sounded. But maybe that was wrong? Maybe Adrian had figured it all out? Maybe he'd set up the lunch as a kind of trap, to test Warren, and then to reveal that he'd been caught out.

Warren told himself that he was getting too far ahead of himself. Way too far. Nothing Adrian had said suggested he had any suspicion of Warren's motives. And even if he did suspect something, so what? There was no way Adrian could know anything about The Weight, so at worst Warren's desire to get Luca in a room with the subforum members would have to seem like a pretty minor and understandable deception.

Warren picked up the laminated menu and scanned the diner's offerings. He knew exactly what he was getting for lunch—the only thing that had changed in twenty years was the prices—but still he found it calming to examine the words on the menu as though he were reading them for the first time. *Spanakopita. Gyro sandwich. Shepherd's salad.* He took the paper cap off the straw in the Diet Coke the waitress brought him and then checked his phone again. Still nothing.

Finally, at five past one, Adrian blew through the belled door with a flushed face and sweat-soaked hair. He was wearing beige pants and a plain white shirt that was damp around the armpits and unbuttoned almost to his sternum. On one wrist he had a bracelet made of wooden beads; on the other, he wore a large and expensive-looking metal watch that looked like it was built for undersea diving or piloting a space capsule.

I'm so sorry, he said as he sat down. *For some reason I thought we'd said one thirty. I ran all the way here.*

It's okay, Warren said.

I've just got so much stuff going on right now, you wouldn't believe it. Miss! Miss! Adrian flagged down the waitress and nodded at Warren. *I've kept this poor man waiting and now he's going to have to get back to work soon. Take his order and I'll be ready as soon as he's finished.*

The waitress was clearly not happy about being bossed around, but she wrote down Warren's order (a cheeseburger, no lettuce or pickles) and waited dutifully for Adrian to make up his mind. After he settled on a chicken salad, he didn't wait for the waitress to leave before telling Warren exactly what he had come to the diner hoping to hear.

So look, man. I read everything you sent me, Adrian said, still sounding like he was out of breath. *Then I went and I read pretty much everything else on that website, most of it twice. I've got a few questions for you, but honestly, I think we should do it.*

Yeah? Warren felt a smile coming on and put a napkin to his mouth to conceal it.

I do. I think it's . . . honestly, I think it's pretty fucking amazing. These people, what they've been through. I showed some of the posts to my wife, and—I mean, first off, you've got to know that she can't see the nimbus and she hates pretty much everything to do with it, like I think she really and truly wishes it never happened—anyway, even she was moved by some of the things people were writing in. I honestly don't know if the nimbus can help them. But if they think so, I kind of think we owe it to them to try. I mean, my god, that woman whose daughter nearly died in childbirth? Or the guy who was ready to off himself before he happened to see us when we took Luca to the chapel? And they're both sure the nimbus helped them.

They're not the only ones. Not by a long shot.

Adrian sat back in his seat and focused on Warren a look of intense inquisition. *Say more.*

Warren understood in that moment what it must feel like to be one of Adrian's students. He tried to break the spell of the gaze with a shrug. *Sounds like you saw it for yourself. A lot of people on that subforum have stories to tell.*

And? What's yours?

What's my what?

Your story.

I'm not sure I have one.

Come on, man. You've seen the nimbus three times. That's more than most people. Probably more than anyone but me and Max and Luca's doctors. You must have some theories about what's going on. I read your posts, you know.

Warren tried not to look surprised. Though he'd sent Adrian an email with a link to the subforum, he hadn't told him which account was his. What else had Adrian figured out? Warren again considered the possibility that Adrian had sniffed out his ruse. *You knew who I was?*

Adrian laughed. *Of course. TimeLord42. I hope you weren't trying to keep it a secret. In one post you said you'd met me at the Div School. In another you said you worked at the University. That narrows it down pretty considerably.*

I guess so.

Adrian looked at Warren with a significant expression. *Like I said, I want to do this. I really do. But if I do it, I need to be careful. I don't know anyone on that subforum except for you. And I'm guessing you don't really know them, either. Except for what you've seen online.*

That's true.

Obviously Luca is my number-one priority. I've got to protect him. From everything I've seen, it seems like people on the subforum are mostly on the up-and-up, but it's the Internet. You never know.

Also true, Warren said. Somewhere deep in his gut he felt an uncomfortable twinge, a belated surge of guilt, maybe, about what he'd planned. He reminded himself what he'd told himself before: for all his patent criminality, The Weight did not seem the type to hurt a little boy, especially not a little boy he believed to possess occult powers.

If this is going to work, you and I are going to have to be partners on this, okay? I need to be able to trust you. So no more secrets. No trickery, okay?

Warren stroked his chin to mask a nervous yawn. *Yeah, sure, of course.*

I can promise you that that will go both ways. I'm going to be honest with you, too. And for starters, I'm going to be honest that I didn't set up this meeting only because I wanted to talk about the subforum. I did want to do that, and I do want to do that. But that's not the only reason I'm here.

Okay, Warren said slowly.

There's something I realized recently, after we saw each other at Afternoon Beer. Something I think you deserve to know.

Warren watched Adrian without speaking, trying to read in his face where this was going.

It's about McGrath.

What? This was not one of the options Warren had considered.

When did you take his class? What year? Do you remember?

It was the winter quarter of my second year in the master's program. So I guess that would have been 1996. January of 1996.

That's what I thought.

Why?

So, look, I need to preface this by saying that I had no idea what was actually going on, and that I feel awful about it. I need you to know that.

Okay . . .

So that same quarter I was TA'ing for the other class McGrath was teaching. And I was thinking about it after I saw you, and I remembered something weird that happened during that time. McGrath came into our weekly meeting one day all jazzed up about something. He seemed happy, really happy, and that was strange, because McGrath was not someone who was ever happy. One of us, me or the other TA, must have asked him what was going on, because it wasn't really like him. I remember this very clearly, because his

*answer was nothing like I expected. He told us he was thrilled because he'd
just caught someone cheating on a paper in his other class.*

My class.

*Had to have been. He said he had the person dead to rights for plagiarism.
I remember his reaction when I asked him how he'd caught the person. He
looked at me with that imperious way he had, like I was a hopeless incompe-
tent. And he said something . . . I don't remember the whole conversation or
anything close to it, but I remember this phrase, because I've quoted it before.
He said, "A good teacher knows his students." He said something along the
lines of: Our job as teachers was to listen to students' questions in class, talk to
them in office hours, read their exams. If we were doing that job well, he said,
we'd know what they were capable of. What they were capable of and what
they weren't. You'd know when something was off, he said, when something
was too good for honest work.*

Warren felt a staticky buzz, like electricity, in the back of his neck
and the upper part of his skull. The rest of his body was numb.

*You see what I'm saying. I wish I could tell you that the accusation both-
ered me. I wish I could tell you that I'd pushed him to show us some kind of
proof—a source, maybe, for what you'd supposedly ripped off. But I'll be real
with you, man. I owe you that much after all this time. I was not about to
cross McGrath. I was scared shitless of the man. Everyone was.*

I don't . . . I'm not . . . Warren pressed his palms against his forehead.
*I remember the paper I wrote for that class. I got a C on it. It was by far my
worst grade in grad school. But McGrath didn't say anything about plagiarism. If he thought I cheated, why did he give me any grade at all? Why didn't
he say something? Why didn't he turn me in?*

*That, I actually know. Me or the other TA asked him if he was going to
haul his alleged cheater in front of the Academic Council, and again he gave
us one of his withering looks. Absolutely not, he said. He'd tried that before,
too many times in his career, and the only thing he'd learned in the process was
that the scales were tipped too heavily in favor of students. I remember him
saying something about how the Academic Council and all the administrative
rules that governed it were an affront to his academic freedom. I didn't really*

follow the logic, but I'm ashamed to suspect that I was probably impressed. I've always taken teaching seriously, and back then I was probably pretty keen on the idea that the bond between student and teacher was something no bureaucracy should get in the middle of.

Warren sat for a long moment in silence until the waitress brought the men their food. The sight and smell of the cheeseburger were nauseating. Finally a question occurred to him. It was an old question, possibly the oldest in human history, a question that—along with the fear of death and the desire for domination—had given birth to every religion Warren could think of. *Why, though?* he said. *Why me?*

Adrian was looking at Warren with a sympathetic expression, but what he said next nearly caused Warren to leave the restaurant. *He was wrong, right?*

What?

McGrath. He was wrong? I mean, that's what I've been assuming. But I figured I should ask.

Of course he was wrong. Warren almost spit the words. His heart was racing and his skin was burning. He told himself to calm down. He told himself to remember why he was here. *It was not a great paper, I'll cop to that,* he said in a quieter voice. *I had a lot going on that quarter, and none of it was good. But I didn't cheat.*

The paper, Warren recalled, was due a few days after his last big blowout with his father, which followed less than a week after he found out that the girl he'd been seeing at the time—the last girl he ever really loved, and the only girlfriend he'd ever seriously considered marrying—had left without saying goodbye. Individually and together, the two events had put Warren in a bad way, and after McGrath denied his request for an extension, he'd stayed up several nights in a row trying to pull the paper into acceptable shape. Warren always figured the paper had something to do with McGrath's animus toward him, but it remained puzzling to him that a single weak essay, in a class that had nothing to do with his proposed course of study, could sink what was, according to Professor Webb, an otherwise attractive doctoral application.

Like I said, that's what I assumed, Adrian said. *But in that case, there's something else that happened that you probably deserve to know about. Another strange thing. It was the same quarter, during final exams, and to be honest I didn't really put it together until the other day. I certainly didn't connect it to what happened to you.*

Warren's whole body was tense. *I'm listening*, he said.

So the way things usually worked was that McGrath would have his TAs read the final exams, take notes, and suggest a grade. Usually he just rewrote our notes as comments in the exam books, without making any modifications. But there was one case, this one young woman, where he ended up being quite a bit harsher than we'd proposed. I don't remember exactly, but let's say he lowered the grade from a B-plus to a C-minus. Something like that. The other TA and I thought it was strange, but then again McGrath was strange. And anyway, as I said before, we were both terrified of him.

Adrian looked down, as though considering something. He took a drink of water and ran a hand through his still-damp hair before continuing. *This is where it got really weird. Just before we handed the exams back, me or the other TA realized that the cover sheets had gotten mixed up. The student who was going to get the C-minus turned out to be this Baptist guy who was angling to do a PhD under McGrath's supervision. McGrath got intensely agitated when we told him, but eventually he settled down. I didn't think anything more of it until the other TA showed me the final grade sheet for the class. McGrath had the Baptist guy getting an A-minus, which should have been impossible, mathematically, with the grade he got on the exam. It was pretty obvious that McGrath had bumped him up, and at the time me and the other TA figured it was because he was trying to do a favor for this kid who wanted to study with him. It didn't occur to us—it didn't occur to me, anyway, and you can bet I've been kicking myself about this for weeks—that it might have something to do with the fact that the Baptist guy was white.*

The woman was not.

For the first time in his telling of the whole long tale, Adrian made eye contact with Warren. *No*, he said. *She was Ethiopian.*

The men ate lunch in silence. Warren still felt sick to his stomach, but one exploratory bite of his cheeseburger encouraged another, and before he quite knew what had happened there were only a handful of fries remaining on his plate.

I know that was a lot to lay on you, Adrian said. *But I figured you'd want to know. Actually let me rephrase that: I figured I'd want to know if I were in your place.*

I appreciate that, Warren said. *I'm glad you told me. I think.* He ate a fry and forced a half smile.

The fry was fine, but the attempt at a smile he regretted immediately. Adrian seemed to think that it meant he was free to leap headlong into another subject. *So that's my thing*, he said. *Now it's your turn.*

My turn for what?

To answer my original question.

You'll have to remind me.

What's your story? Why are you here?

I'm here because you said you'd buy me lunch.

Come on.

You saw the posts. The others asked me to talk to you.

I don't mean that. I'm asking what you think of the nimbus. All those people, what they wrote is very compelling. But they're just civilians, right? You studied this stuff, like me.

I'm a civilian, too, remember? I got a dishonorable discharge while I was still in boot camp.

I wouldn't put it that way.

I would.

Fine, okay. You got fucked. McGrath was a racist and you got fucked. You'll hear no argument about that from me. But that still doesn't tell me what you think about the nimbus.

What do I think about it? I think it's weird.

That much is obvious. But weird how? Natural weird? Supernatural weird? Some other kind of weird?

It's been a long time since I read any Hume, Warren said, *but I'm guessing he would tell us that natural weird should be our default assumption.*

Adrian's face twisted into an expression that was somewhere between amused and incredulous. *If I had to guess, I'd say the people on the subforum haven't read much Hume.*

Warren allowed himself a deep chuckle. *No, I don't imagine they have.*

So it's not religious, then? Not a miracle?

I told you I don't know what it is. But I'm not a religious person, so I think it's fair to say that miracles would be pretty far down on my list.

Adrian leaned forward and looked intently at Warren. He was squinting as though he were trying to read something written in a tiny script on his forehead. *I don't know, man.*

You don't know what?

I don't think you're telling me the whole truth. I think you're holding something back, and I think I know what it is.

Warren was almost certain now that Adrian knew. Not about The Weight, maybe, but about everything else. Somehow he'd figured out Warren's plan. He knew that Warren had started two alternate accounts on the subforum. He knew that with his main account and with his alts, each of them pretending to be a person who didn't know the others, Warren had coaxed the group toward a pair of conclusions: first, that they should all get together in real life, and second, that they should try to get Adrian to bring Luca to meet them. Warren hadn't had to use his alts to suggest himself for the latter task; he had enough credibility with the other members that that happened organically. But still Adrian must have realized that Warren hadn't really been as reluctant as he made himself out to be. He must have figured out that being asked to talk to Adrian was exactly what Warren wanted. He must have guessed that Warren thought he was smart to borrow a strategy he'd picked up in The Mace of Wintermere, which had taught him that most groups of people, most of the time, are waiting for someone to tell them what to do. Adrian must have known that Warren had learned that it didn't take much to get people moving in the direction you wanted: a little deception, some subtle encouragement, and you were on your way.

Adrian leaned back in his chair and put his hands up. *I get it, you don't want to call it a miracle. Fine. It's a big word. Overloaded with Hume and all the rest. I understand. But I think something happened to you. Call it a miracle or don't, I don't care. But I think I know what this is about for you. The nimbus helped you, didn't it? Just like it helped those people on the subforum.*

Oh! Warren said a little too brightly. *Oh, no. No, there's been nothing like that.*

You're telling me nothing is different. No sudden windfalls, no out-of-the-blue love affairs, no wishes granted or dreams fulfilled. Nothing.

I mean, not really. I guess some stuff is better than it was before. But some stuff is worse, too. What about you?

Adrian put his hands up and made a who-am-I-to-say expression. *We're talking about you. But since you're asking, yeah, sure. My whole life has changed. Mostly for the better. Of course, I couldn't tell you if that's because of the nimbus doing something to me or because, you know, it just is what it is.*

The fact of it, you mean.

Mm-hmm.

Warren remembered something. *You know what Augustine said about miracles?*

Don't tell anyone at the Div School, but I don't really know what Augustine said about anything. Except that thing about wanting chastity but not yet.

Well, I think it's Augustine, anyway. If memory serves, he said that if none of the miracles in the Bible were true, it would still have to count as the greatest miracle of all that the Christian Church grew as fast as it did, despite all the reports of miracles being false.

Hmph. Clever. By that logic, though, we should all be Muslim.

Yeah. Or Mormon.

Or Mormon.

Warren ate the last three of his fries. Adrian was still gazing at him intently. *Most of the people on the subforum seem to think it's supernatural.*

Some of them still have questions, but yeah. I think that's fair for most of them.

But it's not fair for you?

I don't think your son is being divinely illuminated, if that's what you're asking. No offense.

Adrian smiled. *None taken. But what's amazing to me is that you're here anyway. You're here, supposedly, on behalf of people who do think that. Why?*

I told you. Because you invited me. Because they asked me to.

Because they asked you to. You're in the habit of doing what strangers on the Internet ask you to? Even though you think they might be crazy? Forgive me if I find that a stretch. Why are you doing this, Warren? What's in this for you?

What Warren said next was not the truth, inasmuch as it made no reference to The Weight or his demands. By any strict reckoning it had to count as a lie of omission. But it was also not false. And though Warren was not a big talker, especially when it came to the most intimate and intense experiences of his life, once he started telling Adrian what he set out to tell him, he found he didn't want to stop until the whole tale was finished.

I told you I'm not religious and that's true. But it wasn't always the case. For a couple of years in my life, when I was young, I was a pretty serious Christian. My father was from Uganda, and he loathed religion. Islam and Catholicism especially. He counted it a point of pride that his ancestors had a hand in the killing of the Uganda Martyrs. But like all good immigrant dads, the one thing he hated more than religion was the thought that his son would get an inadequate education. So he sent me to a Jesuit high school.

Adrian smiled. *Uh-oh.*

I think he expected it to be like it was for him, when he went to Catholic school back in Uganda: I could learn math, I could learn science, I could read all the good and important books they forced me to read, and I would be smart enough to scorn all the religious stuff they threw at me.

I take it that's not what happened.

It was my father's bad fortune and mine that I happened to be a sensitive, introverted, and somewhat anxious kid. Not only that, I was a sensitive kid who spent way too much time, even at fourteen, asking himself impossible questions about the meaning of life. For the Jesuits at my high school, I might as well have been a very fat fish swimming at the bottom of a very shallow barrel. I will insist that they were mostly decent men, in addition to being excellent teachers. As far as I know we had none of the sex stuff that was happening at some of the other Catholic schools in the city. But the whole point of a Jesuit education is to take smart, anxious kids and turn them into smart, stalwart defenders of the faith. My teachers had all been through that themselves, so they knew what they were doing. They knew what we needed to hear. They knew which books to give us when. They could tell who needed to read Chesterton, or Dostoyevsky, or Merton.

How'd they get you?

It's too weird to explain, but I sort of fell into this whole obsession about time.

Time? Like time on a clock?

Kind of. More like time and eternity. Anyway, by the time I got to college I'd decided I wanted to get baptized. But there was a problem.

Your father.

No. Well, yes. But this was a different problem. My problem was that even as I was becoming more and more convinced that the pope held the keys to the one true faith, I nevertheless felt like there was a sort of trapdoor at the bottom of my religious beliefs. If I ignored that trapdoor or pretended it wasn't there, I could get on board with everything else. Like, once the premises were in place, then it was easy to spin everything else out from there. But those premises, if I looked too hard at them I couldn't be sure I actually believed them. And of course I couldn't just ignore that. I felt like I had to deal with it, to settle that score, before I got baptized. Otherwise I'd be entering the faith under false pretenses. And what would be the point of that? Anyway, to make a long story a little shorter, after much agonizing, I confessed this to the priest who was doing my catechism, and he told me I had the wrong idea about faith. To become a Catholic, he said, I did not need to purge myself of every last doubt. Faith was not the same thing as certainty. It was more like an instinct that waxes and wanes for reasons that are not always apparent.

That sounds wise.

It's pretty standard apologetics, not that I knew that at the time. But for better or worse, I took the priest at his word and went ahead and got baptized. Still, though, that sense of a trapdoor was there. At some profound level, I suspected I was just faking it.

And you were how old?

This would have been right around the end of college. I was still on track to go to med school at that point, but it was like I had this itch I couldn't stop scratching, this scab I couldn't stop picking.

So you decided to come to Div School.

It was a little more complicated than that—the time thing had something to do with it, too—but basically, yeah. I thought, okay, I've got one life to live. I've got one chance to try to get to the bottom of things. If I don't do this now, I'm always going to wonder if I missed my chance to figure out what life was all about.

That also sounds wise.

Nah. It's naive. Incredibly naive. That's the way a young person thinks, before he learns that life is long and not so eager to be understood. I thought I was making this grand gesture, leaving behind a good bourgeois life to go on a sort of existential adventure. I bought the idea that you couldn't just go about your ordinary middle-class business if you wanted to learn what God meant to teach you. Jesus was pretty explicit about that in the Gospels, even though Christianity has done its best to forget it. The camel and the eye of the needle. The rich young man who went away sad. If you took that stuff at all seriously, I figured, you had to be ready to give up a lot, and not just money.

Adrian had his eyes closed and was nodding vigorously. Warren went on:

In a weird way, my father's reaction only reinforced that sense. He was naive in a different way than I was, I understand that now. But we shared a sense of the stakes. Like me he was convinced that I was throwing my life away for good. Not just my life but his: he'd busted his ass, after all—he'd actually risked his life—to set me up for success in America, and here I was just tossing it away like it was so much scrap. We had terrible fights, and he stopped talking to me eventually. But you want to know the weird thing? As much as I hated how much he hated what I was doing, I was also strangely flattered by it. For both of us, it felt like everything was riding on my decision. It was just the polarities of our responses that were opposites, if that makes sense.

Adrian's eyes were open again. *It does,* he said. *It really does.*

Plus I had that passage from Luke rattling around in my head. You know, the one where Jesus says no one can be his disciple if he does not hate his father and mother and wife and children. I remember hearing that in Mass one Sunday and listening to the priest try to explain it away in his sermon, suggesting it was just a metaphor or hyperbole. And I remember sitting there thinking, what if it's not?

That's intense, man.

It was, and it took me a long time to understand that the intensity was a large part of the appeal. My mom, for her part, saw things much more clearly. She thought it was fine if I wanted to go to Div School. She said there was time to go and check it out. If I didn't like it I could change my mind. She'd gone through a metaphysical period, too, she insisted, and she thought she was helping me by telling my father that it was something I just needed to work out of my system.

Your dad didn't like that.

Of course not. He thought it was ludicrous. He said it was typical American decadence to think that the world will just wait around for you to make up your mind. But I'll tell you something. I hated it, too. I'll never forget how I felt when she used that phrase, about her "metaphysical period." You've never seen someone so smug. A metaphysical period! There I was, getting ready to throw away all my worldly ambitions. There I was, preparing to toss myself into the mouth of a volcano. And along comes my mom, wanting to talk to me about her metaphysical period? Which, by the way, ended up meaning that she went to this Bible study group for about six months when I was a baby. Anyway, for a long time now, I've been more or less convinced that both my parents ended up being right. My father was right, in that the whole thing turned out to be a disaster, even if he couldn't predict exactly how or why it would end up that way. And my mom was right that I was blowing the whole thing way out of proportion. I wasn't becoming a Desert Father. I wasn't taking a vow of voluntary poverty. I was going to an extremely expensive university to get an extremely expensive master's degree. I was basically giving up one microstratum of the bourgeoisie in favor of another. It was hardly martyrdom I was signing up for.

Adrian smirked. *I don't know. Me and my colleagues are not exactly making fortunes here.*

No, but whatever you're losing in money you're making up for in time to read and time to think. That's a pretty good trade in my book.

Adrian's face grew serious now. *God, man. I'm so sorry about all this. I'm so mad at McGrath, too. You're exactly the kind of person who belongs in the Divinity School.*

Well, thank you for saying that. But I don't actually think it's true. The truth is, even before everything with McGrath went down, I was already getting pretty disillusioned. My classes were all fine. Several of them were very good. A few were outstanding. But even the best of them were all so scholarly. Everything was so intellectual. I know that sounds stupid. What did I expect, right? But I'll tell you: I expected to learn about life, and when I got to Div School all anyone wanted to talk about was books. Not that I disliked books, of course. But even the books that were trying desperately to tell us something about life—the books that, you could tell, were composed in the grips of a crisis of faith as severe as any I'd known—even those books we treated like relics in a museum. I don't know. I guess it's the same old story.

No! Please don't sell yourself short. There's a reason all the best stories are old stories. I get it. I've had that feeling, too, more than I can tell you. I think about it a lot when I'm putting together my syllabi. All this stuff we're asking our students to read, all these sacred texts, week after week we flip through them like so many magazines. But these were books written in blood. Books that were a matter of life or death. Books with the power to save or condemn someone's immortal soul. That's hard to teach, though, you know? Even if you wanted to. And most of my colleagues don't want to.

Adrian looked at Warren as though he expected a response. When none was forthcoming, he took a drink of his water and started nodding again, albeit slowly. *I think I get it now,* he said.

Warren was genuinely puzzled. *Get what?*

Why you're here. What you want from the nimbus. You said you came to the Div School because you wanted to get to the bottom of things. I did, too, for what it's worth. And like you I generally did not find the answers I was looking for. Unlike you, though—or at least that's what it sounds like—I did not stop searching. I played the game, of course. I did what I had to do. But I always told myself that when I got tenure I would drop all the academic non-sense and get back to what's really important. I'm not going to sit here and tell you that I'm certain the nimbus is here to remind me of that promise to myself. But I will say that when I look at my son, when I see the nimbus, I feel like the old questions are still as urgent as they ever were. Sitting here right now, I'd bet you don't entirely accept what your mother said about your metaphysical period. If I had to guess, I'd say some part of you knows . . . how'd you put it? The itch still needs scratching.

Oh, I don't know about that, Warren said. *All that is very much behind me now. All of that was a long time ago.*

Adrian looked unconvinced. He sat quiet for several long seconds. *So what is it, then?* he asked finally. *Why do you care?*

I don't know. I mean, I will admit that there are times when I think that even with everything that happened later, my so-called metaphysical period was the high point of my life. Not the happiest, necessarily. Certainly not the most content or the most satisfied. In some weird way, though, maybe it was the best. But I'm also not under any illusion that I can go back to that way of thinking. I'm not even sure I'd want to. I'd like to believe I settled my accounts with religion a long time ago, and most of the time I feel fine about that. But I guess listening to what people have written on the subforum, seeing how they talk about it, I get the sense that for them, this might be their chance to scratch the itch. For reasons I can't entirely explain, I find myself wanting them to have that chance, even if I can't have it for myself.

There's infinite hope, but not for you.

What?

It's Kafka. "There's infinite hope in the universe," he wrote, "but not for us."

Maybe. Sure. Something like that.

SIXTEEN

Paul, Paul, are you there?

Renata, hey, is that you?

Oh thank god. Please tell me you haven't left yet.

Left what? Left where?

Chicago. You haven't moved? You're still here?

Oh, no. I mean, yeah. Yeah. I'm still here. What's going on? Are you okay?

He's gone, Paul. They're gone. Both of them.

Who's gone? What are you talking about? What happened?

Luca, Paul. Luca and Adrian. Luca started glowing last night, just as he was falling asleep. Adrian got all excited and said he needed to take him somewhere. I told him not to go. I told him he couldn't. We had a fight about it. A bad fight. I told him some stuff I shouldn't have said—

You didn't—

No, don't worry. Not really. I mean, I did, kind of, but I didn't say anything about you. He knows what happened, but he doesn't have any idea it was you.

Wait a minute. What did you say?

It doesn't matter, Paul. This is not about that. This is about Luca. Adrian got mad and he left and he took Luca with him.

Where'd he go?

I don't know! That's why I'm calling. Adrian texted late last night. He said everything was fine but he wasn't sure when they'd be home. I thought he meant he'd be gone an hour or two, but he never came back.

Seriously?

Yep. He took our weekend bag. He took his computer. He did not take our car. No diapers, either, or any clothes for Luca, as far as I can tell.

Jesus.

You haven't heard from him? He hasn't called you?

I haven't heard from him for weeks. He left a couple of messages after the colloquium, but obviously I wasn't really in the mood to talk. I haven't spoken to him since . . . well, since I was at your house.

Oh fuck. Oh god, Paul.

Renata, hold on. It's okay. I'm sure they're okay. Did you call the cops?

I called the cops in five precincts and eight suburbs. I called every hospital within fifty miles. I called both airports, all the airlines. No one has heard anything. The cops say they can't even open a file if it hasn't been two weeks. I swear to god, if that motherfucker took Luca to Texas . . .

Texas? Wait, the Olson guy? Did you try calling him?

Of course I called him.

What did he say?

He didn't say anything. They'd only let me speak to one of his assistants. She told me Mr. Olson was on a hunting trip and wouldn't be back for a week.

You think she was lying?

Yes, I think she's lying. Adrian said the guy was desperate to see Luca. And Adrian . . . I don't have to tell you how obsessed he is with Olson. Fuck. Fuck fuck fuck fuck.

I'm sorry, Renata. I wish I had something more helpful to tell you.

It's okay. I'm just glad you took my call. I was afraid you wouldn't pick up.

What makes you think I wouldn't?

I don't know. I wouldn't have blamed you, though.

Well. Let me know if I can help somehow. I'll call if I think of anything.

Il wasn'l Irue, what Paul said at the end. When his phone lit up with Renata's name on the screen, he had very nearly let her call go to voicemail. Only a few weeks had passed since their hookup, but already that event—which in the moment had seemed both a thrill and a catastrophe, a thrill because it was a catastrophe—felt like a rumor of a memory of a half-forgotten morality tale. When they'd slept together Paul had still been the sort of person who might catch himself unironically uttering a phrase like "the life of the mind," or the sort of person who regularly read books to take a break from reading books, or the sort of person who believed without thinking about it that the difference between an assistant and an associate professor was a matter of existential importance. Now he was someone else. Some*thing* else, if Billy could be trusted: *Dude, you're turning into fucking Gollum,* he'd told Paul just that morning. *It's creeping my freshmen out. It's creeping Salma out. I'll be honest: it's beginning to creep me out, too.*

Paul couldn't deny that it had been a rough couple of weeks. On the morning after his thrilling and catastrophic rendezvous with Renata, he'd left her house before dawn without any idea of where to go or what to do next. In that moment he began to appreciate that his life was unsettled in a way he'd never experienced before. It was an awful feeling. Previously it had always been closing doors and narrowing possibilities that had terrified him, but now he understood that the opposite was so much worse. Broke and broken, homeless and helpless, he felt himself to be free in the worst sense of the word. It was as though he were an exile from his own life, an outlaw, untouchable.

Paul had finally woken Billy with a phone call. For the next four hours, over breakfast at the dining hall, over Bloody Marys at Billy's apartment, and over a succession of generously packed bowls on the roof of his dorm, Billy had listened to Paul unspool the whole absurd and tragic tale. He scowled, he scoffed, he laughed, he joked, he pried for details about Renata's erotic prowess but also commiserated with real empathy. At the end of it all, he told Paul that he was welcome—*fucking of course, man*—to stay as long as he wanted, as long as he needed, in the dorm's common room. The school year was almost over. Summer was almost here. No one would notice him. If they did notice, no one would care.

In the two weeks since, Paul had survived (if that was the word) on a steady regimen of intoxicants, shame, and self-pity. Every day he drank beers for breakfast, smoked shag cigarettes for lunch, and sucked down a slurry of sugar cereal or red Jell-O cubes whenever he got hungry. He worked through his emergency cache of Adderall and muscle relaxers, and when those ran out he started raiding the cedar box where Billy stashed the coke and the acid and the other reminders of his hard-partying days that he wanted to keep out of view of his wife. At night, Paul went up to the roof, played *Master of Puppets* through the tiny speakers of his phone, and punished himself with shots of aggressively umlauted alcohol (Jägermeister, Jeppson's Malört) until he was drunk enough to pass out on the common room's black-pleather couch. In place of real food he gorged himself on social media and cable TV—Twitter, golf, *Survivor*, Facebook, QVC— making himself so screensick that not even pot could chase off the nausea.

Renata's call had caught him at a particularly bad moment. He hadn't shaved for a week, hadn't showered in three days, and was starting to smell bad enough that even he was annoyed at the odor. Just this morning, on his way to a stall in the dorm's communal bathroom, he'd surprised himself in the mirror: he'd lost so much weight, had become so gray and shaggy and grim-looking, that he thought for a moment that some other bearded creep had snuck into the bathroom behind him. He looked like a meth-addicted werewolf. Billy had confronted him not long after that, suggesting, in so many words, that if Paul was planning to bottom out, that was his business. But maybe, he said, he should start looking for another place to do it.

Feeling both gross and ashamed after Renata's phone call, Paul skipped his customary eleven a.m. PBR and took a long shower instead. The dorm's industrial-strength water pressure did not succeed in washing away his indignity, but it did clear his head enough that he remembered something he hadn't thought of while speaking to Renata. When he got out of the shower, he dressed in the nearest approximation of clean clothes he could manage and removed his laptop from his backpack. It required only a few clicks to confirm what he'd suspected: he was still logged in to Adrian's email account.

He called Renata.

You're kidding, she said.

Nope. It's all there.

Can you tell where he is?

I haven't looked. I only just realized I could get in.

Can you send me the password?

I don't know it. Adrian typed it in for me. Without any forethought he added, *I can bring it by, if you want. My laptop.*

Do you mind? I hate to bother you, but I'm desperate.

No problem. Should I come now?

Give me half an hour, but yes, now is good. Max is at school till three, so it's just me here.

Okay. I'll keep looking until then.

Thirty minutes later, Paul was standing once again on Renata's covered porch. He'd done his best to make himself fit for human consumption—his face and neck were freshly shaved, and his armpits were painted in a heavy schmear of antiperspirant—but still he felt substantially out of sorts. Much of the problem, obviously, was biochemical: his body had long since given up trying to modulate the flood of intoxicants he'd ingested over the past two weeks, and the four Advil he'd swallowed before leaving the dorm were having little effect.

On the walk over, however, walking beneath a brilliant May sun that hung high in the cornerless sky, he'd realized that his unease was more than merely physical. The truth was, Paul was not eager to see Renata again. He didn't regret what they'd done, not in the least. Nor did he feel any compunction for the fact (which he now accepted as a fact) that while revenge was not the only reason he'd slept with Renata, it was pretty high up on the list. Yes, he'd been drunk. Yes, he'd been sad. Yes, he'd been desperate for some form of external validation. Yes, his general attitude toward sex resembled his general attitude toward free beer, money, and ice cream, which was to say he took what he could get and didn't worry too much about where it was coming from or why. And yes, it was even possible, as Billy had suggested, that his unconscious had urged him on as a means of perverse self-preservation: cuckolding his adviser might not be the most decorous way to lock the door behind himself on his way out of academia, but it was definitely definitive.

At the same time, Paul's absence of remorse did not mean that he was in any way prepared, especially after the two weeks he'd had, to deal with the aftermath of the affair. For two weeks, the booze and the weed and the pills had helped him hold off any wondering about Renata's side of the equation. They were both adults. They'd done what they'd done for their own reasons. They'd each acted of their own independent accord. What Renata thought of the episode—what Renata thought of Paul—mattered not at all. During their brief postcoital conversation, she'd made it clear that the rendezvous was a one-time-only event, never to be repeated. And while Paul had enjoyed the sex, enjoyed it unreservedly, he was in basic agreement with her verdict. Renata was smart and witty and pretty, and if she was conspicuously bougie she was also interesting and sexy in ways that he never guessed it was possible for a middle-aged mother of two to be. She was living, or so it seemed to him, a life in full. She had kids and a house, a job and (for now) a husband. She had built-in bookcases, for god's sake! She had a life that was as alien to him as an owl's. They had nothing in common, no thread of connection other than their mutual antagonism toward her husband.

Renata opened the door almost as soon as he rang the doorbell. She was dressed in fashionable jeans and a body-fitting T-shirt that probably cost more than Paul's computer, but she did not look well. Her face was pale, almost white, except around her ears and her neck where it was streaked with red lines that looked like scratch marks. Her eyes were pink and puffy, the bags beneath them a bruisy purple. She looked like Paul felt, like she hadn't slept in three days.

She greeted Paul with a sad expression that made him wonder for a moment what kind of affection, if any, was appropriate to the situation. He didn't know what she was expecting from him—he didn't know what he was expecting from himself, really—and so he reached out and awkwardly patted her shoulder. She stilled his hand with her own, holding his palm firm against her clavicle, and exhaled a long, dejected breath.

I'm sorry about this, she said. *I didn't want to drag you back into this mess, but I didn't know what else to do.*

It's okay, Paul said. *I'm happy to help.*

Renata let go of his hand and led him inside, to the large dining table that divided her kitchen from her living room. She took a chair and gestured for him to sit beside her, and he pretended not to notice that this was exactly where they'd been sitting when they'd first started kissing. He took his laptop out of his backpack and flicked the touch pad to wake up the screen.

So, she said, with another heavy breath. *Did you find anything else?*

I did. So, first, there's a guy Adrian's been emailing with quite a bit recently—

Olson, right? Goddamnit. I knew it.

Paul's screen flashed to life. *No. Well, him, too. But this is another guy. His name is Warren Kayita.*

I've never heard of him.

Here, let me show you. Paul typed "Kayita" in the search bar and the subject lines of several dozen email messages appeared below it. *I haven't had a chance to read them all yet, but from the most recent ones, it looks like he and Adrian have been planning something for a while now. A sort of get-together.*

What do you mean a get-together? In Texas?

No, here, in Chicago. Look. Paul clicked open one of the emails from Adrian to Warren. It was dated a few days earlier:

Warren, this is all getting too complicated. Let's just do this. I know everyone is eager to know exactly when and where they should show up, but the nimbus doesn't work like that. It's not predictable. It's not on anyone's schedule. So they're just going to have to be patient.

I still think the chapel on campus is our best bet. It's not open to the public, but my key card will get us in. It's usually empty, and best of all it's close to my house. The next time it shows up, I'll let you know, and you can put the word out. If we get a critical mass of people, I'll bring Luca over and we'll take it from there. Okay?

Fuck, Renata said, putting her head in her hands. *Fuck fuck fuck. I knew it. I knew he'd try to pull this shit again. I'm guessing that's where he took Luca last night?*

That was the plan, I think, but it sounds like they ran into some kind of problem. Paul clicked back to the inbox and opened another email. *You can see here, around eight last night, Adrian emailed this Warren guy to let him know that Luca was glowing.* Paul opened another window and typed in a Web address. *And if you look here, you can see this guy, TimeLord42— I'm pretty sure that's Warren—he posts a message on this forum telling people to be ready to meet somewhere a few minutes later.*

Wait, what is this? Renata pointed at the screen. *I've seen this before.*

It's a forum dedicated to the nimbus. It's private now, so you have to be a member to log in. But Adrian showed it to me a few weeks ago, before they locked it down. I signed up back then and I guess that means I still have access.

He showed it to me, too. It's the one with all the crazy people, right?

Paul couldn't resist a smile. *You're going to have to be more specific. It's the Internet. Of course it's full of crazy people.*

Renata forced a smile of her own. *Adrian was all excited about it, but I thought it was actually kind of sad. A bunch of people who think the nimbus was helping them. Or could help them.*

That's the one.

So what happened after Warren's post?

It's not totally clear. About an hour after that first post, TimeLord42 posted again to say that the meetup would have to be postponed, but he doesn't say why. There aren't any more emails between Adrian and Warren, so I have to assume they were in touch some other way.

And that's it?

No, there was something else. Paul clicked back over to Adrian's email and opened his Archive folder. *I figured he had to stay somewhere last night. He wasn't going to sleep on the street with Luca.* Near the top of the screen was an email from the Collegiate, a hotel in the neighborhood. Paul opened the message and sat back in his chair with a triumphant flourish.

It's for last night, Renata said, once she'd read it. When she turned to Paul her face showed none of the gratitude he was expecting. In fact, she looked pissed. *You didn't think I should see this first?*

Renata got up from the table and walked quickly into the kitchen proper. She scanned the countertops until she found her phone. She came back to the table and read the hotel's number off the email. While the phone rang she crossed the room and dropped herself on her living-room couch. She listened to an automated message and pressed a number on the keypad, and then did this again, and again. When a human being finally answered, Renata spoke in a voice heavy with such exaggerated nonchalance that it sounded almost drowsy.

Yes, hello, this is Renata Bennett. Could you put me through to my husband, Adrian Bennett? He checked in last night. Last night, yes. Yes. No, I don't know his room number. Adrian Bennett. Adrian with an A. Bennett with two n's, two t's. He arrived last night. Yes, with our son. Our young son. That's right. Actually, I'd prefer not to wait. Could you just put me through? I'm afraid it's urgent. No? No, it's okay, I understand. Of course. Of course. I'm sorry, what? He's not available? What do you mean? Did he tell you that? You spoke to him, though, yes? Just now? I'm his wife. What do you mean you can't tell me? Sorry, what was your name? Look, Alisha, I appreciate that you're just doing your job, but like I said, this is an urgent matter. Someone in our family is in trouble. No, I understand. I get it, but it's a pretty silly policy, don't you think?

Renata was already putting on her shoes by the time she hung up the phone. She exhaled another long sigh.

You're going over there, aren't you? Paul said. *Do you want me to come?*
No. Thanks. It's okay.

I don't mind. Really. This wasn't true in the least—the last thing he wanted, now or ever, was to see Adrian again—but Paul felt helpless against the instinct to say it.

Renata finished tying her shoes. She sat without saying anything for several seconds, and then she walked over to where Paul was still sitting at the table. *I'm going to go by myself. If Adrian's there, it's not going to be a pretty scene. The kinds of things I need to tell him are not the kinds of things you or anyone needs to hear.*

Paul stood up. *Do you want me to wait here, then? In case he's not there? It's not like I've got anything else to do.*

Renata closed her eyes. She let her forehead fall against Paul's shoulder, and when his arms wrapped around her she leaned into the embrace. Her body felt warm against his chest and belly, and the shoulder where her face was buried was damp with hot tears. She didn't move for nearly a minute, not even when what Augustine called the *ardoris illecebrosus stimulus*, the lustful prick of Paul's lustful prick, made itself a nuisance between them.

It's too much, she said finally, answering the question that Paul hadn't been meaning to ask. She lifted her head and wiped her eyes. *I'm sorry, Paul. Some other time, some other life. Right now it's just too much. Too much and too complicated. I think it's better if you leave. I need to get over to the hotel.*

SEVENTEEN

I'm sorry, ma'am, it looks like he's checked out already.

But that's impossible. I just called over. Not even fifteen minutes ago. I spoke to someone. Alisha. She told me he was here. She called up and spoke to him in his room.

She did? The young man standing behind the gray-marble reception desk was short and skinny, with dark-brown skin and a high fade. He was wearing a blue suit over a bright paisley shirt, and his face was dominated by big brown eyes that put Renata in mind of someone—an actor, maybe, or a college classmate. She tried to ignore the thought while the man peered into a hidden computer screen and tapped on a hidden keyboard. *It says here that housekeeping has already turned over the room.*

Could I go up to look, just to be sure?

I'm afraid I can't do that, ma'am.

Renata made a split-second decision not to pitch a fit. *Right, the policy. Do you know when he checked out? Did you see him leave? He has a toddler with him. My son. Our son. He's two years old. Blond.*

The young man sucked air through his teeth, giving every indication that he'd sensed, accurately, that he was getting pulled into a drama of which he wanted no part. *I'm sorry, ma'am, it's been a busy morning. I wasn't here when he checked in, so I wouldn't have recognized him. Anyway, this says he paid for his room with a credit card, so everything's automatic. He could have left at any point this morning. I wouldn't know.*

But Alisha . . .

I don't know what to tell you about that, ma'am. She's on her lunch break now. You can wait till she gets back, if you'd like. There's a coffee bar over there by the business workstation, or I'd be glad to get you a water, if you'd prefer that.

No, it's okay, Renata said. An intense heat was burning in her chest. She knew she needed to get out of there before she said something she'd regret. *Thanks anyway.*

On her way home, feeling both furious and flabbergasted at the situation in which she'd somehow landed, she tried to remind herself that the hotel and its staff were not responsible for her predicament. It wasn't their fault her husband had stolen her son.

What she told Paul was true. The fight she'd had with Adrian was as bad as any she could remember, possibly the worst they'd ever had. Both of them had said things the other wasn't likely to forget, not soon or not ever. The fight started when Adrian said he wanted to take Luca out— where and why he wouldn't say, or even for how long. Not that the details mattered. Renata was stunned that her husband wanted to pull their two-year-old son out of bed, and rejected the suggestion in absolute terms. From there the argument escalated quickly, and it was not long before Renata was accusing Adrian of endangering their son for the sake of his own aggrandizement. Meanwhile Adrian blamed Renata, unforgivably, for trying to sabotage his career. And when he'd made the mistake of suggesting that she was still bitter about his affair, she'd compounded that mistake, doubled down on it, by dropping the heavy hint that she'd already evened that score. The fight was so upsetting that Renata locked herself in her bathroom to give herself time to settle down. It never occurred to her that Adrian would take Luca anyway, despite her blanket prohibition.

Walking south toward her house, Renata took her phone from her back pocket and dialed Adrian. When he once again refused to answer, she hung up and called him again, and again, and again, hanging up each time just as the computerized voice clicked on to say that his voice mailbox was full. With each call, the heat rose further into her face, and by the end of her fourth attempt her anger had blossomed into a full-blown rage. Not really aware of her surroundings anymore, she stopped abruptly on the concrete median that divided the four lanes of Fifty-Fifth Street and hammered a long text message into her phone:

I honestly don't understand what you're doing, or what you think you're doing. I've done everything for you. I've paid your bills. I've kept your house. I've raised your children. I took you back when you cheated on me, and even after that I worked my ass off to give you exactly the life you always said you wanted. And this is how you pay me back. This is how you reward me for indulging your every selfish whim: by stealing our son, by stealing MY son. All for what? So that you can use Luca as a circus sideshow to make yourself famous? So that you can trot him out in front of a billionaire who will make you rich? Well, I hope it's worth it. Because it's over for us now. This is too much, even for me. You are endangering our child—my child—and I will not tolerate it even a second longer than I need to. I'm on my way to the police station right now, and after that I'm calling a lawyer. I hope that if you can't manage the basic human decency to speak with me, you will at least text me to let me know Luca is okay. As bad as things are right now, I promise I can make them worse, and if I don't hear back from you, I can assure you that's exactly what I plan to do.

Renata stood on the median while the cars on the divided street cruised in both directions beneath the blinding sun, oblivious to her agony. For several minutes at least she held her thumb a half inch from the button that would end her marriage. It was like holding a grenade, like holding a detonator primed to explode.

Of course she meant every word she'd written. She meant, too, every word she'd implied. She owed it to herself to send the text; really, it was the least she could do. Time had taught her that she could abide Adrian's many faults. She could work fifty-hour weeks as a McKinsey associate, a job she'd hated, so that he could scramble his way out of the adjunct jobs that had threatened to bury his academic career before it even started. She could raise their boys and run their household so that he could devote himself to the teaching and research—to the writing!—that let him get tenure. She could tolerate his egotism and his grandiosity. She could plug up the vacuum of his self-doubts and his insecurities. She could shape herself into the ever-shrinking negative space of his ambition, as though she were a housewife from her grandmother's generation. She could do all of that and more. But what she said in the text was true: this latest thing with Luca was too much, even for her.

All she had to do was press the button. A tap of the thumb and it would all be over. It would not be pretty, she had no illusions about that. Bombs are not implements of beauty. But not until the life she knew was reduced to rubble would she truly be free. One tap was all it would take. And yet she hesitated. To send the message now was to make Luca a hostage. If she could keep her intentions to herself, she reasoned, it was still possible that Adrian might show up at the house without notice, and with her son. It was possible, in fact, that they were both there now.

Renata deleted the message and walked quickly home. As she stepped through the front door into her living room she called out, hopefully, *Hello?*

When no one answered, she wrote another text to Adrian. This one she didn't hesitate to send right away:

A, I know you're angry—so am I—but if you won't answer my calls please at least do me the courtesy of letting me know whether Luca is okay. It's not fair to punish me and make me sit here in a panic.

It only took a few seconds before a bubbled ellipsis showed that Adrian was typing. A rapid string of single-line messages unspooled on her screen. Though they were not what Renata wanted to hear, they at least validated her decision not to send her original text:

I am angry, but I'm not trying to punish you.

Definitely not trying to make you panic.

Luca is fine.

Better than fine, even.

We both are.

Renata ignored the barb in the last line. And when can I expect you to bring him home? she wrote. An hour? A day? A week?

Again Adrian wasted no time in responding:

I can't say for sure.

It won't be an hour. Almost certainly won't be a week.

Somewhere in between.

Maybe a day, maybe three, maybe five.

Just depends.

Depends on what? Renata wrote.

A few things, but mostly on the nimbus.

After a pause the bubbled ellipsis appeared again.

I know you can't understand but this is not about you.

Wait. Let me rephrase.

I mean I'm not doing this because I'm angry.

I'm not doing this to hurt you.

It's something I need to do.

Something I need to see for myself.

We'll be home as soon as we can.

Then we can talk.

When Renata picked up Max from school and brought him home to the empty house, she explained that Luca and Adrian had taken a trip for a few days. At first he was not at all happy to hear this, not least because he decided it meant that Luca was getting lots of ice cream. But after Renata let him eat his dinosaur-nugget dinner in front of the TV and gave him a strawberry Popsicle for dessert—and especially after she suggested, without prompting, that he should sleep in her bed—his anguish about the sudden disappearance of half his family softened considerably. The last thing he did before falling asleep was to ask whether his brother and his papa could stay away longer than the few days Renata had promised him: *How about a week, Mama?*

Downstairs, in the kitchen, Renata reminded herself that she'd hardly eaten anything all day. A watery, inexpert cappuccino in the morning. A banana and a few handfuls of pretzels around ten. A cheese stick that looked as though it had melted and resolidified several times inside its plastic sheath, which she recovered from the bottom of a tote bag just before Paul came over.

She should eat something real, she understood that. She should eat, even though all she wanted to do was sleep. Her head felt fizzy in a familiar way, and she knew that if she didn't put something substantial in her stomach she would wake up with a headache as bad as any hangover. She proposed herself a compromise and, with little in the way of haggling, quickly accepted the deal: she would make an omelet, she would toast two slices of bread, and she would pour exactly one glass of white wine. She would eat, she would drink, and when she was through, she would put herself to bed.

Renata was still working her way through the makeshift meal when her phone lit up with a text from Paul. It was short and innocuous-sounding—crafted, she suspected, for plausible deniability:

Hope you got in touch with Adrian. I haven't heard anything from him.

She set down her fork and picked up her phone. Paul answered before the first long ring was over.

Hey.

Hey. I didn't think I should call.

No, you were right. I appreciate it. Not that it much matters anymore.

You didn't find them at the hotel?

They said he checked out. They wouldn't, or couldn't, tell me when.

Hunh.

Yeah, but Adrian and I texted later. He's got Luca. He's going to be gone for a couple of days. That's all I know.

He didn't say why? He didn't say where?

He didn't say either. Have you looked at his email again?

I tried, after I left your place, but I was logged out. Adrian must have done it after . . .

After I called the hotel, right. Well, so much for that.

Yeah, but it's not all bad news. I've been reading back through that forum I showed you.

Okay.

It's clear they're trying to get people together to see Luca. Warren, this TimeLord guy, said that for security reasons, they were going to have to take the discussion off the forum. They're going to move to email.

Security reasons? What does that mean?

He didn't say.

Oh, god. When do we get to the good news?

. . .

Paul?

I'm sorry. I thought that was the good news. If they're getting people together, I thought maybe we could find them. Or you could, you know, alone. Whichever.

But you can't get into Adrian's email anymore, right?

No, but I emailed TimeLord. Not as myself, obviously. I made a burner email account and asked him to put me on his list.

And?

And what?

And what did he say?

Oh. He hasn't written me back yet.

Great. Wonderful.

But he said it might take a while. In his post. He said not to get concerned if we didn't hear back from him right away.

I see. I guess we'll have to wait, then.

I'm sorry, Renata, I thought—

It's not your fault, Paul. None of this is your fault.

Maybe a little bit.

Not this part. This part is all Adrian.

Okay, fair enough. I'll let you know if I hear anything. In the meantime, if you need anything, I hope you'll let me know. I'm staying up in Wicker Park for the time being, with a friend, but it's an easy trip down.

Thanks, Paul. I'm fine but I appreciate it. I really do.

Two days later, on Saturday around four in the afternoon, Renata got another text from Paul. I think it's happening, the message said. Call me as soon as you can.

Renata put Max on the living-room couch and switched on his favorite show. She decided not to feel any shame, only a mild astonishment, when he complained in a petulant whine that he'd watched too much TV already and wanted to do something else.

Just for a few minutes, Renata said. *I need to go upstairs to take a work call.*

I hate work calls, Max said, but even as he was pronouncing the words the on-screen animation, as capable as any opioid, began to work its effects. His gaze locked in and his eyes went glassy. His mouth hung half-open, as though he'd been struck by a temporary palsy.

Renata took her phone to her office, closed the door behind her, and called Paul.

Paul started talking as soon as he answered. *So I got an email from TimeLord. A few minutes ago. He's being more than a little cryptic, but he says that Luca has started glowing, and that they're going to get everyone together.*

Where?

In Fell Gardens. He said people should meet in the parking lot of the bank on Fifty-Third Street. An hour from now—or an hour from his message, so a little less than that—someone will meet whoever's at the bank and take them where they need to go.

Renata was strung out after too many days of too little sleep and too much stress. Exhausted and exasperated, she heard a strange keening sound escape her throat. *What the fuck is this? What is Adrian doing?*

There was a long pause before Paul spoke. *Honestly?* he said finally, and not without sympathy. *If I had to guess, I'd say he's probably trying to avoid you.*

Renata set the phone on the desk in front of her and put her head in her hands. She listened on speakerphone, mostly without interruption, as Paul sketched out the rudiments of a plan. Probably Warren or whoever would know to be on the lookout for Renata. But they wouldn't know to watch for Paul. He could go to the bank and follow the group wherever it was headed. When he found out, he could call Renata and she could meet him there.

Wait, though, aren't you in Wicker Park?

No, I crashed with a friend down here last night.

And what if Adrian shows up? At the bank?

Then you can come there. That's the whole point, right?

I guess it is. The truth was that Renata hadn't given any thought, now or previously, to what she'd actually say when she saw Adrian again. Her only idea, such as it was, was to find Luca, to scoop him up into her arms, and to never let go of him again.

Anyway, I don't think he will show up. Otherwise why go to all this trouble?

Okay, Renata said, exhaling audibly. *Let me see what I can do with Max. How much time do we have?*

Warren sent the email almost exactly forty-five minutes ago.

All right. That should be enough time for me. After I get Max squared away I guess I'll just wait for you to tell me what's happening?

Yep. I'll keep in touch.

PAUL'S TEXTS ROLLED IN, one after another, while Renata called around to find someone who could watch Max.

> Ok, I'm here. Found a spot where I can see the whole parking lot. I made sure to get here early but I can see a handful of people sitting in their cars. The bank looks like it's closed, so I think it's got to be them.

> I don't see Adrian or Luca anywhere.

> Ok, yep. I was right. A few people walked up on foot and started talking to each other. The people in their cars saw them and got out to join them. You can tell they don't really know each other.

> More are arriving now. I count 18 so far.

> Now 22.

> 25 with 5 minutes to go. TimeLord didn't say anything about who we should watch for, and it doesn't look like the group knows, either. They

keep looking around and checking their phones. A few are chatting. Most are kind of keeping to themselves.

Some more people walked up just as we hit the hour mark. Looks like a family, maybe? They've got two young kids with them. Now 2 more. I think we're at 31 total.

Still no Adrian. Still no TimeLord either, best I can tell.

35 now. No one seems to know what's happening.

Ok wait. Now one of the guys who's been here awhile is talking. Everyone is kind of circling up around him. He's short, balding, middle-aged, darkish skin. He's wearing brown pants and a dark red sweater. Glasses too.

He actually looks kind of familiar but I don't know where I know him from. Oh I bet it's that Warren guy. TimeLord. Still no sign of Adrian, though.

Ok now the main guy is nodding in the direction of the University. I'm tempted to go join them but I think I'll probably just hang back and follow from a distance. It's a big group. Won't be hard to keep an eye on.

Ok they're starting to walk now, all together.

Yep, I was right again. They're headed south across 55th on Kenwood.

Now over to Woodlawn.

Past the dining hall now.

Past the library.

Turning into Main Campus.

Maybe they're just headed for the Div School?

Or not?

God I feel dumb. Of course. They're going into Campbell, next door to
the Div School. Someone just let them all in. I couldn't see who it was.
I'm going to try to sneak in.

So much for that. Doors are all locked. I can't see inside. But everyone
is definitely in there. Do you want to come down? If something's going
to happen, I think it's going to happen here.

Twenty minutes later, after dropping off Max at a friend's, Renata met Paul
in front of the Div School. He was wearing dark pants and a blue shirt.
A black backpack slumped at his feet.

So what now? he said. *What do you want to do?*

I want to find Luca.

I'm guessing he's inside, he said, looking vaguely over his left shoulder.
*Until you got here I was trying to keep an eye on the doors. So far I haven't
seen anyone come in or out.*

I don't think I've ever actually been to the chapel, Renata said. *It's over
there?*

*Yeah, it's just around the corner. I can show you, if you want. Or I can
just point you in the right direction. Up to you.*

No, I'd like you to come. Please.

Paul led Renata to a grassy courtyard with a bike rack and a waterless
concrete fountain. He nodded to a boxy stone building up ahead, whose
broad flank was supported by stepped pillars and shaped by six high
arches. The arches were further subdivided by several panes of stained
glass, which looked, from the outside, as dully utilitarian as any of the
other windows that peered down from the buildings around the Main
Quad.

Paul pointed to a small wooden door under one of the arches.

That's where the group entered. Over there—he pointed toward a cloistered walkway that connected the chapel with the Div School—*are the big main doors. There's a door into the sacristy on the other side. I tried them all. They're locked.*

Did you knock?

Paul shook his head. *I wanted to wait for you to get here.*

Well, I'm here. She looked up at the small door. *I guess I'll try that one. You want to wait here for me?*

Paul looked at Renata and pursed his lips. *I think I should come. At least until you get inside.*

Renata thought for a moment and decided Paul was right. *Okay,* she said.

They began to walk in the direction of the gray cloister, but before they'd taken three steps, Paul stopped Renata with a hand on her shoulder. *Wait,* he whispered.

Together they watched a small group of people—Renata counted five—approach the wooden door. One of them tapped something on her phone, and a minute or two later, the door opened and they went inside.

Renata was running before she quite knew what she was doing. She beat Paul to the door, and was already pounding on its hard wooden surface with her fist by the time he caught up to her.

The door opened, but not by much. A youngish Latino with glossy black hair and wide brown eyes put his head into the narrow gap. *I'm sorry, this is a private event,* he said. *The chapel is not open to the public right now.*

Yes, I'm supposed to be in there, Renata said. *I need to get in there.*

Can you tell me who invited you?

I don't need an invitation. My son is in there. My husband . . . Renata stood on her toes and strained to look over or around him. There were candles burning inside, and she could make out the silhouettes of a few people all looking the same direction. She could not see Luca or Adrian.

I'm sorry, ma'am. He began to pull the door closed.

Wait, TimeLord! Paul shouted over Renata's shoulder. *TimeLord invited us.*

The door opened again. The young man looked at Renata, and then at Paul, and back at Renata. *Okay*, he said finally. *You can come in.*

Renata.

Renata heard her husband before she saw him. As she stepped into the stone chapel she felt like she was entering a cave. It was cool inside, and dark—dark enough, anyway, that despite the candles, it took a few disorienting seconds before Renata's eyes were able to forget the brilliance they'd just left behind. Her ears, however, needed no such adjustment.

Renata, Adrian said again, his voice louder now and more imperative. This time she was able to follow her name back to its source. On the dais in front of the altar she saw Adrian standing frozen with his arms spread wide, as though she'd caught him in the middle of a lecture about angels or pterodactyls. He was dressed in the same clothes he wore on his teaching days—pleatless khakis, a gingham button-up, white low-top sneakers—and on his face was an expression that showed neither anger nor surprise. Instead he wore a prim close-lipped smile that Renata recognized as the mask he put on whenever he felt the need to steel himself for some public ordeal.

And he was in public: Renata saw that. So was she. In front of him, in front of her, were some three dozen people, surely the same group Paul had followed from the bank. A few of them had glanced at her on her way into the chapel, but now all of them were looking intently at her and at Adrian. Their faces, upturned and expectant, made it clear that they knew that something of significance was happening, even if they didn't know what.

Luca was nowhere in view. Renata scanned the crowd, hoping to see his blond head bobbing among the wooden pews. *Where is he, Adrian? Where's Luca?*

Adrian dropped his arms and put up his hand in a familiar, infuriating gesture of pacification. *He's here. He's fine. Don't worry.*

Adrian, I'm not kidding. Where is he?

Renata was still watching Adrian, still glaring at him, when she heard Paul speak her name in a low voice behind her. She turned as he stepped forward to close the distance between them. *I think I know*, he said quietly. *I think I know where Luca is right now. Follow me.*

EIGHTEEN

It had all been going so well. One moment, Luca was sitting at Warren's feet, glowing steadily and drawing with a fat marker on a stack of colored construction paper. Adrian was out front, in the boxy nave of the chapel, delivering a lecture that he'd insisted was imperative to establish the proper mood and context before he let the crowd see the nimbus. The Weight was in the pews, waiting quietly if not exactly patiently for his turn to bask in the boy's glow and absorb whatever otherworldly power he imagined it might confer. Warren, for his part, was beginning to let himself believe that the crisis of the past eight months was nearing its conclusion.

An instant later, all that calm gave way to chaos. The door to the chapel slammed open, hitting its paneled backside hard against an ancient wire coatrack. A pale woman with red cheeks and wet eyes— Adrian's wife, it turned out—came storming into the tiny carpeted room. Without so much as a glance in Warren's direction, she dropped to a knee and scooped her son into her arms.

She was crying, heaving in heavy breaths, but Luca seemed no more bothered by her distress than he'd been surprised by her appearance. He stood patiently while she squeezed him and covered his blond head in kisses. Finally he pulled away and directed her attention, with much pride, to the tangled scribble he'd drawn on the colored paper.

Warren was watching this little reunion with something approaching extreme discomfort when Adrian appeared in the doorway, looking both angry and distraught. He was talking to his wife—talking at her—hissing in the violent whisper that rich white couples use when they argue in front of their children. *I wish you would just relax for a minute*, he said. *Renata, would you please just let me explain.*

Renata ignored Adrian until he was standing over her. She stood and, though several inches shorter than her husband, looked him square in the eye. *It's over, Adrian. It's too much.*

What do you mean? Too much what?

I'm getting a divorce, she said, in a tone that suggested she was delivering the news to herself for the first time. *I'm leaving. We're leaving.* She tugged Luca up onto his feet and then lifted him onto her hip. As she stepped around Adrian, she appeared to notice Warren for the first time. The look on her face made him feel complicit in a crime that he hadn't realized he was committing.

Renata was almost out the door when Adrian stopped her with a question. *It was Paul, wasn't it? That's why he's here. You fucked my graduate student.*

Seeing her silent response, Adrian ran a hand through his hair and allowed himself a bitter laugh. *God, of course. Of course. After everything I did for him, too. I guess no good deed goes unpunished.*

Renata spoke without turning around. *You flaked on him, Adrian. You abandoned him. You ended his academic career.*

"Ended his academic career?" What? Is that what he told you? I'm the only reason he has an academic career to begin with. You know that, right? He told you that, too, I hope? He told you how I held his hand and coddled him at every stage along the way? He told you I got him into the Div School, and convinced his professors not to let him fail his qualifying exams,

and handed him a dissertation topic on a silver platter? He told you I was well on my way to getting him an extremely lucrative fellowship from John Olson? But hey, I missed a meeting. So, sure, totally, absolutely makes sense that he would feel honor bound to sleep with my wife.

Renata turned back now, still refusing to look at Adrian. *It wasn't only him,* she said quietly.

What? There were others?

No, I mean, it wasn't only up to Paul.

Oh, I see. I get it. This was your choice, is that what you're trying to say? This was revenge for you, too?

That's not what I mean.

Bullshit. I know you've never forgiven me.

Maybe you're right, Renata said. Finally she looked over her shoulder at Adrian. *But it wasn't just that. It wasn't only that.*

I didn't do this to you. You know that, right? Adrian said. His voice sounded less aggressive than it had before. His question sounded like a genuine question.

Renata didn't answer. Instead, she looked down at Luca, who was resting with glazed eyes against her shoulder, half asleep. She kissed him on the forehead, and then she turned and carried Luca out of the sacristy.

Warren watched Adrian watch her go. He barely had time to begin to reckon the disaster that had just befallen him—the collapse of all his plans, the end of all his plotting—when there was a scream from out in the chapel. It was a woman's scream, and then there was another, and another after that, and then there was a man's voice that followed them all. The voice belonged to The Weight:

I'm not going to hurt you, lady, he said, loud enough that Warren had no trouble hearing him. *I'm not going to hurt you. But I can't let you leave with that boy.*

Warren felt an odd physical sensation as he watched Adrian sprint out of the sacristy. It was a strange internal shiver, a flutter of trembling unease that shuttled back and forth through his body like a rebounding wave. He tried to ignore the feeling as he stood up, a painful process that required permission from his unhappy knees and his disgruntled lower back, but the shiver intensified as he rose, and refused to let itself be forgotten. It grew in magnitude as he moved toward the screaming and shouting coming from the open door—he heard Adrian's voice, and The Weight's, and Adrian's wife's, and many others—and made him wonder for a moment if he were about to faint, or worse.

The odd feeling, and the foreboding it inspired, reinforced Warren's reluctance to see what was happening out in the chapel. It was an old and well-established principle of his, after all, not to get mixed up in other people's problems. The bespoke troubles that life liked to tailor were hard enough to deal with; he saw no reason to go around adopting secondhand miseries as his own.

Even so, whatever he might prefer to think, and as skilled as he was in the more advanced techniques of self-delusion, Warren could not bring himself to believe that he was exempt from the drama taking place on the other side of the door. It was Warren, after all, who'd cut a deal with The Weight in the first place, and Warren who'd told him in a text an hour ago that he should come to the chapel if he wanted to see the glowing child.

Warren passed through the sacristy door just in time to see the last members of the subforum crowd, two elderly women and a man with a cane whom Warren remembered from the bank, doing their best to hustle out the back door of the chapel. The pews in front of the altar were all empty now, but the air between the tall stained-glass panels still felt unsettled from the recent commotion. On the dais, off to his left, Warren saw Adrian, his wife, his glowing son, and a young man he didn't know. All of them were standing in a tight cluster.

Behind them, blocking their path to the chapel's side door, was The Weight. His long face was set in a grim expression until he noticed Warren, at which point it brightened horribly.

Aha! There he is, he said. *The man of the hour. The reason we're all here.* He lifted both arms in a gesture of mock welcome, and it was then that Warren saw the pistol. The Weight was not aiming the gun—in fact he was holding it fairly casually in his right hand—but the sight of the weapon froze Warren in place.

Everyone in the cluster, save Luca, turned to look at him.

Warren, who is this guy? Adrian said. *He said you invited him here.*

When he tried to speak, Warren discovered that his tongue was suffering the same mild paralysis as the rest of his body. The shiver, he noticed, was still with him, but it was no longer moving, no longer a traveling wave. At some point it had stopped cresting and instead spread itself, like a spill or a rash, into each of his limbs. His whole body was quivering now, and he understood that this must be the belated arrival of his father's instinct for trouble.

A loud electronic noise outside the chapel snapped Warren out of his reverie. When he and everyone looked up to see what it was, and where it was coming from, they saw blobs of blue and red light sweep across the panes of the interdenominational stained glass. The Weight understood what was happening before the rest of them.

Motherfucker, he said, landing hard on the third syllable. The pink in his cheeks turned into bright red splotches that dappled his face, and pretty soon his whole body was vibrating with anger. He looked over at Warren and aimed the pistol at his chest. *Was this you? Was this your idea? Did you set me up, you fucking cog?*

Warren put up his hands instinctively. *No,* he sputtered, even before he fully understood what The Weight was asking. *No, please,* he said, pushing the dry words out past his heavy tongue. *I have no idea what's happening.*

The police lights continued to chase each other across the stained glass. There was another noise: one of the heavy doors creaking open at the other end of the chapel. The Weight spun and fired his pistol twice into the wood above the vestibule.

Luca shrieked at the loud double bang, and then laughed and clapped his hands.

Fuck! The Weight turned back and waved the gun at Warren. *Warren. Bring that boy over here.*

No! Renata yelled. She put Luca on the ground and stepped in front of him. *You're not going to touch him! Adrian . . .*

Adrian put his arms out wide in front of him in a pacific gesture. *Let's just calm down, now. Everyone just relax.*

The Weight cut him off. *I don't need to hear any more from you, Professor. Not now and not ever.* He turned to Renata. *I'm not going to hurt the boy, lady. I promise. I just want him over here. Warren, now.* Again he waggled the gun in Warren's direction.

Warren moved slowly to where the other group was standing, and as he got closer, Renata moved, too, shifting her position, and Luca's, to keep the boy between her and her husband. Warren felt nothing but a tingling numbness where the shiver had been. He looked at Adrian's wife, and then he looked at Luca. The boy was not oblivious to the tension, as he had been back in the sacristy. He was not oblivious, but he also did not appear to be frightened: he knew that something was happening and seemed curious about it. When he saw Warren approach, he peeked out from his parents' legs and hooted a happy welcome.

Warren looked at The Weight, who nodded back impatiently. *What the fuck are you waiting for, man?*

Warren reached down, hoping to take Luca by the hand, but Renata turned to block him before he made contact. *He's not going*, she said. *Adrian, tell him he's not going.*

Lady, will you chill the fuck out? I'm not a monster. I'm not going to hurt the kid.

That's right, she shot back. *You're not going to touch him.*

Warren, get the boy.

Still numb, Warren looked helplessly at Renata. Her face was white, actually white, except where it hung in dark pouches under her eyes.

I'll go, she said. *I'll take him.*

Do you want me . . . Adrian started to say.

No. I'll go.

Renata picked up Luca and carried him over to where The Weight was standing. She did not set the boy down again; as she got closer, in fact, she adjusted her hold to wrap him even tighter. The Weight approached them both. He held his hands up close to the nimbus, with the gun pointed away from Luca, as though he were warming his palms at a campfire. Luca looked at him skeptically, and then he put his hands up, too, mirroring The Weight's.

See, The Weight said, with a quiet chuckle. *See, this is all I wanted.*

While The Weight was doing whatever he thought he was doing with the nimbus, Warren took the opportunity to glance at Adrian, who returned his look with an almost invisible nod. Affecting nonchalance while keeping his eyes on The Weight, Adrian bumped the elbow of the young guy, Paul, and then he reached up and scratched the front side of his shoulder. When he was sure that The Weight wasn't watching him, he tapped his collarbone twice with his middle finger.

That this was a signal of some kind, Warren had no doubt. What it was supposed to mean, he had no idea.

Professor! The Weight took a step back from Luca and looked at Adrian. *How are we going to get out of here? There's this door and the ones in the back. Are there other ways out?*

I'm sorry, Adrian said. *I don't think I know.*

Is there a basement?

Again, I'm sorry. I couldn't say.

What about you? The Weight said to the young man. *You're the one bonking the professor's wife, did I hear that right?*

The young man flinched. He looked away and said nothing.

It's okay, I don't care. More power to you. But I want you to tell me how we're going to get out of here.

Let them go, Adrian said. *You can keep me and I'll help you get out of here. I can make some calls, tell them it was all a big misunderstanding. But let everyone else go.*

The Weight appeared to consider the thought, and then he nodded in the direction of the vestibule. *They got cops out there. Cops aren't big on misunderstandings.*

I'll bet you good money those are University police, but it won't stay that way for long. The University police aren't like the CPD.

The Weight spat on the chapel floor. *What the fuck do you know about police, man? Cops are cops. And these guys down here, I've heard about them. These aren't rent-a-cops. These guys are deputized.*

A scraping sound came from the side door of the chapel, just behind where The Weight was standing. It was a key, Warren realized, someone trying to unlock the door. The Weight noticed the sound, too, and when he did he stepped back to the door and put an ear to the thick wood panels. With his right hand still holding the gun, he used his left thumb to hold the dead bolt closed until whoever was working the lock gave up. He seemed pleased with the effortless success.

As The Weight examined the door, looking for some way to keep it barricaded, Adrian scratched his shoulder again. He made eye contact with Warren and with the other guy, Paul, and then he risked a single small signal with his index finger. This gesture also puzzled Warren, but then he got it: he understood what Adrian was planning to do, just as Adrian was starting to do it.

It happened quickly but not chaotically. Time retained its iron grip on events, forcing cause to yield to effect, and on right down the line. Warren saw Adrian run toward The Weight, and he saw Paul run immediately after him. He saw The Weight look up from the lock, and turn, and lift the pistol. He saw Adrian leap at The Weight, and he saw The Weight fire the pistol, twice, while Adrian was already in midair. He saw Adrian land heavily on The Weight and crumple as he made contact. He saw Paul hit a second later, his shoulder slamming into The Weight's chest. He saw Paul recover his balance while The Weight was still staggering, saw him reach for the wrist that held the black gun.

Warren knew that this was his moment. Calmly and for the first time maybe in his entire life, he understood exactly where he fit in. Without a thought for his bad knees or his tender feet or his crooked back—without thinking, even, of any danger to his own life—he ran over to where Paul was grappling with The Weight. Recalling a distant lesson he'd learned from the bullies who ruled his middle-school playground, he punched The Weight hard in the groin, and then he went to work on the gun. The Weight fired twice more, without effect, and then Warren prized it free. He took three steps back, held the warm pistol grip in both hands, and spread his feet shoulder-width apart, like he'd seen in the movies.

I got it, he yelled to Adrian and Paul. *I've got the gun.*

Renata screamed just as Warren made his announcement, and Paul took the opportunity of The Weight's temporary distraction to punch him once more in the gut. He stepped back, out of Warren's way, as The Weight folded over in pain, and then he noticed what Renata had seen: Adrian was on the ground, breathing hard, in a puddle of dark blood.

Renata swept Luca into her arms and carried him over to Warren. Through tears she told the boy to wait right there, and then she rushed over to help Paul minister to her husband. She kneeled next to Adrian, pleading with him, beseeching him, not to die, while Paul stripped off his T-shirt and tried to stop the bleeding. Warren kept the gun trained on The Weight, who was breathing hard and leaning with his back against the chapel's stone wall.

Warren felt a tug on his pants. He risked a glance away from The Weight and saw Luca holding tight to his left leg. He was still glowing, if more faintly than before, but he was not smiling, or hooting, or clapping. He had a finger in his mouth and was staring at his mother, watching her desperately try to revive his father. Warren did not stop in that moment to consider what Luca understood about what he was seeing. Nor did he wonder whether two years old was old enough to retain even a repressed memory of that sort of trauma. Still, the boy clearly understood that something was wrong. Warren knew he had to do something.

Nodding at the side door, he said to The Weight, *Come on, let's go. Outside.*

The Weight looked up at Warren from his slumping crouch with a glowering expression.

Come on, outside, Warren said again.

The Weight stood, slowly, and limped to the side door, leaning against the wall as he went. He flipped the dead bolt and was pulled outside by several hands as soon as he opened the door.

Warren exhaled and closed his eyes when he saw him go. He took two deep breaths and was about to take a third when the door flew open and a brilliant light flooded the chapel.

Put the gun down! someone shouted. *Step away from the boy and put the gun down!*

Warren opened his eyes and peered into the brightness. *It's okay*, he said. *He's gone.*

Step away from the boy and put down the gun. Now.

Warren had no idea who they were talking to or what they were talking about. They had The Weight; he'd seen them take him outside. The boy was safe, and the gun . . .

And the gun, he realized, was still in his hand. And his hand was still closed on the grip. And the barrel was still pointing at the open door, where The Weight had last been, where the riot-geared police were now. Warren understood; he saw the root of their confusion. He opened his mouth to explain, but his first word—*Wait!*—was silenced by a loud *pop.*

How odd, was his first thought, after the stone floor of the chapel jumped up and smacked him broadside. How strange that the floor would leap up to hit him like that. How weird that it would want to. Granted, Warren had never been particularly solicitous of the many floors he'd walked on, but he couldn't think of any reason this one should take special offense. Certainly no reason it should insist on compounding its initial assault by pressing itself so hard and inconsiderately, as it was now, down the length of Warren's aching body.

It was not so bad, was Warren's second thought. For a moment his pain was excruciating, as the multipart injury delivered by the floor—his hips, head, shoulder, and elbow were all throbbing in protest—joined the agony that was already convulsing his abdomen. It did not take long, however, for shock to set in, for his mind and his body to go their separate ways. The disjoint between what he was thinking and what he was feeling was such that it took him a few seconds or minutes or hours before he guessed the nature and origin of the red spillage that covered his hands and his belly and made them warm when the rest of his body felt so cold. The aches where the floor hit him receded, and the burning in his belly took on a local quality, as though the flesh it was tormenting existed in a nearby but separate room. Warren could visit that room, he could look in on it, he could submit himself to its ferocity, but he was surprised to find that he could also leave it.

He'd been shot: on that point he was not deceived. Disoriented as he was, he understood that all that blood outside his body could only mean one thing. Was he dying, too? Had he reached the invisible date on the calendar that had stalked him for more than four decades—the long, fatal shadow that was cast, ineluctably, on the day he was born? As a younger man, even a brief thought of that moment was able to set him spinning—heart racing, breath catching, skin at once sweaty and cold—into a breathless panic. But dying, if that's what this was, turned out to be different than Warren expected. It was simpler, somehow. Easier.

He saw no bright lights or long tunnels. No angels or devils appeared to welcome him into the afterlife. No ancestors or saints showed up to resolve for him all the deepest mysteries of existence. Everything was black, and quiet, and still.

Warren was halfway convinced that this was how it was all going to end—assuming that it had not all ended already—when he heard a distant whooshing. He recognized the sound. It was the same whooshing he'd heard as a boy when he felt time rushing past him like wind. Except now it was Warren who was moving: propelled by some invisible force, he was being pushed forward, carried forward, as though on a river determined to empty itself over a waterfall.

As the current grew stronger and faster, as the whooshing increased in pitch and intensity, Warren felt an intense pang of an unpleasant and unfamiliar emotion. It was not fear and it was not sadness. It was not anger and it was not even really regret. It felt like anxiety but worse: more taut, more tense, more distressing.

Pricked by the strange sentiment and certain now that he was about to die, Warren saw fit to utter a simple prayer. *Forgive me for everything I've wasted*, he said without saying. *Forgive me for wasting everything.*

The whooshing stopped as suddenly as it started. Warren opened his eyes. He saw that he was still in the chapel, and he saw that it was empty now, except for a single figure: a man, in his thirties, maybe, sitting in the front row of the wooden pews. His face was instantly familiar, but it took Warren more than an instant to identify him as his father, for he looked younger now than Warren had ever known him in life. He watched Warren for what felt like a long time, and then he began to nod, and then he began to smile. Warren felt a flood of deep calm wash through him. *It's okay*, his father said in a soft and familiar baritone. *It's all over now. You don't have to worry anymore. You're going to be all right. Everything is going to be fine.*

SUMMER QUARTER

NINETEEN

"How can I keep silent? How can I stay quiet?
   My friend, whom I love, has turned to clay,
   my friend Enkidu, whom I love, has turned to clay.
   Shall I not be like him, and also lay down,
   never to rise again, through all eternity?"
   Said the tavern-keeper to him, to Gilgamesh:
   "O Gilgamesh, where are you wandering?
   The life that you seek you never will find:
   when the gods created mankind,
   death they dispensed to mankind,
   life they kept for themselves.
   But you, Gilgamesh, let your belly be full,
   enjoy yourself always by day and by night!
   Make merry each day,
   Dance and play day and night!
   Let your clothes be clean,
   Let your head be washed, may you bathe in water!

Gaze on the child who holds your hand,
For such is the destiny of mortal men."

Paul finished reading and looked up one last time at the crowd out in
front of him. They were gathered on the lawn next to Harrison—sitting
in the same two columns of the same white folding chairs where the
Div School's muted graduation ceremony had taken place a week earlier. Nearly all of the faculty were out there, and more than a few of
the students, even though summer break was officially underway. He
caught significant glances from Professor Hart, and Billy, and Salma, and
another from the Dean.

Marcus Doran was there, too, Paul noticed, about four rows back on
the left side, but the sight of his erstwhile antagonist had no effect on him.
In the three weeks since Adrian died, Paul had found it easy to complete
the task he'd started after his dissertation colloquium. In his own mind,
if not yet in the University registrar's, he'd cut himself off from graduate
school completely. He was done, well and truly done, and he didn't care
in the least whether Doran interpreted his decision as a victory. Doran
could have his rigor; Paul would keep his dignity.

They'd tried to talk him out of it, of course: several of his professors,
the Dean, even the Chancellor of the University, who had invited Paul to
his massive office to receive something called the Chancellor's Award of
Special Merit. In fine academic fashion, the award came with no money
or tangible benefit—at least, no benefit to Paul. (In fact, he could find no
evidence that the award was a real award at all: the certificate looked like
something the president's executive assistant had whipped up in Word
and printed on a spare sheet of diploma parchment.)

It was not hard to guess the reasons for the Chancellor's solicitude.
The bloody event in the chapel was a PR disaster for a University that had
spent tens of millions of dollars on property, police, and publicity trying
to convince prospective students—and, more to the point, their parents—
that a campus situated on the South Side of Chicago was not, ipso facto,
unsafe. After news stories of the events cast Paul, alongside Adrian, as

one of the heroes of the occasion, however, someone in the University's Communications Department must have spotted their chance. Within a few hours of the impromptu ceremony, one of the pictures Paul had been asked to pose for, along with the ghostwritten quote he'd been asked to approve, were front and center on the University's home page.

(For his part, Paul still thought there was nothing heroic about what he and Adrian had done. Nothing heroic, and a lot stupid. Obviously if they hadn't rushed the killer, Adrian might still be alive. But the journalists and everyone else evidently needed some virtue to balance out the villainy of The Weight and the tragic incompetence of the police.)

The Chancellor had not believed Paul when he said he was leaving the Div School. Maybe he chose to mishear. *Take some time off,* he said during their conversation, nodding with an almost theatrical solemnity while the photographer snapped pictures. *Don't rush it. A traumatic experience like that, it's like a broken bone. You need to make sure it heals right in the early days, so it doesn't give you problems down the line. But whenever you're ready to come back, we'll be happy to have you.*

The Dean, who'd heard from Professor Hart what happened at the colloquium, understood the situation a little better. He, too, called Paul into his office. He, too, said that Paul was welcome back if and whenever he decided to return. *You wouldn't have to work with Doran, you know. I've already decided that this is the last straw for him here at the Div School. We'll obviously get you a new adviser, too. Believe it or not, we actually do have plenty of faculty here who understand that the job is to teach our students, not to torture them. And if money's an issue, you should know I've already started arranging a memorial scholarship in honor of Professor Bennett. I'm sure nothing would please him more than to know that you were the first recipient.*

Paul had kept it together, barely, when the Dean told him this, but he had not been able to resist reporting the conversation to Renata over text as soon as the meeting was over. They had not seen much of each other since the chapel. In the immediate aftermath, Paul had volunteered to help her out with the boys and/or the postmortem logistics, whatever needed doing. But he couldn't really blame her for rebuffing his offer. Even he couldn't be sure that he didn't have ulterior motives, and he appreciated that Renata probably had complicated feelings about his role in her husband's death.

Still and all, she had written him back right away after he texted her news of the Dean's offer. Amazing, she wrote, with a laughing-crying emoji as punctuation. A few seconds later, she wrote more:

You should take him up on it.

I'm not kidding.

Assuming you want to stay.

I don't, but come on, Paul wrote back. I know you don't think I'm a good guy, but that's a bridge too far even for me.

You're a very good guy, Paul Harkin. Don't let anyone tell you otherwise.

I'm not just saying that because I have a favor to ask you.

But I do have a favor to ask you.

Sure, he wrote. Anything.

The Div School is planning a memorial service for Adrian.

They asked me if I wanted to say something, and the answer is no.

But I'd like it if you said something.

I know it's a big ask, after everything that happened. I won't hold it against you if you don't want to, or if you'll already be gone.

But it would mean a lot if you did it.

Would mean a lot to me.

It doesn't have to be a proper eulogy. Even a reading would be great.

Of course, Paul had written back. Of course I'll do it. I'd be honored to.

Paul didn't think too hard about whether that last part was true. Nor did he wonder too much about why Renata wanted him to speak at the memorial. But he also didn't hesitate to select, for his tribute, an extended version of the passage from *The Epic of Gilgamesh* that he'd heard Adrian recite back in college. The passage included a section Adrian had left out: the rebuttal by the tavern-owning goddess Shiduri, who warned Gilgamesh that the only plausible end for his flight from death was more death. Whether this was willful subversion or a suitable farewell to Adrian and the Div School was another question Paul didn't bother sorting out, though he had taken care to omit something himself: a line in which Shiduri tells Gilgamesh to enjoy his wife's repeated embrace.

He had not dared to look at Renata while he was reading the passage or even in the quiet moment after. It was only after he'd taken his first step away from the lectern that he glanced over at where she was sitting in the front row, red-eyed in a pretty black dress, with her besuited boys on one side of her and her elderly mother on the other. She returned his look and dipped her head gratefully.

Paul might have liked to see her after the ceremony ended, but he didn't want to wait for the line of well-wishers to disperse. Still less did he want to stand in line and pretend he was no different than they were. He texted her instead: Sorry I bailed, but it didn't seem the best time or place for a goodbye. I'm around for a few more days, though . . .

From across the lawn, he watched her conclude a long handshake with the Dean and then look down at her phone. She read the message, looked up, and scanned what was left of the crowd until she found Paul.

Before the next of the well-wishers was upon her, she tapped a quick response: Ok. I'll call. THANK YOU it was perfect.

Paul turned to Billy. *Let's go to Dylan's.*

Wait a second. Billy said, slamming his pint glass down on the sticky wood table. *The kid was there. Adrian's son, with his wife . . .*

Billy and Paul were sitting in a booth in the back room of Dylan's, not far from a stroboscopic pinball machine that was done up in a superhero motif. Salma had joined them for the first two drinks, but when she saw where the afternoon was headed, she excused herself in the name of male solidarity. Paul looked across the table at his best friend. *Yep*, he said.

What about the nimbus?

Paul bit his bottom lip and nodded. *Apparently it hasn't shown up again since Adrian died.*

But I thought she couldn't see it. Isn't that what you told me?

I did. She couldn't. She can't. But her other son, Max, could see it.

Wait, so what the fuck?

I don't know, man.

Billy's eyes narrowed. *Was it Adrian? Was it something he did? Was it all a hoax?*

I'm telling you, I really don't know.

It would make sense, though, right? I mean, maybe not actual sense. But more sense than the alternatives.

Paul took a deep breath, and then a long pull from his beer. *You're not the first person to wonder. But as I sit here right now, hand to heart, I really don't think so.*

So what was it, then?

Dude, I'm telling you, I don't have any fucking clue. At this point I'm not even sure that I want to know.

Billy finished the last of his beer and wiped the foam from his beard with the back of his hand. *Fucking hell, I can't believe you're really leaving. Wednesday, right?*

Paul nodded.

And the job starts when?

The Monday after that.

How much are they paying you?

More than I've made in the last five years, easy. On the strength of a tip from an old acquaintance, Paul had scored a job at a digital-media start-up. It's a gold rush, the acquaintance had told him, a land of catered lunches and free beer and flowing kombucha.

Where you going to stay when you get there? Billy asked. *Gonna find another dorm to crash in?*

Nah, Paul said with a smile. *I got lucky. Someone I knew before I came to the Div School is doing a PhD at Columbia. She got in touch again after she saw me in the news. She's leaving soon on a Fulbright to Namibia. She's got a rent-controlled apartment and two cats and doesn't want to give up it or them.*

Aren't you allergic to cats?

Not in rent-controlled apartments, I'm not.

Around the time Paul was getting started on his seventh or eighth drink, he got another text from Renata.

Hey, she wrote. I'm sorry I didn't catch you earlier. Any chance you could swing by to say a quick goodbye? I just got the boys down, and I've got something I'd like to give you before you go.

Paul looked at the time on his phone. He hadn't realized how late it was. He and Billy had been drinking for nearly three hours. He did not feel hammered, but he was clearly in no shape to see Renata. Sure, he texted. Half an hour?

It was still light out when he and Billy left Dylan's, but not by much. The sky was a deep blue-purple and the clouds were a silver gray. *Want to go back and play FIFA?* Billy said. He was swaying as he spoke, or Paul was, or both of them were.

I do, Paul said. *But I've got to go do something first.*

What? How long?

I don't know. I'll text you when I'm back at the dorm.

On the walk over to Renata's, the alcohol in his bloodstream helped Paul imagine a little too excitedly what might be waiting for him. He read and reread her message several times while he swerved down the sidewalk, and with the help of his drunken hermeneutics he decided to ignore the word "quick" and lay all the stress on the last sentence of the text.

Not wanting to wake the boys and spoil whatever surprise Renata had in mind, Paul texted her when he arrived. She opened the front door, still in her black dress, and stepped out onto the porch in bare feet.

Hey, she said, before adding with a wry smile, *You all right?*

Yeah, yeah, Paul insisted. *I'm fine.*

So it would seem, she said, chuckling quietly to herself. *I was going to say that I was sorry I couldn't have you in for a glass of wine, but it looks like you're set for the night.*

No, really, I'm okay . . . Paul started to protest, but Renata cut him off.

Anyway, my mom is here, and after what happened last time, I think it's probably better for both of us this way.

Paul tried not to show his disappointment.

But I'm glad you came over. I wanted to say goodbye in person. I also wanted to give you these. From behind her back, she produced a manila envelope. *I'm going to be moving, too, in a few weeks. I've been going through some of Adrian's stuff, trying to figure out what I want to keep.* She handed the envelope to Paul. *He had a folder with your name on it in his filing cabinet, and of course I had to look. It sounds like you've made up your mind, but just in case, I thought you might like to see what was in there. He could be such an asshole, but he really was a big fan of yours.*

Paul looked down at the envelope. He didn't know what to say. *I'm sorry it all went down like this*, he managed finally.

I am, too, she said hoarsely. *But it wasn't your fault. Please never forget that.*

Maybe some of it, Paul said.

No, Renata said forcefully. She stepped up on her toes and kissed him, not long and not hard, on the lips. She patted his cheek with her palm. *Not any of it.*

Paul opened the envelope as he walked through the park at the end of Renata's street. The papers inside, he saw, were letters of recommendation that Adrian had written for him at various stages of his aborted academic career. He'd never seen them before, and he was a little surprised to see how comprehensively Adrian had praised his scholarly aptitude. It was enough to make Paul wonder for a moment if he'd erred in accepting Doran's judgment over Adrian's, if leaving the Div School was a mistake he'd regret for the rest of his life.

Nah, he decided. Who was he kidding? He dropped the letters in a trash can near the park's kiddie playground and went back to Billy's.

TWENTY

Mama Mama Mama Mama Mama Mama . . .

Renata looked up and heard Luca's footsteps coming fast down the hall from the front room.

In here, buddy. I'm in my room.

Luca pulled up short when he reached the doorway. He was wearing his favorite outfit, a diaper and a mask of blueberry yogurt, and was carrying a plastic light saber. He put the end of the toy in his mouth and eyed the duffel bag that Renata had been packing on her bed.

What's up, Luke?

Mama, where you going?

I'm just going out for a little bit, bud. I'll be back in a few hours.

Where, Mama?

I'm going to swim, buddy. Mama's going for a swim.

I want swim.

Not today, Luke. Maybe later this week. Maybe tomorrow.

Luca looked down at the light saber and appeared to consider this information. *Where Luke go?*

Mariela's coming, sweetie. I told you that, remember? At breakfast?

Luca's eyes grew wide. His face broke into an incredulous smile. The same expression had brightened his face the first time he heard the news, an hour earlier. *Mariela?*

Yeah, buddy. Remember? She should be here soon. Why don't you go wait for her out front? I'll be done here in just a minute.

Luca dropped the toy and spun on his heels. Renata smiled to herself as she heard him go thunder-waddling down the hall, calling out for his brother the whole way. *Mac! Mac! Mariela coming! Mariela coming!*

Renata finished packing her duffel and brought it out to the living room, where she found Mariela greeting the boys. Renata hugged her hello and told the boys to be good. At the last minute, she remembered something she meant to bring. She ran back upstairs to Adrian's office and found what she was looking for. On her way out again, she kissed the boys and said goodbye.

Of all the disorientations that had affected Renata's life in recent months, the fact that Luca was talking now had to count as pretty minor. Obviously Adrian's death was at the top of the list. The disappearance of the nimbus was a not-so-distant second. Far behind those two came all their many consequences and ramifications: the planning for the funeral and the memorial; the dealings with the police, the hospital, and the DA; the settling of accounts with the life-insurance company; the signing and initialing of forms, so many forms, *RPB, RPB, RPB* over and over again; the professional divorce (for that's what it felt like) from the University; the preparations for the double trials (criminal and civil) of Adrian's killer; the packing for the move to Seattle; the selling of one house and the buying of another; the scouting and selection of new schools for the boys; the permanent winding-down of her consultancy; and then all the other little and not-so-little logistical novelties that had to be managed, maintained, ameliorated, or otherwise taken care of. None of it—none of that—was in any way interesting or appealing, and it was no consolation that even in her post-traumatic haze Renata was doing a respectable job of handling it all.

In the immediate aftermath of the worst day of her life, of course, this had not been the case. For about two weeks she had felt literally sick with grief. A brutal headache had hunched right behind her eyes like a tiny angry ogre wielding an ice pick, and a persistent nausea had made it impossible to keep anything in her stomach more substantial than saltines. She'd been groggy and lethargic, like she'd saddled herself with a permanent hangover, but also found it impossible to sleep more than three hours at a stretch.

Maybe the worst part of that acute period of her mourning was that it seemed like it would last forever. *This is my life now*, was something she told herself more than once. *I cheated on my husband, and then I killed him, and now this is the life I will have, and will deserve, forever.*

She was wrong about that last part, as it turned out, just as her mother had assured her. The grief did not go away. It did not even really abate. But it did undergo something akin to a phase change, like a concentrated liquid toxin sublimating into something gaseous and diffuse. The enervations of the early days gave way to a dull anesthesia. No longer did she feel like it would take an impossible effort to get out of bed in the morning. No longer did she feel like the prospect of feeding the boys, much less feeding herself, would take from her every last erg of available willpower. No longer did she feel much of anything, in fact. She could answer the door and answer the phone. She could fill out forms and sit for recorded interviews. She could manage her mother and the boys. (Her mother had insisted on coming to Chicago to help—or "help"—before Renata had regained the energy to send her back to New York.) She could sign papers and scan documents and respond, however briefly, to the condolences that came in from friends and acquaintances. She could do what Adrian always joked, not always joking, that she did best: she could deal. She could take care of what needed to happen. She could accomplish what needed to get done. Who cared if she didn't feel anything while she was doing it? Who cared if everything seemed to be happening in a gray, narcotic haze?

Then, out of nowhere, Luca started talking. *Mama, I'm hungry* were the first words he said, and while this, too, was a change from what came before, it was at least a nice change, unlike all those others. It was something Renata could feel something about—something, more to the point, that she could feel happy about. So much in her life had gone wrong, but at least this little corner had righted itself. That was something, she tried to remember. So much had gone wrong, but at least Luca, her little boy, was turning out okay.

The Undergraduate Athletic Center was virtually empty. Renata stripped down to her bathing suit in the locker room and stashed her clothes, along with her phone, her keys, and her duffel, in one of the painted lockers. She checked her face in the mirror on the way out to the pool, astonishing herself all over again at how frail the woman in the glass appeared: how hollow and how old. Though she'd always heard that stress could age you—just look at the president, creased and gray after barely a half-decade in office—never had she suspected it could happen so fast.

The morning after her affair, still riding the high of the occasion, she'd congratulated herself for the compliments Paul had lavished on her thirty-nine-year-old body. She wasn't supposed to think that way, she knew, even if she couldn't exactly remember why. But even though she felt a little silly about it, she had not denied herself the pleasure of knowing that she had won the admiration of a man still in his twenties. Now, though, god: now she looked fully middle-aged.

Renata pulled on her cap and walked barefoot to the pool. She stepped off the deck into the warm water. After a few easy laps, she started her workout in earnest, alternating between freestyle and breaststroke. She pushed herself harder with each set, for it was only at maximum exertion that she had any chance of escaping for a few moments the guilt that she'd been carrying since Adrian died.

The guilt was somehow worse than the grief. It was with her constantly, even when she was otherwise numb. There was no question in her mind that she was responsible for Adrian's death. The therapist she'd started seeing had of course disagreed, and in the strongest possible terms. But Renata knew better. Maybe she hadn't been determined to fan the flames of an insane little pseudoreligious cult. Maybe she hadn't invited a hardened criminal to come and gaze upon her son. Maybe she hadn't pointed the gun and pulled the trigger that fired the bullets that killed her husband. But so what? If she had not tried to leave the chapel with Luca, to take just one possible counterfactual, then the thug who killed her boys' father might very well have left them all alone. Anyway, it was her job to keep her family safe. It had always been her job to keep her family safe. And in that task, she had failed.

What it meant to live with this failure was a question Renata had only recently been able to formulate for herself. (Forget answering it.) She'd noticed, however, that one of her instincts was to do what everyone else was doing: to make Adrian the hero of his own demise. This was the story she'd told the police, when they'd interviewed her at the campus station next to the bookstore. It was the version she'd told the Chancellor, when he invited her to his office for tea. And it was the version she'd told the public-radio reporter, whom she'd invited to her house for an exclusive interview. There was nothing in that story about intramarital arguments or extramarital affairs or antimarital quasi-abductions of glowing children. There was not a hint that her marriage had ended a few minutes before the fatal shooting; there were no threats, in her telling, that had not come from the thug with the gun.

This was the version of the story she knew that everyone wanted. It was the version she knew that Adrian would have liked for himself, as well. Long after he'd learned that the idea of the hero's journey was too crude and too unsophisticated to be cited approvingly in academic company, he never gave up his private fondness for the notion that life— his life, at least—ought to be lived on the model of the ancient myths he loved so much.

Obviously everyone wanted to know about the nimbus, too. They'd all heard the rumors. They'd seen what the Internet had to say. They all wanted to know what Renata made of the stories going around that suggested something strange and supernatural was going on with Luca. Renata didn't deny that she'd heard the stories, too. She didn't deny that Adrian had been interested in them. He was a scholar of religion—what did they expect? But she could say with untainted honesty that she'd never seen anything unusual happening to her son, and so she had to assume that the whole thing had been a misunderstanding that got way out of hand.

It was tempting to believe all of this. In the two months since Adrian died, after all, there was really nothing she wanted to hear more than that she'd been wrong about her husband all along. The chain of causality that would buttress such an accusation could only work backward, but that was not a problem, not for her. Because Renata was responsible for Adrian's death, her reasoning went, she must have erred in reacting so strongly to his embrace of the nimbus, and because she had erred in that reaction, she had been too hard on him in general. Her punishment proved her crime.

It was tempting, too, to believe the story that she was telling about the nimbus. Tempting and made all the easier because it had gone away as mysteriously as it had, supposedly, arrived. It was, Renata knew, a cliché to say that the nimbus was beginning to seem like something out of a half-remembered dream. But that's how it felt to her. It was like those times when she'd be cooking dinner—chopping cucumbers, maybe, or poaching chicken—and would remember, not well but suddenly, that a bare eighteen hours earlier, while sleeping, she'd been soaring over a snow-covered mountain pass with only her arms for wings. Or maybe it was like being sick: like having a bad head cold and trying to recall what it felt like six months later. She could call to mind the signifiers of her distress with no trouble (the panics, the crying, the fights) but it was getting more and more difficult to summon any memory of the experience itself. Was it really so bad as all that?

This was the guilt talking. Renata knew that. Her omnipresent inter-locutor. Every story starts with a lie, and the lie that her guilt wanted her and everyone to believe was that Adrian's death, a little like Christ's, transfigured everything that came before it. As though a single decision—however futile, however fatal, however heroic—could redeem all the others. The guilt wanted Renata to believe it. The journalists wanted Renata to believe it. The academics at the University and beyond wanted Renata to believe it. Daily, hourly, sometimes minute by minute they made their case that she and everyone else were only minor characters in the tragic tale of a professor who gave up his life to save his extraordinary son.

This was the story her boys would grow up hearing, undoubtedly. When they were old enough to appreciate that what had befallen their father was not merely, as it seemed to them now, a spontaneous and ter-rible misfortune but something he'd chosen, they would understand why so many people had told them so many times over the past two months that their father was a great man. Renata was not going to take that away from them. Not now and not ever. They'd lost their dad; that was too much already. And while it was certainly true that she was still angry at Adrian, for so many reasons, she didn't want to let that anger make her petty or pusillanimous. If the story of Adrian's heroism could ease the pain of her sons' grief even a little, then she would tell them that story every day and every night for as long as she lived.

Still, though. Some part of Renata—maybe it was a weak part, cer-tainly a quiet part, but somehow, also, it was an ancient and essential part—could not go along with it. She had no idea if she would ever be able to shake herself free of the guilt, but she was not ready to believe what it wanted to tell her. Adrian and his ambitions had subsumed her while he was still alive; she was not ready, not yet, to let herself be sub-sumed by his death.

Renata finished her cooldown and climbed out of the pool. She took a shower, and then she changed into her clothes, and then she patted her hair dry as best she could with one of the thin striped locker-room towels. She ventured another look in the mirror and decided things were not as bad as they'd seemed. She took her phone from her duffel bag and sent a brief text.

Yeah, Warren responded a few seconds later. Now's as good as ever. I'm still in the Rehab Department. Still in room 422.

TWENTY-ONE

Do you miss it? Warren heard himself say.

Renata, Adrian's widow, winced at the question. She was standing at the foot of the hospital bed, and her gaze fell away, over to the curtain that divided Warren's room in two. After a moment's pause she collected herself and looked back at him with pursed lips. *I miss him every day. Every hour, just about. I know you heard us in the chapel. Things weren't good between us. But I can tell you honestly: whatever I wanted, it wasn't this. It wasn't anything like this.*

I'm sorry, Warren said. *I'm very sorry. But that's not what I meant. I was asking about the nimbus.*

Renata's expression softened. She exhaled loudly, making a sound that was halfway to a laugh. *Honestly, if I never heard that word again, it would be too soon.*

I take it it still hasn't shown up again? Not since . . .

No, she said quickly. *Not since Adrian died.* She folded her hands in front of her face and touched her thumbs to her lips. After a silent moment, she lifted her head and squinted at Warren. *Why do you ask? Do you miss it?*

No, Warren said truthfully. *But it was not really a part of my life. Not like it was for you. You lived with it for so long. And . . .*

Yes?

Don't take this the wrong way, but I got the sense that Adrian liked having it around.

He definitely did. That was part of the problem. A big part of the problem.

Warren felt an urge to defend Adrian, which he saw no reason to restrain. *I can't say I blame him.*

Really? Renata allowed herself a small smile. *I found it very easy to blame him.*

It's certainly not something you see every day.

It was not something I saw any day, Renata said.

Warren accepted the correction with a nod, and both of them sat several long seconds while a silence passed between them. *Did you want to?* Warren said finally.

See it? Not really, Renata said. *If there were times when I wanted to, it was only so that I could know what we were dealing with.*

What you were up against, Warren offered.

Something like that.

But you didn't think it was real.

Oh, no. Not really. Do I believe people when they said they saw something? Yes. Do I think they saw what they wanted to see? Yes again. Do I think Adrian especially wanted to see something? Absolutely.

But?

But do I think my son was illuminated by a strange magical force that conferred blessings on its beholders? No.

You think people saw the nimbus because they wanted to?

Renata sighed. *Wish fulfillment is a hell of a drug. But I don't know. You tell me. What do you think?*

It's not my theory. But sure, I guess it's possible. That raises another question, though: Why?

Renata was quiet for a moment, and then she looked up and smiled again. *Life, friends, is boring. We must not say so.*

You're quoting someone.

John Berryman, the poet.

I don't read much poetry.

No one does. They especially don't read him.

Renata watched Warren for a response, though what she was hoping for he couldn't say. He held his face blank and said nothing.

Renata slipped the tote bag from her shoulder and set it on top of a rolling cart. *I brought you some stuff. When you told me you didn't have any relatives around, I thought maybe . . . I don't know.*

Oh. Warren was so surprised that he didn't know what to say. *You shouldn't have. Really.*

It's the least I could do.

Warren felt an acid-like burn at the base of his esophagus. *No. I mean it. I don't deserve anything. Certainly not from you. I'm the reason I'm here. I'm the reason Adrian isn't.*

Renata stepped forward and touched Warren's foot through the thin hospital blanket. *I told you last time, you need to stop thinking like that. Please. You've suffered more than enough for whatever you think you did. Which, to be clear, I do not accept. I saw what happened. You saved Luca, you saved me. You did not kill Adrian.*

But The Weight . . . I'm the only reason . . .

No. Absolutely not. I reject the premise. Maybe you invited him, maybe it's even true, as you suggested, that you set the whole thing in motion. But none of it would have happened without Adrian. He's the one who took Luca, even after I begged him not to.

I hope you know I had no idea. He didn't tell me—

I do know, and that's why I'm insisting that it wasn't your fault. Adrian wasn't going to give this up. I don't know why. He was so lucky. We were so lucky. I mean, obviously we had our challenges. Everyone does. But our life before this stupid thing turned up . . . It was pretty good. Not perfect, but pretty good. I don't know why he couldn't be happy with what he had. I don't know why he couldn't be satisfied. The world was not enough for him.

Another quote. More poetry?

Renata gave a little laugh. *James Bond.*

When the door closed after Renata's departure, Warren pulled the rolling table over and looked into the tote bag she'd left behind. She'd visited him twice before, and on one of those previous visits she must have asked the nurses about his cravings. This time she'd skipped the flowers and brought him instead a big bag of fun-size 100 Grands, a dozen Honeycrisp apples, a quart of cold buttermilk, and a warm falafel sandwich from the Lebanese place Warren loved so much up on Fifty-Third Street.

Warren rolled up on his left side, careful not to put undue pressure on any of his several wounds. The right side of his lower back, where the cop's bullet had left his body after tearing through his small and large intestines, was especially sore. He reached over with his right hand, which was still bruised on top from where the IV port had been taped down for two weeks, and tugged the outer edge of the table toward his lap. When that task was accomplished, he worked the buttons on the bed's remote until he found a position that reasonably approximated sitting.

He took the sandwich from the tote and ripped the foil down halfway, like a burrito. His guilt over what happened in the chapel was too deep to let him accept Renata's absolution, but he appreciated her attempt to let him off the hook. Ignoring the burning behind his sternum, he took a big bite of the sandwich, and then another, and then another. It was everything he'd hoped for, and so much more. A miracle, he was tempted to tell himself, until he remembered that a miracle, or something like one, was the reason he was here.

Warren allowed himself a small chuckle at the thought, even though laughing was painful. He wondered idly what all this must have been like for Renata. Awful, obviously, was one answer. Awful and probably not helped by anything she'd said to her husband in the sacristy before he died. But it wasn't that part Warren was wondering about. It was the sudden change in her circumstances that made him curious.

He believed her when she said they'd been lucky. By every indication she and Adrian were the kind of people who moved from strength to strength, who knew failure only as a distant rumor. Everything came easy to them: money, looks, intelligence, social grace, worldly success. (Maybe not marriage, but after his parents' relationship Warren saw no reason to count divorce as a misfortune.) While they lived, people like the Bennetts were life's champions, and when they died—especially when they died a death like Adrian's—they were remembered as paragons, pillars of civilized society.

What was it like for Renata to see all that change in an instant? What was it like for her to come late to the knowledge that affluence is no antidote to worry, that all the human and financial capital in the world is no proof against sudden disaster?

Warren wasn't about to count it a point on his side of the ledger that he suffered no such surprise when he'd come to consciousness in the ICU, still groggy after his surgery. That he would be shot, that he would be shot by a cop, that he would be shot by a cop who was gullible enough to accept what The Weight told him, causing him to mistake Warren for an armed kidnapper: none of these were events that Warren ever hoped or expected to experience in his life. But neither were any of them especially surprising. Unlike Renata, unlike his father, he had always been one of the unfortunate ones: *l'anime triste*, as Dante had it, whom mercy and justice disdain.

While he enjoyed the undeserved bounty that Renata had brought him—after he finished the falafel sandwich and drank half the buttermilk and ate a handful of 100 Grands—Warren wondered if Renata was right about the nimbus. Was it just wish fulfillment? There was something to the thought, obviously. Warren could admit that, at least in the privacy of his own skull. Though Warren did not share Adrian's apparent taste for the esoteric, though he liked to think of himself (as everyone did) as a clear-eyed realist about the state of the human situation, he could not honestly say that he was content with the idea that life in general, and his life in particular, were the sadistic cosmic jokes they seemed.

Certainly he could acknowledge that he'd let himself marinate for too many hours, too many weeks, too many years in the memory of his past failures and slights. Definitely he would concede that he'd told himself too many times that life was an omnishambles barely worth living. But even during the most intense of his existential agonies, there had always been some part of him that could not accept that all the collected strivings and sufferings of humanity were no more than a random flutter in the quantum fabric of space-time. Even during the lowest moments of his life, some part of him still wanted to believe.

Was that all the nimbus was? A projection of that small but durable desire? A psychologically motivated hallucination? Warren could accept the suggestion in theory, just as he could accept in theory that his near-death vision of his father was a kindred phenomenon.

In both cases, however, Warren had reasons to doubt his skepticism. With the nimbus, it was his first encounter with Luca, in the hospital hallway, that made him wonder. Like Paul, like The Weight, Warren had had no cues or prompts before his first sighting of the nimbus, and yet still he'd seen what they and so many others had seen as well.

With the vision of his father, Warren's counterproof was vaguer but still enough to keep him from signing on to the wish-fulfillment theory entirely. Obviously it was true that the words he'd heard were words he badly wanted to hear. But it was also true that the feeling of absolution and tranquility that had accompanied his father's benediction had stayed with him as something more than a memory. Maybe some cocktail of neurochemicals had conjured the scene and the feeling to soften the torment of what was looking very much like they might be Warren's last moments alive. Maybe. But then why did he still feel, even now, at a level deeper than ordinary emotion, that a breach had somehow been healed?

Anyway, Warren considered, if metaphysical mystery was what his subconscious was craving, nothing so strange as signs and wonders were necessary. Nothing so peculiar as a glowing boy or a paternal apparition. Every morning of his life so far, for four decades running, Warren had woken into an experience of the world that was logically and scientifically nonsensical. Fourteen, sixteen, sometimes eighteen hours a day he'd seen time do its best and oldest trick, merely by spilling from one moment implacably into the next. If mystery was what he wanted, it was enough to watch day become night, summer become fall, months and years and decades slide by without surcease. It was enough to hum a song, to speak a word, to remember that even the slightest sough or sigh depends on the impossible flow of time.

Warren balled up the falafel wrapper with his napkins and the apple stem inside. He recovered his phone from the far side of the table and typed a phrase into his Web browser. A picture of Pierce Brosnan appeared, and now he remembered, sort of. According to a film-review website, *The World Is Not Enough* was one of the lesser Bonds, a poorly plotted effort that was distinguished mostly for its attempt to assuage the confused imperatives of the Clinton era by casting Denise Richards as a super-hot nuclear physicist named Christmas Jones.

The title of the film, he read, was borrowed from the fictional Bond's real-life ancestor, Sir Thomas Bond, an English baron who used the phrase *orbis non sufficit* for his family motto. And here Warren saw that Renata was wrong, or at least not entirely right: the phrase had, in fact, been poetry before the real Baron Bond got hold of it. Lucan had used it in his *Pharsalia*, and then Juvenal had borrowed it for his *Satires* to mock the ambitions of Alexander the Great:

A world was not enough for that youth from Pella, Alexander,
Seething with discontent at the narrow confines of his universe,
As if trapped on some rocky prison isle, tiny Seriphus or Gyara:

But once he's entered that city, Babylon, built of brick and clay,
He must be content with it as his coffin. For death alone reveals
How small the remnants of a human being.

Warren ate another 100 Grand, and then he clicked over to The Mace of Wintermere. A few days earlier, a University lawyer had called to ask if he would be open to discussing a settlement for the University-sponsored shooting. Warren still had no idea how much money that might entail, but he'd used the call as an excuse to treat himself to a fifty-dollar Maxi-pack of Winterbucks.

While the game loaded, he finished off the carton of buttermilk. On his screen appeared a small village full of peaceful civilians who were unlucky enough to possess a plot of territory he wanted for his fief. With a silent salute to Soame Jenyns, he prepared to send his freshly outfit-ted warrior-monks to slaughter the peasants. Just then, however, Warren heard the door to his room open again. He looked up and saw the nurse arriving with his noontime pain meds. He put the game on pause and buried his phone among his bedsheets. The digital massacre could wait.

Time, for once, was on his side.

ACKNOWLEDGMENTS

Thomas Merton says somewhere that "the great work of the solitary life is gratitude." I don't know if that's true, but I do know that the solitary work of writing this novel has made me immensely grateful for everyone who still believes in the miracle of fiction.

Thanks also to:

Amelia Atlas, my brilliant agent, for her intelligence, enthusiasm, loyalty, and care.

Tim Duggan, whose thoughtfulness won my allegiance long before I was lucky enough to call him my editor, for turning an ancient dream into a reality.

Nell Freudenberger, for expert advice at too many crossroads to count.

Catrin Einhorn, Justin Vogt, and Jon Cox, for their crucial feedback on early drafts.

Andrew Miller, Zoë Affron, Hannah Campbell, Emily Mahar, Gabriel Guma, Sonja Flancher, Carolyn O'Keefe, and everyone at Holt who helped make this book a book.

My parents, Michael and Susan Baird, and my sisters—Kelly Crowe, Betsy Baird, and Colleen Baird—for their unyielding love and unflinching encouragement, no matter how winding the path.

Henry and Felice Yager, for welcoming me into their family with warmth and generosity.

Lelvin, Carter, and Savannah Crowe; Alison Yager, Andrew Elmore, and Phoebe and Sage Yager-Elmore; Monty and Blaire Erwin; and my extended Skalla and Yager families, for their affection and good cheer.

Annie Dillard, for showing me how it's done.

Wendy Doniger, Bernard McGinn, David Tracy, Arnold Davidson, Richard Rosengarten, Rebecca West, and especially Françoise Meltzer, for teaching me what I needed to know, and then some.

Brian and Nora Abrams, Elliot Ackerman, V. Joshua Adams, Martin Amis, Andrea Andersson, Elizabeth Angell, Jonathan Blitzer, Victor Brand, John Cable, Ben Calhoun, Kevin Campos, Lizzy and Lucas Carmichael, Christopher Cox, Ryan Coyne, Matt Crystal, Joriah Dering, Anand Desai, Vanessa Diffenbaugh, Cesar Dimas, Rob Fischer, Eric Gross, Sarah Hammerschlag, Evan Hughes, Matthew Hunte, Jilan Kamal, Patrick Radden Keefe, Ashley and John Kemper, Joshua Kotin, Mark Krotov, Ross Land, Sarah Larson, Eric Laufer, Duncan Long, Anthony Madrid, Andrew Marantz, Wyatt Mason, Betsy Morais, Stuart Nagae, Mary Norris, Eric Nudleman, Woo Jin Park, Adam Pollet, Robert D. Richardson Jr., Tracey Rosen, Jim Rutman, Dylan Saake, Sonya Schneider, Ryan Stotts, Megan Twohey, Adelle Waldman, Danny Webb, David Wolf, and Elisabeth Zerofsky, for their friendship and support.

Mieke Pierre and Nicole Boudinot, for helping me find the time.

Amelia and Ollie, the best kids a father could hope for, who make each day a wonder, and who need no nimbus to glow.

This novel is dedicated to JY, my love and my light. Thank you for keeping the faith.

ABOUT THE AUTHOR

Robert P. Baird grew up in Northern California, studied mechanical engineering and human biology at Stanford, and earned a PhD from the University of Chicago Divinity School. He has worked as an editor at *The New Yorker*, *Harper's Magazine*, *The Paris Review*, *Chicago Review*, and *Esquire* and has published journalism, essays, and reviews in those magazines and other outlets. He lives in Brooklyn with his wife and children. *The Nimbus* is his first novel.